THE
PECULIAR
GIFT OF JULY

THE
PECULIAR
GIFT OF JULY

— a novel —

ASHLEY REAM

DUTTON

DUTTON

An imprint of Penguin Random House LLC
1745 Broadway, New York, NY 10019
penguinrandomhouse.com

BOOK DESIGN BY Lorie Pagnozzi

page ii art: pie icon © Shutterstock

LIBRARY OF CONGRESS CATALOGING-IN-PUBLICATION DATA

Names: Ream, Ashley, author.
Title: The peculiar gift of July: a novel / Ashley Ream.
Description: New York: Dutton, 2025.
Identifiers: LCCN 2024035082 | ISBN 9780593853726 (hardcover) | ISBN 9780593853740 (ebook)
Subjects: LCGFT: Novels.
Classification: LCC PS3618.E2247 P43 2025 |
DDC 813/.6—dc23/eng/20240802
LC record available at https://lccn.loc.gov/2024035082

Printed in the United States of America
1st Printing

The authorized representative in the EU for product safety and compliance is Penguin Random House Ireland, Morrison Chambers, 32 Nassau Street, Dublin D02 YH68, Ireland, https://eu-contact.penguin.ie.

To Austin and Abigail
More than there are stars in the sky

THE
PECULIAR
GIFT OF JULY

CHAPTER ONE

There was no end to the oddments that washed up on Ebey's End. So far that winter, the official list, which was kept pinned to the wall of the local tavern, included half a wooden rowboat sawn neatly down the middle and a Maytag wringer washing machine. Some teenagers claimed to have found a Styrofoam cooler full of condoms, but this was unverified as the condoms were not in the cooler by the time it made it to the tavern. As a result, the school nurse had made an announcement over the loudspeaker concerning the dangers of relying on prophylactic flotsam.

This would've been notable in most places, but Ebey's End was and had always been different. A green speck of an island so far north and west of the Northwest, folks were in danger of having to learn the metric system and the Canadian national anthem. It wasn't near anything or on the way to anything, and those who came and stayed had their reasons.

Two blocks inland, Anita was standing at the checkout ringing up one of her regular customers and wondering what had become of his life. He picked up each item from his basket and set it individually in front of her. Three frozen burritos, all chicken. One box of cornflakes. One quart of two-percent milk. Coffee, ground. An apple.

She held it up. "One?"

Mr. Daly nodded, his hands in the pockets of his gray suit. He was the only man on the island who owned more than one and the only man who wore it outside of a coffin.

"Well, you wouldn't want to overdo it," Anita said, and put the apple in the paper sack.

"I've thrown out the last three," he admitted. "I keep forgetting about them."

Anita, who took groceries very seriously, stopped what she was doing. "Do you keep them in the fridge or on the counter?"

"I've tried both." He thought for a moment. "The last one rolled behind the toaster. By the time I found it, it had grown a kind of . . . fur."

"Fur?"

"White fur, like a mouse," Mr. Daly said, rocking back on the heels of his dress shoes, the backs of which had worn down from the habit. "It was sort of sweet, really."

He smiled at her, but it was not cheering.

Preston Daly had gray eyes and gray hair to go along with his gray suit. He was a head taller than anyone Anita had ever met, with limbs so long he gave the impression of constantly needing to fold and unfold himself to fit anywhere.

She knew he lived alone, and she knew he did not have visitors, at least not the sort who stayed for food. This had been true for a long time, but the situation seemed to be getting worse.

Anita had spent all forty-four years of her life in the store. It belonged to Mack, her father, who'd bought it from a couple whose only son had died in the Korean War. A picture of him in uniform had hung next to the front door over the stack of hand baskets for decades, and her father, out of respect, had left it until first the man and then the woman died, and then the picture had quietly come down and been thrown in the trash.

The building, which her father also owned, was 120 years old and had always housed some version of the store. Coffee, sugar, and flour had been for sale here since the first white settlers had sailed across the Salish Sea from Seattle, pulled west into the far reaches of the San Juan Islands by the promise of virgin timber. With a breathtaking disregard for the native people, the logger barons built a bunkhouse and then a saloon and then Anita's store.

Not much had changed. Nowadays the gray light outside filtered through the front windows, partially blocked by hand-colored signs advertising a special on chicken thighs ($1.29/lb) and potato chips (2/$5, select varieties only). The wood floor was untouched, darkened from a century of wet boots, with a slope that went from front to back. Gaps had opened between the boards wide enough to jam in a nickel, which children sometimes did. The shelves, too, were wood, lighter in color and too close together, so one person reaching for oatmeal might step back and bump into another choosing jam.

The space was four times deeper than it was wide and didn't lend itself to the long, regular aisles found in modern stores. By necessity, the Island Grocery was arranged more like a bookstore with sections and nooks, which made even the half-sized rolling carts seem bulky. Overhead, metal fixtures like overturned washtubs shone down pools of yellow light. These were irregularly spaced so that the cereal section was bright as noon while both the wine and the "international foods" lived in a permanent dusk. Anita's regular customers often pulled out cell phones, which worked only sporadically on the island, to use as flashlights over the labels.

Refrigeration had been installed but not air-conditioning. She did not carry fifteen kinds of flavored mayonnaise or whole pomegranates, because people did not really want to buy those things. Not in Ebey's End. Not at the Island Grocery. And if Anita knew anything, it was what her customers wanted.

She had started sweeping the floors after school when she was six. Her father paid her in quarters, which she used to buy candy from the bulk bins at half off, her unofficial employee discount. She'd moved on to stocking shelves and then working the cash register once she could see over the top of it. That was when she learned the secret of the grocery business, the truth of its bloody, beating heart.

People shopped how they lived. They ate how they thought. They used food to show—or withhold—love, from themselves and from others. She could see who was hosting holiday dinners and who was alone, who had been told to watch their cholesterol and who had fallen off the wagon. She knew when there were houseguests and who was on vacation. She could tell when someone in the house was sick or pregnant, when their New Year's resolutions began and when they ended. She could tell by the food in their carts when her customers were depressed, and she could guess why. She knew when money was tight and when it wasn't. She could predict birthdays, engagements, and, on at least two occasions, divorces. Anita could read people's shopping carts as clearly as if they had handed her their diary.

Having that kind of information was a responsibility she took seriously. She kept her customers' secrets, and she never interfered. People came to her for margarine and canned corn, not a lecture.

Still, Anita was worried about Preston Daly. Or, more precisely, she worried about his heart. He seemed to have left it out on the counter, forgetting about it until it grew fur—white like a mouse, sweet, really, but gone off just the same.

She sighed and gave him the total. He paid in cash and left the change, more than ten dollars, in the cup for stray pennies. He always did. "For whoever might need it," he'd told her once, and she'd been careful to use it that way since.

Preston was president of the town's bank, which had a name but didn't need it. His father had been the bank president before him and his grandfather before him and his great-grandfather before him, all the way back to whoever had first cleared the trees from the spot where it stood. He was good at his work, but he did not enjoy it. Anita didn't think he enjoyed very much, although not for a lack of wanting. He did, after all, keep buying the apples. Hope in fruit form.

"Mr. Daly," she called as he was walking out the door.

He stopped.

"Maybe eat the apple now," she said.

He smiled, and again it did not travel up his face, but he retrieved the apple from the bag and bit into it. She could hear the crunch and snap of the breaking pink-and-yellow skin from where she stood.

As he left, he stepped aside for Carol, who pushed down the hood of her coat and nodded to Anita as she came in. It was raining outside, a heavy drizzle that started in October and marched with head down and shoulders hunched right through April. No one carried an umbrella. Suffering was a point of civic pride.

Carol had written a single book a number of years before, which had done well. She was married to Henry, who most people called Doc. They had been married for forty-one years, and for two of those years, Anita had been sleeping with him.

It had not been the two most recent years. It had, in fact, been more than twenty years ago, but it was still the first thing Anita thought of each week when Carol came to do her shopping. Always on Monday afternoons, always with a list, on the back of which, Anita could see, she had written out all the meals she would make for the week. Carol did not shop from one side of the store to the other. She started in the center, going through the canned foods, cereal, and snack aisles, then to dairy, then to produce so her tomatoes and strawberries would not be bruised, then to bread so her loaf would not get crushed, and finally to frozen foods so her ice cream would not melt. Carol was a woman who thought things through, and recently, she was a woman who bought Pepperidge Farm Milano cookies.

When their two children were living at home, Carol had bought cookies, mostly Toll House or Oreos. But when the younger, Declan, had gone to the mainland for college and had not come back, she had stopped. Years had gone by cookie-less. Then, three months ago, Carol started buying Pepperidge Farm Milanos. Anita had always been careful to keep them in stock. They were Gordy's favorite.

Gordon Whitehead ran the post office, such as it was. The entire island was only about twenty square miles, long and curved with bays, coves, and inlets cutting into every bit of shore. It looked, from above, like something that had been chewed on. There were, at last count, a few thousand full-time residents and significantly fewer households, which wasn't enough to justify home delivery. So twice a week, everyone made the drive into town to see Gordy and collect their mail. There was nothing precisely wrong with Gordy, so much as there was little to recommend him. He ran the post office like it was his own personal kingdom, enforcing his own rules, which sometimes did and sometimes didn't have anything to do with postal regulations. He was not married. He had a medium-sized rambler house built in the 1960s and not touched since, except for the chicken coop.

"Coop" didn't really do it justice. Gordy had a predator-proof high-rise of poultry, complete with fenced, reinforced chicken runs, which wove in and out of the giant evergreens that, despite the previous logging, still covered nearly all the island.

"Chickens," he'd once told Anita, "like trees."

Gordy would know. He had several dozen chickens, perhaps more. No one was really sure, but it was far more than his residential lot was zoned for. This caused some amount of fuss with the neighbors, but no one had gone so far as to alert whatever authorities one alerts for an out-of-control chicken situation. Partially this was because Gordy was Gordy, and people needed their mail—all of their mail— more than they needed to not hear squawking. But partially it was because this was Ebey's End, and people had a certain way of doing things. Calling the county wasn't in character. Small-caliber explosives were.

Exactly what the cookies meant, Anita couldn't yet say. She was careful never to ask anything that would give away how much she noticed. It would make people uncomfortable, and now that the Blue Bird Market had opened just two miles away, Anita couldn't afford to make anyone uncomfortable.

The phone rang. Anita knew she had approximately twenty minutes before Carol would want to check out, and so she answered it.

"Is this Anita Odom?" the voice on the other end asked, marking herself as an outsider, most probably a mainlander, and not one of Anita's usual suppliers.

"Yes," Anita answered. "Who's calling, please?"

"This is Lee Overton from the Washington State Department of Children, Youth, and Families. I'm afraid I have some unfortunate news."

When Anita hung up, a buzzing like a dial tone filled her head. Her limbs felt as though they were connected to the rest of her body by frayed bits of string that might give way at any moment. It was only because she had been working a cash register since she was nine that she could work it then. The call had taken much longer than she'd expected, and so Carol was already unloading her cart when Anita hung up.

She took each item as it rolled down the half-sized conveyor belt and scanned it. She dropped one thing after another into one sack and then another and then another, paying no attention to what each item was. She told Carol the total, and Carol paid. Anita wouldn't be able to say how later, only that it was usually a debit card, the kind Anita didn't consider secure because it took money directly out of the owner's bank account.

Carol had not caught enough of Anita's end of the conversation to know what the call had been about, only that it was formal and serious and had left her looking dazed. Carol wondered if it wasn't something to do with Mack, but they didn't have the sort of relationship that would allow her to ask. Instead, she murmured her thanks, which Anita didn't seem to hear, and headed for the door.

Carol's hair had been fading slowly from blond to gray, but she still wore it long and gathered in a twist, as she had every day for the past fifteen years. For the two weeks before Christmas, she had come into the store wearing very small candy cane earrings. They had been no larger than the lobes of her ears, small enough that they seemed to be apologizing for themselves. But it was now the first part of January, and the candy canes were gone, replaced by plain gold balls, even smaller and more apologetic. It was another thing Anita didn't notice but that Gordy would later.

CHAPTER TWO

Carol drove her car into the garage. She and Henry had lived in the same house for thirty-nine years, which did not mean it had been the same house for those thirty-nine years. It was set back from the water, up a small rise, with views they couldn't have afforded if they had to buy it again. They were surrounded by dense evergreen forest on three sides, and while they had neighbors, they were too far away to see.

The outside of the house was painted the same color as the paper grocery bags she unloaded, two by two, from the trunk and carried through to the kitchen. It had always been that color, popular in the early '80s and not since. Five years before, when they'd last had painters come, she'd suggested blue. Henry had asked if she was having a midlife crisis.

She thought about that a lot. Almost every day, in fact. Exactly what he'd said. Exactly how he'd said it. She'd not replied at the time, but it was still there, like a piece of gravel wedged fast into the tread of her shoe, pressing into the ball of her foot with each step.

It wasn't as though there hadn't been plenty of other reasons to be mad over the course of a marriage. She'd been more than mad when she followed him to Anita's apartment all those years ago. She'd sat with her car idling in the alleyway between the grocery store and what had been the old movie theater. He could've looked out the window and seen her down there, but he hadn't. And seized by a sudden terror of having to confront him and *do* something about the situation, she'd thrown the car into reverse and backed out, nearly getting in an accident.

The kids had been in junior high back then. Old enough to know what was going on, although she'd done her best to keep it from them.

So, yes, she'd been plenty mad then, but she'd made her decision. She'd decided to let it go, and after a while, she saw that it had ended. If there were others, she didn't know about them, which was for the best. It was hard enough getting herself together every week to do the shopping in that woman's store, which was the only grocery store in town at the time.

Doing her hair and just a little makeup, gathering up her list and walking in, right past Anita, there in that apron, had been an act of defiance. Anita might have been sleeping with Henry, but he was married to Carol. She had the house and the children. Anita had been barely twenty, still living with her parents above the shop.

Now that Carol's own children had passed that age, she understood how young twenty really was. Young enough that she had to wonder how culpable Anita had been. Some, of course. But not half as much as her husband. Carol no longer shopped at Anita's store because doing so was defiant. She did it because they had a history together, even if neither of them acknowledged it.

All of which was to say that she understood that Henry's comment—dismissive and rude as it was—was hardly the thing to blow up a marriage about. And yet it was the thing she could not let go.

Carol unpacked the groceries, sliding the bag of Milano cookies into the back of an upper cabinet behind the Christmas china, and then set about making dinner.

Just before seven, the meatloaf with tomato glaze was done. The mashed potatoes were covered on the back burner to stay warm, as was the buttered sweet corn that had come from a can. She stirred the gravy every few minutes to keep it from forming a skin while she listened to the Seattle NPR station with her laptop. It was the tail end of *Marketplace*, which she didn't much like, and after that would be *Fresh Air*, which she did.

There was an apple pie on the counter from Tiny's Bakeshop. Anita sold some in her store, but Carol preferred to make the trip two streets down to the bakery itself on Main. She would have said, if anyone had asked, that she made the extra effort because the pies at the bakery were the freshest, which they were. Or she might have said it was because that was where you could get the widest variety, which was true. If you wanted apple or pumpkin, you could get those at Anita's. If you wanted a citrus custard tart with almond crust or French silk with four inches of meringue domed on top, you went to the bakeshop. Carol bought nothing so exotic—she bought apple because Henry liked apple, even in the middle of summer—but she went to the bakeshop anyway because she liked Tiny.

She liked her, and if Carol were being honest with herself, she envied her. Pastor Chet would have cautioned her against being covetous, but Carol didn't think that applied in this situation, and anyway, she took Chet with a grain of salt. It wasn't that Carol wanted to get up at three a.m. and make pies, but when she saw Tiny there in her own space, running her own business, there was a longing in Carol's chest, a small, sharp thing like swallowing an aspirin and having it get stuck halfway down. Tiny was her own person, that was all, and Carol wasn't. Carol belonged to others. Her children, who were grown. Her husband, who was rarely home. She hadn't meant it to be this way, and frankly, it embarrassed her. It felt as though she'd made some very shortsighted decision, probably an entire series of them, but while that was allowable, saying she had done so was not. She couldn't say she wanted something else, something in addition, without being accused of not valuing what she had. At least she couldn't say it to anyone she knew. That was another pain, a second aspirin-sized pellet lodged somewhere behind her sternum that she could do nothing about.

Fresh Air with Terry Gross came and went. Except it hadn't been Terry but someone else. She wondered if Terry was on vacation. The fill-in host didn't say, which bothered Carol. She knew she didn't deserve an explanation, but she wanted one.

Henry hadn't called. She stopped stirring the gravy.

At eight, she made herself a plate, which she had to warm in the microwave. It had taken her an hour to cook dinner. It took almost no time to eat it, sitting alone at the kitchen table. The back of the house was one big wall of windows looking out over the water, but it got dark at four o'clock in the winter. And so she sat looking at a reflection of herself, spooning mashed potatoes into her mouth for eight minutes and then pie for four minutes after that.

At 8:30, she put everything in the fridge still in the original pots and pans, shoving the milk and margarine out of the way to cram it all in. When she slammed the door, the phone rang. She glanced at the caller ID and then let the answering machine get it, watching herself in the black window listen to her husband's voice.

"I'm obviously late tonight. Nate Stevens broke his arm at basketball practice. I just finished setting it, and I've still got an hour's worth of paperwork I have to file. You should go ahead and eat without me."

Henry hung up.

They had been married for forty-one years. She'd stopped counting for a while, and now she was again.

They'd had this house built with money her father had loaned them. It had five bedrooms, which had been a ridiculous size for two people, but they'd wanted children. The house had shrunk with the kids, but they were gone and had been for some time. The house was too big again, and she couldn't see out of it. There was no "out" out there, only herself in her loose-fitting jeans and pale blue turtleneck looking back in.

The person who was not Terry was gone. Carol didn't know what show was playing. She wasn't listening.

She opened the sliding glass door and stepped out onto the deck. The cold mist landed on her face and soaked up through her socks from the boards under her feet. It wasn't cold enough to snow, but it would be later, small flurries that would melt when they touched the ground.

Outside, she could see beyond her own face. The clouds were thick and low like a dingy blanket thrown over the island. No moon. No stars. Almost never were this time of year, but still, she could make out the surface of the water. Hear it. Hear it all the way to Canada. The trees that circled the house were sharp, jagged triangles in the dark, black against charcoal, the difference barely discernible. Trees looked bigger at night. They lost their individuality, became a solid mass, closing in. They reminded her of those movies her son had liked, the ones with the orcs, millions of orcs coming over the horizon, running straight for her.

She looked over her shoulder into the house. The kitchen was lit up like a diorama. A museum example of what an upper-middle-class kitchen would have looked like thirty-odd years ago. Only the appliances had changed and only slowly. Once every twenty years. Now there was a laptop. A small television by the table so they didn't have to talk. Not the flat-screen kind but an old one that weighed a ton.

The house didn't have window shades. There was no one close enough to look in. It would be, Henry had said, a waste of money.

Anyone could see her in there. No one did.

The rest of the house was dark. Empty. Carol turned away from it, walked in her wet socks across the deck and down the short set of steps to the grass and around the side of the house until she could see down the road.

Narrow, barely two lanes. A lane and a half. It would be hard to pass if someone were coming the other way, but someone never was. There were only three houses on this street, and the street was a mile long, nothing but a part in the trees, with Carol at the very end.

She walked through the grass until she got to the driveway, and then she kept on the grass, walking alongside the light strip of concrete, the brightest thing she could see. At the end, she stopped. There was no curb, only a strip of gravel and dirt that separated the lawn from the road. She uncrossed her arms, reached down, and unbuttoned her jeans. They were loose and fell to her ankles. She kicked them off. The cold mist attacked her shins and her thighs, her dimpled saddlebags that hung below her butt whether she skipped the pie or ate it, and so she ate it.

She picked up her jeans and folded them and then dropped them by her feet again and took off her underwear. Carol's pubic hair was medium brown, even as her hair had been blond and now blond washed almost to gray. She reached up, pulled the clip loose, and let the strands fall past her shoulders. Long hair was unacceptable at her age. Why wasn't clear, only that it was, and so she wore it up. The same style every day. She took off her turtleneck next, pulling it up by the bottom hem over her head. The mist had its way with her stomach and her back while she turned her shirt the right way out and folded it, too, dropping it on top of her underwear on top of her jeans. She unhooked her white bra, three hooks for a wide band. Her breasts were not small, but they were not large, although her nipples were very prominent. They'd gotten that way after she'd breastfed both of her children, and they'd stayed that way all these years, like her body thought she might still find some need for them.

She was starting to get cold. Truly cold. And so, leaving her clothes there on the dirt-and-gravel strip, she ran. In nothing but her thin beige socks pulled up to her shins, which were beginning to show varicose veins, she ran. Her boobs swung and bounced, pulling on her skin. Her hair blew back from her face, trailing behind her, beginning to stick to her scalp from all of the wet.

In the dark, her skin was white and luminous. She looked down. She was not moving as fast as she felt herself to be moving, but that was fine. The feeling was the important thing. Now she was the brightest thing she could see, that anyone could see if they looked.

CHAPTER THREE

Anita had offered to meet the social worker at her office on the mainland, but she had insisted on coming to Ebey's End, and so Anita had offered to meet her at the ferry, but she had insisted on coming to Anita's house. Anita explained that she didn't have a house. She had a grocery store and lived in the apartment above it. The social worker had said that was fine. She was still coming. It had been less than twenty-four hours since that first call, and Anita was sitting on her father's sofa with the television off, holding on to a cold cup of coffee and waiting for the knock.

Before leaving the store the night before, she had picked up a box of Froot Loops, ground beef and a jar of Prego, half a gallon of milk, white bread, peanut butter, two apples, two oranges, and two bananas. She'd started in the produce section, and she hadn't made a list. Upstairs, she'd put it all away except for the fruit, which, for the first time in her life, she'd arranged in a bowl and set first on the kitchen table, and then on the coffee table, and then, when that seemed strange, back on the kitchen table again.

She'd given the social worker directions, which included going down the alley between her store and the building next door, which had a FOR LEASE sign on the marquee. The woman would have to climb the steep wooden stairs along the outside to her door, which was plain and white and marked only by a black-and-gold sticker that said PRIVATE.

It was not entirely true that Anita didn't have a house, although it depended on your definition of "house." She had purchased three acres of land and the sort of double-wide trailer that, with the addition of a porch, a carport, and some bushes, could pass for a house. When her elderly father had had his stroke, she'd moved him there with her. He could no longer manage the stairs above the shop or the shop itself, and at night he needed someone with him.

Anita had expected a long, slow decline, but Mack had other ideas. He did the exercises the physical therapist had shown him. He got out of the house, pestering Anita to drive him to town, where he would spend the day at the store, no longer doing much work but looking over her shoulder, correcting what didn't need correcting. When he'd pushed Anita nearly to the point of patricide, he would walk over to the diner, order coffee and a plate of contraband French fries, and talk to whoever came through the door.

It had turned out to be a surprisingly effective recovery plan. He still could not manage stairs or the store. He still got around with one of those rolling walkers that had a built-in seat and hand brakes, and he still lived in Anita's trailer. But he did not need her with him quite so much, and so, for both of their sakes, she'd moved out, taking over the apartment where she'd grown up. And because her furniture fit in the trailer, and his furniture fit in the apartment, they had—for the most part—left things that way.

When Anita sat on the sofa, it was her father's sofa. When she lay in bed, it was her father's bed. She used his dishes, swept with his broom, and ran his store. And there was certainly a lot any two-bit psychiatrist could do with that.

Ms. Overton, the social worker, had said to expect her at three o'clock. But it was 3:20, and then it was 3:45, and then it was four. Anita went to the kitchen, poured the cold coffee down the drain, and made a peanut butter and banana sandwich. She had scrubbed the apartment that morning, changed the sheets on the guest bed, which had been hers growing up, and then, when the logistics of the situation dawned on her, ran downstairs for a new toothbrush and tube of toothpaste. She left both by the bathroom sink, the toothbrush still in its packaging to show that it was new. Anita knew it was inadequate, but she didn't know what else to do.

Anita ate her sandwich over the sink to catch the crumbs and looked out the window. Across the back alley was a secondhand clothing store, which was not precisely a thrift store. They didn't take donations. They paid people for what they brought in and wouldn't take what they couldn't sell, not that the unscrupulous didn't try to get around that. They came after hours and left sacks full of unwanted things by the back door in violation of the ever-larger sign that told them not to. Anita sometimes heard the perpetrators pull up at night. The telltale popping sound of a trunk and the scuffle of feet. If she was in the kitchen, she'd look down. She couldn't always tell who it was, but sometimes she could and she filed it away. It wasn't grocery behavior, but it still told her something. She never said anything, not to them and not to Lynette, who owned the store and had to cart it all away. Every business had a downside. Anita cleaned up a lot of broken eggs.

At 4:15, there was a knock on the door, and Anita jerked back like the counter was electrified. She'd been anxious at one o'clock and two o'clock and three o'clock, but a nervous system can only be on high for so long. Nothing she was worried about had happened, and in the past hour, she'd entered a liminal state. The cat was in the box, both alive and dead. Until it wasn't. Until it was knocking at her door, demanding to get in and have a go at the furniture.

She didn't have time to wash the plate and knife and was forced to leave them in the sink like questions at the end of a test she hadn't had time to get to. She wiped her hands on her jeans, wished she were an entirely different person, and then, on an exhale like pulling a trigger, opened the door.

The social worker stood on the small wooden landing, but Anita didn't see her. Her eyes traveled over her to the girl by her side. On the phone, Ms. Overton had said she was fourteen, in good health, and that her name was July.

Anita had been too stunned to ask anything else, and now she realized how inadequate the description had been. It was like saying, "It's an animal. It has fur and four legs." That might be a dog, but it also could be a horse or a gerbil or a snow leopard. July, likewise, could've been any fourteen-year-old girl in the world, but she was not. She was this very specific one, and Anita's brain whirled trying to replace the horse it had expected with the unknown creature in front of her, who was studying her right back.

Growing up, Anita had a best friend, who had a cat. In fourth grade, she got a second cat, which had to live in the bathroom for a week so the two could sniff each other under the door. Anita had forgotten that until now. At the time, it had seemed an unnecessarily prolonged introduction, but now it made complete sense.

Ms. Overton interrupted.

"I'm sorry we're so late. I tried to call, but I couldn't get any cell service."

"It comes and goes," Anita said, which made the woman's brow crease, and Anita wondered if that counted against her.

"I'm Anita," she said, holding her hand out to the girl.

July hesitated but then took her hand out of her coat pocket. It was slim and cold, and she didn't shake so much as she allowed Anita to hold the ends of her fingers in a sort of Victorian courting gesture, saying nothing.

A heavy mist was coming down, leaving a sheen of moisture on their coats. (In Ebey's End, it should always be understood that it is raining or drizzling or misting or just generally wet unless it is August or specifically stated otherwise.)

July had the hood of her wool coat up. The hood rested on the top of her head and flared out before gathering in at the collar like Little Red Riding Hood if Little Red Riding Hood had preferred gray. The coat itself went down past July's hips and flared out slightly as though it might decide to become a dress. The social worker's outerwear was more prosaic, a faded burgundy parka of the sort that could be worn skiing but almost never was. It had a faux-fur-lined hood, which the woman had left down despite the weather. She was soft and middle-aged with a heavy workbag over her shoulder. She wore no makeup, as was the local custom, and had light brown hair with a soft, natural curl that was slowly becoming matted to her head.

"Come in," Anita said, and stepped aside. "I can take your jackets."

July began to undo her oversized black buttons, but the social worker declined. "I'll keep mine, thanks."

Anita wondered if that meant she wasn't planning to stay long. She had no idea how this was meant to go. Such a thing had never happened to her or to anyone she knew. She couldn't even recall seeing it happen on television, which hardly seemed possible.

July, who was more inclined to stay, handed over her coat. It was heavy, and Anita had to fight the urge to sniff it.

Under her coat, July wore black leggings and an oversized black sweater. Her socks were red and heavy and came up over top of her shiny green combat boots.

Anita motioned toward the sofa. She couldn't say for certain what someone would picture when told she lived in an apartment over an old grocery store. But in reality, it was like someone had taken a standard suburban home from a 1952 Sears catalog and shrunk it to half size. Just inside the front door was a small dining table with a pendant lamp hanging over it, and beyond that was the living room, which opened into the kitchen. The single hall led to the bathroom and three small bedrooms. There was a linen closet in the hall and clothes closets in each of the rooms. That was it. Anita had to keep the vacuum and Christmas decorations in the spare bedroom that served as the grocery's office. She carried the girl's coat to the dining table and draped it over a chair. Eventually July would have to hang it in her bedroom, but they hadn't gotten to that yet.

Ms. Overton unzipped her coat before sitting down. July took the seat next to her but not too close, while Anita took the only other chair, her father's wooden rocker.

"How was the ferry?" Anita asked because you always asked.

"A bit rough, actually," the woman answered, and closed her eyes briefly, as though reliving the trauma.

There was something on the woman's sweater, right in front between the zippered panels of her coat, that might have been a small trickle of dried vomit. Anita tried not to look at it, but out of the corner of her eye, she thought she saw the girl's mouth twitch as though suppressing a smile. When Anita turned to look at her squarely, though, the flat, unreadable expression came back.

"I didn't realize the trip would be quite so long," the woman went on.

Anita sympathized. Once or twice a year, going to the mainland would become unavoidable for one reason or another. The ferry schedule gave the appearance of strict regularity but in practice was more like a weather forecast. There was a fifty percent chance of you making the two-hour crossing and a fifty percent chance the engine would break, or some necessary crewman would be unavailable, or the waves would be too high, or maybe it was Tuesday, so to hell with it all.

Ebey's End was the terminus of the route. Once aboard, you would stop at Friday Harbor (unless it was actually Friday) and then Orcas Island and then Shaw and then Lopez, unless you skipped them (see above reasons). Then, once you got to the mainland, you were not actually in Seattle, which was where most people needed to be. The drive from Anacortes, where the ferry docked, to the city was another hour and twenty minutes, unless it was two and a half hours, or if there was an accident, you would never find out how long the drive was. You would simply have to abandon your car on the road when it eventually ran out of gas.

Anita understood this was God's way of telling her not to go. She had been warned, and if she persisted, she should expect no help. Obviously no one had explained this to Ms. Overton.

"First," the social worker said, even though it wasn't first. They had been speaking for at least two minutes. "Let me say that I am sorry for your loss."

The loss was Catherine, Anita's cousin on her mother's side, a woman Anita had met two or three times when they were children and not since. Her death, in a car accident, was sudden. Ms. Overton used the word "unforeseeable," which Anita silently objected to. Everyone dies. It is the most foreseeable outcome possible.

Anita's family had always been small, which had not made them close. In fact, it seemed to have done the opposite. Her mother and father had each had one sibling. Those siblings had married and each had a single child. A trio of trios that had floated off like bits of dandelion fluff to live independent of the others.

When Anita's mother had died, her father told her he had tried to notify Catherine, but all he had was the address book his wife had kept. When he called the number written there, it was no longer in service. When he called directory assistance, they couldn't find anyone by that name, which was when he remembered hearing Catherine had gotten married, but no one had written down her new name. This was before social media, and so that was it. She was gone from their lives forever.

That is until Ms. Overton's call the day before. It turned out Catherine had gone on to become a professor of ancient history. She had gotten divorced and only afterward adopted a child, taking their traditional family structure of three persons down to two.

Catherine's parents, Anita's aunt and uncle, had already passed. Their branch of the family tree, spindly to begin with, was now cursed, a sickly thing trying its best to die. And Catherine, in a stunning lack of foresight, which Anita would forever judge, had passed without a will. As best as anyone had been able to determine in the past two weeks, she had made no arrangements at all for her daughter's care. It had taken the state this long to locate Anita, the girl's closest living and able-bodied relative.

Anita hadn't known July existed twenty-four hours ago, but the social worker had made it clear that it was her or foster care. The last time Anita had pictured herself a mother was when she still played with dolls. She might have married if a suitable opportunity arose, but her opportunity had been married to someone else. There were other men in Ebey's End, but she viewed them like she viewed the trees. Nice to have around but not something you brought into the house.

Ms. Overton had pronounced the words "foster care" in the same way she might have said "battlefield amputation." So would Anita consent to guardianship? They needed an answer. It had already been two weeks.

Anita didn't know to whom those two weeks had belonged, but

they had not been hers. She had not had two weeks. The universe had had two weeks. The state of Washington had had two weeks. Anita got twenty minutes and a description of a child who could also have been a horse.

But Anita had watched a lot of *Law & Order* and had a wildly irrational fear of what could happen to a girl on the edge of not-being-a-girl in such a situation. Or it might have been a perfectly well-proportioned fear. She would never know. July would live with her because Anita could not bring herself to refuse.

Still, she did not think it was a good idea. She did not consider herself prepared or suitable. This whole thing was almost certainly not in the girl's best interest—or Anita's, for that matter. Anita would not, she was sure, be anything like a real mother, which would probably leave them both psychologically damaged in the following four years. (She was assuming the girl would leave at eighteen, although, if she'd considered it further, she might have remembered that she and her father lived in each other's houses.) Nonetheless, in the twenty minutes she'd had to contemplate the situation, she'd decided that the girl, abandoned by her birth mother and orphaned again by her adoptive one, was obviously so far past any hope of mental well-being that any additional damage Anita could do would be superfluous.

Anita herself did nothing but work, and when she wasn't working, she sat on the couch and watched television, eating whatever she happened to have off the plate in her lap. She could go a week without leaving the building. She was going to die alone, her body in a heap by the frozen foods. Her only contribution to the world would be an infallible personality test reliant on packaged foodstuffs. It wasn't much of a future to be protective of, and so here they were.

"Shall we go over everything?" Ms. Overton asked, pulling several thick manila folders from her bag.

"Yes," Anita said.

"It will be something of a process," Ms. Overton told her.

Anita looked over at July, who had her hands pressed hard between her knees. She was looking at the stack of papers like it was a test. It was, of course, but not for her. Probably she didn't know that. If it had been Anita at that age, she'd have been inconsolable.

Anita looked back at the social worker. "I would imagine so."

CHAPTER FOUR

nita had called her father immediately after she'd gotten the news. She could hear the diner noises behind him. He had been silent at first, as stunned as Anita had been. When he finally spoke, it wasn't encouraging.

"I think someone else should take her."

"Thanks, I think a lot of you, too."

It wasn't that Anita disagreed, but it was different coming from her own father.

"You don't have any experience."

There was a voice she couldn't place, and Mack pulled the phone away from his mouth to answer. Anita knew this was the moment when word would begin to spread. Measles was less contagious than gossip in Ebey's End.

"There is no one else," Anita said when her father came back.

"There's always someone else."

"Who, Dad?"

He didn't have an answer, and so he'd said, "I'm calling Pastor Chet."

"Great, tell him to pray for me."

Anita hung up a little harder than she should have but only half as hard as she'd wanted to.

. . . .

Anita did what she thought she should do. She showed July her room and offered to help her unpack her suitcase and boxes. July thanked her and declined in the fewest words possible. Anita ordered pizza because everyone knows kids like pizza. They walked through the drizzle together to get it because, if mail doesn't get delivered, you can pretty much forget about anything else.

They ate at the kitchen table on the plates Anita had been eating off her whole life: thin white Corelle dishes with the gold butterfly pattern around the rim. They'd been government issue in 1975 and were both hideous and indestructible. Anita was afraid the dishware wasn't making a very good first impression. Nothing in the apartment made a very good first impression because the impression was that the occupant was an eighty-year-old man who bought Bengay in the economy size and had a deep knowledge of Medicare supplement plans.

Anita explained about the apartment and the dishes and her father and the trailer, although she avoided using the word "trailer." July looked up when Anita spoke. She stopped chewing. She put her hands in her lap. She listened like someone who'd gotten lost and needed directions. It made Anita uncomfortable. Nothing she was saying was important. The girl needed to eat, but she would not while Anita talked and so Anita stopped talking. Eventually July picked up her piece of pizza again. She ate only one, and it was so quiet between them that Anita could hear the muted sounds of the store below, the last customers of the day running in for milk or eggs or something quick for dinner. If she tried, she probably could have figured out who they were and make a pretty good stab at what they bought. It made her a very good grocer but not a particularly good anything else.

. . . .

Anita woke in the middle of the night with a witch's brew of anxiety and pepperoni grease churning in her stomach. The acid had crawled back up her esophagus and, if her nervous system was to be believed, had caught fire. Sitting up helped but not enough. Grudgingly, she threw back the covers and put her bare feet to the cold wooden floor.

She moved past July's room as quietly as she could, pausing to listen for any noises behind her closed door, and then continued into the kitchen in search of a glass of milk. Moving in the dark, she opened the refrigerator, reached for the carton, and froze.

Sitting square in front of the milk was a half-empty bottle of "assorted fruit" Tums, the same bottle she was certain had been in the medicine cabinet.

Anita hesitated before reaching for it. When she did, the plastic was as cold as anything, and when she opened the top and poured two—and, on second thought, one more—into her hand, they were cold, too. The medicine, however it had gotten there, had been there for a while.

Without putting the tablets in her mouth, Anita turned and looked through the gloom toward the bedrooms. There hadn't been any noise earlier, and there wasn't any now. Nothing but the low hum of the refrigerator, which was, in its mechanical way, telling her to stop being ridiculous. She carried the bottle with her to the bathroom, closed the door, and opened the medicine cabinet. Inside was a blank space where the bottle should have been.

Anita tried to remember the last time she'd taken any. The truth was she took them a lot. She went through a bottle every few weeks and had for some time. Her father's stroke had come two weeks after the Blue Bird had opened. It got to be she reached for the bottle every time she started to worry, imagining she could feel the stomach acid burbling up before it actually did. She took the fruity little tablets preventatively, habitually. She figured they couldn't hurt. She'd certainly taken them the day before and more than once. She just didn't remember putting them in the refrigerator. She couldn't think how she would have done that. She always dumped the bottle into her hand right there in the bathroom, and if she *had* carried the bottle to the kitchen, wouldn't she have noticed earlier?

Unless, of course, she hadn't with all the running around, worrying and waiting, making up the guest room and going back and forth down to the store. Maybe the veneer of calm she'd spackled to her outsides had been thinner than she'd realized.

Anita put the bottle back on the shelf where it belonged, closed the cabinet, and, with only the briefest tingle of hesitation, tossed the three tablets—two pink and a yellow—into her mouth. They tasted exactly as they always did. They weren't even cold anymore.

. . . .

The next morning, July came out of her room fully dressed in more leggings and another sweater. Her hair was light brown and parted down the middle. She'd tucked it behind her ears, which was an upgrade over the night before, when it had hung on either side of her face like a curtain about to close. Anita noticed her eyes were hazel, and she had a small cleft in her chin. She still had the flawless skin of childhood with a slight roundness in her cheeks, even though her legs and arms were so thin her joints protruded. The purple half-moons under her eyes were darker and more bruised-looking than they had been the day before, and Anita wondered if she'd slept at all.

She offered eggs or oatmeal or cereal, and July chose cereal. Anita produced the box of Froot Loops, secretly proud she'd thought to buy it.

"If you don't like this, you're welcome to anything downstairs."

"This is fine," July said, reaching for the box and then stopping. "Thank you," she said, glancing up at Anita, checking. Anita didn't know for what.

"You're welcome," she said, and only then did July pick up the box and pour the cereal into her bowl.

Anita hadn't had Froot Loops possibly ever and certainly not in the past twenty-five years, but in solidarity, she poured her own bowl, determined to make this meal different from the last.

"I'm going to talk," she said, "but you should keep eating."

July set down her spoon. "Okay."

Anita raised her left eyebrow. It was a thing she could do, bring it almost all the way up to her hairline. She waited, brow up. July hesitated but picked up the spoon. Anita felt like she'd won something.

"I'm going to say something about me, and then you say an equivalent thing about you. It'll be like a party game."

It was less like a party game and more like a corporate icebreaker, but it was the best Anita could think of, certainly better than a drunken round of Never Have I Ever.

Anita picked up the milk and poured it into her bowl. "My middle name is Ann."

She set the milk down and looked at July.

A beat passed, and then the girl said, "Constance."

Anita nodded. "Good."

She would've thought "Constance" had fallen out of common usage sometime around the Salem witch trials, but what did she know. Anita picked up her own spoon and was about to say the next thing when July spoke again.

"I've never liked it."

This was almost a conversation. Anita tried to act natural in case the girl spooked.

"I've heard worse."

Anita took a bite of cereal. It did not taste like fruit. It did not taste like food. She couldn't believe she sold this to people. She couldn't believe they bought it. She tried to chew without letting it touch her tongue. This did not work, but the girl was eating it, and Anita would have plowed through a bowl of splinters to keep from insulting her.

"What?" July asked.

Anita had taken a mouthful of coffee and was holding it with chipmunk cheeks, trying to slosh it around. She swallowed and feigned innocence. "What what?"

"What's worse than Constance?"

"Oh, uh . . ." Anita's brain whirled like an overtaxed hard drive. She hadn't come prepared with examples.

"Chester," Anita said, the name rushing out. "The pastor here is named Chester, which makes him Pastor Chester."

July gave a small smile.

Encouraged, Anita pushed on, babbling. "People here mostly stay in the family business like me. So his father was the pastor before him and his father before him."

July ate another bite, chewing normally, watching Anita and listening.

"That means Chet's parents knew what he would grow up to be, and they named him that anyway."

"Malice aforethought," July said.

"Exactly," Anita said, impressed.

July looked down at her bowl, dragged her spoon through the floating neon Os without scooping any up. The milk had turned gray.

"My mom used to say that sometimes. 'Malice aforethought.'"

The air around them got heavy. Anita didn't know what to say, and July didn't look up. Outside, a gull screamed. They were only a couple of blocks from the water. Everywhere in Ebey's End was only a couple of blocks from the water.

"I'm sorry about what happened to her and to you."

July raised a shoulder and then dropped it. "Thanks."

Whatever conversation they were going to have was over. Anita gave up on the cereal and picked up her coffee.

"I'm sorry, too," July said. "That you got stuck with me."

"I didn't get stuck with you," Anita said.

It came out quickly and automatically, a lie but a necessary one. She tried to think of something else to say, something to prove it, but she couldn't and the silence went on too long.

"When you're ready," Anita finally said, "I'll show you around the store."

July put down her spoon. "I'm ready."

. . . .

Anita showed her the stockroom where she kept cases of dry goods waiting to be shelved and a folding table pushed into the corner they called "the break room." Then on to cold storage, stacked high with milk and eggs, and over to the walk-in freezer she used to keep cases of ice cream and TV dinners, separate from the smaller freezer just for meat. Anita introduced her to the handful of part-time clerks, all women over forty, who manned the register when Anita didn't. And she purposefully did not introduce her to the high school boys, who stocked shelves early on weekends or after six o'clock when the store closed on weekdays. They came and went so often Anita was always hiring. It was a decades-long chain of interchangeable young men between the ages of sixteen and eighteen, wiry in their ball caps and T-shirts, who smelled like sweat and, in the past few years, the sickly sweet fumes from their vape pens.

Later that day, she went to enroll July in school, taking with her the thick files of paperwork Ms. Overton had left behind, not knowing what she would need. In the end, Anita ended up handing it all over to the woman in the school office to sort through. She was familiar, a customer but one who tended to come when one of the other checkers was on duty. Still, she smiled at Anita, her left eyetooth a little crooked, and nodded and said she'd been expecting her. It had been twenty-four hours since July's ferry had docked, plenty of time for news to make the rounds.

She walked Anita through a dozen forms, filling them out for her "to speed things up" and handing them to Anita to sign, which she did, largely without reading them. Anita had had no idea how many forms were required to send a child to school. It was like applying for a mortgage. Between this and the social worker, Anita had signed her name more times in the past twenty-four hours than she had in the preceding forty-odd years, and they weren't done. July would have to choose electives and be slotted into classes, which were already full. Her transcripts had been good. She could take the advanced math, if she wanted, but that would mean classes with older kids. The registrar/attendance secretary told Anita to think about it, and to talk through the elective choices with her.

"We don't have as many as she's probably used to, but still," the woman said, "if she's college-bound, it'll matter."

Anita had never gone to college. She didn't know anything about it, but she didn't say so. She probably should have asked for more help—different help—than filling in lines on forms. The forms she could've figured out on her own.

Would July be participating in sports? the woman asked. Any after-school clubs?

More things Anita didn't know. She asked for a list to take home. They didn't have a list. The woman rattled them off. There were at least a dozen, some of which sounded less like extracurriculars and more like obscure governmental agencies. (What the hell was a DECA, and did her taxes pay for it?) Anita wouldn't remember anything but "girls' soccer" when she got back to the car. She didn't know if July played soccer or wanted to. She didn't know anything whatsoever.

It was a Wednesday. July would start the following week. It wasn't much time to get her act together.

"And finally, will she be riding the bus?" the woman asked.

"Yes," Anita said, jumping on a question she felt qualified to answer.

The store was miles from the school, too far to walk, especially in the rain, and Anita had to work. Scheduling was hard enough as it was. The woman handed her another form.

. . . .

On the drive home, Anita's heart, usually reliable, got ahead of itself, a little at first and then more all at once. It beat faster and faster like it was running for a bus while the rest of her was forced to stay still behind the wheel of the car. She thought about pulling over and didn't. She thought about dying and didn't. She thought about calling someone and dismissed that entirely.

By the time she parked, she was panting. Her hands were unsteady, and she missed the gear shift the first time she reached for it. Before she opened the door, she pressed her lips together. Her chest rose and fell noticeably, so she zipped her coat.

Upstairs, July was in the guest room—her room—with the door closed. Anita hurried to the bathroom and shut herself inside. Leaning against the sink, she flicked her eyes up to the mirror. Her makeup-less face was pale under bright pink cheeks. She looked like a corpse that had caught a fever.

There was a knock on the door, tentative and without rhythm. July called out almost too quietly to be heard: "Anita?"

Anita took a breath and put her hand to her chest. She avoided looking in the mirror again. "I'm okay," she called back.

July didn't say anything, and Anita reached for her washcloth, yellow and starting to fray at the edges. It was stiff. It didn't dry soft on the towel rack anymore, and she didn't know why, but it probably wasn't good. She turned on the tap and threw it into the bottom of the sink. When it was soaked, she wrung it out, sank to the edge of the tub, and pressed it against her face. It didn't smell sour, but it didn't smell good either.

The small voice came from the other side of the door again. "Anita?"

"Yeah."

A pause. "I have to pee."

"Okay." The washcloth muffled her voice.

"Really bad."

Anita stood up and started for the doorknob, but before she got there, she doubled back for the medicine cabinet. She flicked it open and stared at the shelf. The Tums were where she'd left them. She grabbed the bottle, dumped out two, and was still wiping the tablet dust from her hand off on her pants when she opened the bathroom door.

CHAPTER FIVE

July wore a green apron identical to Anita's. Her cousin had already shown her how to sweep the floor, straighten the shelves, and sack the groceries. The sacking lessons took a long time. Anita did a lot of explaining. She incorporated visuals. There was a trial period. Sacking groceries was an art. You had to think about weight and structure. You wanted to minimize the number of bags a customer had to carry, but if the chips were crushed or the peaches bruised, that was on you. Eggs were a world unto themselves. And you had to work fast. No one wanted to stand around watching someone hem and haw over what to do with the extra-large tub of spinach.

There wasn't one stock boy Anita had hired in the past five years who she would've allowed to sack. July figured it out the first day. By the next, she could go as fast as Anita could, and something Anita didn't yet recognize as pride pricked inside of her.

With her arms crossed, Anita waited for the next customer to walk in. July saw where she was looking and looked, too. Neither of them said anything. They didn't have to wait long. When the glass door swooshed open, it was Felicia who hurried in.

Anita leaned toward July. "Watch her," she whispered.

Felicia worked the front desk at the sheriff's department, which shared a building with city hall. If you needed a permit or to file a report or were just looking for help with your tinfoil hat, Felicia was the first and usually last person you talked to. There was not a level of crazy that existed in Ebey's End that she had not seen and dealt with personally. It implied a certain level of competence, which made her home life a wonder.

Felicia was divorced and had four boys between the ages of eight and sixteen, every one of which teachers hoped they didn't get. The backseat of her car looked like a homeless person lived in it, and Anita had heard her house was worse.

"Morning," Felicia said. "Afternoon. Whatever."

She grabbed one of the rolling carts, which stuck to the next one in the row. She yanked and yanked again and then cursed when it came loose and ran over her foot.

"You okay?" Anita called.

"No," Felicia answered without looking up, "not really."

She speed-walked to the far side of the store and disappeared down an aisle, pushing the cart ahead of her like it was a battering ram.

Anita handed July a broom. "Keep an eye on her, but don't let her know it."

"Why?" July whispered, her eyes darting toward where Felicia had gone.

"I'll explain when she leaves."

"Shoplifter?" July asked.

"Jesus, no. She works for Bill," Anita said, without explaining who Bill was. "Go on. You're missing stuff."

July took the broom and stepped away from her post at the checkout. With one more look over her shoulder at Anita, she pretended to sweep, making her way to the far side of the store.

Thirty minutes later, after Felicia had crisscrossed the store three times, she and July were both back at the register.

"I'd swear it was a goddamn full moon," Felicia said while Anita ran her items quickly over the scanner.

She'd filled the cart to the top, mounding things toward the center like she was building a mountain out of freezer pastries and Ritz crackers. In the little-kid seat by the handle, she had six dozen eggs.

"That kind of day?" Anita asked dutifully, showing interest but not too much.

"You have no idea."

Anita scanned canned spaghetti, canned fruit cocktail, canned green beans and canned corn, packages of chicken thighs with the skin on, and pounded cube steak. There was toilet paper and aluminum foil and three loaves of bread. The items kept coming. Sack after sack full. Anita's hands moved in a steady rhythm, never once having to turn an item to search for the barcode. *Beep, beep, beep,* the register went like a heart monitor.

She gave a glance over to July to see if she was keeping up. Once or twice, she struggled, getting behind when she had to grab another sack from the stack and they stuck together. Anita slowed her rhythm a little to let July get her legs under her and then picked it up again. On it went until the last items, the eggs, as always.

Felicia handed Anita a couple of coupons, two of which were expired and that Anita let go anyway. She always did for Felicia. It was a private merit system. Anita read off the total, several hundred dollars, and Felicia paid in cash.

"It just goes up and up, doesn't it?" she said when Anita handed her the change.

"Always."

Felicia looked over at July, who was trying to fit the last bag into the cart for her to roll out to her car. It was precarious.

"You're the new girl?"

It was the first time Felicia had acknowledged her presence.

Anita wasn't sure July was going to speak, but she pushed her hair back behind her ear and said, "I'm Anita's cousin."

"Well, welcome, Cousin," Felicia said. "I'll tell my boys to keep an eye out for you at school."

July nodded, not yet knowing if this would be a good or bad thing. Anita figured it could go either way, protectors or tormentors. Probably both.

"Do you need help out?" July asked.

"No," Felicia said. "I'd rather deal with it myself."

They watched her go. When the door slid closed, Anita turned to July. They were alone in the store.

"Tell me about her."

"Tell you what?"

"Anything. What did you learn?"

"She bought a lot," July said, testing her answer by Anita's expression.

Anita nodded but didn't say anything.

"She was in a hurry, but she kept going back the way she'd already been. I don't think she knew what she wanted."

"Anything else?"

"She threw stuff into the cart. Like really threw it."

"What does that tell you?"

"She's not careful or doesn't have time to be."

"And?"

"She has a big family."

"Anything else?"

July opened her mouth and then shut it. Anita raised her eyebrow. "Go on."

July shook her head.

"You've got something else," Anita said.

July shook her head again and looked down. Whatever it was, she didn't want to say, so Anita took over.

"She bought two cake mixes and two cans of frosting, both different flavors. You know she cooks, but not a lot and not from scratch. You saw the canned goods, so probably she's not making a multi-layered cake. She needs two different ones, but it's just after the holidays. Most people aren't buying cakes right now. New Year's resolutions. We're in the diet trough for a couple of weeks, so probably it's a birthday. Could be two cakes for two different birthdays or two because her family can't agree on a flavor."

Anita knew it was two birthdays, but she had an unfair advantage. Felicia had been shopping at her store for as long as Anita could remember.

"She bought the chicken thighs and the cube steak, the cheapest cuts of meat we've got. But she bought name-brand cereal. So she economizes on things without a label but spends more on things that have one. She had coupons. Fifty-five cents on a three-hundred-dollar order isn't much, but she bothered. Money is tight, but she doesn't want it to show."

Anita paused to see if July was following.

"She bought a lot—big family, like you said—and she knew it would be expensive. You can tell because she had a lot of cash on her. Way more cash than most people carry, so there has to be a reason for that."

"She doesn't have a credit card?" July posited.

"Or she doesn't like to use it. But you're right. You'd have noticed eventually when you saw her open her wallet enough times. No cards."

"Why doesn't she have one?"

"Good question."

Anita knew but didn't say. The cards had disappeared around the same time as the divorce. Felicia's situation was difficult but hardly unique. There was a saying on the island: You either had three jobs or three houses. In other words, you were a local and hardships were expected, or you were a summer person, an invasive species upon which they'd come to rely.

July stared at her, not open-mouthed, but it was close. "Do you do that with all of your customers?"

Anita had never shown anyone what she could do. It wasn't meant to be a party trick. But she had spent her entire life behind a cash register. She wasn't good with people like her father was. She wasn't natural, and so she'd had to develop other ways of knowing folks. It was a skill, and she was good at it. More than good. It was the thing she did best in the world, and also the thing she hid.

"Whatever you do," she said, sidestepping the question, "don't let the customer know what you know."

A small furrow gathered at July's brow. "Why?"

"People don't want to know you're paying that much attention to them. They come in. They do their business. They leave. That's it."

July eyed her but didn't respond.

"Spit it out."

The girl pulled her sleeves over her hands and then put her hands in her apron pockets. "I'm pretty sure all anyone wants is for someone to pay attention to them."

"Not everyone," Anita said, her voice like a sinking stone.

July looked like she wanted to say more, but she kept her lips together. Then the door swooshed open, and the next customer walked in.

Anita wondered, later, what July had known about Felicia that she hadn't wanted to say. Whatever it was, she decided it said something positive about the girl's character that she'd kept it to herself.

CHAPTER SIX

t was 7:30 in the morning, and the sun was still not up. July stood at the end of the block, waiting for the bus alone. There were no cars on the street. No cars in the parking spaces angled off the road. No one going in and out of anywhere. Nothing moved. It felt like the rapture. July's whole life felt like the rapture.

Downtown Ebey's End was three streets deep and three blocks long and looked like the set of a black-and-white Western minus the horses. The buildings were more than a hundred years old, including the library, which was in a fussy Victorian house at the end of the street.

Each business was painted a different color. Anita's store was yellow. The shuttered movie theater next to it was brown with a marquee that jutted out. (FOR LEASE, it said, with a phone number.) The bakery was pale blue, and next to it was the tavern done in dark green. Across the way were the pizza parlor, which was light purple, and the ice cream parlor, which was red and only open on weekends. It seemed to July those two ought to switch colors, but there wasn't any rhyme or reason to things here. The pharmacy was white, and the diner was black. Nothing was gray except everything was gray. The clouds, the sky, the mood.

The only exceptions to the old-timey rainbow effect were the bank and the post office. Both were relatively new glass-and-concrete buildings. Standard issue in any mainland suburb, but here they stood out, and July noticed for the first time how ugly buildings like that could be.

She had been waiting for twenty minutes, fifteen minutes past when the bus had been due. She thought about walking back to the store, but she was afraid the bus would come if she did and she'd miss it. She didn't want to bother Anita, who'd been at the computer in the spare room when she'd left, frowning at a spreadsheet.

July spent all of her time trying not to bother Anita, who was family—at least to her mother—but felt to her like a stranger with an extra bed. July knew she was a thing that had happened to Anita. She'd fallen on her like something pushed out a window. And the same was true for July. All of this had fallen on her, too. Not one thing but many things. She tried not to think about it during the day if she could help it. Anita expected her to get up, to function, to say words and put on clothes. But each thing—pants, socks, underwear, shoes— it was all an effort. Sometimes she had to stop halfway through with one leg in her pants and one leg out. She'd sit down on the edge of the bed, and it was hard to start again. She was expected to sit at the table and pick up her fork and put food in her mouth, chew and swallow it. It was a dining death march she was barely surviving, and she *wouldn't* survive it if she let all that had happened to her crowd her mind. It had to be kept far off to the side during waking hours, something she could only just see out of the corner of her eye. It felt like a betrayal, but it was the only way. She could think of her mother, or she could breathe. Not both. Not at the same time.

From under the hood of her wool coat, July had watched the morning's mist turn heavy, condensing into rain. Her backpack was wet. Her jeans from the knees down were wet. Her canvas high-tops had gone from tomato red to the color of drying blood. Her socks were soaked and turning pink from her shoes, something she wouldn't find out until later.

She heard it before she saw it. An engine coming from the other direction. She stepped closer to the curb, picked her head up, thought, *Finally.* But when it came around the corner, it wasn't a bus but a black sedan at least ten years older than she was. She expected it to continue by, but instead, it slowed and, in fits and starts, pulled up to the curb six inches from her feet.

The window rolled down to reveal a teenage boy who did not really look old enough to be driving. He was pale and wore a dark gray hoodie under a thin brown coat. The inside of the car was steamy, all of the windows fogged but for the half-rainbow shape the wipers made on the windshield. From where she stood, she could smell the sickly vanilla air freshener hanging from the rearview mirror. She stepped back.

"Bus didn't come?" he asked, both hands still gripping the wheel tight like he was afraid to let go.

Back home, she'd have turned and walked away, gone into a shop with other people for protection.

"I guess not," she said, looking over her shoulder.

She put her hand in the pocket of her coat. Anita had given her a set of keys for the apartment and the store. July threaded her fingers through them like her mom had taught her.

"My name's Malcolm," he said. "My dad's the pastor."

He pointed over his shoulder with his thumb like the man was behind him. She looked. No one was there.

"Pastor Chester," she said.

Malcolm made a noise like a snort. "Well, everyone calls him Pastor Chet, but yeah. He wanted me to drive by in case you didn't get picked up."

"I didn't."

"He figured. But the good news is he let me borrow the car, so now neither of us have to take the bus."

She looked at the faded side panels and the green moss growing on the rubber gaskets around the windows.

"This is your dad's car?"

"Technically it belongs to the church."

July thought about not getting in. If her mother had found out she'd gotten in a stranger's car, she'd have killed her. But her mother was dead, and Anita was busy, and Malcolm seemed to be who he said he was. And if the worst had not already happened, it felt like it had. She got in.

"So is your dad psychic or something?" July asked when she'd put her wet bag at her feet and buckled herself in.

Malcolm smiled. He had a line of zits along his hairline at the temple, evenly spaced like perforation. His hair was the same medium brown as hers but curly. Big, soft ringlets fell down over his forehead. He probably hated it, and one or two girls secretly—or maybe not so secretly—loved it.

"The bus is always kind of a disaster. Sometimes it shows up. Sometimes it doesn't."

July didn't say anything, but she thought about the ferry and wondered why no one around here got fired.

"My mom was, though," he said, checking the side mirrors and rearview three times before pulling out onto the empty street. "Psychic, I mean."

July looked at him. It went on a little too long, and he shifted in his seat.

"Just, like, a little bit," he amended.

They were out of downtown and past the smattering of old houses that clung to the outskirts. He turned on his blinker, signaling to no one, and then made a right onto the two-lane highway that split the island down the middle. Huge evergreens grew up on either side like canyon walls. The only way to see the sky was for July to lean forward and crane her neck all the way up.

"A little bit how?" she asked.

"She just knew stuff."

He shrugged. July waited.

"Okay, like, I'd lose my favorite pencil on the way to school, and then I'd open my lunch box and find a dozen new ones in there along with a peanut butter and jelly sandwich."

He paused to see if she was following.

"Okay."

"That's amazing, right?"

She gave it a second but probably not long enough. "Was that the first time you'd lost your pencil?"

He blinked. "Well, no."

"Do you lose your pencils a lot?"

"Maybe, I guess. Sometimes." He was getting flustered.

"The first time you lost your pencil, did she know it would happen?"

"Okay, that's not the point," he said, adjusting his already tight grip on the steering wheel.

July knew she'd pushed it too far. She was sorry, sort of, but too embarrassed to say so. Back home, she'd have slunk away. Here there was nowhere to go. She gave the skin on the back of her hand a hard pinch, a reminder to do better. No one here knew her. She had one shining chance not to screw it up.

He had the windshield wipers on low, and they made a scraping noise each time they swished by. He or his dad or the church or somebody needed to replace the blades. She reached over and pushed the defrost button for the front and back windows. After a few seconds, the fog began to clear, and the air inside stopped feeling like a vanilla-scented sauna.

"Oh," he said, like he had no idea cars did that. "Thanks."

She looked at him out of the corner of her eye. He was blushing.

Malcolm was older than her, but it was starting not to feel that way. She wondered if it was an island/mainland thing.

"'Knew stuff,'" July said, rewinding the conversation. She wanted another chance, but she kept her tone casual. It was important to sound like she didn't care, in case it didn't work. "Why past tense?"

"She died," he said matter-of-factly.

July kept her head turned like she was interested in the scenery. Something like a softball had wedged itself under her sternum.

A quarter mile went by before she said, "Mine did, too."

The trees started to push back from the edges of the road, and then, with what felt like a great suddenness, fields came into view. It was like coming out of a tunnel into the sky. Each farm was marked with a house so far off in the distance, it was hard to say what color it was. July wondered what they grew but didn't think to ask.

"I know," Malcolm said. "That's the other reason the pastor sent me. Fellow member of the Dead Moms Club."

He was the first person she'd told who hadn't said he was sorry, which took some of the awkwardness out of it. He'd also called his own dad "the pastor."

"Is that an official thing?" she asked. "The Dead Moms Club?"

"It could be."

The softball in her chest was shrinking. "How many members?"

"Two, I guess. We're kind of exclusive."

He glanced at her and smiled, but then yanked his eyes back to the blacktop, which made the car jerk.

"So I make three," she said.

"No, it's just us. I inducted you without your permission."

She thought about that. "Do you think your dad wanted me to make you feel better about your mom being dead or you to make me feel better?"

They finally passed another car. It was going in the opposite direction on the other side of the double yellow, but Malcolm slowed way down anyway, tapping the brakes in a way that upset her stomach.

He shrugged. "Honestly? I think either one would be fine with him."

Up ahead was a school bus. She wondered if it was the same one that was supposed to pick her up. They had to be getting close, and the nerves she'd had at breakfast came back. She started to jiggle her knee. All she wanted was to slide in behind everyone else, find one or two people to eat lunch with, and otherwise go entirely without being noticed for as long as she was stuck here. The less people knew about her and her . . . stuff, the better.

Malcolm turned on his blinker a quarter of a mile before the bus turned off onto the blacktop drive, and they followed it.

A wheat-colored building sat close to the road. It was a single story with a roof that extended too far past the walls, making it look like it was huddled against the rain. The sign out front, low to the ground, said EBEY'S END JR./SR. HIGH. Below that was movable type like on the abandoned movie marquee.

WELCOME JULY HARRIS

"What the shit?!" July yelled. She turned her head, watching the words as they passed in hopes they would pop out of existence.

Malcolm flinched, his whole upper body pulling in on itself like a turtle.

Other cars were filing in after them. They moved slowly toward a gravel lot surrounded by chain-link fencing. There were no marked parking spots. Everyone was making it up, some better than others. Malcolm kept his eyes on the bumper in front of them, giving it his full attention.

She looked at him like it was his fault. "Do they do that to all the new kids?"

Gravel crunched under the tires as he slotted the car in a little too far from the one next to them but didn't make a move to fix it. He put the car in park and took the keys out of the ignition.

"I don't know," he said, blowing out a puff of air. Clearly he sympathized. This was bad. "We've never had one before."

"Never?!"

"Well, probably not *never* never, but not in a long time."

July didn't move to open the door. He didn't either. Around them kids were getting out of cars. They didn't look exactly like the kids she'd known her whole life, but they didn't look entirely different either. Same genus, different species.

"What was your old school like?" he asked.

"Bigger, obviously," she said, watching two girls walk to the front door and disappear inside. They looked older than her. "There were five hundred and fifty kids in my grade."

"Wow." He sounded impressed. "We have two hundred and four."

"Two hundred and four kids in your grade." She was doing the math in her head. Two hundred per grade, four grades in the high school, three in the junior high, that made—

He stopped her counting. "We have two hundred and four *total*."

She stared at him.

"The junior and senior high put together." He paused. "Not including the teachers."

After everything that had happened in the past month, it shouldn't have mattered, but it did.

"How many of them do you think already know everything about me?" *Or think they do,* she finished in her head.

"Well, not everyone. I mean, Kevin is out with mono, and Julian is nonverbal, so it's hard to say what he knows." Malcolm stopped to consider it. "I think it's a lot. People don't give him enough credit."

July didn't know what to say.

"Don't worry," he said, opening the driver's door. "You'll be fine. You already joined a club and everything."

She looked at him blankly.

"The Dead Moms Club, remember?"

Her stomach rolled over like it was trying to eat itself.

"Come on," he said. "I'll take you to the office, get you checked in before the welcoming assembly."

"The welcoming assembly?!"

"Kidding! Kidding!" he said, and then, realizing he didn't actually know if he was kidding, he smiled harder, trying to keep the expression from melting off his face. It made him look like a murderer.

"Oh my God."

"Do you want to pray?" he asked.

She still hadn't gotten out of the car. "No!"

"Okay."

"Do you?" she asked.

"Honestly, I'm just trying to get you to open the door, so whatever it takes, really."

The parking lot was full of cars but empty of people. They were the last ones left.

He gave her another smile. It was sort of sad, which felt normal. Smiles shouldn't just be one thing. She reached for the door handle and heard him let out a breath.

CHAPTER SEVEN

'm your great-uncle Mack, and these are your cousins Samson and Gideon."

"Dad," Anita said on a sigh.

They were standing outside of Anita's house, which was also her father's house, which July saw wasn't actually a house but a trailer, albeit a nice one on a cleared piece of land that might have once been farmed but wasn't anymore.

She and Anita were both getting wet because Samson and Gideon, two oversized German shepherds, were taking up all the space under the small porch roof, trying to get close enough to sniff both July, who was new, and the bags of groceries, which were also new. Mack, with his rolling walker, took up the doorway, keeping anyone from changing positions.

Each dog was the size of a small bear. They were identical, except one had his tongue lolling out and the other didn't, a difference that July suspected would not hold.

"What?" Mack said. "I can't make introductions? She's family."

"To you, yes," Anita said.

Mack turned his attention to July. "She discriminates on the basis of species."

"Dad . . ."

Mack didn't look at his daughter. "She's also very close-minded."

"Dad!"

"What's that?" Mack indicated the grocery sacks.

"It might be dinner if we can all go inside."

It was five o'clock and already full dark.

"No, the sacks. Those aren't my sacks."

"I ordered new sacks," Anita said.

"You ordered different sacks."

July was moving her eyes from one to the other, noticing all the ways they looked alike. Same rangy bodies, although Mack's was slightly stooped. Same broad forehead, same nose, same pale skin. Mack's hair was shorter and grayer but not that much shorter or grayer. On both of them it was thick and a little wavy and looked like they put their hands in it a lot.

July had never lived with anyone who looked like her, and she'd never had to think about that before.

"These are better," Anita said.

"They're more expensive."

"Because they're better. Inside. Now. Please."

Mack gave a look to indicate this wasn't over before reversing slightly and executing a three-point turn. July half expected one of those truck back-up alarms to sound.

Samson and Gideon held their places, and Anita pushed through the pack, following her father. They let her go, but when July tried, they pressed against her so that all three of them went through the door at the same time. Each dog was nearly a hundred pounds, which was about what July weighed. It was like being the toothpaste squeezed out of the tube.

Anita kicked off her shoes inside the door, and July followed, stepping on the backs of her red Converse to get them off. She was knocked off balance first one way and then the other by the dogs.

"Samson, Gideon," Mack said, snapping his fingers. "Let her be."

The one with, she saw now, the slightly smoother coat sat, giving the appearance of obedience, while placing one paw on her left foot to hold her in place. The other, who she suspected was Gideon, feigned deafness. His tongue still hung out of his mouth, and he was looking up at her with a hopeful friendliness she found hard to resist, even as she could see the serrated edges of his teeth.

She reached down and petted the dense ruff of fur around his neck, curling her fingers and scratching under his leather collar. Samson's butt sprang up off the floor, and before mayhem could ensue, she scratched him, too.

Both were medium brown with black muzzles and black saddle markings. They had upright ears, heavy coats, and tails powerful enough to hurt when they smacked her leg. July intensified her scratching, moving from their ruffs up behind their ears until both pairs of golden-brown eyes started to droop.

Mack, who was dressed in a black-and-red flannel shirt tucked neatly into loose jeans, made his way to the round dining table in the eat-in kitchen, his blue velour house slippers making a *shh-shh* noise on the cream-colored carpet. One of the chairs was already pulled out at an angle, and he lowered himself into it. The day's paper was spread out in front of him, as much as it could be spread. July had seen the *Island Examiner* for sale in the store. It came out twice a week, sold for $1.50, and was twelve pages long. The main story was about a small motorboat that had capsized near the ferry terminal, causing a delay. There was a photo that looked like it had been taken from a long way away on someone's phone.

"Just push 'em off you," Mack said. "They usually have better manners."

Anita, who was unloading the expensive sacks at the kitchen counter, snorted.

Mack gave her a look but didn't say anything. July ignored both of them and sank down on the carpet in between the two dogs, who dropped down, too, lying on their bellies. Samson laid his head on his paws. Gideon, with the rougher coat and the "in it for a good time, not for a long time" attitude, put his chin on her knee.

The house smelled like peppermint and wet dog. July couldn't see what Anita was doing behind the breakfast bar, but she heard the opening and closing of cabinets, the sink turning on and off, the chopping of vegetables on a cutting board. After a minute, there was the sizzle of meat in a pan.

"What is it?" Mack asked.

"Turkey chili."

"You can't make chili with turkey."

"Well, then I'm working a miracle."

July smiled like smiling was something she was only testing out.

It had been a hard day. She'd had to stand up and introduce herself in every class, some of which she had with kids a grade or even two ahead of her. People stared at her when she said her name and where she was from and then went on staring even after she sat down. So many kids kept turning in their seats to catch glimpses of her that one teacher made July move to the front row, so at least everyone would be facing forward.

Lunch would've been a whole other circle of hell if it weren't for Malcolm. He'd waved at her from his table as soon as she'd gotten her tray, and she'd hurried over to him, her ears hot under her hair.

"How's it going?" he whispered when she'd sat down.

She'd moaned theatrically, and he'd nodded.

What Malcolm had said in the car was true. Almost everyone, if not actually everyone, knew about her mom and Anita and that she was an orphan twice over, which, it was agreed, had to be some kind of record.

"Seriously, what are the *odds*?" another ninth grader had said in the locker room while they were changing into their gym uniforms. The other girls had nodded and kept a good distance in case such colossal bad luck was catching.

July didn't have a uniform and had to borrow one with "Prop. of EE Jr/Sr High" written in permanent marker across the back of the T-shirt and the butt of the shorts. The shorts were too tight and kept crawling up her crack, so all anyone could read was "Prop . . . High."

It was horrible, and it wouldn't have been that surprising if she'd been forced to wear it for the rest of the year. But the teacher had handed her an order form at the end of class and told her to bring it back with cash or a check by the end of the week.

Samson flicked his eyes to her, and she ran a hand over his skull between his ears, telling him she was okay. She wasn't really, though, and he seemed to know.

July had expected Mack to quiz her like all adults did, as though the only way to make conversation was a rapid-fire rundown of grades, school subjects, sport participation, and, if it was later than April, summer plans. But Mack was watching his daughter and treating July like nothing new.

"Saw the price of milk went up," he said.

"Always does." Anita kept cooking.

"You seeing any effect?"

"Organic sales are down but not much."

"People might switch if it keeps up."

Anita didn't answer.

"You should be keeping track."

"I'm always keeping track, Dad."

Mack had his forearm on the kitchen table. July watched as he started to drum his fingers. He looked over and caught her watching him.

"She thinks it's her store," he said out of the corner of his mouth.

He acted like he was trying to keep Anita from hearing, but he spoke loud enough to be sure she did.

Anita didn't say anything, and the silence started to develop weight. July couldn't see Anita from where she sat, but she could see Mack. He was watching his daughter, expecting her to say something, and when she didn't, he turned to July.

"Bill said they put your name up on the school sign."

July still didn't know who Bill was.

"Yeah."

Mack chuckled. "Bet you didn't like that much."

"Not much," she agreed, her ears getting red again.

"Anita graduated from there, you know."

Mack looked again at his daughter. July could hear the sound of a spatula breaking up ground meat in the pan. The sizzle had quieted down, and the peppermint in the air had given way to onion and cumin. In the store, Anita made small talk with everybody, saying a little more or a little less depending on the customer. But she wasn't saying anything to Mack. There was something between them. July just didn't know what it was.

"Did you?" July asked him, trying to cover the silence.

Mack let her, going on like there wasn't anything to notice. "Nope. From Ohio originally."

"Why did you move here?"

"Got discharged, went home, didn't fit in anymore, started driving. Stopped when I ran out of country."

"Dad's a Vietnam vet," Anita said.

July and Mack both got quiet, making space for Anita to come back into the conversation. After a minute, she did. Sort of.

"Dinner in thirty minutes."

"You can't make chili in thirty minutes," Mack said.

"Maybe you can't." Anita's voice was flat.

There was the sound of an electric can opener, and then the sputtering sizzle of something wet hitting a hot pan.

"I don't want a salad," Mack said, swiveling his body back toward the table and picking up the paper. He didn't glance at it before tossing it on one of the empty seats.

"We're having salad," Anita said. "You need the roughage."

"I'm already shitting like a goose."

"Dad!"

July laughed. That she still could was a bit of a surprise.

Mack looked over at her and made a farting noise with his lips. Anita threw down her knife, and July, despite feeling she ought to know better, laughed harder. Gideon and Samson both picked up their heads, but it was Samson, always eager to better his brother, who pushed up to his haunches.

Anita moved to the end of the counter, where July could see her. "I'd like to tell you we're better than this," she said, "but obviously we're not."

Mack grinned and made another farting noise. He reminded July of a kid looking for attention.

"Yes, Dad, thank you. We got it."

When Anita turned her back, Mack's face relaxed, transforming from a giddy kid to an adult. July was watching him, and when he noticed, he winked.

Mack ate the salad after Anita added a generous helping of croutons and blue cheese dressing, which was a different brand of blue cheese than he'd previously ordered for the store. This led to ten minutes of tense conversation having to do with whether deceased actors were qualified to make condiments and whether this was really relevant to customer-buying habits. Anita pointed out *she had data*. Mack said sometimes customers don't know what they want until you don't give them a choice about it. She pointed out the Blue Bird gave them choices whether Mack liked it or not.

Gideon's concerns were more prosaic. He used the salad debate as cover, belly-crawling like a Navy SEAL toward the table. When he was close enough, July broke off a piece of cornbread and held it down for him. He inhaled it in such a way that she jerked, afraid for her fingers, but Gideon was a precision eater when he needed to be, and he licked her hand both for crumbs and reassurance.

Watching his brother be rewarded for breaking the rules was too much for Samson. He popped up and hurried over. The tags on his collar jangled like sleigh bells, attracting everyone's attention, including Anita's. She scolded him, and Samson hung his head. But Gideon only looked at July from the corner of his eye, solidifying their alliance vis-à-vis table scraps.

After dinner, July got up to help with the dishes. At home with her mom, she always had to be reminded, but that felt like a luxury she didn't have anymore.

"Leave those," Mack said to July, pushing himself up from the dinner table with his walker.

July was already standing with dirty dishes in each hand. She looked from Mack to Anita, unsure of what to do. Anita reached over and took them from her.

"Go on," she said. "Humor him."

July followed Mack at his pace from the eat-in kitchen to the living room, which was furnished with a soft cream-colored sofa, an oversized chair, and an ottoman. The only thing it had in common with the living room in the apartment were the words "living room."

Mack was pointing to the far wall next to a fake fireplace surround. In matching matted black frames were color photos of teenage boys all in baseball uniforms standing for the obligatory team photo. In each was a small black sign propped at the players' feet. EBEY'S END COUGARS, it said, followed by the year. There were at least fifteen of them.

"The store sponsors the team every year," he said. "Preston over at the bank does the football, and the Elks Lodge has the soccer—boys' and girls' both."

July looked obediently at the photos, which were remarkably similar over so many years, only the quality of the pictures improving slightly with time. Malcolm had told her lots of kids played sports on the island because it meant getting to travel for games, usually only to the other islands, but still, it was something. The photos went back longer than she'd been alive, which added up to a lot of kids all just trying to see something different.

"You know what team the Blue Bird sponsors?" Mack asked.

She shook her head.

"None of 'em."

He turned toward the sofa, which was just far enough from the coffee table for his walker to pass. He took the far cushion, letting himself into it with a whoosh of air between his lips. He patted the space beside him, and July followed, while he reached forward for the remote.

The television was in a large hutch across from them, and she expected him to turn it on. But the remote stayed loose in his hand. A second passed. Five. Ten.

It had started to make her uncomfortable when he took a deep breath and said, "It's been a trauma, everything that's happened to you. And that's partly my doing. Connie and I—Connie was your great-aunt—we didn't keep in close contact with the rest of our kin."

He turned the remote over in his hand.

"Self-reliance to the point of isolation kind of runs in the family."

He jerked his chin toward the kitchen, where Anita was loading the dishwasher.

"But after Connie died and now Catherine—" He cleared his throat. "Well, we might not deserve forgiveness, but I hope you might see your way to it anyhow."

It had never occurred to July that anyone was at fault but her. She was the reason all of this had happened, but she couldn't say that. It was too much to explain, and it would sound crazy if she tried.

"It's okay."

He smiled without meaning it and reached over to pat her knee, quick but warm. "It's not, but I appreciate you saying so."

Mack pushed a small red button on the remote. "You like college basketball?"

She didn't.

"Sure," she said.

CHAPTER EIGHT

B efore they left, July had to use the restroom. It was down the hall, and when she finished, she dried her hands and opened the door. She hadn't meant to do it quietly, but she must have because Mack and Anita didn't stop their talking.

"You see those purple circles under her eyes?"

"Of course I see them," Anita said, keeping her voice lower than her father's.

"She's not sleeping."

"I realize that."

"You should talk to Doc, see if he can give her something."

The last thing July wanted was a sleeping pill. That would only make it harder to stay up. She hurried out into the hall, making her presence known and stopping the conversation.

"I'm ready," she said, and Anita reached down for their things.

. . . .

July had intentionally stopped sleeping the day her mother died.

She had always known things without being able to explain how she knew them. Sometimes it got her into trouble. Her third grade teacher had accused her of stealing a reading quiz out of his desk when she'd asked about one of the questions before he'd handed them out. She'd been sent to the principal, who'd called her mother, who asked, in her most professorial voice, if there was any proof. Could it not be, Catherine had demanded, that the quiz questions were so painfully obvious even a third grader might have guessed them? July had been sent back to class without punishment but also without apology.

Her mother changed the hiding places for her Christmas presents every year because July could, without fail, point to each wrapped gift and say what was inside. Their last Christmas together, Catherine had kept them all at a friend's house. It hadn't mattered, but July pretended like it did, guessing wrong on purpose when her mother handed her each present on Christmas morning. Her mother had wanted to surprise her, and it was neither of their faults that she couldn't.

The day it happened, July dreamed her mother had died in a car accident. She woke with a pain like a punch to her chest and ran to her mother's room. She shook Catherine awake and begged her not to drive the mile to campus that day. Her mother told her it was only a dream. She hugged her and did not complain that it was six o'clock in the morning.

July did sometimes have bad dreams, but this felt different. It was different from a regular dream, and more intense than her usual knowing, which had always been about small things. Her "talent," as she thought of it, had always felt like remembering, only her mind ran the clock backward. She just *knew* in the same way other people knew what they ate for breakfast. And like normal remembering, she didn't necessarily get to choose what she would know and what she wouldn't. There were times she wanted it and didn't have it, and times she wished she didn't know things she most certainly did.

That morning, July would not be consoled, and she would not relent. Her mother must not, under any circumstances, drive to work. Catherine, exhausted by her daughter and the early hour and all she had to do that day, had parted the curtains and looked out the window next to the bed.

They'd lived in a rented two-bedroom apartment made from half of the upper floor of a formerly grand home that had been subdivided and made much less grand decades before. It was December 20. Final exams for the winter quarter were done. Catherine was planning to go into her small, windowless office to take care of some paperwork before Christmas and also to pick up the presents she'd hidden there. It was cold but, for once, not sleeting. If she left early and did not stay long, the weather would hold. And besides, they'd been baking cookies and eating cookies, and Catherine, who was soft and round, had complicated feelings about that, which she tried to hide from her daughter. The walk, she thought, wouldn't hurt things, and if she brought a large enough bag, she could carry the gifts home.

She was killed at a crosswalk. She'd had the right of way. The driver had stayed, dialed 9-1-1, and attempted to render aid, none of which had mattered. It was very late in the day when someone, a police officer accompanied by Ms. Overton, finally came to the door.

Despite everything, Catherine had died in a car accident, an accident she would not have been in if it weren't for July. July told that to the police officer, after the two of them had calmed her down. It had been important that he know because she needed to be arrested. She had killed her mother, not directly, but she had contributed to her death, and that was against the law.

He said it wasn't. He said it had not been her fault. The person had made a right turn on red without looking for pedestrians. He said it happened all the time. He said people shouldn't be allowed to make right turns on red.

She said she shouldn't be allowed to dream. Ms. Overton had patted her back. July had not been comforted by either of them.

. . . .

Anita couldn't take more Froot Loops. She would buy July all the Froot Loops she wanted. She'd let her live on Froot Loops if that made her any happier, but Anita was drawing the line. She made oatmeal for herself and offered some to July, who shook her head mutely and instead poured herself breakfast from the rainbow-colored box.

Anita sat across from her, added brown sugar and half a sliced banana to her bowl, and watched July spoon cereal into her mouth without speaking or looking up. Her hair hung in its curtain formation with a slight wave around her face. Anita was beginning to guess that meant it was going to be a hard day. Hair behind the ears, face revealed, meant there was still hope.

The tender blue skin under the girl's eyes was worse that morning. Or it wasn't, but her father pointing it out made it seem worse. It made it seem like Anita was not seeing to the basic things a guardian should see to: shelter, food, education, health and safety. Surely sleep fell under health and safety. She should call Henry like her father had suggested. She probably should have called Henry immediately. Children needed doctors and checkups and shots. Anita had July's vaccination records, which she was somewhat disturbed to learn were kept not by her doctor but by the state. Anita didn't think about government more than she absolutely had to, and she preferred the government didn't think about her either.

Still, she should call Henry's office and speak to his assistant at least. Get some idea of what she ought to be doing and when. She'd mention the lack of sleep casually, enough to elicit the necessary treatment but maybe not so much that Henry would think badly of her. She shouldn't care. It shouldn't be part of the equation. But she did care, and it was.

"Do you carry quiche?"

Anita blinked. She'd been lost in her own thoughts, and the slight disorientation of being pulled back into relationship with another person always took a second to resolve itself.

"Quiche?" she asked.

"Yes, in the store. Do you have it?"

"No."

July was holding her spoon over her nearly finished bowl. The utensil was hovering like a helicopter waiting to land. This tangent appeared to have been as unexpected an interruption to her as it was to Anita.

"Are you sure?"

There was a furrow in July's otherwise perfectly smooth skin. It was the sort of skin that no amount of cream could return to you after the age of twenty-five, not that Anita had ever tried. Anita couldn't remember the last time she'd worn mascara. High school, probably.

"I'm positive. Why? Do you like quiche?"

Quiche would be an infinitely better breakfast option.

"No," July said, and dropped her spoon into the now-gray milk in her bowl.

It was Anita's turn to furrow her brow. "So you were just taking inventory?"

"I guess," July said.

She put her elbows on the table and pressed her eyes into the palms of her hands. Her fingers curled up toward her hairline, and she left her head there for a long time like it was too heavy to pick back up.

Anita was definitely calling Henry.

. . . .

After July left for the bus stop, Anita went down to the store, which wouldn't technically open until nine, but she always instructed any stock boys she had on the early-morning schedule to leave the front door unlocked when they came in and to put out the honesty jar, which she kept stocked with a sufficient quantity of change. She wouldn't do that during tourist season, but she trusted her regulars. If anything, they overpaid.

Just as Anita had finished culling the bagged salad for anything past its sell-by, the front door opened and Tiny called out to her.

Anita checked her watch. It was after eight, which meant Tiny had left out her own honesty jar to make her deliveries. She had an even harder time getting help than Anita did.

"In produce!" Anita called back, throwing the last of the out-of-date Caesar into a cart.

Tiny met her at the end of the aisle. She was pulling the old metal utility cart she always used.

"You want some old salad?" Anita asked, holding up a bag.

Tiny was four foot ten on her tiptoes and wore boy's sweatpants and running shoes every day of her life. Under her coat was a striped apron that went down to her knees and a gray muscle shirt that showed off her biceps. She kept her dark hair short and her skin tan. She did not look like someone who baked for a living. Despite her size, she looked like someone who led Outward Bound expeditions and knew how to fix a carburetor, which Anita bet was also the sort of person who wouldn't mind a little floppiness in her romaine.

"Sure," Tiny said, "I'll take some."

Anita congratulated herself on, once again, knowing her customer. "What have we got this week?" she asked.

Tiny tossed the salad in with the pies. "There was a screwup with my egg order, and now I've got 'em coming out my ass. Everything is gonna be custard and meringue for the next week."

She reached in and started sorting through her signature blue boxes.

"I know you usually take the sweet stuff, but I brought some quiche, too. A few ham and Swiss, a couple spinach with feta—" Tiny looked up at Anita's face and froze. "All right, fine. Don't take 'em."

Anita didn't know what she looked like, but her head felt like someone had turned it upside down and given it a shake.

"Did you tell anyone you were making quiche today?"

Tiny lifted an eyebrow. "What do you mean, 'tell anyone'?"

"I mean, did you tell anyone you were going to make quiche?" It came out a little more strident than Anita intended.

"No."

"Did you make quiche yesterday?"

"I didn't get the eggs until yesterday afternoon."

"Did you tell anyone about the eggs?"

Tiny put both hands on her sweatpants-covered hips, which looked more like those of a fifteen-year-old boy than a middle-aged woman. "Anita."

"What?"

"I don't know what your thing is, but it's weird and I got shit to do. Do you want the quiche or not?"

Anita hesitated. "I want the quiche."

Tiny walked away, pulling the utility cart and shaking her head. Anita didn't follow, but a moment later, she could hear her in the cold foods section stocking the boxes.

At nine o'clock sharp, Anita went upstairs to call Henry. Shannon picked up the phone. She'd been his assistant since her youngest was old enough to go to school full-time, which meant about five years. His old assistant, the one he'd had when he and Anita had been seeing each other, had retired, which was a relief. Anita didn't think she'd known about them, but assistants know a lot.

"Doc's office," Shannon said.

Anita identified herself and asked after Shannon's kids, one of whom had recently broken his arm. Anita got the play-by-play, which took a good ten minutes. On the island, it wasn't possible—or at least not advisable—to jump right into business, not unless something was actually on fire and then only if it was a big fire. Every conversation needed to include a preliminary exchange of information. This was how news was had on the island. The twice-weekly paper served only as backup, and if what you heard from your neighbor was contradicted in print, you believed your neighbor.

"Heard you got yourself a new family member," Shannon said after she'd wrapped up her story.

"That's what I was calling about."

"Listening."

"I was wondering if there was some sort of initial exam I should bring her in for?"

"Initial exam?"

"You know," Anita said. "Like when you get a new puppy."

Shannon was quiet for a second. "A new puppy?"

Anita didn't like having all of her questions answered with questions. "To make sure everything is okay."

"In case she's got worms or something?"

"Something."

Anita heard Shannon adjust herself on the other end of the line. "Okay, you want to tell me what's really wrong?"

Anita didn't know if she was easy to read or if Shannon had been at this job long enough to smell a rat or if it had something to do with her having three kids. Anita was betting on the latter.

"You keep patient information confidential, don't you?" Anita knew she was insulting Shannon by asking because she was asking to remind her, and Shannon wasn't stupid.

"I do." Her voice was neutral.

"She's not sleeping."

"She's been through a lot."

"I know, but she needs to sleep. I thought Henry might want to prescribe her something."

"At fourteen?"

Anita didn't appreciate her tone. People needed different things to get through life. It wasn't like she hadn't noticed Shannon bought a tub of Duncan Hines chocolate icing every week and never, not once, anything that might be made into a cake.

"I'll pass Doc the message, if you want," Shannon said, the implication being this was her last chance to keep her incompetence to herself.

Anita didn't take it.

"I do. Thanks."

. . . .

After school, July worked in the shop, sweeping and bagging and straightening. If Anita pulled a stack of cans forward to fill an empty space, she'd see July pull a stack of cans forward. If Anita grabbed a mop to wipe up wet footprints on the hardwood floor, she'd see July do the same not fifteen minutes later.

At six, they closed up. Anita checked out her own groceries— buying whatever they were going to have for dinner that night—

before totaling out the register and putting the cash into a vinyl banker's pouch that she took upstairs. She cooked while July started her homework. Pork chops with a side of stewed cinnamon apples and boxed stuffing that came out dry. July didn't mention it. Her hair was still hanging down around her face.

When Anita asked how school had been, July said fine. When Anita asked if she liked her math teacher, she said she was fine. When Anita asked if she was going to join any clubs or teams, July said no, which was still only one word but a different one, at least.

Anita couldn't tell if July was sad and exhausted in a way that anyone would be or if she had crossed a line into something worse. She was worried it was worse, and slowly, over the course of one hour-long TV drama, she became convinced it was. By the time July shut her door at ten o'clock, Anita felt almost as bad as she imagined the girl did.

Anita needed Henry to call her back. She needed her own mother to be alive. She needed someone to tell her what to do.

CHAPTER NINE

A t first, it had been easy for July not to sleep. Sleep was too terrifying to imagine, but while the fear remained, it was no longer enough. She had to keep moving. As soon as she stopped, her mind would snap shut. It wasn't that she drifted off so much as she fell into a sudden, coma-like state that her fear would jerk her out of, like someone pulling violently on the reins of a horse. It had started happening during the day, even while she was standing. She'd started making up games to keep herself awake. Mimicry mostly. She'd see if she could cross a room with the same number of steps Anita used. If she could drink a glass of water in the same number of sips, wash a dish with the same number of wipes. She tried to be subtle. So far Anita hadn't mentioned it.

Not that July trusted her mind anymore. She'd been awake so long she'd started to see things. She saw a black cat walk through the front door of the store, but when she went to call it to her, it had disappeared. She couldn't read, which had been her favorite thing, because the words would swim on the page, twirling around one another like dancers and then coalescing into one counterclockwise swirl of ink that disappeared into the center of the page like a flushing toilet. And even that couldn't keep her awake.

July took a cold shower at night, which helped. She'd say good night to Anita afterward, go to her room, and close the door. And then July waited, pacing to stay awake until eleven, when she felt sure Anita was asleep. Then she was out of her room, out of the apartment, down the stairs, and into the store. It was easier to stay awake in the store. But it was obvious that just walking around, like she had been doing, wasn't going to be enough.

And so, on this particular night, she took a Snickers from the rack by the register and peeled open the wrapper, eating it on the way to the soda aisle. She pulled a can loose from the plastic rings of a six-pack and opened it, chugging the sugar and caffeine so fast the carbonation made her eyes water. She didn't know if this was stealing or not. The store belonged to Anita like the apartment belonged to her and the kitchen and the food inside of it. When July had hesitated in front of the refrigerator on her first full day, Anita had told her to take whatever she wanted. This might be the same, and it might not. She'd never shoplifted before, not even a pack of gum.

She took what was left of the soda and the candy bar to the refrigerated storage room in back where Anita kept the crates of milk and cases of yogurt and cheese before they were unloaded onto shelves by the stockers, who July could already see would not stick around long. Mostly high school age or close to it, they carelessly tossed boxes of merchandise. They slit open cartons with utility knives, slicing through the top layer of goods inside, so yogurt spurted out of containers and chips spilled from bags. Instead of pulling the expired cottage cheese, they pushed it farther back, stacking new ones in front. July saw all of it and said nothing. She stepped around them without speaking, and in turn, they didn't speak to her. Their conversations stopped when she appeared and picked up again, usually with a snicker, when she passed.

Every hour since her mother died, July had heard her voice, always saying the same thing: *It's just us, kid.*

In life, she'd said it all the time. She said it on Father's Day, when July would make her a card like she had the month before for Mother's Day. She said it when July slammed her bedroom door and when the toilet overflowed. It was the all-occasion sentiment for a single mom. They were in it together. They would make it work because they had to. There was no white knight in their story, and if one had shown up, they'd probably have kicked him out.

"It's just us, kid" wasn't a bad thing. It was a point of pride.

The only person who ever could have separated them was July, and she had in one complete and stunning blow. The pain and guilt of it was so big that, if she'd felt it all at once, it would have killed her. And so it dripped into her slowly and continuously like an IV bag she pulled along beside her and would, she guessed, for the rest of her life.

July sat down next to a tower of blue milk crates. Cold from the concrete floor seeped through her flannel pajama pants and numbed her butt. She pulled her legs up and wrapped her arms around them, resting her forehead on her knees. She was starting to shake, but at least she wouldn't have to worry about falling asleep. She was too cold. She'd had sugar. She'd had caffeine. She'd be fine.

. . . .

Anita was too worried to sleep, and so she heard when July opened her bedroom door. Anita listened as her young cousin walked down the hall and through the living room. When she opened the front door, Anita sat up. When it closed, she got out of bed.

In her own pajamas—a gray T-shirt that barely covered her rear end—Anita walked to the front room. She listened as July descended the wooden stairs, which creaked under her weight. At the kitchen window, Anita watched as July slipped into the alley and opened the back door of the store with the key Anita had given her. When Anita couldn't see her anymore, she went back down the hall to the third bedroom that served as her office.

She shook the mouse to wake the computer screen and pulled up the feed for all six security cameras. She watched July, who was wearing shoes but no coat, walk to the front of the store and take a candy bar from the rack. She peeled open the wrapper on her way to the chip and soda aisle. Anita watched her disappear from view, emerging a minute later with an open can. She tipped it back. Even on the grainy, black-and-white video, Anita could tell she'd nearly drained it in one long, glugging gulp.

July wiped her eyes. (Was she crying?) And then she made her way to the back, past the sign that said EMPLOYEES ONLY and through the swinging door. Anita didn't have any cameras in cold storage. She waited, her foot jiggling under her. Whatever July was doing, she wouldn't be long. It was thirty-six degrees in there unless she'd gone farther, pushing through the second door into the walk-in freezer, where it was zero. Anita looked at the clock in the corner of her screen. A minute went by. Two. Five.

Anita pushed the rolling chair away from the desk and hurried out, stopping only long enough to grab the day's jeans from the floor of her room, putting them on one leg at a time as she tried to keep walking toward the front door. She didn't bother with shoes.

She found July curled up on the floor behind a stack of crates. It had only been a few minutes, but she wasn't moving. She wasn't shaking. She wasn't anything but dead. Obviously dead. Or dying. Maybe only dying. Anita leaned over and grabbed July hard by the bicep, prepared to drag her out, start chest compressions, call 9-1-1. Then July jerked up, and her head slammed into Anita's face.

"Jesus fucking Christ!"

Anita stumbled, her hand cupped around her nose. She heard July gasp, was aware of her scrambling to her feet. Not that she could see this. She couldn't see anything.

"Oh my God, are you okay?"

"I thought you were dead!" Anita pinched her nose, trying to stem the bleeding. It didn't work, and it made her sound like a cartoon character.

"Why would I be dead?"

"Why would you be passed out in my refrigerator?!"

Anita tipped her head back, trying to reverse the flow of blood and, if possible, time. Her hands, face, and T-shirt were covered in gore, and it was a struggle not to drip on anything salable.

"I was trying to stay awake!"

July hadn't meant to be honest. Exhaustion, shock, and worry had broken whatever part of her brain was in charge of lying.

"It didn't work!"

"I know!"

They were both shouting, and the shouts were bouncing off all the hard surfaces. Refrigerators were nothing but hard surfaces.

Anita's head was still tilted back, but she could hear July crying.

Anita assumed fourteen-year-old girls sometimes shouted, but she didn't shout. She preferred to seethe inwardly until her stomach hurt. She tried to take a breath and couldn't because of her nose, which hurt more than anything she could remember.

"Please don't cry," she said, and then regretted it.

July had every reason to cry. Anita had a few reasons herself, but she was still trying to impersonate an adult, and none of the adults she knew were criers. Mack, she was fairly certain, had had his tear ducts removed at birth.

"You know what?" Anita said. "I take it back. Cry as much as you want. All day. And if anyone gives you any crap, I'll withhold their groceries."

It was still hard to see, but Anita thought July might have stopped sniffling.

"I'm serious," Anita went on. "I'll go to their house and repossess every crumb I've ever sold them. That floppy celery from two weeks ago is coming with me."

The edge of desperation in her voice was obvious even to Anita. She'd told the girl to cry and was now saying anything she could think of to stop her.

Anita felt a hand on her arm. July was turning her around and pushing her gently toward the door.

"I'll steal ice cubes for you."

"I don't need ice cubes." July wasn't laughing. She didn't even sound happy. Tired, maybe. Resigned. "You might, though, for your face."

Upstairs, Anita put July to work making hot chocolate while she went to the bathroom to clean up. It helped less than she'd hoped. The bridge of her nose was swollen, and purple bruises had started to bloom under both eyes.

On her best day, Anita bore a passing resemblance to Frances Mc-Dormand during her later, no-makeup years. She wore jeans and flannel shirts that she sometimes tucked in and sometimes didn't. She'd been known to cut her own hair with kitchen shears. She didn't think of herself as vain, but now she looked like a boxer who'd lost his last-hope fight and was on his way to sleeping in a car.

A small rivulet of blood kept seeping out her right nostril. Every time she thought she'd stopped it, it started again. She gave up, twisted a piece of toilet paper like she was rolling a joint, and shoved it up her nose, letting the end dangle free.

It would be sensible to call a doctor. But Anita didn't do that. For July, yes. For herself, only if a bone was sticking out, and she had someone to watch the register.

· · · · · · · · · · ·

July told Anita about the dream because she couldn't think of anything else to say that would make any sense, not that she expected Anita to consider what she said sense. She told her about the police officer and the crosswalk and Ms. Overton at her door. She said she hadn't slept—or not much, not more than a few minutes at a time—since.

Anita listened and watched as tears flowed down the girl's cheeks, soundless and continuous like the blood that came from Anita's own nose.

"If it wasn't for me, she would still be alive," July finished.

"No," Anita said. It came out like the shutting of a door. Solid and final.

"She was walking because I asked her not to drive."

"And if you hadn't said anything, she'd have driven, and something else would have happened. And you'd still be here."

Anita put down her mug, which she had finished, despite the slight taste of salted iron in the beginning. Preston Daly had given the cup to her years ago when she'd opened a savings account. The name of the bank wrapped around the outside in a heavy serif font.

"You don't believe that," July said.

Anita met her eyes. "Actually, I do."

"How?" The word came out fast.

Anita took her time answering.

"Because you loved your mother. You tell me you foresaw her death? Okay, fine. I've heard weirder things. But you didn't make a stranger drive through a crosswalk. You don't have that kind of power. If she was going to die in a car accident, she was going to die in a car accident. Hers or someone else's. That day or some other day. Knowing it and being able to control it are not the same thing."

The girl's pajamas were too big for her. They made her look smaller than she was, and she wasn't big to begin with. The purple moons under her eyes looked almost as painful as Anita's.

"You're not afraid of me?"

"Of course not."

"Because it could happen again."

"I doubt it, but in any case, it still wouldn't be your fault. Not any more than my dad's stroke was mine."

"You can't know that."

"I can," Anita said. "And I do."

July looked down at the table, which, like everything else, was Mack's. She ran her thumbnail down a deep gouge in the surface. Anita had made it when she was about her age. It was just after Easter. She'd gotten a particularly large chocolate bunny in her basket. It had been solid and heavy, too unwieldy to eat. And so, while her parents were downstairs in the store, she'd gotten out her mother's largest kitchen knife. She'd meant to chop the rabbit into bite-sized pieces, but it rocked under the knife just as she pressed down her hardest. The blade slipped. She'd been lucky it hadn't gone into her hand.

"You're really sure?" July asked.

"I'm really sure."

"You have to be sure."

Anita couldn't imagine an adult believing so much in another person's answer.

"I am absolutely and completely sure."

They left the dirty mugs in the sink.

The doors of their two rooms were next to each other, and they stood in between them, paused, awkward. Some other woman might have been able to reach out and hug July, but Anita's arms didn't know how. And so when July said "Good night," Anita said "Good night," and that was all.

. . . .

July was in her bed, which was not her bed but might eventually come to be with time. She'd turned off the light overhead and the lamp on the nightstand. She'd spent the last weeks fighting not to fall asleep, and now that she had permission, she couldn't make her eyes close.

Down the hall, she heard the floorboards creak. A car passed outside. The refrigerator's compressor switched on. The inside of her skull felt like it had been scooped out with a grapefruit spoon. She looked up at the ceiling, and then over at the window. She could see the green numbers from the alarm clock reflected in the glass. She could tell the time, albeit backward, without turning her head. It was a stupid thing to think about it, but it was what she was thinking about when her door popped open.

The sound—a scrape and a snap, as the door, not quite fitted square in its frame, rubbed along the jamb and then came free—made her jump.

"Sorry," Anita said, whispering even though there was no need.

She was carrying a pillow and a blanket that dragged on the floor.

Without saying anything else, she dropped them both on the oversized braided rug by July's bed and lay down on it.

July looked down at her. Anita had settled herself on her back with her eyes closed. Even in the dark, July could see the bruises, now fully formed, blooming across Anita's nose and under her eyes.

"Are you sleeping?" It was a stupid question, but July asked it anyway.

"I don't sleep much."

"Because your nose hurts?"

"My nose will be fine. I never sleep much."

July was quiet for a moment, but she didn't lie back. Not yet. "Why?"

"I never have."

"Why?"

Anita knew young children were supposed to ask "why" a lot. She'd imagined July would be past that. On the other hand, no one had ever asked her why she didn't sleep. Her parents had only told her to sleep, and Henry had offered her drugs to make her sleep. Neither of those were the same thing.

"I don't know," she answered honestly, her eyes still closed.

"Are you afraid?"

"Constantly."

Anita expected her to ask "Of what?" and she didn't know how she would answer. But instead, she heard the covers shift and the mattress squeak as July lay down. Thirty seconds passed, which was a long time in the dark on the floor on a braided rug, which would leave red patterns branded into her skin the next day.

"It's okay," July said. "I'm here."

And as ridiculous as it was, that did make Anita feel better, and eventually both of them did fall asleep. Maybe not well. Maybe not for very long. But the bar, in both of their cases, was low, and they got over it together, and that was not nothing.

The next morning, when Anita knew that neither Shannon nor Henry would be in the office yet, she called and left a message canceling her request for sleeping pills.

CHAPTER TEN

I t was after nine o'clock, and Anita was at the register when the front door swooshed open, and a gust of cold, damp air blew in along with Pastor Chet.

He was closer in age to Henry than to her. Pam, his deceased wife, had been notably younger and had made him a first-time father later in life than was standard. He always looked hurried and sometimes harried. That morning, he stopped and glanced around, looking not toward her but toward the aisles where other shoppers might be. Anita wondered who he was avoiding, but, as always, she didn't ask. She assumed she'd figure it out in relatively short order, anyway.

"Morning, Chet," she said, dragging his attention in her direction.

"Good morn— Are you all right?"

A night spent on the floor had not done Anita much good. The bridge of her nose was black and purple like smeared ink, as were the half-moons under her eyes, spreading down to her cheekbones, which faded into green. All of it was slightly swollen and changed the shape of her face in a way she would not have chosen. That might have been fine. She didn't look in the mirror much anyway, but every time she bent forward, she could feel her heartbeat in her nasal cavity. And the pain radiating out of her sinuses had mass and dimension in a way pain should not.

That morning, she'd carefully spooned oatmeal into her mouth, trying not to chew too much. She hadn't realized that chewing moved so many facial muscles, as, unfortunately, did speaking, smiling, and frowning. Sneezing with a broken nose was a circle of hell previously unknown even to Dante.

Next to her bowl, she'd poured out both ibuprofen and Tylenol like she was sprinkling salt and pepper over eggs. It had not helped as much as she'd hoped, so she'd taken to holding a bag of frozen peas to her face when no one was looking. (Birds Eye in the sixteen-ounce bag for $2.99.)

Was she all right? Clearly not. But it also didn't seem to be the sort of injury that would flare up years down the road every time the weather changed. She hadn't had a stroke, and no bones were visible. She was inconvenienced but not permanently damaged.

"My cousin moved in with me. We accidently bumped heads."

Chet came close enough for her to see the spray of lines radiating out from the corners of his faded blue eyes. She'd known him her whole life. He was a friend of her father's, but that proximity had not made them close. Chet and Anita were poorly suited to each other. It was a benign incomprehension, like a moose trying to negotiate with a woodchuck. But what they lacked in mutual understanding, they made up for in politeness, which was all anyone really needed to get along in the world.

He looked from one side of her face to the other and grimaced.

"Have you gone to see Doc yet?"

"I don't need to see him."

Anita watched Chet suppress a sigh.

"You're trying not to move the top half of your face," he said.

"Untrue. I'm trying not to move my whole face."

"Anita, you need to go to the doctor."

He sounded tired, like her injury was something he could not possibly be expected to deal with, but deal with it he must.

"I'm fine. I have peas." Anita held up her peas.

"Do you also have a medical degree?"

"No, but I have Google. Same thing."

Anita understood Pastor Chet did not need one more thing in his life. Already he hosted the AA meetings and the grief support group, played basketball with the at-risk kids, visited the sick and the old and the sick and old. He ran the food pantry, counseled newlyweds, hosted a weekly spaghetti supper, and found time for Sunday school, Christmas pageants, and Easter egg hunts. If you needed to be married, buried, or baptized, he would see to it.

It was hard to say if Chet had walked into all of that responsibility or if it had been yoked to him. Probably both. Maybe if he did less, he'd be better off. Or maybe it was the only thing keeping him alive. Anita didn't know.

Twice Chet had climbed over the railing up on Widow's Pass, prepared to jump. Twice he'd been talked down. That had been seven years ago, but it wasn't the sort of thing you forgot. When it came to Chet, everyone held their breath and hoped for the best.

"How's Malcolm?" she asked to change the subject.

"Well, thank you. I spoke to your father recently."

"He said he was going to call."

She expected he would say something about that. Maybe tell her he'd said an extra prayer in her direction, despite her lack of church attendance, but he did not. She expected he would extend an invitation to July through her. There were youth group meetings of some kind at the church, Anita was sure. But again he did not. His eyes had drifted over her shoulder and lost focus.

"She's a good kid," Anita said to bring him back.

He looked at her and pulled himself up a little straighter, as though he'd just remembered where he was or maybe who he was. He nodded and cleared his throat.

"They all are, Anita."

She could see he meant it.

He took a step back. "You really should call Doc."

"I know."

"But you won't."

She shrugged. He didn't need any more problems. She'd keep hers to herself.

"All right, then," he said. "I best . . ." He gestured to the shelves without finishing the sentence.

Chet and Malcolm lived in the parsonage and got most of their food from the church-run food bank, which was really a walk-in closet off the fellowship hall. (Anita was a regular contributor, just as her father had been before her.) Chet, she knew, made so little money they easily qualified for the church's own charity. This was supplemented by various members of the women's ministry, who took it upon themselves to drop off casseroles and pans of box-mix brownies on a regular basis.

When Chet did shop, he tended to buy things like milk, salt, lettuce, and toilet paper. He carried a list folded up in his pocket with the items written in several different inks and by two different hands, which he sometimes struggled to decipher.

"Anita, what would you guess that word is?" he would ask, pointing to some chicken scratch on his crinkled piece of paper. Dutifully, she would lean in, but there was never any point. If he didn't know, she certainly didn't.

He was usually in a hurry, coming back from visiting a parishioner and running off to a meeting. He was in and out in less than ten minutes and paid with folded bills from his wallet, shoving the change in his pocket as he hurried out to the church's elderly black sedan.

But that morning, he did not pull a list from his pocket. He darted from shelf to shelf like a hummingbird, picking up something and then putting it down, heading to the next aisle. Anita did her best, while holding the bag of peas to her face, to not look like she was looking.

When he came back, only five minutes later, he had three bananas, a bottle of gluten-free soy sauce (neither he nor Malcolm suffered from celiac disease), a box of Brillo pads, and some off-brand marshmallows. It would have made more sense if the pastor had walked up and handed her a pregnancy test and a coupon.

Still, she took each item as it came, ran it across the scanner, and slid it into a bag. Chet kept his eyes on the screen while she did it, avoiding her gaze like they were strangers in an elevator.

"Take care of yourself, Anita," he said when she handed him his change.

"You, too, Pastor," she said, and watched him go.

When the door shut, she put the peas back to her face and wondered what in the hell that had been about.

. . . .

That afternoon, when Mr. Daly walked in, July was pulling old magazines from the small display by the register and replacing them with the February editions. He picked up a small basket, as usual, said "Hello" to Anita as usual, and stopped to exclaim over her face, which was not usual. After she reassured him, Anita gestured to July and introduced them.

He took the girl's hand, which she offered in the old-fashioned way, and he all but bowed.

"You're living with Anita?" he said with genuine surprise and interest.

No one had told him. No one told Preston anything that was not expressly and directly related to money. There was something about him that kept other people at bay despite his politeness and even gentleness. The usual banter did not extend to him. This was both his fault and not his fault, as all such things are.

When July confirmed that she was indeed living with Anita, his face lit up from the cheekbones down.

"How marvelous," he said.

He was back at the register in short order and set down his two apples—giving Anita a small smile over these—his three frozen burritos, a box of cornflakes, and a quart of two-percent milk. No coffee today, she noticed. He didn't always buy it. There was only one of him, after all.

She rang him up, and he paid, dropping too much change into the penny cup. He was out the door when July sprang up from her crouch at the magazine rack and ran after him, a copy of this month's *Martha Stewart Living* in her hand.

The door closed between Anita and the two of them, blocking the sound, but she watched as July handed him the magazine. He looked down at it, puzzled. Words were exchanged. More than a few. July was obviously insisting.

Anita felt one of her eyebrows try to make the trip toward her hairline, but the bruises objected and she returned to neutral as Preston slid the magazine into his sack and July walked back inside.

"What was that?" Anita asked.

July shrugged. Anita thought she recognized the shrug. It was her shrug.

"He just . . . needed it," the girl said.

"The bank president needed a women's magazine?"

"Yes."

Anita started to say something, stopped, and then started again. "You remember what I said about not interfering with the customers, right?"

July was looking at the gum display, and for a moment, Anita thought she wasn't going to answer. "I remember," she finally said.

"Okay," Anita replied.

"Okay."

CHAPTER ELEVEN

Maggie put her hand over the mouthpiece and hollered over to the front booth where Mack always sat. His plate of shoestring fries wasn't anything but a smear of ketchup by then, and he was on his third cup of coffee.

"What is it?" Mack hollered back, trying to see around Lynette, who'd come by with a sweater from her shop after hearing from two different people that July had been seen wearing one like it.

"Bill says the guys all have shit to do, so if you're coming, do it now."

Laughter burbled up from the surrounding tables, and Lynette rolled her eyes.

Mack looked at his watch and got a little jolt through his hindquarters.

"I'm coming!" he yelled back. "Tell 'em I'm coming."

He scooted out of the booth and grabbed his walker as quickly as he could manage it, which set Lynette to fussing. She draped the sweater over the front bar, and he pushed it down the sidewalk that way, setting off the bell over the bakeshop's door not five minutes later.

"She's out of apple," Doc hollered from where they all sat. "And I wouldn't bring it up if I were you."

Tiny, who was not in the mood, raised both her middle fingers in Doc's direction.

Tiny was the one who'd dubbed them the Old Philosophers' Club. She had not meant it kindly, but they'd taken up the moniker with enthusiasm nonetheless. It gave their meetings an air of legitimacy, made them feel a bit like the Freemasons, which the island did not have, or the Shriners, which they also did not have.

There were four regular members now, all men of "a certain age," as Chet put it. It was a concerningly small number. There had been six, but Al got shipped off to the mainland to live near his daughter in one of those memory care places. (The thought made them all want to throw a pinch of salt over their shoulders.) Then Donald passed not six months later. Pneumonia at seventy-nine. With the possible exception of Doc, they hadn't expected him to die. They hadn't gotten around to thinking of themselves as vulnerable enough to die of things young people got over with cough medicine.

Mack, who was now the oldest member by more than a decade, waved that they should continue on as he pushed his way to the counter, Lynette's sweater threatening to slip to the ground and tangle around his feet at any moment.

The bakeshop was in a building nearly as old as the grocery. The floors were the original wood, worn and patched in places. To the right was a scattering of café tables and booths that lined the far wall along with bookshelves and baskets that had been turned into display cases. Inside were cellophane bags full of the chocolates, marshmallows, and brittle Tiny made herself when she wasn't also churning out every kind of pie under the sun. She tried to keep a selection of muffins, cookies, and premade sandwiches going, but that ebbed and flowed depending on how much help she could hire. The shop had been short-staffed and Tiny overworked for so long, she was starting to have what folks were calling "her little mad fits," which didn't seem so little if you were on the receiving end of one.

Mack scanned the day's remainders. "That pecan?" he asked.

"Chocolate pecan."

Mack didn't approve of mixing flavors, but he kept it to himself, ordering the buttermilk chess instead.

She poured a slug of hot coffee into a heavy white mug without asking and shoved it toward him, sloshing a bit over the side, before reaching into the case.

He picked up the coffee, dripping some on the sweater, and set it awkwardly on the walker's little seat. Tiny came around, pie in hand, and scooped the mug up. Crossing the dining room in four strides, she dropped it and the plate on the table between Bill and Chet. Mack nodded, and she turned away with a grunt.

"What are we talking about?" Mack asked, dropping himself into the chair that Chet pulled out for him.

Doc caught Bill's eye, who glanced at Chet, who looked sideways over to Doc, who glanced over his shoulder. The white saloon-style doors that separated the kitchen from the shop were still swinging, but Tiny was nowhere to be seen. There was a high school kid Mack didn't recognize in the far corner booth with a laptop open in front of him. The headphones clamped over his beanie cap had ear pads the size of bagels. Otherwise the shop was theirs.

"You tell it," Doc said.

He was the only one of the four who didn't have pie in front of him. He'd been summarily denied following the apple upset.

"You sure?" Bill asked.

"Go on," Doc said, waving a hand.

Bill was serving his third term as county sheriff and pretending to be unsure about running again next year. It did, if nothing else, give the boys something to talk about on slow news days, but this wasn't one of those.

He shifted his weight, and the stiff leather of his gun belt creaked. "About eight p.m. last night, dispatch got a call from one of Doc's neighbors reporting a naked woman in the street."

Mack had the first bite of buttermilk chess in his mouth, which about fell out when his jaw dropped. "All-the-way naked?"

"Apparently."

"Who?" Mack asked, too pleased with the new gossip to notice Bill's hedge.

The sheriff looked to Doc, but he'd closed his eyes.

"Carol," Bill said, sounding sorry for it. "Neighbor said they wouldn't have called, but apparently this wasn't the first time."

Mack, for once, didn't know what to say. Ebey's End had its share of eccentrics. He could think of at least three people he would not have been surprised to hear were running around town showing their privates, and that didn't include the teenagers. He might even have put Tiny on that list, depending on the day, but Carol was a substitute Sunday school teacher. She was certified in first aid and CPR, and her Christmas cards arrived no later than December 15.

"Is she all right?" Chet asked.

Bill shrugged. "Deputy drove out. Street was clear, so he knocked on the front door. Carol answered. Said there was nothing wrong, so he left it at that. Called me, and I called Doc."

Bill picked his coffee mug up and took a long swallow, surrendering the floor.

They all looked at Doc.

"When I got home, she was in bed with a book. Said she'd been having a hot flash."

Mack remembered when Connie had been going through the

change. She'd walk right out of the shower and into the kitchen, open up both the refrigerator and freezer doors, and stand there, holding open her towel and flapping it like bird wings. That hadn't been altogether normal, but it wasn't dropping trou in the frozen foods and waving her nethers at the Otter Pops either. You had to understand these things on a continuum.

But that was for a later discussion. At the moment, Doc was in need of support, and they were honor-bound to give it.

"Well, it's squirrely, I'll give you that, but that's the way it is with those hormones." Mack buried the tines of his fork deep in his pie. "She'll be back to normal soon enough."

The others followed Mack's lead and murmured their assent. A second passed in uncomfortable silence, and then Bill spoke up.

"Barbara's grandmother came to the Thanksgiving table once in nothing but a bra and pantyhose." Bill had his arms crossed but still managed to hang on to his coffee mug. "No underwear or nothin'."

The other three looked at him.

"Her dementia was real bad by then."

"This was the '90s?" Mack asked.

"Early aughts, it would've been. She didn't last much longer after that."

"I don't think Carol has dementia," Chet said.

"I'm not saying Carol has dementia. I was saying . . ."

They went on, but Doc wasn't paying attention. He had a napkin in his hand. He hadn't had one before, but this one had appeared without his knowing and he was balling it up tight. He didn't argue the situation, but he knew that Carol, at sixty-three, should've been past all that. In all likelihood, anyway. The truth was he didn't know. She'd come to him with remarkably few medical problems over the years, and if he'd thought about that at all, he'd have put it down to his good influence. Preventative care by osmosis. If she was having symptoms of something, he expected her to tell him. And if she didn't tell him, he expected her to act normal. The whole thing felt like a violation.

"How's Anita doing with everything?" Bill asked, trying to change the subject.

"Doing her best." Mack picked up his own mug, remembered the three cups he'd already had at the diner, and put it back down. "It's a hard situation."

"Sure," Bill said. "Sure. Would be for anyone."

"She's never really been around kids, you know, and with Connie being gone."

It didn't sound like the end of a sentence, but it was and they all knew it. Connie, Mack, and Anita had been like three legs on a stool. It wasn't that Anita and Mack hadn't gone on, but they were wobbly without her, even all these years later.

"I heard July's a real good kid," Bill said. "Sandra was telling Felicia at the station the other day."

"Good as gold," Mack agreed, puffing up.

"It'll turn out," Doc said, pushing aside his own problems for the moment.

"It will," Chet agreed.

"Could be she'll need a little help, though, settling in and all," Mack said.

"Not a problem." Bill picked up the hint.

"We take care of our own," Doc agreed.

Mack looked around the table. A cop, a doctor, and a pastor. Between them, there wasn't anything they couldn't sort out, and being in their company gave Mack confidence. It would be fine, like they said. And if there were still things keeping him up at night, well, he was probably overreacting. That was all. No need even to bring them up.

CHAPTER TWELVE

That evening, after hamburgers and Ore-Ida curly fries from the freezer section, July sat at Anita's computer doing homework. She finished and tapped the requisite keys. The printer, which was also on the desk and so close she barely had room to work the mouse, whirred and beeped to life. While she waited, she opened a browser window and then her email account. No one her age used email if they could help it, and she wasn't surprised not to find anything. She didn't even have email addresses for most of her friends. They all chatted on their phones, but her mom had said fourteen was too young for one, even though literally no other parent thought that. Fifteen *maybe*, her mother had said. She hadn't lived that long.

When July had last seen her classmates, things were good, and then the worst happened, and she never saw them again. No goodbyes. No nothing. Her school cleaned out her locker. Ms. Overton had picked up the grocery sack they'd dumped her things in and brought it to her. There was nothing she wanted, and she'd thrown the whole thing away.

That was less than a month ago, and it felt like a year. July couldn't remember her locker combination anymore. She could barely remember her old class schedule. She imagined her friends texting each other about her and about what had happened. They'd have sent one another prayer-hand emojis and crying faces at first. Now they probably didn't talk about her at all.

July thought about them, but she wasn't sure she'd want to see them even if she could. They'd been her friends most of her life, but they wouldn't have known how to deal with any of this any more than she did. They'd cluster together, and she'd be on the outside. No one from back home was a member of the Dead Moms Club, and they certainly didn't want to think that, with one bit of bad luck, they could be.

Not that things were much better here. Her new school felt like a big game of musical chairs, but the song had stopped before she'd ever shown up. Years before. Long enough that everyone had forgotten they'd even been playing in the first place. As far as any of them knew, they'd been born into those chairs. As far as she knew, they had been.

Malcolm was the only one who'd gone out of his way to make space for her, and while she appreciated it, she suspected the space had always sort of been there. He didn't hang out with anyone at school. When she sat with him at lunch, no one else at the table talked to either of them. When they rode the bus, Malcolm sat alone until she took the seat next to him.

He didn't seem to mind, but July did. She wanted a place where she fit. She wanted that click when a puzzle piece slides into the right spot, not the pressing and smacking of trying to force it. She wanted that thing she'd seen the first time she'd gone to Mack's with Anita, when July had looked from one to the other and known they belonged to each other.

July reached into her backpack and pulled out the social worker's card. She'd been thinking about this since those two weeks when Ms. Overton was running around, trying to find someone to take her. She thought maybe the woman would bring it up, but she hadn't, and July had been too scared to ask. Even now, thinking about it made her heart beat fast.

July set the card on the desk and rubbed her knuckles on her thighs. The longer she waited, the harder it would be, for her and for everyone.

She tucked her hair behind her ears and then clicked COMPOSE. She typed Ms. Overton's address into the box, which was the easy part. She looked at the subject line, tried to think if there was a reason not to type what she wanted to type, and then typed it: "My birth mom."

The email itself was only a couple of sentences, but she read and reread it half a dozen times, deleting something only to type it right back exactly the way it had been before. It was hard to concentrate. Anita could walk in any minute. July was trying to listen for her, but *Law & Order* was on. She couldn't trust she'd hear her cousin get up. The best thing was to finish before a commercial break, and there were a lot of commercial breaks. Internet speeds on the island were crap. Anita didn't have a single streaming service. She watched everything through satellite cable. Commercials, set schedules, no binge-watching. It was like having to wash your clothes in the creek.

July was running out of time. She hit SEND. Then it was gone. Quickly she closed the browser. It felt like tiny carbonated bubbles were popping in her blood. She was nervous, but it was an excited nervous.

She stood, and the desk chair wheeled back six inches, which was the farthest it could go in the cramped room. It had a wedge-shaped pillow on the seat and a lumbar pillow on the back, attached with a webbed belt. At some point, a dog had chewed it.

She pushed the button to turn off the screen, grabbed her unzipped backpack off the floor, and almost forgot Ms. Overton's business card on the desk. She snatched it up and shoved it back in the depths of her bag before heading down the hall to shower and pretend like everything was fine.

· · · · · · · · · · · ·

It was 9:30 when Anita heard a knock at her door.

She couldn't remember the last time someone had come over unannounced. It was possible it had never happened, so naturally she inferred doom. Something was wrong. Probably down at the store. There was a fire, a break-in, a sinkhole, a bear. Two bears. She was so certain calamity had struck that she reached for her coat before she turned the knob.

Once she got the door open, she stopped. It was worse than she had feared, and she didn't know what to do. She stood there, stunned at the sight before her. There were four people crowded together on the tiny landing, which was at least three more than it was meant to hold.

"Evening," Harley said, raising his hand, which stopped in midair. "Gosh, are you okay?"

Anita's mind was so full of possible disaster she didn't know how to answer. After a second of confusion, he pointed toward his own face.

"Oh." She had to stop herself from touching her nose, which still hurt in a stiff breeze. "Accident in cold storage. It looks worse than it is."

Mary Alice, his wife, stood next to him and leaned in. "It looks pretty bad."

Anita wasn't sure what to say to that, but Harley went on. "You taking any ibuprofen?"

Harley looked like a lumberjack with a full beard and shoulders that strained his shirts. In reality, he was the town pharmacist, and Anita wouldn't have been surprised if he'd pulled a bottle from his coat pocket.

"I am," she assured him.

"Every four hours," he said.

"Sure." She had no idea how often she took them. Whenever the thought struck her and as many as were to hand. She was thinking of pouring them into a candy dish.

"We're sorry to bother you so late," Mary Alice said.

Mary Alice was all motherly hips and bosom. She hadn't always looked like that, but she had for so long it was hard to remember what she'd looked like before. It was as though she had evolved into her final and fullest form, a woman who had reached her true potential.

Harley, Mary Alice, and Anita had all been in the same graduating class, but even then, it had been clear they were on different paths. Mary Alice had had an engagement ring on her finger at the same time she'd had a diploma in her hand. It had seemed to Anita then, as it seemed to her now, that Mary Alice had known where she was going and how she was going to get there, and she would just as soon get started.

Anita, on the other hand, had done the thing directly in front of her and then the thing directly in front of that and so on. But instead of a breadcrumb trail, it had been an assembly line. The tasks came to her, and she stayed put. Seeing Mary Alice there on her doorstep with her family, Anita felt . . . passed by. It was a sensation that came up more than she cared to admit, an amorphous feeling that settled like a dark filter over things. Perhaps that was why, without thinking too much about it, she'd always avoided Mary Alice. And Harley. And all the other people on the island close to her age.

"Were you going somewhere?" Mary Alice asked.

Anita looked down at herself. Her coat was in her hand, and her father's old slippers, several sizes too big, were on her feet. Ketchup from dinner had splotched onto her sweatpants.

"Not exactly."

"Good, then," Mary Alice said, and thumped both her children, who made up the other members of the quartet, on the shoulders. "Say hello," she commanded.

"Hello, Miss Odom," the children, a teenage girl and slightly younger boy, said in an obedient monotone.

"Hi . . . there." For the life of her, she could not remember their names.

All four of them blinked at her expectantly.

"Did . . . you need something?" she asked, trying to make some sense out of this. "From the store?"

Mary Alice laughed and waved the thought away. "Oh, no. This isn't business."

She seemed to view this as good news. Anita wasn't so sure.

It was a quirk of Ebey's End that, although Harley and Mary Alice were universally referred to as the Connors, their last name was actually Brown. Mary Alice had been born a Connor, and a few years after marrying Harley, she had taken over her family's business. Connor's Pharmacy had been Connor's Pharmacy for more than sixty years. It had been started by Connors and run by Connors, and no one seemed to think that ought to change, current facts notwithstanding.

"We felt bad we hadn't been by yet," Mary Alice said. "Didn't we?" She turned to Harley, who nodded. "Bill stopped by the store tonight, and, well, it was a good reminder."

Anita wasn't sure she was following, but if Bill was involved, her father wasn't far behind.

Mary Alice tapped the girl again, which was when Anita noticed she was carrying a repurposed cardboard box that said "Clairol 16 units" on the side. The girl held it out.

"This is for July," Mary Alice said. "Just a little care package we put together. Madison and Cole helped."

"Oh," Anita said, taking the box. "Thank you."

Harley shifted his considerable weight, and the old wood of the stairs creaked.

"You should come in," Anita said, casting a worried eye at the landing under their feet.

She imagined the whole of the staircase coming loose from the side of the building and crashing into the alley below. It would surely kill them, wiping the town free of Connors and Browns both, and leave her with no way to get down to the street.

They all squeezed in, standing awkwardly in the small front room, making it feel several sizes smaller. The boy—Cole—pressed up against the dining table, and Harley clasped his hands in front of him while Madison scanned the furnishings like an insurance appraiser.

Anita was trying to figure out if she should offer them drinks or cookies and then wondered if she had cookies or if she should leave them and run down and get cookies, and did they want cookies at almost ten o'clock? Were Froot Loops an acceptable alternative, and maybe she shouldn't have asked them in at all because the kids needed to be in bed, but now they were inside and how did she get them back outside? Which was when July came in.

She was wearing flannel pajama bottoms and a long-sleeved T-shirt with her wet hair combed back from her face.

"July!" The relief in Anita's voice was palpable. "These are the Browns . . . Connors . . . Browns."

"Either is fine," Mary Alice said, beaming at July, who looked only slightly less uncomfortable than Anita felt.

Madison, perhaps to avoid being thumped again, spoke up. "We brought you some stuff."

"Oh," July said. "Thanks."

Madison glanced at her mother, who nodded, and then all five of them looked at Anita, who only then realized she was still holding the box. She handed it over.

"So," Mary Alice said. "Have you girls gotten to know each other yet?"

"We're in the same lunch period," Madison said.

"Oh, that's fun! Maybe you two could sit together."

"She sits with Malcolm," Madison said.

"Well, then you could *all* sit together."

Madison gave her mother a look that suggested otherwise, but she didn't say anything and for a moment neither did anyone else.

"Okay, well, it's late," Mary Alice said after a beat, which allowed all six of them to let out the breath they'd been holding.

The Connors filed out the door, with Mary Alice taking up the rear. Anita was holding it open, repeating "thank you, good night, thank you, good night" to each as they passed like she was a stewardess and everyone was deplaning. It wasn't the most awkward thing she could have done, but it cracked the top five.

Unlike the rest of her brood, though, Mary Alice stopped and reached out a hand. She put it on Anita's arm, squeezed, and didn't let go. "We're just down the way," she said. "Anytime. Anytime at all." And then she was gone, which was good because somehow, at those words, tears pricked Anita's bottom lashes. It was ridiculous, but still, she had to blink to clear them before shutting the door.

Anita looked at July, who looked at her. The only thing she could think of to say was "What's in the box?"

The answer turned out to be "whatever you could grab off the shelves of a small-town pharmacy if the seas were rising and you only had five minutes." There was shampoo that smelled like grape popsicles, a cheap pair of rubber flip-flops, leftover Christmas candy, a stapler, a box of sanitary napkins, dental floss, and one roll of athletic tape.

"That's nice," Anita said because she imagined that was what her mother would've wanted her to say, and she was trying to be a good role model.

"Okaaaaay," July said, which was the more appropriate response.

They both looked at the hodgepodge of sundries now spread out on the kitchen table. Anita remembered running down to her own store and buying a toothbrush and fruit when she'd found out July was coming. This wasn't so different. For the first time in a long time, she felt a kinship with Mary Alice.

"We're okay, right?" Anita asked. "We're doing okay?"

She didn't like the tone of her own voice. The reassurance was supposed to run in the other direction.

"Sure," July said.

"You've got everything you need?"

"Yeah."

"Because you can tell me."

"I'm fine. I've got staples." She opened the stapler. It was empty.

Neither of them said anything. Anita understood there was something she should say, something not about staples. But knowing you should say something and knowing precisely what that something might be were two different kinds of knowing.

While July was putting the shampoo and pads away in the bathroom, Anita slipped into her own room and wrestled the queen-sized mattress off her bed, which was significantly more difficult than she expected. She'd gotten it out into the hall when July opened the door, toothbrush in her mouth, and stared.

Anita was hunched over with the mattress falling down across her back, her arms wrenched behind her, trying to grip the edges and drag it like a dead body. She froze.

"Everything's fine."

July raised an eyebrow much like Anita tended to do, and for a moment, before she remembered they were not blood relations, Anita thought it was genetic.

July closed the bathroom door again, slower this time, and Anita continued, pulling and dragging until she got all 150 pounds of it down the short hall and into July's room. By the time July came in, Anita had the mattress wedged between the twin bed and the closet door, which would no longer open. She was breathing hard and had both hands on her hips.

Anita hoped July would go first, but she didn't.

Finally, Anita said, "I figured, since night isn't great for either of us, we could go on keeping each other company for a while."

July didn't answer. She was staring down at the mattress, which was now the entirety of the bedroom floor.

"If you're not okay with it, I can—"

"I'm okay with it," July said.

Anita paused. "You sure?"

July nodded.

"You wouldn't rather—"

"No."

"Okay."

July didn't say anything else.

"I'll get some blankets, then."

CHAPTER THIRTEEN

A reasonable person might have said that the last thing Preston Daly needed was another periodical. He had copies of the *Seattle Times*, the *New York Times,* and the *Island Examiner* going back six months. They were stacked on the dining room table, on the coffee table, and on the floor by the sofa where he sat when he wasn't at his desk. Preston made it a point to leave the bank at the expected hour, so that the people who worked for him and did have families and lives and interests beyond the moving and trading of money would feel they could also go home. But going home for Preston was simply exchanging one workspace for another, with the occasional stop for milk and apples in between. (He had recently graduated to two apples, so no one could say he wasn't making progress, although it was difficult to suggest that apples made a life.) He also had many, many issues of *The Economist, Fortune,* and *Money* along with several hundred *New Yorker*s, which seemed to arrive in his mailbox with alarming frequency and which took up whatever space, mostly on the floor, that the newspapers didn't. Their slippery covers turned the piles into avalanches more often than not, which he left more often than not.

Where there weren't periodicals, there were books, more than he had read or could possibly read. They had started in the bookshelves, which lined the sitting room and his office and the spare bedrooms. (It could be argued that all the bedrooms, including his, were spare.) But those, too, had breached the borders.

A layer of furry gray dust had settled over much of it, creating a sort of geologic record indicating when something had last been touched, and Preston touched little.

The trash did not go out as often as it should, which was not the catastrophe it could have been as he did not bother to throw out much, nor did he eat much, so there wasn't a lot in the way of smells that might have forced his hand. Not that there wasn't *a* smell. There was, but it was the sort of musty odor any unlived-in dwelling takes on in time. Preston would've thought such a thing would be impossible. His home—a large, not very well-kept Victorian on a hill, which overlooked the town and also the sea in the distance—was not unlived in. Except maybe it was. Maybe what Preston was doing there did not count as living, and the house and the smell knew it.

Preston existed, and he worked. He worked more than he existed, but technically he did both. Neither made him happy. But neither was he so unhappy that he had done anything to change it. He put one foot in front of the other. He did his job. He spoke when spoken to. He wore his suits. He drove his car, although only, really, along the two-mile triangle delineated by the bank, the grocery store, and his home. (He did not have to drive to the post office. It was next door to the bank.) When he wasn't working, he sat on the sofa until it was time to sleep, and then, most of the time, he slept there.

He did, he thought, manage to keep up appearances. His suits were clean and pressed. His hair was trimmed. He shaved. He cut his nails. He fulfilled his side of the public bargain. He no longer really expected to do anything else. This was the way things were, and he did not have the energy or even any idea of how he might change it.

And if he did change it, what would it change into? What did he want? The whole thing was simply impossible.

And so, that night, he had come home, driving through the black wrought iron gate that he always left open and which was an extension of the wrought iron fence that ran all the way around the quarter-acre property. If he'd bothered to check, he'd have found the gate was actually rusted into position and couldn't be closed, but he didn't bother and didn't know. He was only sure he didn't want to close himself in or anyone else out. Not yet.

He left his car in front of the old carriage house in back, which was intended to function as the garage but was so full of stuff—he didn't even know what—that it couldn't be safely opened, let alone used. And then he carried in his small bag of groceries. He put one of the apples and the milk in the otherwise empty fridge and the burritos in the almost-empty freezer. (He did have one of those blue ice pack things in case of a twisted ankle. The magazines were a hazard.) He put the cereal in the cupboard, which was otherwise a graveyard of graying spices and moldering tea. And then he took the other apple and the girl's gift into the sitting room and to his spot on the sofa.

He ate, and he flipped through the magazine, intending to drop it into one of the piles as soon as he reached the apple's core. He had never in his life read a copy of *Martha Stewart Living*. He might have had a vague idea that such a thing existed, but most of his knowledge of the older woman's existence centered on insider trading. He didn't have much of an opinion about the case, although he believed, in general, that it was illegal for a reason. All of which was to say, he knew next to nothing about what he was holding and wasn't particularly looking forward to becoming better informed. He was simply passing the three minutes it would take to eat his fruit, which was also his dinner. He was, he supposed, planning to look at enough of the pages that he could say something polite to the young girl the next time he saw her. He did very much want to be polite.

She had given him the January issue, which seemed mainly to be about fixing the mess you'd made of your life the previous year. The first article was on home organization, helpfully broken down into twenty tips. The first was to organize vertically. This made no sense to Preston. He read on. The article told him to put his most-used items at eye level and heavy things down low. Little-used things should be "elsewhere." He glanced around the sitting room and wondered what here was not "little-used." He kept reading.

The article told him to use grease-proof paper plates inside his cast-iron skillet to keep the retained oil from transferring to other skillets he might want to stack inside. Preston had no idea if he owned a cast-iron skillet and why it would retain oil if he did, but the pictures were strangely compelling. Clean, bright white and marble kitchens. Close-ups of cabinets and closets that were full of matching clear containers and woven baskets. He read about how woven baskets could change his life. He wondered how many baskets exactly he would require to enact such a change. He wondered if there were that many baskets in the world.

He was instructed to toss expired products, which led to his first understanding that products could expire, and was told to "reassess" his storage needs every six months. He learned he had need of four inboxes, and that was just for paper. He looked at photographs of offices that looked nothing like his office. He learned about purchasing magazine holders if he absolutely could not toss old issues but was reassured that he really should. He considered the fact that this very article was in an old issue. He tried to scoff and didn't quite manage it. He learned the word "demilune." He read an article about paint colors that would "be everywhere this year" and another about all the proper ways of making a bed. He could not remember the last time he'd made his. He also could not remember the last time he'd slept in it, which only partially made up for the fact that he also couldn't remember the last time he'd washed the sheets.

The apple was long gone. He didn't remember finishing it, and he didn't know where the core had gone. He didn't think about it. (He would eventually find it, albeit days later.)

Before he knew it, Preston Daly had read the entire issue. When he put it down, when those clean, neutral-colored interiors were no longer in front of his face and his own home was, he had a feeling like a hand pressing on his chest. He bent forward and dropped the magazine onto a stack of other magazines. The stack fell over. He almost left it there. He started to, and then he bent over and picked it up, all of it. He got the stack standing again, which required getting up off the couch and squatting down—down being a greater distance for someone of his height than for others. He stood up. He looked at the neat stack. It was better. He started to turn away, and then he didn't. He bent over and snatched the *Martha Stewart* off the top, dropped it on the sofa, and gathered up all the rest in the pile and carried them out the back door to the bin. They made a satisfying *thump* when they hit bottom. The hand that was still pressing on his chest let up the tiniest fraction, a quarter of a millimeter at most, but he felt it. It was not nothing.

He went back inside. He thought about sitting on the couch. He thought about going so far as to walk up the stairs to his bedroom. Instead, he bent over and picked up another stack. The floor underneath was an entirely different color. He went back to the bin.

CHAPTER FOURTEEN

Anita was not at the register when Henry walked in. She was on her way there, and when she saw him through the glass door, her feet raised the possibility of turning her body around and carrying it in the other direction. They proposed doing so as quickly as possible.

It wasn't as though she didn't see him. Henry was her father's friend and his doctor. He was everyone's doctor, unless something was very wrong and you had to go to a mainland doctor, and then he was the doctor who arranged for that. Henry was the person she'd called when she'd found her father after the stroke. He was the person she spoke to every day from the hospital and then the rehabilitation center and then in her home, where he came to check on Mack each evening for two weeks. He came until Mack told him to knock it off. From then on, Anita took Mack to Henry's office when required. It was required less now, which was good because it was getting more awkward. At first, she'd been too worried about her father to think about anything else. But when it became clear that he was not on death's door, other thoughts snuck in. She tried not to have them. She had them anyway. It was such a long time ago. She ought to be over it by now. And anyway, it was too late to run. He'd spotted her.

"Henry," she said as he stepped through the door, "what brings you in?"

"You," he said, and held up his bag.

Henry only made house calls under dire circumstances. He was the only primary care doctor in town, and he didn't have time to be "going all over creation." He didn't have time to do much. He was the only person Anita knew who worked as many hours as she did. Maybe more. Anita, after all, had several employees. He had Shannon.

"I was informed of your injury."

Anita let out a sigh she didn't bother trying to hide. "Dad?"

"Among others."

Henry had crossed the distance between them and bent to put his bag on the floor, which wasn't precisely a bag but something more like a tackle box. He stood up and took another step—the last possible one—toward her. He was close enough for her to feel his breath. She leaned back, but he reached up and took her cheeks in his hands. Anita's heart was pounding so hard, she was afraid he'd feel it through her skin. She didn't know what to do, and she didn't know where to look.

Henry, for the briefest moment, looked her in the eye. His were hazel with a small speck of darker brown in one like a defect in a photograph. It had been there years ago. She'd noticed it when they lay in bed together. It had not faded. Then he was looking at her nose, turning her face one way and then another.

"I'll be as careful as I can," he said.

She felt the words, a warm bit of air on her lips when he spoke. She wondered if she should close her eyes. She started to—

"Jesus Christ!" Anita jerked back.

"It's broken," he said, letting go of the bridge of her nose. "Fortunately, the cartilage isn't misaligned."

"Great."

It probably was good news, but Anita wasn't in a grateful sort of mood.

"Ice it four times a day. Tylenol as needed, and keep your head elevated at night. It'll heal in about six weeks. You're going to want to avoid bumping it until then."

"I would imagine having someone yank on it isn't so great either."

He gave her a small smile. His hair was thick but gray, a little wiry. His brown-check shirt showed a small belly that hadn't always been there. He'd missed a spot shaving, right under his left nostril.

"Chet said you bumped heads with your cousin. Is she okay?"

"I'm okay."

It was Martin Luther King Day, and July was out of school. She had materialized next to Anita's left arm, making Anita turn her head too fast, which made the already throbbing appendage hurt more.

"You must be July," Henry said. "Mack told me you are, and I quote, 'the best thing since penicillin.'"

He held out his hand before noticing July's were full. She was carrying a pale blue pastry box that everyone in town knew.

"Quiche," she said.

"So it is."

She shifted her weight from foot to foot. "It's for you."

Henry's eyes flicked to Anita, who was trying to kill July with her mind.

"Carol used to love quiche. I don't think we've had it in years."

"You should take it to her," July said.

She was still shifting her weight from side to side, and Henry wondered if she didn't have to pee.

Anita tried to interrupt, but July talked over her. "For lunch."

"I'm afraid this"—he gestured at Anita's nose—"is my lunch break."

"It would only take a minute."

A flush had spread up the girl's neck to her cheeks and was creeping across her forehead, making the small white scar there stand out like it had been drawn on with Magic Marker.

"July—" Anita started.

But Henry was thinking about it. Carol was obviously having problems. Stopping in to check on her—with the quiche as an excuse—wasn't the worst idea in the world. In fact, it was probably a very good one.

"You have a thoughtful girl here," he said to Anita.

Nosy was more like it, Anita thought.

"All right, young lady, I'll take you up on your offer. But so you know, when my wife asks what on earth I'm doing home in the middle of a workday, I'm blaming you."

July gave him a smile, a genuine one big enough to see that one of her incisors was crooked. He found it charming. Too many girls tried to be too perfect. He smiled back and then raised the box in Anita's direction as a thank-you.

"Ice," he reminded her. "Tylenol."

"Right."

"I'll tell your father you'll live," he said, picking up his bag.

"Have Shannon send me a bill."

Anita didn't think he would, but she didn't want to presume. She didn't want him to think she would.

He walked away, and she watched him go. July tried to leave at the same time, but Anita reached out and grabbed the sleeve of her oversized sweater.

When the door shut, she said, "What was that about?"

The heat in Anita's face—from the pain, from Henry, from July doing whatever the hell this was—burned.

"He needed to see his wife."

"And you know what he needs?"

July's neck was so red it looked hot. She pulled her arm free and turned her back.

Instinctively, like reaching for a thrown ball, Anita grabbed the girl's shoulder. She knew she shouldn't have as soon as she'd done it, but it was too late.

July swung her head around and glared hard. Her nostrils flared. A wave of adolescent anger washed over July, hotter than anything she'd been expecting. Anita was mad, too, but her anger took the side streets of her brain, doing a rolling pass through the logic center.

"You know what else I know?" July said, her voice loud enough to be heard from one side of the store to the other.

Anita said nothing. She breathed in and out, feeling the pressure of the air through her broken nose. She waited for it to come. The words looked ready to bust out of the girl's chest. Like the power of them was too much to keep inside such a small body.

"Aaaagh!" July yelled, closing her eyes tight.

She reached for the nearest shelf, grabbed a package of pink Hostess Snoballs, and threw them as hard as she could.

Anita stepped out of the way, but she needn't have bothered. The package smashed into a soda display, missing her by several feet. She didn't know if that was on purpose or not. She didn't get a chance to ask because July turned and ran out of the store without, Anita noted, a coat.

"Well, that was something," a voice said over her shoulder.

Anita didn't look to see who it was. She knew.

"Done with your lunch break?" Anita asked.

"Yep," Peggy answered.

Peggy had spent most of her career working for the county and had retired with a nice pension three years before, only to discover

retirement made her crazy. She'd been working part-time for Anita
ever since.

"I'm going to step out for a bit," Anita said, her embarrassment and
irritation making her voice clipped.

"Yep."

Peggy had raised three girls herself and now had so many grand-
kids she sometimes lost track. July's outburst did not surprise her.

Anita picked the Snoballs off the floor. They'd exploded on im-
pact, the marshmallow coating split and chocolate cake smeared inside the wrapper.

"You want these?" she asked.

"Jesus, no," Peggy said, walking around the check stand to take
her place at the register. "They look like a baby's behind. Makes me
think of diapers every time I see one."

. . . .

It wasn't that Anita wasn't concerned about July, but the island was
small. The girl had no good way off of it, and everyone she might
come across would know who she was and where she belonged. So
after walking up and down the handful of streets that made up
downtown, Anita had gone back to the apartment and called Mack.

She didn't tell him exactly what had happened, but she told him
enough and asked him to put the word out. He called Pastor Chet,
the diner, and Bill, who put out an informal BOLO. Anita called
Tiny, Lynette, and Jim, the librarian. And then, after thinking it over
for a moment, Mary Alice at the pharmacy. She asked them to keep
an eye out and call her if they saw anything. Everyone would. Everyone understood.

"Teenagers," Jim had sighed.

Anita thought it was a little more than that, but she didn't correct him. Mostly she was just glad the social worker wasn't around to see this. For half a second, she wondered what would happen if she were, and then Anita pushed it out of her mind.

. . . .

Doc drove with the quiche on the seat next to him. HAM & CHEESE was written in marker across the blue pastry box with the cellophane window. Tiny's handwriting, he presumed.

The road to his house was narrow without so much as a curb or a ditch separating the asphalt from the trees. They were so close to one another he imagined their roots touched and tangled under the black road beneath his tires. When another car came from the other direction, both vehicles had to hug their respective edges, half a tire in the few inches of gravel that edged the pavement. It would be easy to have an accident, easy to jerk the wheel a little too hard to the right. He imagined the front end of his old BMW smashed into one of those old-growth trunks. Not every day. Not even most days. But sometimes.

Doc turned into the drive. He'd been lost in his own thoughts, which was probably why he didn't see Gordy's old truck until he was parked beside it. Everybody knew Gordy's truck. The joke around town was that he'd had it painted that color to match the rust. Doc wasn't sure there wasn't truth to that.

He couldn't think of any good reason Gordy would have for coming to his house. The last time he'd seen him in the clinic, they'd had a disagreement. Doc had drawn some blood, telling him he was checking his cholesterol and "whatnot." The "whatnot" was Gordy's liver values, which Doc hadn't liked the look of. Gordy didn't want to hear it and had left shouting that Doc hadn't had any right to run the tests in the first place. Later, he'd gone out to the tavern and told everyone who'd listen that Doc was guilty of malpractice.

It had given a fair number of people a lot of pleasure to tell him about it. Didn't seem to occur to them that Doc might not have wanted to hear it, but it was what it was. If Gordy wanted to stir up some imaginary feud, fine. Doc had done what he had to do. It was up to Gordy to save himself. Doc didn't run the AA meetings. That was Chet's job.

Having Gordy turn up at his house, however, was another thing entirely.

Doc leaned over the steering wheel and looked up at the windows. There weren't any lights on. Nothing moved. He squeezed the wheel and his jaw. He was either making himself paranoid or not moving fast enough. Both were equally plausible.

Doc turned off the windshield wipers and the engine, pushed the garage door opener, and climbed out, leaving his case and the quiche where they were. He walked into the garage, across the smooth concrete floor, past Carol's car. He opened the door that led into the mudroom and stopped to listen, but the house was silent. Normally, he'd have kicked off his wet shoes before walking through into the kitchen, but the hairs shaved close to his neck weren't lying down the way they should, so he kept his shoes on, leaving damp marks and pine needles on the linoleum.

The back side of the house was a wall of glass that looked down the grassy slope to the dock that pointed like a gray finger toward the empty horizon. He didn't see a living thing outside. Not even a gull.

"Carol?" he called.

There were two half-full coffee mugs on the kitchen table. In front of them, the chairs had been pushed out and left that way. Carol always straightened things like that, and the last time she'd walked off and left dishes on the table was when she'd had the flu.

"Carol?!"

He walked fast, moving into the formal dining room, around the table and out the other side, stepping down into the sunken living room. He checked the bathroom and his office. Nothing else was out of place. He heard a quiet *click* as the heat switched on.

Doc moved to the front of the house, past the entryway. There was a pair of men's shoes, black and heavy-soled, he didn't recognize by the door. One had fallen over on its side.

Doc grabbed the banister and swung himself around and up the stairs, taking them two at a time. When they'd built the house, Carol had wondered aloud if they shouldn't put the master suite on the first floor for when they got old and stairs were too hard. He'd told her the wife of a doctor got enough medical care to take the stairs at ninety, but he was breathing hard at the top.

When he got to the landing, he stopped. He'd thought he'd heard something. He closed his mouth and tried to quiet his panting enough to listen. That was when he noticed the door to their bedroom at the end of the hall was closed. All the other doors in both directions stood open. They rarely closed anything but a bathroom door, especially now that the kids were gone. It impeded airflow and made hot and cold spots. Their HVAC system was old enough to run for president.

He heard it again.

He was down the hall in ten long steps. He didn't call her name this time, and he didn't knock.

CHAPTER FIFTEEN

It was cold and wet, and July had left the store without her coat. She'd started out running because she was angry and upset and afraid and kept at it because it was the only way she wouldn't freeze. She ducked down one of the alleys between two of the buildings, made a left and a right, and then kept going. She didn't have a plan, and she only sort of knew where she was. But the downtown was small, which was a good thing and also not. She came to the edge quickly and kept going.

She passed some of the newer buildings on the outskirts, including a tiny strip mall circa 1970. It was clad in dark brown shingles and housed a dentist, an optometrist, and Doc, the entirety of the island's medical services. Past that were houses, small and old but well-kept. If she'd headed right, which she didn't, she'd have passed a handful of old Victorians, including Preston's, which was undergoing a quiet but miraculous transformation.

The houses petered out almost as quickly as the businesses, and the road she was on slalomed up. It wasn't very steep, but it was steep enough that July, who wasn't much of a runner, had to stop and put her hands on her knees. The mist was light but persistent, wetting the outside of her clothes, while the layer of sweat she'd worked up wet the inside. She had to get moving or freeze, but her heart was hammering and her lungs burned, and she needed a break. Two cars passed. She thought one of them slowed and was maybe going to stop, which gave her a sharp hit of adrenaline she would sooner have done without. July hadn't been out of the city long enough for a car pulling alongside of her to feel like anything but a threat. Fortunately, the car didn't stop and neither did the one after it, and she kept going, moving as fast as she could up the slope, not really running anymore but not walking either.

She passed an out-of-season farm stand, empty and vacant, and beyond it a low-slung concrete bunker with a sign out front that looked like it had been done with house paint: EBEY'S END AUTO REPAIR. Two junkers were parked out front, including a pickup with three wheels and a jack that kept it from leaning to the side. There were no people in sight, and the jack looked like it might have rusted in place.

Meadow gave way to woods. And July started thinking she needed to step off the shoulder and into the trees because there, at least, she'd have some shelter from the wet, even though it looked dense and dark, and she was a city kid. The truth was she'd have been more comfortable in a homeless encampment under an overpass, but Ebey's End didn't have either of those things—homeless encampments or overpasses. And even if she did hide in the woods, she couldn't stay there forever. Anita probably wanted to send her back now, and soon Ms. Overton would be on the ferry, throwing up in the bathroom and then tromping through the evergreens looking for July, who, by that time, would probably have been eaten by a bear.

It was because of the trees that July didn't see it sooner. The church was the second largest building on the island, right behind the junior/senior high, but still, the uppermost tip of the cross barely cleared the firs.

There were double doors painted white on the front of an A-frame sanctuary, which might have had its charms if it weren't for the additions. It was as though several manufactured homes and a 1960s-era elementary school had blown into the side and stuck there. Past those was a children's play structure, the bright plastic faded and one of the swings dangling from a single chain, along with a small basketball court that only had one hoop. That there wasn't a net went without saying. The parking lot was gravel and empty. She looked it all over twice and then one more time, hoping the old sedan she only now realized she'd been looking for would materialize.

It didn't. She wasn't that lucky.

Numb, she walked forward anyway, because even if she ended up curled on the wood chips under the cracked slide, at least there wouldn't be any bears.

Movable type told her worship services and Sunday school were at nine and a spaghetti supper started at six. ALL W LCOME. She tried the door and nearly cried when it swung open.

Inside was still and quiet and smelled like orange furniture polish over stale coffee. She stood shivering on a large black industrial mat designed to soak up the worst of what a whole community's worth of sodden shoes could do. Beyond it, the carpet was low-pile and dusty red. A rolling rack of empty hangers was to her left, and a bulletin board tacked with announcements was on her right. There was one for the AA meetings and the single-parent support group and the women's ministry, which needed volunteers for a spring cleanup planned for March. A guest book with room for names, addresses, and phone numbers was on a small table. Her fingers were blue and too stiff to use the pen. And no one else had either. The page was blank.

Ahead of her, one of a pair of doors was propped open, a brown rubber doorstop shoved into place. Inside, rows of pews stretched into the darkness. At the far end, a low stage held a wooden podium draped in a white cloth, and behind it hung a cross that went nearly to the ceiling. A brass sunburst radiated from it. She took a tentative step forward, off the all-weather mat.

Inside the sanctuary, the floor was wood, the same color as the pews, with runners down the aisles. Hymnal racks ran along the back of each bench with mismatched blue and red books clustered inside, unstraightened from the last service. She took two steps and startled when the lights blinked on. She spun around but was still alone.

July didn't know churches had motion-sensor lights. She knew almost nothing about churches at all. She'd only been to one wedding, held in the university chapel. The chapel had been brick and modern inside but for the alabaster Jesus hanging in perpetual agony over the groomsmen.

There hadn't been anything like that at her mother's service. It had been held at the faculty club. There was no body. Not even ashes. Ms. Overton had taken her. The dean of the history department had spoken. July had never met him before, and she couldn't remember anything he said, except afterward when he'd apologized there weren't more people. He blamed it on winter break. July had thought there had been plenty of people until he'd said that, and then it didn't feel like enough anymore.

She had a hard time remembering most of what happened during that time. It was like the film in her brain had been corrupted, leaving staticky bits that were almost never things you would want. She could remember eating a tuna sandwich in her downstairs neighbor's kitchen the day after her mother was killed. She'd stayed there for the two weeks. Ms. Aquino was a surgical nurse at the children's hospital. She didn't go to work the whole time July stayed, which July hadn't thought about at the time.

Together, she and Ms. Aquino ate sandwiches and Ruffles plain potato chips. The TV had been on a lot. It was easier than talking. Sometimes they both stayed in their pajamas. Ms. Overton had called or come by every day. Maybe that was normal. July didn't know. Ms. Aquino said July could go upstairs to her own apartment whenever she wanted but not by herself. Ms. Aquino would go with her. July didn't really know why, but she never went. She stayed in Ms. Aquino's guest room and didn't sleep and watched Animal Planet at three in the afternoon. They didn't celebrate Christmas. Ms. Aquino didn't have any decorations up, and she didn't mention it at all. And so July forgot about it until it was over, which was good. She couldn't have lived through the holiday if she'd known it was happening.

"Hello."

The voice made July jump. She grabbed the front of her sweater and smacked her hip into the side of a pew hard enough to raise a purple bruise by the next day.

"Oh," he said when she faced him.

The man was wearing a puffy coat unzipped. She could see the white clerical collar at his throat.

"Sorry," July said.

"No, it's . . ." He gaped like a fish for the next word and didn't find it.

"The door was unlocked," she said. "So . . ." It was her turn to trail off.

"Yes." He was on firmer ground here. "Almost always. Unlocked, I mean. You're welcome. Anyone is."

All W lcome.

"I thought maybe Malcolm would be here?"

July thought she saw his shoulders drop like someone who'd been let off the hook. She could've been wrong. It was a very puffy coat.

"Let's see," he said.

She followed him out of the sanctuary and down one hallway, around the corner, and down another. They passed classrooms and a large multipurpose room, along with several closed doors that might have been storage and one that was marked PASTOR'S OFFICE.

The last turn took them down a narrower hall with only one door at the end. The walls were paneled with fake wood, and the deep grooves between each made stark vertical lines that messed with July's perspective, turning the corridor into an M. C. Escher drawing.

She had to blink and turn her head to keep from getting dizzy. On her left was a row of framed eight-by-ten portraits, first in black and white and then becoming color as the photographs moved through time. They were all men. All white. All dressed in the same black shirt and same white collar. Some wore glasses. Most wore black suit jackets. The man in the last photo, the same man who walked in front of her, didn't. Little brass plaques on each were engraved with the title "Pastor" and then a name. Pastor Chet's last name was Liddle. So was the name of the man before him and the man before him.

Chet stopped at the door and took a ring of keys from his coat pocket. There was another plaque here. It said PRIVATE.

"Malcolm," he called when he got the door open, "are you home?"

They stepped into a living room as locked in the past as Anita's apartment. The walls were covered in the same wood paneling. The carpet went from red in the hall to orange inside, with only a thin brass strip to mark the threshold. The couch was low with squared-off arms covered in a dull gold brocade worn in places from decades of arms and backsides. Two TV trays sat in front of it, and an old vacuum tube television set was on a small cart in front of those. The kitchen was in the far corner, open to the rest of the room, much like Anita's but larger, with enough room for a dining table in the middle. Anita's table, though, had room to eat on, while this one was covered with books and notepads and loose sheaves of paper. It reminded July of her mother's desk. Or what had been her mother's desk.

Someone else would've taken it over by now. She was always saying there wasn't enough space in the department for everyone. July knew it wouldn't have been left like a shrine. Hot tears seeped up to her lower lashes. Her arms were crossed over her chest, and she had to squeeze her biceps and hold her breath to keep the tears from falling.

A door on the opposite wall swung open. Malcolm was barefoot, wearing gray sweatpants, an unzipped black hoodie, and a T-shirt July would later learn was from a Christian summer camp, now defunct.

"You have a visitor," Chet said.

"Hi." He looked surprised but not that surprised.

"Hi." July lifted a hand in a half wave. The tears came back. This time she couldn't stop them.

"Oh, uh, you want to come in?" Malcolm took a step back and waved toward his room.

"Leave the door open," Chet said as July hurried around him.

Malcolm's room was cleaner than she'd expected. The bed, which had a blue-and-white plaid comforter, was technically made, even if the corner of the top sheet hung down crookedly almost to the floor, and the pillows were scrunched up by the headboard like someone had been lying there recently. The only other furniture in the room was a wooden desk and chair, both of which were piled with textbooks, paperbacks, and notepaper, making them look an awful lot like the kitchen table she'd just passed.

"Here, let me just . . ." Malcolm grabbed up the things from the chair and deposited them on the foot of his bed. "There you go."

July sat. Malcolm did, too, on the edge of the bed, which made his pile slump over.

Outside the room, a door closed. July wondered why it mattered whether Malcolm kept his room open if Chet was someplace else, but she didn't say it.

"You're pretty wet," he said.

She had almost forgotten, but she could feel her hair now, sticking to the sides of her face. Her sweater was heavy, and if she'd tried to take off her leggings, she'd have had to peel them off like sausage casings. Her high-tops were, once again, soaked through.

"I ran here."

"From Anita's?"

She took a breath, and it came in stuttery, so she had to blow it out through her lips, doing her best to hold herself together. She wiped her face with the sleeve of her sweater.

"We kind of had a fight."

Malcolm nodded, looking down first at his pants, which had a small hole in the knee he was picking at, and then across the room to the window. The blinds were open, and the broken-down children's play equipment was on the other side.

"I hope it's okay I'm here."

"Yeah, it's okay." He looked back at her and gave a small smile.

"You might be busy," she said.

"I'm not busy."

July pulled the cuffs of her sleeves down over her hands.

"Do you want to talk about the fight?" he asked.

"Not really."

July didn't know what she wanted to talk about. She didn't think she wanted to talk about anything. She was looking down at her hands—or the sweater sleeves where her hands had been. When she looked up, Malcolm was holding a tissue out toward her. She didn't even know where he'd gotten it from.

"Thank you. Sorry. Maybe I should . . ."

Nobody here could finish a sentence, including her.

"It's okay," he said. "Really. I have fights with the pastor, too."

July balled the tissue in her hands. She had a hard time imagining that. "Why do you call him 'the pastor'?"

Malcolm shrugged. "I dunno. I guess because everyone else does? Sometimes I call him Dad. Just, you know . . ."

She thought he was about to say more, but he swallowed it and they sat together in the quiet for a minute. It was less uncomfortable this time.

She looked at the desk by her arm, scanning the books. They weren't the same as the ones for her classes. He was a couple of years older than her, even if it didn't really feel like it when they talked. She hadn't read any of the paperbacks either, but she'd heard of them. There were a couple by George R. R. Martin, which she thought was a little odd. She didn't need to have read them to know they had a lot of sex in them. She wondered if Pastor Chet knew or cared.

"Is that your mom?" July pointed to the one photograph in the room.

The picture was on the far corner of the desk, small, framed in faux silver and almost obscured by detritus. July moved a stack of papers a few inches to the left to see the woman's face more clearly. She was pretty but not striking with brown hair that she wore long and unstyled, parted down the middle. The photograph had been taken on a beach with evergreens in the background and a cloudy sky.

"Yeah," Malcolm said. "That was before I was born."

"How old were you when she died?"

"Nine. She died on my ninth birthday."

"Jesus."

"Yeah, kinda ruins cake and ice cream basically forever."

July knew a canned dead-mom joke when she heard one. She wondered how many times he'd told it, and if it did what he wanted it to.

"My mom died five days before Christmas," she said, "but that's not as bad."

"It's close," Malcolm allowed.

"What do you remember about her?"

Malcolm shrugged. "Not as much as I want to."

"Did she cook? My mom cooked."

"Yeah, I think so. I remember pancakes. She tried to make them in heart shapes but, like, just by pouring the batter, so they were always sort of funny-looking."

"That's nice," July said.

"Yeah."

July pulled the sleeves of her sweater tighter around her hands, balling the cuffs up in her fists. "What other things did she do?"

"You should ask my dad. He remembers more than me."

Pastor Chet hadn't seemed very comfortable in her presence, and she didn't think he'd welcome a lot of chitchat about his dead wife from her either.

July picked up a Martin book. "Any good?"

"Not bad," he said, "but it's not my favorite one."

Malcolm told her what his favorite one was and why, and she told him about her favorite books, some of which he'd read and some he hadn't. They might have gone on talking like that for a long time, but there was a sharp knock on the frame of the door and both of their heads jerked up.

"Uncle Mack."

The front wheels of his walker were just over the threshold. He wore a baggy olive-green coat—what July thought was called a mackintosh—over more or less the same outfit she'd seen him in at his house, jeans and a flannel shirt, neatly tucked in.

"I see you found God," Mack said before greeting Malcolm, who called him "sir."

July didn't know what to say to that, so she didn't say anything. She was more embarrassed in front of him than she would've been if Anita had shown up. Anita she could be mad at it. With Mack, she felt childish.

"If you're done saying your prayers, I think we best be heading back. Dogs are in the car doing Lord knows what to the upholstery."

July stood up, and so did Malcolm. She raised her hand in a small wave, and he did the same, looking a bit embarrassed himself.

She followed Mack back out into the main room of the parsonage and found Pastor Chet standing by the sofa.

"Thank you much," Mack said, nodding to him.

"Happy to help. Hope Anita's healing up all right."

"She'll manage. She's waiting on us."

Chet reached in front of Mack and opened the door. It was polite, but July got the sense he was happy to be rid of them. Out in the narrow Escher hallway, she heard him close the door, but she didn't look back.

"He called you," she said.

"'Course he did."

The space was too narrow for them to walk side by side. July stayed a step back, grateful she didn't have to look him in the eye.

"Sorry you had to come get me."

"Anita is the one who came." His voice had a heavy seriousness she hadn't heard from him before. "I tagged along for the ride."

Outside, Anita's station wagon was parked across three spots in front of the main doors. It was still misting, but both passenger windows were rolled halfway down, the top halves of two German shepherds shoved through the cracks. Gideon's tongue was hanging impossibly long out of his mouth, and even Samson looked happy, moving from side to side as far as the frame of the door would allow.

Mack took the handicap ramp off to the side, and rather than face her cousin alone, July followed him. She was relieved when he opened the front passenger door for himself, pushing Samson into the back as he did.

"Why'd you let him sit in front?" Mack said, lowering himself into the fur-covered seat and then bending over to fold his walker. "Take this, will you?" he said to July.

She reached for it as Anita popped the trunk.

"Weirdly," Anita said, "I decided not to let your dogs fight to the death over a single window when I possess many windows."

July wedged the walker into the trunk and then opened the back door, pushing the two dogs out of the way to get in. Her heart beat too fast, flooding her body with more blood and oxygen than it could use, but Anita didn't acknowledge her. She didn't, as far as July could see, look at her, even in the rearview mirror.

It might not have mattered. All she would've been able to see was dog—a muzzle, an ear, a tail. There wasn't enough room for both of them and July, too, back there, and they wouldn't sit still. They were everywhere and on top of her, and she, too, could only see a piece of each of them at a time, an assemblage out of order.

"You coulda rolled down the *other* back window," Mack was saying.

Anita looked at her father as she shifted into gear. "Do you think that possibility escaped me?"

Mack huffed. "Well, you did go ordering the expensive sacks."

"Dad, I swear to God—"

Gideon had won the shoving match with Samson and, as the victor, had placed his two front paws on July's thigh before shoving his entire upper body up to his armpits out into the cold winter air.

"Neither of them *wanted* the other back window," Anita said.

"What do you mean, they didn't want it?"

July was so nervous she felt sick. Anita had to say something eventually. She had to do something. July had thrown food in the store. Anita could send her to foster care for that. She could send her for any reason or for no reason. No one had come asking for July. No one had particularly wanted her. It had taken the state of Washington itself to find someone it could bully into taking her. She was being *allowed* to stay, which was the third shittiest thing you could feel. The second shittiest was not being allowed to stay. And the winner of the shit race was not knowing which it was going to be. Getting sent back would actually be better. Not that anyone in the car seemed to understand this or even to notice it, especially Gideon.

Ninety pounds of dog were screwing down through the skin and muscle of July's leg at the two small points of his paws. It was like being pinned under the little rubber feet of a refrigerator. Meanwhile, Samson was nosing around his brother's haunches, readying himself for another skirmish.

"I mean neither of your spoiled dogs wanted to use that window. Apparently that side of the car is subpar."

July, who was trying to push Samson toward that other window, was coming to understand the deep truth of what Anita said.

Mack reached for the temperature control, turning up the heat and making the windshield fog. "They're pack animals. You have to establish dominance."

July didn't know how to establish dominance. The three of them were approximately equal-sized, but she was the only one strapped to the seat. And if any real violence broke out, she didn't like her chances. She tried to push Gideon off, but he fought back, grinding his paws in harder. She didn't think he meant her harm, but accidental injury didn't hurt any less.

"Dominance?" Anita asked.

"Guys . . ." July started.

Samson made his move, forcing his snout and then the rest of his shaggy body between July's face and his brother, muffling her pleas.

"Every pack needs a leader," Mack said.

July thought she heard Anita snort, but she could no longer trust her senses.

"Right, and as the alpha, you choose to let the dogs sleep on all the bed pillows, *my* bed pillows."

July was desperate to turn her face away, but the side of Samson's body had her head pinned, filling her nose with reeking wet fur, grown extra dense for the winter. He whimpered. He shoved. Gideon shoved back. More paws were on her. More weight. A hundred and eighty pounds of ruff, tail, fur, and muscle were locked together in a canine sumo match for window supremacy.

It was no longer possible to force them off of her. They took up all the space—all the air—between her and the back of Mack's seat. They were wedged in. There was nowhere to go. She couldn't feel her arms.

"That's right," Mack was saying.

It was becoming increasingly clear that July could die. She might actually be dying. This was the end of her. And no one, not even the dogs, noticed. (This was the fourth shittiest thing. Still not number one.)

"And it's not *all* of the pillows."

July's world was going black.

"I keep half of one for myself."

"Hey!" Anita shouted. "What's going on back there?"

July could no longer see, but she felt the car swerve to the side of the road and the sudden jerk as Anita stepped hard on the brake.

"Dammit!" Mack shouted. "Samson, Gideon, knock it off!"

July heard a door open.

Anita's voice was farther away. "I'll kill both of them!"

"They don't mean anything by it!"

July heard the latch and then felt the cold air that whooshed in as her door flung open.

"Out!" Anita shouted, pulling both dogs down onto the gravel shoulder by their collars. "Bad dogs! Bad!"

With the sudden lifting of their weight, July's eyes opened. She took a shaky breath.

The bruises on Anita's face were still stark. On another woman, they would've suggested she'd been a victim, but not on Anita. On Anita, they made her look tough.

"You all right?" she asked.

She was bent over, her hands on her knees, peering in at July. It was the first thing she'd said to her since the store and the Snoballs.

July nodded.

"I'll shoot them if you want me to."

Anita's face was deadpan, but July smiled.

"Don't joke about that," Mack said, twisting around in his seat to get a look at them.

"Who's joking?" Anita asked her father.

Behind her, Samson and Gideon had their tails and heads down low, their eyebrows bunched together, the vision of repentance.

"They're sorry," Mack said. "Look at them."

"They're sorry they got caught."

"Now, that's just not true. What do you think, July?"

July wasn't stupid. She knew this was a scene the two of them were acting out for her. If she wasn't exactly being forgiven, she wasn't being thrown out either. Not yet.

"I think they're sorry," July said.

She had a part in the scene now, too, and she wasn't talking about the dogs.

Anita looked at her. Mack looked at her. Both of them nodded.

It was a weird way to fix things, sideways and with substandard materials. But maybe families did it that way when there were more than just two people in them. July didn't have any way of knowing.

CHAPTER SIXTEEN

Sarah was standing in the kitchen, which would've been too small at twice its size. She had her phone pinned between her shoulder and her cheek and was slicing coins of cucumber into a salad bowl, stopping the dull knife with her thumb. The sink was full of dirty dishes, and every inch of counter space was taken over by the toaster oven, compost canister, spoon rest, and other life necessities, layered over by her kids' homework, craft projects, and the newspaper she never had time to read. In her ear was Carol, her mother, who, in a voice much calmer than Sarah could imagine, was explaining that she was moving out.

"I take responsibility," her mother said. "Your father is very upset, and it's only right that I be the one to leave."

Sarah wasn't sure that was true. She was trying to be as calm as her mother was, at least on the outside. She was trying to be a modern sort of daughter who could hear that her mother had been having an affair without acting like a child. What she was feeling on the inside was a whole other thing, but she hadn't gotten to her insides yet.

At the moment, she was trying to get food on the table in thirty minutes because Ariel had a walk-on part in the school play, which they were definitely going to be late for. Her husband, stuck in the usual Seattle traffic, wasn't even home yet, and her seven-year-old, who heard everything anyone said within a four-block radius, was in the living room watching *Bluey*. So whatever Sarah said had to be indecipherable.

"I spoke with Declan," her mother said.

Sarah's radar pinged. Why would her mother have called her brother before calling her? "He's going to come out and stay with your father for a while," Carol went on.

"Of course he is."

Sarah couldn't help herself. Her brother had been through three jobs in three years. He was desperate to look for a way not to grow up and take responsibility. He'd probably crawl right back into their mother's womb if he could.

She heard her mother take a breath. "I think it's a good thing."

Sarah let it go. "What about you? Where are you going to stay?"

"I haven't decided."

Sarah had finished with the cucumber. She put the knife down, took the phone back into her hand, and closed her eyes.

Her mother hadn't ever worked. Not really. She'd written that book when Sarah was in high school, which, you know, good for her, but she hadn't written another one. It wasn't exactly a career. And now she was retirement age and had no money of her own. She'd get something in the divorce. (Obviously there would be a divorce.) But Sarah doubted it would be enough, which meant all of this was now *her* problem.

"You know you can always come here, Mom."

She said it because she had to. There was no way of not saying it, even though it would be a nightmare and a half. Sarah and Kurt had bought the two-bedroom bungalow as a starter home, only to have prices shoot through the roof five years later. Compared to their neighbors, their mortgage was practically nothing, and their house was worth two and a half times what they paid for it. But it didn't matter, because all the other houses had gone up two and a half times, too. They could never leave these one thousand square feet because they'd never in their lifetime be able to buy anything else.

Her kids shared a bedroom smaller than some people's closets. Jack kept falling off his loft bed in the middle of the night, but neither kid could have a regular bed because then they couldn't have anything else, including a dresser or a desk or a damn dust bunny in there. So being the good parents they were, they'd decided their child could keep getting concussions, and now—NOW—she had to cram her mother in, too.

She'd have to sleep on the sofa. It was the only possibility, which meant no one else could really use the living room, and— Why did her mother have to do this to her? *God.*

"Thank you, sweetheart, I appreciate it, but you've got your hands full."

Sarah's shoulders sagged. Was she supposed to argue? Was that what they were doing? Like that *Sex and the City* episode when Charlotte converts and has to go to the rabbi three times or whatever?

"You're sure?" Sarah asked.

"I'm sure."

"Okay, well, Ariel has the school play tonight."

"Then you better get going."

"You're okay?"

"I am."

. . . .

Carol hung up and looked out over the water. Small waves rolled steadily up the rocky beach, spraying and hissing and then running back the way they'd come as fast as they could go. They reminded

Carol of kids playing a game, daring one another to pull some prank and darting away in a chorus of squeals. She was parked off the side of the two-lane road that ran along the water. It was beautiful but usually empty, especially this time of year. The sand was too rocky for people to want to walk for long, and the wind coming off the sea was icy and wet.

She opened her car door and stepped out, every joint in her body protesting its treatment. Some of her hair had come loose from its twist. The wind grabbed hold of it, blowing it sideways across her face. Last night was the first night in Carol's life that she'd slept in a car. When she'd walked out of her home carrying an overnight bag, she hadn't known where she would go. She assumed an idea would present itself by the time she made it to the end of the road, but no idea had. Or rather many had and all had been discarded. Ebey's End had a motel, but it was closed for the season. Carol had friends, but nearly all of her friends had husbands and nearly all of the husbands were friends of Doc's. Carol and Doc were a couple, and they had couple friends—in the past, anyway. Over time, they'd socialized less and less, which made it even more awkward to ask for favors.

Mainlanders had been buying second homes on the island recently, and she knew some of them rented those houses out. So she'd pulled over once she could get a decent signal on her phone and poked around the internet, searching for rentals. She'd found three different websites. There were fewer houses for rent than she'd hoped, less than a dozen, and all of them wanted some $300 a night. She didn't know what she'd expected, but what was acceptable for a few nights' vacation wouldn't do in the long term.

It had been too late by then anyway to make any arrangements, and so she'd found a place to park and had, she was ashamed to admit it, cried herself to sleep. She had too many feelings, and they were all exhausting. Shame and embarrassment were there. Of course they were. And so was fear. She had been thrust into the unknown, not just for the night but for the foreseeable future, and it wasn't hard to imagine a very difficult life ahead. It was awfully late to be beginning again, and she wasn't sure what sort of resources she might end up with.

It had been kind of Sarah to offer her a place, even if Carol had heard clearly in her voice that it had been obligatory. That was fine, even if it didn't feel particularly good. We all want to be wanted. (That's how she'd ended up in this mess, after all.) But if we are any sort of decent, we often do things because we *should* do them, especially when it comes to family. She'd been the one to tell Sarah and Declan for all their growing-up years that they didn't need to like something to do it. Lord knew, as much as she loved her children, she hadn't relished most of the daily tasks they'd required of her. How much pee and vomit had she cleaned up? How many baseball games had she sat through when all Declan had done was ride the bench? Meals cooked? Toilets scrubbed? Sheets washed? It had been endless.

Obligation was underrated. Obligation was the glue that held people together. Not that it couldn't fail.

Carol had heard—she couldn't remember when or where—but she had heard that people often subconsciously want to get caught. She couldn't swear to what her subconscious did or did not want, but she could say for certain that, in forty years, Henry had never before come home for lunch.

The bedroom door had flown open. She and Gordy had not been actually in the act, thank God, but there had been no denying that they had been. There had been all manner of shouting and stomping, the gathering of clothes and the slamming of doors. Gordy had gotten out as quickly as he could, and Henry had followed him, yelling and red-faced. Their vehicles were both in the driveway, side by side, and as Gordy was getting his truck started, which took more than one try, Doc had opened his own car and pulled out, of all the things in the world, a quiche. He pulled it from the pastry box and hurled it overhand at the truck. Pastry bounced off the windshield and splattered onto the hood before sliding down onto the concrete as Gordy pulled away.

Carol had been standing in the open front door in her sweater and underwear, having run out behind the two men, ready to throw herself between them if it had come to that. It hadn't. She wasn't the sort of woman men came to blows over, not at her age and not in the past either.

Later, when she was leaving with her bag in hand, she'd seen the bent, disposable pie plate still there, wet and crushed. Most of what it had contained had been knocked out and smeared across the driveway, but some amount remained, enough to tell what it had been. The blue box, too, was there, blown farther down and caught by the pole of the mailbox. It said HAM & CHEESE in marker that was smearing in the drizzle. Carol couldn't remember the last time she'd eaten quiche, and she could not imagine why her husband had bought one at all, let alone in the middle of a workday. She would probably never know. They hadn't exchanged very many words after Gordy had gone. There'd been so little left to say, which was, she thought, the saddest part of all.

Now here she was, looking through the strands of her own gray hair at the sky, heavy with dark clouds. And she had absolutely no idea what she was going to do. None at all.

CHAPTER SEVENTEEN

Cashier duty?" Mack asked, pausing by the door to pull his gloves from his hands and shove them into the pockets of his waterproof jacket, releasing for a moment the handles of his walker to do it.

July didn't recognize it as showing off, but it was.

"Yep." She tried not to act like she thought her promotion was a big deal, but she did. "How was your Philosophers meeting?"

"Oy." Mack shook his head. "A doozy. Doc—" He paused, not sure how to proceed around innocent ears. "Well, he's having a rough time at home."

July pulled her hands up into the sleeves of her sweater. She'd heard what had happened. Every customer who'd come in the door had said something about it—not to July, of course. They spoke to Anita and Peggy; to Darryl, the part-time butcher; and to one another. But July still heard them. It wasn't a very big store, but there were plenty of places to hide and listen.

She didn't know if Anita blamed her. She hadn't said a word about it, and July tried not to say too many words at all.

She hadn't known what Doc was going to find at home. She didn't know he was going to find anything. She just knew he needed to go. Now all of this had happened, and maybe it was for the best and maybe it wasn't. And maybe it depended on who you asked, but July felt a little sick over it.

Anita had told her flat out that knowing things didn't make them her fault. She said July didn't make cars run over people, and if that was true, she probably didn't make Carol sleep with the mailman either. That was what July was planning to say if she had to. So far, Mack was the only person who'd mentioned it to her at all, and the fact that he had was a relief. It was like July had been holding her breath, and he told her she didn't have to anymore.

"I heard what happened," she said.

Mack blushed. He certainly hoped that wasn't the case. He'd gotten, if not a complete picture from Doc, then enough to imagine the scene himself. It wasn't the sort of thing a young girl ought to know about. He'd like to think Anita didn't know anything about it, but he supposed, at her age, if she didn't, that was another sort of problem. There never had been much in the way of boyfriends in her life, and after Bill's girl, who was also one of his deputies, came out of the closet, Mack had wondered.

"Yeah, well . . ."

He pretended to inspect the Valentine's display, which had grown steadily in recent days. There was the usual chocolate candy, along with pink-stuffed Oreos and a proliferation of plush animals, including a frog wearing a crown. Cellophane-wrapped bouquets squeezed together in black plastic buckets, and heart balloons floated on curly ribbon leashes. One had gotten loose and bobbed up at the ceiling, drifting lazily around the perimeter of the store, as though in orbit.

"By the way . . ." July said, pushing some buttons on the new register's touch screen, an unauthorized addition that had come after

Mack's stroke. The cash drawer dinged open, and she lifted the top dividing insert, pulling a handful of checks and large bills from the bottom. "Anita wants you to take this to the bank."

The vinyl deposit pouch with the bank's logo printed on the side was tucked beside the register. July pulled it out, dropped in the money, and zipped it closed before holding it out to her uncle.

He looked at his watch. "Bank's nearly closed, for Christ's sake."

"Probably should hurry." She gave the pouch a little waggle.

He didn't reach for it. "We've been making our deposits first thing in the morning for fifty years."

July tried not to look overly invested. "I think it's important . . . to Anita."

Mack pressed his lips together and let a puff of air out through his nostrils. He did not believe in change for the sake of change. And if something else was going on, he expected to be consulted.

"Doesn't want my opinions, but she'll take my help, I suppose."

He reached out and took the pouch, holding both it and the handle of his walker in the same hand. He turned toward the door, not bothering with his gloves. It wouldn't take long, but that was hardly the point.

He'd only been gone a few minutes when Anita came down from upstairs, having begun and then rationalized the abandonment of a stack of paperwork.

She watched as July finished ringing up Mr. Prince—ground beef with the 50% OFF sticker, which meant it would need to be used up tonight; tinned grapefruit; a Baby Ruth; name-brand saltines and off-brand sandwich spread, the pink kind with visible pickle relish. Even if Anita had never seen him, she could have said from the receipt that the customer was a man between seventy and eighty, likely unmarried. In this case, that would be wrong. Mrs. Prince sat in her wheelchair in front of their living room window from breakfast through to dinner. She hadn't left the house in fifteen years. She certainly didn't cook. Anita wasn't even sure if she still ate.

After Mr. Prince left, July, who had more homework than usual that night, stepped away from the register, and Anita took her place.

"Goulash tonight," she said, because she wasn't in a position to ignore the discount beef either.

July made a face.

Anita knew July would only pick at a dinner she didn't like, professing not to be hungry, and then, an hour later, would eat two bowls of sugared cereal. Anita also knew that, while she was not a great cook, she was a serviceable one. Her food was fine, and she didn't spend all day on her feet and then go upstairs and stand in front of a stove for the fun of it. She certainly wasn't doing it for herself, and eventually they were going to have it out over this. But not that night.

"You didn't slip Mr. Prince a life-changing banana, did you?"

Anita had meant it to be a joke, but July didn't smile.

"No."

"No peanuts to make him run away with the circus?"

"*No.*"

It was the closest they would come to discussing the thing they were not discussing.

. . . .

Upstairs, July stripped off her coat and shoes and went down the hall to the linen closet. Standing on tiptoe, she pulled a set of cotton sheets from the top shelf, barely able to catch the edge with her fingertips so the whole of it tumbled down on top of her, half unfolding in the process. She gathered the pile up off the floor and carried it to the sofa.

She tucked the fitted sheet, yellow and worn soft, around the bottom cushions, doing her best to make it look at least a little neat, and when that failed, she spread the flat sheet over top and unfurled an orange, yellow, and brown afghan from the 1970s over all of it. That was neat, if not actually nice, and would have to do.

Hungry, she went to the kitchen and pulled a box of Froot Loops from the cupboard, pouring them into a bowl without milk. She was ruining her dinner, but dinner that night would be ruined anyway, so it didn't count.

In the kitchen next to the sink was the easiest place to hear voices coming up from downstairs. July didn't know if it was the pipes that carried the sound or what. Anita heard all kinds of things from downstairs no matter where she was in the apartment, so much so that July wasn't sure if "heard" was the right word. It was as if she and the store were tuned to the same frequency.

July took her bowl and slid down the bottom cabinets until her butt was on the half-circle rug in front of the sink. She gathered a small handful of cereal and dropped it into her mouth. It would be hard to make out individual words unless there was shouting, but there was a good chance of shouting. She folded her legs crisscross and tucked her feet under her thighs, eating and waiting and thinking.

She wasn't sure how long it would take Mack to return, but he would. He was as tethered to the place as Anita. They were the same that way and yet entirely different. The store served him, not the other way around, which didn't mean he didn't love it. He did. Just for altogether different reasons.

It wasn't any surprise to July that he'd chosen to buy the one kind of shop everyone had to visit, the items inside all necessary and perishable. Mack, no matter how personable, could never have sold cars or vacuum cleaners. How often did anyone buy a vacuum cleaner? It wasn't only that he wanted to be around people. It was that he wanted to be around the same people over and over until his life was interwoven with theirs, and theirs with his, and if he had to control the island's supply of Cocoa Puffs to ensure it, then so be it.

Anita, on the other hand, had turned the store and the apartment above it into a self-sufficient island with, until recently, a permanent population of one. It was safe and comfortable and distant. The checkout stand was a two-foot-wide barrier that no one crossed. Anita knew everyone and was friends with no one, a condition July was not certain her cousin had even noticed. She had, July thought, confused knowledge *of* people—factoids gleaned from the purchase of pickle relish and Tampax—with actually *knowing* them. That those were different things was obvious to July and would soon, she imagined, become clear to Anita. The only real question was how much trouble July would be in in the meantime.

CHAPTER EIGHTEEN

The bank was one of the few businesses downtown that had its own parking lot. It was large enough to hold six cars, if you counted the handicap space, which was a tad optimistic. In his whole life, Mack had never seen more than three customers there at a time. And on this day, aside from the cars he knew belonged to Preston Daly and that young man who worked for him—his name slipped out of Mack's mind like a greased eel every time he heard it—there was only one other: Carol's.

"Well, shit on toast," Mack said under his breath, and wheeled his walker over.

It was out of his way and none of his business, but he went right on. He didn't even look around to see if anyone was watching.

The inside of the old white BMW—Doc had bought them matching ones fifteen years before, in the grips of what everyone assumed was a midlife crisis—was neat, Carol would never allow otherwise, but neatness didn't hide the truth. In the backseat was an overnight bag and next to it a folded blanket and pillow, things Mack might have been able to ignore. But in the front was a brown sack with the goddamn Blue Bird logo printed right on it. It might as well have been a middle finger. With a puff of air that made him sound like an old bull, Mack pointed his walker toward the front door.

The lobby was empty but for the boy. His name tag—where would the world be without name tags?—said JEREMY. Jeremy smiled at Mack, and Mack was forced to smile back and wheel his way over. He handed him the zippered pouch and waited for his deposit receipt.

The bank was small: a cluster of upholstered chairs around a coffee table spread with magazines, where no one sat; a counter with room enough for three tellers, which was more than the bank employed; a glass-walled conference room for the signing of documents; a vault where they kept the lockboxes; and Preston's office.

There were a lot of reasons a bank president might need to shut his office door, but Preston didn't encounter many of them. In fact, when he'd closed it that day, the whole lobby had taken on a slightly unfamiliar feeling, as though the furniture had been rearranged.

The boy, nameless again in Mack's mind, handed over his receipt. With no more business to conduct, Mack considered he might have to take a seat in one of those lobby chairs. His bony behind might be the first behind to ever lower itself onto their pristine surfaces, which, to his mind, was fitting. But he'd not made it halfway across the commercial tile flooring when Preston's door opened halfway, and Carol, who was holding herself tighter than a coiled spring, slipped out.

The skin under her eyes drooped, and she had a wadded-up tissue clutched in her fist like someone was going to try to take it from her.

Mack looked from her to the door, but Preston didn't emerge.

"Carol," he said, turning his walker to head in her direction.

She nodded, but her eyes flicked away from his, an attempt to acknowledge him without having to engage. But he was on her heels, and no one—no matter how distraught—could let the door slam on an old man with a walker. She had to stop and wait for him, and she did.

"Carol," he said again, when they were both outside.

"Hello, Mack," she said, squeezing her tissue tighter.

He nodded to her car. "You shop at the Blue Bird now?"

She opened her mouth, a look of surprise on her face, and then shut it, took a breath. "It was on my way."

"On your way where?"

"I was driving by."

"Hogwash."

Carol didn't even bother to open her mouth. She was a smart woman, smarter than most people realized, and she wasn't going to walk into his trap.

Mack kept both hands on the walker's brakes. It gave him something to squeeze.

"You're gonna freeze to death sleeping in that car," he said.

The stillness that came over her was palpable. It wasn't only that she didn't move. It was that she seemed incapable of doing so. A whole section of hair had come loose from the twist at the back of her head, and her coat hung from her shoulders, threatening to slide in a black puddle to the ground. Her hands didn't move to fix any of it. They weren't even gripping the tissue anymore. It hadn't yet fallen from her fingers, but that had more to do with the tissue than with her. It was hanging on the best it could.

"Why don't you come stay at my house?" Mack said.

Carol looked over his shoulder at the side of a building across the way. "Thank you, but I'm fine."

"You're not."

She didn't argue with him. She had more dignity than that. "It's nice to see you," she said, and went to step around him.

He pushed his walker in front of her feet, nearly upsetting his own balance and hers.

"No," he said. "No, if I let you sleep in that car one more night—"

Carol opened her mouth then, and he held up a hand. He wouldn't allow her to fib. It would only embarrass them both.

"Not even the Lord himself would forgive me."

For the first time that afternoon, Carol looked him in the eye and said exactly what was on her mind. "You're not letting me do anything, Mack. This isn't to do with you at all."

Mack pressed himself up straighter without letting go of his walker. It pushed back his shoulder blades and puffed out his chest like a robin redbreast.

"The only person in this world I know better than you and Doc is my own daughter, and if you don't think that means something, then you've got your head screwed on backward," Mack said, meaning every word.

"Maybe I do," she said, "but I can't stay with you."

Lord, but she was a stubborn woman, Mack thought.

"Why not?"

She bored her eyes into his. "I am deathly allergic to dogs."

Mack paused. "You are not."

Mack didn't believe in allergies. He considered them to be a nervous condition brought on by participation trophies and too much fluorescent lighting.

"I am."

"You never said so before."

"Why would I have?"

Mack didn't have an answer for that.

Carol looked, if it were possible, more tired than when they had begun. "My parents had to give away our cocker spaniel when I was two because I wheezed so bad."

It was Mack's turn to look away.

"Fine." He tried not to sound irritated. "You'll stay with Anita, then."

Carol let out a loud and sudden bark of laughter devoid of actual humor.

"What's wrong with Anita's place?" Mack demanded, meaning, of course, his own place.

"Nothing's wrong with it."

Carol didn't really know if anything was wrong with it. Unlike Henry, she'd never been in the apartment.

"Then why not stay with her?" Mack asked.

She tried not to sigh. She wasn't in a position to be sighing. She obviously needed help. It was only that she didn't want it to come from Mack. Who it should come from, she didn't know, but not him.

"Because Anita isn't the one asking," she said.

He waved a hand and made a noise that had too much mucus in it.

"It'll be fine. She could use the help anyway."

"Help with what?" Carol asked.

It was a reflex question. She didn't really care. She was thinking about how Mack felt free to speak for Anita. Carol wouldn't dare speak for Sarah, but maybe that was because Sarah had grown up and moved out and Anita never had.

Mack, though, had grown suddenly reticent. She watched as he pressed his lips together, flattening them out like a frog. It was an interesting gesture for a man known to be one of the town's most inveterate gossips. (*Philosophers' Club, my patootie,* Carol thought.) His eyes traveled down the street toward the store, and without meaning to, he squeezed his hand brakes.

She could've waited him out, but the payoff wouldn't have been worth it. She'd heard about the girl running away, however briefly. Everyone had.

"July is turning out to be a handful, I suppose." Carol kept her tone neutral. She'd raised Declan, after all.

Mack cut his eyes to her and then went back to staring down the road. "She's a good kid who's been through a lot. It's not her fault."

"Of course not," Carol said, and meant it.

Carol was not the sort of woman people automatically thought would be good with children, but she was. She spoke to them respectfully and told them the truth whenever possible. She didn't get down on her hands and knees to play pretend, but she did talk to them, and she took their responses seriously. It was an unusual quality in an adult, and she'd not yet met a child who didn't appreciate it.

She expected Mack to say more, but he was still worrying those hand brakes of his.

"Well," she went on, "even if she's setting the drapes on fire, I don't think Anita is going to want me as a houseguest."

Now Mack really was affronted. First his dogs and now his daughter. "Why not?" he huffed.

Carol stared at him. He really didn't know.

Well, of course he didn't.

Doc was his best friend. Anita was his daughter. They weren't going to tell, and she never had. People supposed there were no real secrets in Ebey's End, but it wasn't true. Every place has secrets. On an island, you just had to work a little harder to hide them.

"Only the usual reasons," she said.

Mack narrowed his eyes. He didn't know what the hell that meant, but he wasn't going to let it keep Carol sleeping in a car. And he certainly wasn't going to have her shopping at the Blue Bird, for Christ's sake. The last thing he needed was for that to catch on.

"The walker folds up," he said. "It'll fit in your trunk if it's not full of what all."

Carol looked at him, and he looked right back. He did his best to exude the sort of influence he'd once had, afraid as all get-out that he only looked ridiculous.

"Fine," she said.

Mack tried not to be surprised.

"We can have this conversation with Anita."

"Like I said—" he started.

But Carol cut him off. "I heard what you said. You need to hear what she says."

Mack looked like someone had knocked him slightly off his center. Not wholly. Not so that he could argue. But a little.

Good, Carol thought. He needed it.

She was almost proud of herself before realizing what she'd have to do now. It shouldn't have mattered. She saw Anita every week. She'd gotten over it, or at least she'd decided to get over it, which was perhaps not exactly the same thing, although it ought to be. She'd put enough effort into it. Years of effort, and now, with Gordy, well, goose and gander and all that.

And yet.

Carol squeezed the balled-up tissue she discovered in her hand. Maybe her husband had been right. Maybe she was having some sort of crisis. *Shit.*

. . . .

"Carol needs a place to stay for a while," Mack said.

Anita had the cash tray out of the register and was doing her totals when they walked in. The store, which didn't close for another fifteen minutes, was empty. Mack looked around. There ought to have been two or three customers, at least, running in for a few things after work. It was something else for him to worry about.

Anita had a small stack of fives in her hand. It was very small.

There wasn't as much cash as there should have been in the till, and she was having trouble switching from one rather serious problem to whatever this was going to turn out to be.

"What?"

Mack raised his voice like she was hard of hearing rather than busy doing the things he no longer had to.

"I said Carol needs a place to stay. So I told her she could stay in the apartment with you."

That did get Anita's attention, and her mouth fell open.

"She can take the extra bedroom," he went on.

"I don't have an extra bedroom."

"'Course you do."

"I have two bedrooms, and July is in the other one."

She was talking to him like Carol wasn't standing there. She wasn't even looking at her.

"I know how many bedrooms my own apartment has, Anita. There are three."

"That's the store office."

"It doesn't have to be."

The truth was, while Mack hadn't forgotten about July, he had forgotten she'd be sleeping in the other bedroom. His brain did things like that sometimes, and he didn't know if that happened to everybody or if it was the stroke. But the last thing he wanted to do was admit it.

"Dad, it's full of files and the computer."

"You'll figure it out."

The way her father waved off problems made Anita quietly homicidal. His waving them away didn't actually make them go away. It just meant he wasn't going to deal with them, so she would have to—along with everything else.

"Why can't she stay with you where there's actually room?"

"I'm allergic to dogs."

Both of them looked at Carol. It was the first time she'd spoken.

In the car, before she'd gotten out and fetched his walker from the backseat—the trunk had had some things in it, although not as many as you'd expect—she'd fixed her hair. She'd smoothed it all back into the twist she always wore and refastened it with a large barrette. Mack had watched her. She didn't even use a mirror. She'd left her bags in the car, but she'd taken her pocketbook. While he got himself situated with the walker, she'd stood waiting, buttoning her coat up to the neck so it looked dignified, setting her purse strap onto her shoulder. Carol always could pull herself together, and Mack appreciated that in a woman.

Now they were both standing here in front of his daughter, who wasn't half so put together.

"I can see this is a problem," Carol went on. "Please don't worry about it."

She turned and started toward the door.

"Carol—" Mack said, and then, deciding there was a better target, turned to his daughter. "She's sleeping in her car!" he hissed.

If he'd meant to keep his voice low, he hadn't succeeded. Carol flinched but didn't stop. If anything, she walked faster.

Anita's lips parted and then closed. She was busy. She had responsibilities. Crushing responsibilities that were not this. This was not hers to take on. And it was Carol, for God's sake. *Carol.*

Mack stared at her gaping like a fish.

"Anita Ann!" His daughter had never given him reason to feel shame, and he could hardly believe she'd decided to start now. "What is wrong with you?"

Anita looked at him and then at Carol and then at him again. She was painted into a corner, and she knew it. If she didn't relent, there would be no end to it. Mack would see to that.

"Carol, wait." The words came out pained.

Carol was nearly to the door, standing under the blank space where the soldier's photograph had hung. She stopped but did not come back.

"You don't have room. I understand."

Anita sighed. She couldn't help herself. "I've been sleeping in July's room anyway."

Mack raised an eyebrow. He wasn't sure that was appropriate, although he couldn't have put his finger on why.

Anita caught her father's look. "I put my mattress on the floor."

"Why?"

Anita opened her mouth to smart off, but Carol got her words out first.

"Children don't stop needing you just because you'd rather sleep."

Anita blinked. It was the first time anyone had come close to saying she was doing things right. The two women looked at each other. It only lasted a moment. Carol said her next words to Mack.

"When Declan was thirteen, he got pneumonia. I put his old Boy Scout sleeping bag down on the floor and stayed there next to him for two weeks."

"July's not sick," Mack said.

"That doesn't make her well." Carol pulled her purse strap up higher.

Mack shuffled his feet inside the frame of his walker. "Anita hasn't been getting her to sleep like she should."

"Dad!"

"What? Everyone knows anyway just looking at her."

"It's not as bad as it was." Anita's jaw tightened. "We're making progress."

Carol really had been planning to leave. She had no idea what she was going to do once she left, but the insanity that had seized her back at the bank had lifted. She needed a real plan, and standing in that overcrowded store, breathing in overripe bananas, she knew this wasn't it. But listening to the two of them, she found herself stuck. She needed to go, but the moment for going didn't feel like it was getting any closer. The feeling only worsened with every bickering word, and if she were even half as smart as she thought she was, she would walk away that very second.

"Is someone helping you?" Carol blurted.

"Is someone helping me do what?"

Tension was coming off Anita like heat off freshly laid asphalt.

"With the day-to-day," Carol said.

"I'm fine."

A look passed over Mack's face, and Anita stared him down, daring him to open his mouth again.

"Well," Carol said, after a bit too much time had passed, "you're a wonder."

Anita had a pen in her hand. She was pulling on the plastic pocket clip with her thumb, bending it back farther and farther without even realizing until she felt it give way with a snap between her fingers. It was loud enough for the other two to hear, but neither of them acknowledged it. Anita pushed the pen and the broken cap into the pocket of her apron.

"Yeah, well, July's a good kid, so . . ."

"Right," Carol said. "I've heard."

Anita didn't want help. Carol wanted help, but getting it this way was its own humiliation. Both roads came to the same place. Carol felt her feet start to come loose from whatever had held her in place. She was done here, and anything that came after wouldn't do her any good.

"Stop." Mack raised the frame of his walker three inches from the floor and slammed it back down again. "Stop it, both of you."

"Dad."

"No." Mack held up his finger and then turned away from her. "Carol, Anita asked you to stay with her. She didn't ask the way she should've, I know that, but we are pretty much up to our ass in alligators with this kid."

"Dad!"

"But the bigger problem is you freezing to death in that car. So you can stay with Anita, or we can start going door to door right now, but we are going to work this out."

The hum of the store's refrigeration was loud in the silence that followed. Mack turned to his daughter. He didn't say anything. He didn't need to.

Hating him more than she ever had, Anita took a breath. "It's possible I could use some help. Temporarily."

Carol wasn't sure she liked Mack any better than Anita did in that moment, but every graceful exit had been sealed shut and spackled over. She adjusted the strap of her purse again. It was turning into some kind of tic.

"If you're sure," she said.

Anita looked her in the eye. "Yep."

Carol looked right back. "Great."

. . . .

Even if Anita wasn't sleeping in her room, she was still sleeping on her mattress. Carol said the sofa would be fine, which sounded magnanimous, but it left Anita without a place to sit in the evenings. Not that she said so.

July was at the kitchen table with her books when the two women came through the door. She only nodded at the news, which might have been a clue, but Anita missed it. Then she looked over at the sofa.

Anita left without saying anything. She still had her father, whose fault all of this truly was, to deal with. She went back down the stairs to the alley, where Mack was waiting for her to drive him home. Her mouth was so full of the words she'd like to have said that they tangled together and none of them would come out. She pulled out of her usual parking spot in front of the store, stepping hard on the gas and harder on the brake. They made it to the end of the road before either of them spoke.

"You're welcome, by the way," he said.

Anita was mid-turn when she stopped the car, managing to block two streets at once.

"What are you doing?" Mack looked behind them.

"I'm *welcome*?!"

"Yes, you're welcome."

Anita wasn't sure she'd ever been this angry. "What exactly should I be thanking you for?"

She had her fingers wrapped around the steering wheel so tight blood couldn't get through them.

"I made the deposit."

Anita stared at him. He stared back.

"What?"

"I made the deposit."

Anita looked at her father like he had bats flying out of his ears. "*What* deposit?"

"The cash out of the register. July told me you wanted me to take it to the bank before it closed, so I did. Gave it to that boy, whatever his name is."

"Jeremy." She said it automatically. He'd been one of her stock boys years before.

"Right, I've got the receipt somewhere," Mack said, but didn't make a move to look for it.

Anita tried to loosen her fingers from the steering wheel and found she couldn't.

"July asked you to," she repeated.

"No, she said *you* asked me to. Said it was important for some dang reason."

Anita had done no such thing, but it explained where all the cash had gone. It felt like her brain was trying to catch up, but somewhere it had made a wrong turn. It was no longer quite so clear what was happening or who she could blame for it.

A car came up Second Street behind them, waited half a second, and gave a small honk. For a moment, Mack didn't think Anita was going to move, but then she did, releasing the brake and putting her foot to the gas.

Mack understood there was something he'd missed, but he also had the feeling he was better off not asking. Everything had gotten sorted, but the glue on that arrangement hadn't yet dried. It would be better if nothing got bumped.

CHAPTER NINETEEN

J uly sat at the table with Carol, who sipped hot tea and ate toast with peanut butter and sliced banana on top. She was already dressed and had taken all the bedding off the sofa and folded it up, doing her best to make things look normal. She didn't mention Anita or glance toward the office. And she didn't pull out a phone and stare into it like July's mother had in the mornings, although Catherine had never sat down for breakfast. She ate a chocolate chip granola bar over the sink while reading the *New York Times* on her phone.

Carol sat looking out the window, but the window next to the table only looked out on the alley that separated Anita's building from the empty one next door. She was looking down toward the ground where cars sometimes parked and where the store's dumpster sat. If the stock boys didn't close it all the way, seagulls would come. If two or more showed up, they'd make their mournful *mah-mah-mah* calls.

The first time July had seen those birds, she'd thought they were bleeding. They all had red splotches on their beaks that looked like injuries, but Anita had told her they were supposed to look like that. It was the kind of bird they were. But that morning, there were no birds or cars or people, nothing to look at, but Carol went ahead and looked anyway.

By the time July had carried her bowl to the sink, the air in the apartment was so still and heavy she could hardly stand it.

. . . .

July and Malcolm were sitting on the floor next to the gym doors, making themselves small so no one rushing by would trip on their feet. The big dust brooms the janitors used left a trail of dirt and grit close to the walls, so when July put her hands down to shift her weight, she had to wipe her palms off on her pants. The morning bell hadn't rung yet, and she was waiting until the last possible moment before going into the locker room.

"Maybe you have to be eighteen or something," Malcolm said.

His head was leaned back against the cinder block wall that had been repainted so many times it looked rubberized.

"I'm pretty sure she'd have mentioned it."

That morning, while Anita showered, July had gone into the office to check her email in private. There had been one non-spam message, and it was from Ms. Overton. When she'd seen it pop up, bolded, at the top of her inbox, her heart had started throwing itself against her rib cage like a feral cat caught in a trap. Part of her hadn't wanted to open it, but that part was never going to win.

If you adopt a dog from one of those rescue groups—Save the Poodles or whatever—they make you promise, if you decide you don't want the dog anymore, that you'll bring it back. Apparently it didn't work that way for people. July had asked if someone could contact her birth mother and tell her what had happened, but Ms. Overton replied that that wasn't possible. She didn't say why not. She said if

July had more questions, *Anita* could contact her. In July's head, it was a door slamming.

Malcolm's backpack was on the floor between them. He unzipped it and pulled out a Rice Krispies treat cocooned in plastic wrap.

"For you," he said, handing it to July.

One of the women's ministry ladies had made them for a committee meeting and had let Malcolm have the leftovers. He'd been rationing them, and this was his last one. He'd been planning to eat it during study hall.

"I thought these were your favorite," July said.

He shrugged. "They're okay."

They were his favorite, but he couldn't say that or she wouldn't take it, and it was all he had to offer.

July unwrapped the plastic, broke the square in half, and gave him the larger piece back.

After the bell, he had to run to make it to English class, his open backpack flopping on his shoulder the whole way. They were supposed to be reading *My Ántonia*, but so many of the class weren't actually reading it that Mrs. Schwartz had started giving quizzes for each chapter.

Malcolm slid into his seat and reached into the front pocket of his backpack for his pencil. It wasn't there. He felt around frantically and then reached into the main part of his bag, even though he always put his pencil in the little pocket. They only got five minutes to take the quiz, no exceptions, and he was losing time.

His hand closed around a thin box. It wasn't anything he recognized, and when he pulled it out, his stomach flipped. It was a box of ten pencils with a note taped to the outside.

In honor of the Dead Moms Club

Malcolm spent so much time staring at the box that he only had two minutes left to take the quiz and only then because Mrs. Schwartz yelled at him to get a move on.

. . . .

Mr. Daly slid his hands into his suit pockets and rocked back on his heels while Anita rang up his groceries. Coffee, two apples, one quart of two-percent milk, one roast chicken. Anita's hands, moving quickly through the motions, stuttered. She glanced up at the banker, who gave her a small smile. Unsalted butter, mixed greens, whole wheat bread, sliced cheese, one tomato out of season.

Anita pushed the food over the scanner, tapping the PLU codes into the touch screen for the fruits and vegetables. She glanced over at July, who had two paper bags open and was carefully setting each item in one or the other.

Eggs. Anita opened the carton to be sure none were cracked. She couldn't remember the last time he'd bought eggs.

"July, get Mr. Daly another carton of eggs, please. Large."

Anita set the carton on the counter next to the register while July jogged off toward the back of the store.

"Oops," he said. "Thought I checked those."

He probably had. They were fine.

She took the last item off the belt. The latest *Martha Stewart*. Anita reached over and slipped it into one of the bags, pulling the bread over to hide it.

"Anything special coming up?" she asked.

"Oh, no, nothing special," he said. "I'm just trying to do things a little different."

He looked over to where July had disappeared.

"How are the apples?" Anita asked.

"The apples?"

"Any more fur?"

He blinked, confused, and then the memory bloomed across his face. "Not in a while. Thank you."

July came back with a new carton of eggs. He smiled at her as she slid them into one of the bags.

"Are you baking?" July asked.

"What?" Preston was so surprised by the question it took him a moment to understand it. "Oh, no, no." He took his hand from his pocket and waved the idea out of the air. "I don't bake."

Anita raised an eyebrow at July and wondered if there was some miraculous chocolate chip cookie recipe in that magazine. Maybe next Preston would give up banking and go work for Tiny. The bank would close, and everyone in town would have to start keeping their money under their mattresses.

She totaled his order.

"Do you?" Preston asked July. "Bake?"

She shook her head, reaching up to tuck her hair behind her ears. Anita saw she had a white scar above one of her eyebrows and wondered how she'd gotten it.

"My mom did, though. Cookies mostly. Sometimes pie at Thanksgiving."

"Oh, I love pie." He rocked back again.

"Seventy-eight dollars and ninety-six cents," Anita interrupted.

Mr. Daly reached for his wallet.

"What kind?" July asked.

She was shifting the items in the bags. She might have been settling them for transport, but Anita was suspicious. She tried to keep one eye on her while making change.

"Coconut cream," he said, clapping his hands together. "Coconut cream is wonderful."

Anita jumped at the sound, and when she looked up, he smiled. She saw joy in his gray eyes and remembered how he'd been just a few weeks before. *Oh, hell*, she thought. *If it means that much to him, let him bake pie for the rest of his life.*

"Chocolate," July said. "That's my favorite."

Anita handed him the receipt and his change.

As always, he took a ten and dropped it into the penny cup before putting the rest back in his wallet.

July slid the bags toward him. "Have a good day."

"You, too, young lady. You, too."

CHAPTER TWENTY

Declan sat parked in front of the Island Grocery. He'd sat there so long his windows had fogged up, and he could no longer see the store.

He was back in Ebey's End, which he did not want. Soon to be back in his childhood home, which he also did not want. Sleeping in his childhood bedroom, which he definitely did not want. Doing . . . he did not know what.

Not that he wasn't trying to spin it. He was "helping out" his father. He was "being supportive." He was "regrouping." In truth, he was so deep in the shit he didn't know which direction to swim in, but he was keeping that to himself.

Two weeks ago, he'd been given "the opportunity to resign" from his most recent job. His boss, who was several years younger than he was, had the nerve to say to him, "We both know you're not happy here."

The unhappy job that he no longer had to be unhappy about, which was surprisingly more unhappy-making, had been as an "accounts receivable specialist." In other words, a bill collector. No one wants to be a bill collector. Bill collectors are, by definition, unhappy. They are unhappy to the point of needing to medically intervene in their unhappiness, which requires health insurance and pharmaceutical benefits, which means working longer as a bill collector, which increases their unhappiness. It's a death spiral.

Shortly after his involuntary resignation, Declan had been on his sofa in the middle of the afternoon still wearing the shorts he'd slept in. He was playing *Call of Duty* and eating a bag of mini powdered sugar doughnuts, which was his way of calming the panic. Then his mother had called.

He'd been surprised to find he didn't actually care that she'd been sleeping around. Declan didn't want to hear about it. Not at all. Not ever. But he didn't *care*. Doc had been treating her like an employee since Declan was a kid, so this seemed like fair play. He'd have preferred it wasn't Gordy, but he supposed his mother's options had been limited.

She'd finished the story by saying, "Your father threw a quiche at him."

Declan wasn't sure why there was a quiche, and he wasn't going to ask, because, in this case, the fewer details he had, the better. But he was thinking about it when she said, "I was hoping you could check on him."

"Gordy?!"

"Of course not. Your father."

Declan paused and then said the only thing he could think of: "Why?"

Carol had been through a lot, and so she had to take a breath and ask God for patience. Then, when it didn't come, she had to pretend that it had.

"Because someone should and it can't be me, and when he talks to Sarah, they end up fighting."

"Are you . . . worried about him?" Declan had asked.

It was a question Carol hadn't expected. Not that any part of this felt like something she'd expected. In fact, none of it felt entirely real. She had the strange sensation of not being herself, as though she might pull her driver's license from her purse and find she had been quite mistaken. It was surreal, and it had been that way for some time.

Her mind was wandering, and it took her a moment to remember the question.

"He will want someone to be worried about him."

Declan didn't say anything. He wasn't sure he'd ever heard a more depressing sentence. *Pretend*, she was saying. *One of us has to pretend.* It was then Declan realized it wasn't just his parents' marriage that had broken down. All of their relationships had broken down. They were, all of them, a mess. It was sad and also a little bit of a relief because it wasn't only him. He wasn't the only screwup in the family. They were all screwed up. They were all unequivocally and equally a disaster.

Digital blood representing the death of his character was splattered across the television. He was no longer playing but had forgotten to pause.

"I have an idea," he'd said.

It had been spontaneous, as most of his ideas were, a way to solve his immediate problem and maybe all of their problems. Or at least make them better. His mother's response, measured as it was, might have tempered his excitement, but he'd stopped listening.

The thing about Declan's ideas was that they tended to burn hot, and that kind of excitement was hard to maintain. They also tended to obscure certain other realities. In this case, what it would mean to come back to Ebey's End. Driving onto the ferry had felt like squeezing into old clothes he hadn't worn in fifteen years, and he had the unsettling sense that the moment he got out of the car, he wouldn't be able to take them off again.

. . . .

Anita had gone upstairs, and July was alone in the empty store.

She'd started out standing behind the register, but after about twenty minutes, she'd slid down onto her butt. Anita kept one of those squishy standing mats on the floor, which made it a comfortable enough spot. Around her were the little hidden shelves with extra paper bags, bright orange PAID stickers, a stapler, register tape, and a small trash can with three of Peggy's diet soda empties. Peggy only drank diet soda, as in exclusively and in lieu of all other liquids. July was certain that if water crossed Peggy's lips, it was an accident, like swallowing a raindrop or gargling at the dentist.

July had peeled several of the PAID stickers off the roll and was covering the left knee of her leggings with them when she heard the front door swish open. She grabbed a roll of receipt tape so it would look like she'd had a reason for being down there and stood up just as the man by the door was grabbing a handbasket and turning in her direction. He jumped like in a cartoon.

"Jesus!"

"Hi, sorry," July said. She held up the register tape.

He switched his basket to the other hand and shoved the empty one into his jacket pocket.

The man looked both incredibly familiar and not familiar at all. There was something disheveled about him. Not dirty but not quite together, the sort of look people had when they were woken in the middle of the night in the middle of a dream, except it was four o'-clock in the afternoon and he was in a grocery store.

"Can I help you find something?" July asked, feeling the skin under her hair start to prickle.

"Uhh . . ."

He looked around, and July looked at him. He hadn't shaved in a few days, and the strip of shirt visible under his coat had a crisscross of wrinkles like it had been left too long in the dryer or maybe he'd slept in it. But his coat was one of those expensive expedition brands, and she recognized his shoes as the ones all the tech bros wore standing in line for bánh mì and boba.

"No," he finally said. "No, I'm good. I used to live here. I'm just, you know, trying to remember."

"Trying to remember living here?"

He smiled, but it wasn't sincere. "No, I usually try not to remember that. But I'm here, so . . . I guess I'm looking for the alcohol."

"Past the Valentine's candy, go around the shampoo, then make a left. It's against the far wall."

He blinked.

"Yeah, it doesn't make a lot of sense at first, but then it does."

"Right."

"If you get lost, yell, but I don't think Anita moves stuff very often, so wherever it was when you lived here is probably where it still is."

He made a noise at the mention of her cousin that July didn't know how to interpret. "Is Anita around?"

"Not right now. Did you want to talk to her?"

"No, not at all. How about her dad . . ." He paused and July could see him fishing in his memory bank. "Mack?"

"Nope, just me at the moment."

He nodded, and July realized that, for the first time since moving here, she was talking to someone who had no idea who she was. It felt like an opportunity, but for what, she wasn't sure.

When he moved off, she tried and failed to crack her knuckles, picked at a hangnail until it was at the edge of bleeding, forced herself to stop, and then, when not doing it became impossible, she followed him.

He was pulling a six-pack out of the beverage fridge. There were a few sodas in there and some little bottles of milk, too, all absurdly overpriced, that Anita told her they sold mostly to tourists in the summer.

"So you're from here?" she asked.

"Born and raised," he said without looking at her.

"And you're back for a visit?"

"Sort of."

"Sort of back or sort of visiting?"

He closed his eyes, basket in one hand and beer in the other, and let his chin fall forward onto his chest.

She waited. Ten seconds passed. Ten seconds was a long time to stand in silence with someone who might be having some kind of mental break. Three months ago, she wouldn't have stayed, she would've been afraid of him, but a lot had happened, and she wasn't afraid of very much anymore.

"You okay?" she asked.

She wasn't sure he was going to answer, but he did.

"No, not really." He opened his eyes. "I'd kind of forgotten this part."

"What part?"

"The part where you can't buy a beer without it becoming a community event."

"Well," she said, looking over her shoulder, "it's just me, and I wasn't planning to tell anyone."

The man's face fell into something adjacent to contrition but not quite. It was the same look her classmates got when they screwed up and got caught, and the getting-caught part was what they were sorry about

"Shit. I—" He stopped and took a breath. "I'm not usually like this. Things are just— It's weird right now."

She felt the tingling again. "You never know. Might be a good weird."

When he laughed, it was sincere, and it came out like a snort. "History isn't on your side, but you have to keep trying, right?"

"Right," she said.

He looked down. "You know you've got a bunch of PAID stickers on your pants, right?"

She did know, although she'd forgotten. It actually was a lot of stickers, which she wasn't a hundred percent sure were going to come off. She was probably going to have an increasingly dirty patch of adhesive there for as long as she owned these pants, which might be a really long time. She wasn't sure if part of Anita's commitment included things like new clothes.

"I guess it's like you said, things are kind of weird right now."

She left him there with the usual niceties and wound her way to the opposite side of the store. Anita kept the candy near the dog food, which gave the corner a weird smell—like hay mixed with beef jerky and chocolate.

July skimmed past theater-style boxes of Sour Patch Kids, Mike and Ikes, Milk Duds, and Junior Mints, letting her fingers touch each one until they fell on the last box on the bottom shelf. It was slightly dented and pushed into the corner, half hidden and probably expired. No one would miss it.

Five minutes later, the man, whose name she still didn't know and who still didn't know hers, put his beer and his basket on the miniature conveyor belt.

"Technically I'm not supposed to sell you that."

He looked down at the bag of name-brand tortilla chips, jarred salsa (mild), and Double Stuf Oreos. "What if I promise to eat a salad?"

She pointed to the beer. "You have to be eighteen to sell alcohol."

"Wow," he said. "You really are a kid."

She shrugged, too interested in what would happen next to be offended. "Anita's upstairs. I can call her to come down."

He pressed his lips together, clearly trying to come to some decision, then leaned across the conveyor belt and fake whispered, "What if I steal the beer but accidently drop a twenty on the way out?"

July cocked her head. "You really don't want to see her, do you?"

"It's not personal," he said.

"Sure."

He tried to think of something to say that, if repeated, because it would be repeated, would be both benign and not a lie, and which would not make everything worse because, of course, he was already walking into a gossip minefield.

"Twenty-seven dollars and forty-four cents."

The girl had interrupted his reverie.

"What?"

Without his realizing, she'd rung up his purchases, including the contraband beer.

"Twenty-seven dollars and forty-four cents," she repeated as she bagged the order: salsa and beer on the bottom, cookies in the middle, tortilla chips on top for optimum transport.

"Oh," he said, reaching for his wallet. He swiped his credit card. "Thanks. I hope I didn't get you into any trouble."

She tore off his receipt and handed it to him wrapped around the dented box of Hot Tamales she'd stashed next to the register. "Not for this," she said. "And these are on the house."

He took the candy and smiled when he unwrapped the receipt.

"These were my favorite back in high school."

"Yeah?" She tried to sound surprised.

"I worked next door," he said, flipping the box over and looking at the back. "I used to take them from the concession stand."

"At the theater?"

He nodded.

"It's closed now," she said.

Declan looked up. "Really?"

It was her turn to nod, and his shoulders slumped.

"I practically lived there my senior year. It was a miracle I graduated."

July kept quiet, and he looked back down at the box.

"I think it was the last job I actually liked."

He'd slipped back in time to a place well before her with a look on his face that suggested there was something about Ebey's End he'd missed, if only a small thing.

Sometimes, she knew, small things were enough.

It was only when she pushed the bag toward him that he came to.

"Right, thanks," he said.

"You're welcome."

CHAPTER TWENTY-ONE

Anita was in the computer room. She had, without meaning to, surrendered every other space in her life. Her father was in her house. Her mattress was in July's room. Carol was in her living room, her bathroom, her kitchen, her every damn place. Two months ago, she'd been thinking of getting a cat for company, and now her life felt like an elevator with people coming in and in and in until she was pressed into the corner with nowhere to go and not enough air. She was edgy, and it was starting to show.

"She having night terrors?"

Anita jumped.

"Sorry, I didn't mean to startle you."

"You didn't," Anita said, then took her hand from her chest. "What did you say?"

Carol nodded toward July's room across the hall. Anita's mattress still blocked the door. "I thought she might be having night terrors."

"Not exactly."

Even if Anita had wanted to explain what was wrong with July, she wouldn't have been able to. Not without making both of them sound crazy.

"Small favors, then. Sarah had night terrors. They went on for years."

Carol was holding a mug with a tea bag dangling from the lip. It was one of Mack's mugs, black with a chip in the handle and the name of the local funeral home on the side from when her mother had died.

Carol raised it slightly. "I helped myself. I hope you don't mind."

"It's fine."

"We got one of these when Henry's father passed away."

The mention of Henry's name was like a poke with a sharp stick.

Carol's eyes flicked to Anita's monitor. She'd been playing spider solitaire. A rolling score was in the corner. She'd been playing for a while. Anita was self-conscious about getting caught. She didn't usually play games in the middle of the afternoon, but saying so would only make it sound like it was all she did. She had to fight the urge to close the program, like stubbing out a purloined cigarette.

"She's probably having bad dreams, though," Carol said.

Anita turned back to the monitor. "Nights are hard."

"When Declan was a baby, he'd scream anytime you put him down. Didn't matter for what. He could be sound asleep, but the minute I tried to lay him in a crib, his eyes would pop open and he'd howl. Henry worked all the time, and I had Sarah to look after, too."

Carol was not one of those women who feigned confusion over postpartum tragedies. If anything, she was surprised new mothers didn't throw themselves out of windows on a regular basis.

"I started hallucinating I was so tired. I saw bugs crawling up the walls and thought I was going insane."

"Guess it's a good thing July's not a baby."

Carol went quiet, and Anita kicked herself.

"Sorry," she said. "That wasn't . . ."

"It's okay."

"It's not. I'm . . ." *Thinking about running away,* she thought. ". . . tired, I guess." Saying it made it true. Anita's eyes hurt. She went to rub them and flinched. Her face looked better, but everything from her brows to the white peach fuzz of a mustache over her lip was still sore.

Carol watched her, and Anita had the unnerving feeling the other woman knew what she was thinking.

"I thought I'd make dinners while I'm here, if that suits you."

Anita played a ten of hearts and then was stuck. She was out of moves.

"If you want," she said.

She'd liked to have gotten up, but she didn't have anywhere else to go. And there were schedules that still needed doing, bills that weren't going to pay themselves. She was trapped. She closed the game and turned partway toward the door. "You don't have to."

"I'm supposed to be helping. It was our agreement."

Anita raised an eyebrow despite herself, and Carol snorted. It wasn't a sound Anita imagined would come out of her.

"It's the agreement we both have with Mack, then."

Anita rolled her eyes. "Dad doesn't know how to mind his own business."

"Oh, he does," Carol said. "He just thinks everything is his business."

"Especially where I'm concerned."

Carol nodded. "I noticed that."

Anita didn't have a civilized response and was reduced to grunting.

"All right," Carol said, stepping back from the door. "Let me know if you need anything else while I'm here." There was a small pause. "It won't be for long."

"Okay," Anita said, careful to keep her voice neutral.

Carol turned.

"I am sorry," Anita said, catching her. "About earlier."

Carol didn't respond, just waved a hand in the air and went back down the hall.

. . . .

Declan walked back out to his car—or near to it. He couldn't help stopping and looking over at the theater. Sure enough, there was a FOR LEASE sign up on the marquee. A light mist was falling, dampening his hair and the shoulders of his jacket, but not so much he needed to do anything about it.

Without exactly deciding, Declan turned and started toward the dark, full-length windows that lined the front of the theater. He set his groceries down on the dry pavement under the marquee and cupped his face against one of the windows. It was too dark to see much, but what he could see was disheartening. Empty but not entirely empty. The candy case was there, the popcorn machine, the double doors that led into the theater itself. The parts of the thing were still intact, but the soul was gone.

He took a breath and dropped his hands. He'd pushed the box of Hot Tamales into the back pocket of his jeans, and he took them out then and popped open the seal, pouring a handful into his palm. It felt like the repast after the funeral, except he'd missed the funeral, which was just as well. He'd have hated to see the lights turned off, the doors locked for good. Better, he thought, to have the feeling of having missed it than to see the last gasp.

Declan leaned his back against the glass and put a small handful of the spicy, sweet candy into his mouth. Hot Tamales are a lot, flavor-wise. When he'd worked the counter, people didn't usually buy them, and when they had, it was to go along with something else—popcorn sometimes but usually nachos. There was something about Hot Tamales and nachos that worked for people. But Declan could mainline a whole box the way other people could shoot whiskey. He'd stop only long enough to rinse the sticky red goo out of his teeth with a gulp of Sprite from the cup he kept under the counter.

He'd liked the flow of things in the theater—the trickle of the early arrivals, usually older people who didn't have anything better to do than sit for twenty minutes, watching the same five movie-trivia questions cycle across the screen. Then there was the rush. Tickets and candy, popcorn and soda. The whole town would come streaming in on a Friday night. He saw everyone—his friends, his teachers, kids he wanted to impress and kids he knew were impressed by him, the waitress from the diner, old Mr. Connor, Mack and his wife before she'd died, Tiny, Chet and Pam, his own parents along with his sister sometimes. Everyone in the whole town for one showing or another. It was a fire hose of people, and everything had to happen in fifteen minutes. Then, *boom*, he could always hear the start of the previews, and the last stragglers grabbed their popcorn buckets and hurried into the dark. The doors to the theater swung shut and stayed shut, and it was quiet, idle. He could catch his breath, take his time. He'd liked it like that. He'd liked the rush and then the hard stop. The tide coming in and then out. Not everyone did. Some people got frazzled by it, but he'd liked it. It was almost like getting high, a jolt of adrenaline, a big event. Even if "big" was relative in Ebey's End. He was still in the center of it, making it happen.

Unfortunately, it wasn't possible to sell movie theater concessions for the rest of his life. Even he wasn't that much of a wreck. And even if he were, the theater was closed. Gone. And it was just him, leaning against the cold glass with sticky red goo in his teeth, which were now full of fillings, probably not a coincidence, and wishing he had a Sprite.

CHAPTER TWENTY-TWO

July had spent the past two weeks watching Carol and Anita skirt around each other. The air in the apartment no longer crackled, but it had been replaced with a strained overpoliteness that didn't feel comfortable either.

That afternoon, Mack had asked her out for ice cream, and she'd jumped on it. They were sitting side by side on a weathered gray bench outside of the ice cream parlor. They both had cones. His was two scoops of strawberry, which had already dripped on his pants, and hers was one scoop of cookie dough.

"You going to get a stomachache?" he asked, eyeing her as she licked a drip that was running fast toward her fingers.

"No, are you?"

He pointed to her cone. "When Anita was little, Connie wouldn't ever let her lick the cookie batter off the beaters. Said it would make her sick."

"Raw eggs," July said.

She had the hood of her coat over her head and a scarf that belonged to Anita or perhaps Mack. It had come out of the back of the closet, so it was hard to say.

Gideon and Samson were on either side of their humans, doing their best to look emaciated and pitiful. Samson, bred to be majestic and powerful, was trying to suck in those five extra pounds while Gideon drooled on himself. Neither took their eyes off the treats.

It had been an unusually dry—if not warm—day, and when the clouds broke enough to reveal actual sun, folks came stumbling out of their homes, stunned and slightly disoriented. They were like bears woken from their hibernation in February, not sure what to do but determined to do it. As many as half a dozen people had walked or driven past, all within fifteen minutes. It was practically Manhattan, Mack thought, not quite sure if he was going to be irritated about it or not.

"Did you lick the beaters?" he asked.

"All the time."

He nodded. "I always thought Connie was being ridiculous, but you know how it is with women."

July scowled at him. Mack, if he thought twice about what he'd said, didn't show it.

"They don't put eggs in this, though," she said. "So your wife was probably right."

It was Mack's turn not to comment. Instead, he cleared his throat, which had been for show, but turned into a cough so hard that Samson, who had sunk down to his belly on the cold sidewalk, pushed to his feet, alert and ready. Gideon was up shortly after, and Samson, without breaking eye contact with the strawberry ice cream, scooted over, boxing his brother out. A small shoving match ensued, both dogs trying to be as subtle as possible to avoid a reprimand. Samson stamped on July's foot and then stumbled when she pulled it out from under him, creating an opening for Gideon, who wiped drool on July's pants in the process.

Mack recovered without dropping his cone, and July, who had stopped eating, went back to hers without comment. It was her way of punishing him for being sexist.

He started to clear his throat again, thought better of it, and just said what he'd meant to say.

"So you've been keeping company with Malcolm, then?"

July had worked her scoop of ice cream down so it was level with the cone. She took a bite out of the edge. It was stale. Maybe no one but them bought ice cream in the winter.

"We're friends, I guess."

Friends had proved harder to come by in Ebey's End than she'd imagined, but truthfully, even back home, friendship had been a slippery and changing thing. When she was younger, it had been easier. She remembered calling anyone who sat next to her a friend. She called the volunteer crossing guard who stood in front of her elementary school her friend simply because she remembered July's name and greeted her each morning. That had been before she'd realized her name was what was memorable and not her.

It wasn't that way now, and it hadn't been for a long time. Friendship was something that was traded in exchange for a place in the pecking order. It was like how her mother had explained historical marriages to her. If someone was an asset to your position, you tried to hang on to them in whatever way you could. Maybe it turned out you actually liked them, but plenty of people didn't get that lucky.

Malcolm was different, though. When he'd picked her up on her first day of school, it felt like he'd already made a place for her even though they'd never met. He was like Mack that way, like he was glad to see her, glad she'd moved here. He didn't act like her bad luck was catching because he'd had really bad luck, too. There were things she didn't have to explain to him. And after everything that had happened, that was a lot.

Not that she would say that to Mack.

"Just friends, then?"

Mack wasn't looking at her. She didn't want to look at him either.

"Why?" she asked, taking another bite of the cone, even though she didn't really want to.

Mack cleared his throat again, and she looked over to see if he was going to have another coughing fit but he managed himself.

"He's quite a bit older than you is all."

July shrugged. "Two years."

She said it like it wasn't anything, although obviously it was.

"It's not only the years that count."

July's hood was still up. She could use it to hide part of her face if she wanted. She did the same thing with her hair sometimes, something her mom had pointed out to her. After that she tried not to do it too much. She didn't want to look shy, even if she felt it. It wasn't good for the pecking order thing.

"What's that mean?" she asked.

Mack shifted on the bench. Old people got bony butts. She remembered that from somewhere. She looked down at his feet. He wore gray Velcro sneakers, the same gray as his walker. She wondered if it was some kind of subconscious choice to make his walker like his feet or if old-people shoes only came in one color.

"I'm just saying you shouldn't be anything more than friends, if you catch my meaning."

"Gross," July said, because it was sort of true, and also it was the thing that would end the conversation the fastest.

Mack relaxed. "Keep that attitude until you're about twenty-five, and you'll be all right."

July turned her head the other way. Someone had parked in front of Tiny's Bakeshop and was walking inside. No one she recognized, but she watched anyway. She could feel a tingle run up her scalp like gooseflesh.

"You done?" Mack asked.

She looked back, distracted.

"It seems like you're done," he said, nodding at her ice cream. What was left in the cone had melted and was soaking through the napkin wrapped around the bottom.

"I'm done."

"Me, too," he said. "Cone was stale."

July stood up, and he scooted his walker closer to stand up, too, rousing the dogs. She would've taken his leftovers to the trash for him. But there weren't any. He'd eaten the whole thing, and she didn't know where his napkin had gone. Maybe he'd eaten that, too.

It was when she turned toward the trash can that she saw Jim coming down the sidewalk. He stopped in front of Tiny's and swung open the door. July fought the urge to run after him.

"Can we go to the bakery?" she asked, looking back toward Mack, who was pulling himself up and unlocking the wheels of his walker.

"You still hungry?"

"I wanted to get something for Pastor Chet," she said, pushing her hands deep into the pockets of her coat to keep from fidgeting. "As a thank-you—for what happened."

"Oh." Mack was taken aback. "Well, I suppose that would be nice."

He said the last part of his sentence to her back. July was already walking toward Tiny's shop, stopping to toss what was left of her cone into a trash can along the way.

She waited for him by the bakery door. Mack was walking as quickly as he dared, the dogs keeping to his pace, but her legs ate up sidewalk like it wasn't anything. He watched her, knowing it didn't matter how much physical therapy he did, he wasn't ever going to move anything like that again. Everything was hard for Mack now, and it always would be. Hard was the best he could hope for. Hard was staving off impossible.

By the time he caught up, Mack was breathing fast and trying not to show it. Doc would've given him a lecture, but July only opened the door, waiting for him to go through with Samson and Gideon at his heels.

The baked goods were in a long glass display case, and July made for it, scanning the whole pies. Winter meant citrus tarts, chocolate meringues, maple and walnut, shoofly and buttermilk chess. Key lime if you were lucky, but ask for cherry, and Tiny would have you out on your ear. Especially that day. That day was fixing to be a good one for having a fit. She'd barely gotten over the egg disaster, and now the dishwasher had broken down. She'd tweaked her shoulder in the weight room at the YMCA, and here was Mack with his god-damn dogs.

"Odom," she hollered, pushing through the white saloon doors that led into the back kitchen. "How many times do I have to tell you about those dogs?"

"They are service animals."

"What service would that be? Crotch sniffing?"

"Only if you ask nice."

Tiny raised her middle finger just as July, who had been crouched down to better see the bottom row of pastry, stood up.

"That wasn't meant for you, hon," Tiny said, which was the closest anyone was going to get to an apology that day.

As for Samson and Gideon, it wasn't that they were oblivious to Tiny's mood so much as they were willing to ignore it. The smell of food—sweet and savory—that made human mouths water was driving them out of their minds. Their tails, long and muscular, thwapped back and forth so fast and hard July had to scoot farther down to avoid a bruise. Gideon whimpered, and Samson shuffled his front feet. He was fixing to bite or pee, either of which would probably get Mack banned for life.

To avert an island-wide diplomatic incident, Mack said, "Give me two of them mini chicken pies, would ya?"

Tiny scowled at him but reached into the case.

"No," Mack said when she turned toward the toaster oven. "No reason to warm them up."

Tiny stopped, a pie in each hand. Chocolate was smeared on her gray apron, and her tanned biceps bulged out of her sleeveless shirt.

"Are you going to give my pie to *dogs*, Odom?"

"I'm buying the pie, which makes it my pie and none of your business."

"The hell it isn't."

It was after lunch, and only a few of the tables were occupied. Jim, the librarian, was sipping a latte and eating biscotti on his break. The hospitality subcommittee of the women's ministry was having their monthly meeting in the corner. And one or two folks Mack recognized from the checkout line were scattered around with their laptops and empty plates. All of them, even the women's ministry, had gone quiet. They watched and listened, secretly counting themselves lucky to get this bit of gossip firsthand. Everyone, that was, except Jim, who was the only one watching July.

The girl's face had gone red from the collar of her coat up to the roots of her hair. No one had ever prayed so hard for the floor to open up beneath them, and neither Mack nor Tiny was paying her even the smallest bit of attention. And so Jim, who couldn't bear to see a kid hurt in any way, pushed back from his table as easy as he could and walked up beside them.

"Excuse me, Tiny," he said, interrupting Mack, who was about to say another fool thing. "I'd like to buy those pies, if it's all right."

Tiny, who looked ready to throw them rather than sell them, raised an eyebrow.

Jim lived in a single-story rambler house that had a ramp out front instead of stairs. His sister had gone to a party her freshman year of college. When someone dropped her off in front of the emergency room with alcohol poisoning, she didn't have a pulse. She'd been a finance major and had walked on to the university's tennis team. Her name was Samantha. Samantha could no longer say her own name. She couldn't walk or use her arms very well, and she couldn't control her bowels. Jim had taken custody of her four years ago when his parents, with their own health problems, were no longer able to care for her. He went to the library, and he went home. He played video games online after putting Samantha in bed with a fresh diaper. He took his breaks with a latte and a biscotti. He did not get involved in public arguments, but he was stepping into this one.

Jim looked Tiny in the eye and then over to the girl, without shifting his head, and then back to Tiny. Mack caught it and felt the appropriate amount of shame. She'd get used to him and to Tiny, not to mention Gordy, Bill, and all the rest, but she wasn't yet. And he wasn't used to considering himself from an outsider's perspective. Jim was the best of all of them on that day—and plenty of other days, too.

"Go on, then," Tiny said, dropping the pies at room temperature on top of the case. "Y'all do what you want. I got other problems."

Jim reached for his wallet, and Tiny waved him away. Mack went to pick up the pies.

"Let me," Jim said.

Outside, he set them on the sidewalk next to the bench in front of

Tiny's window. Mack dropped onto the seat, and the dogs fell on the food.

"Thank you," Mack said, "for all of that."

Jim nodded, brushed crumbs from his hands, and started to go back inside.

"We meet here on Wednesdays at three o'clock," Mack said, catching Jim as he reached for the door.

"Pardon?"

"We call it the Old Philosophers' Club, but that's BS. It's just a bunch of men sitting around complaining, but still and all, you should come if you can. You'd be welcome."

Jim knew what the Old Philosophers' Club was. He wasn't sure it was possible for there to be a cool kids' table when the kids were in their sixties and seventies, more the age of Jim's father than Jim. But they were the men in town who had standing for one reason or another, and Jim had no expectation he'd ever be asked to join them. No one asked Jim to do much of anything. They knew about his sister. They assumed he had his hands full. They didn't want to bother him. Jim was being not bothered straight into a serious depression. The only friends he really had thought he was an orc named Gr1m3ly.

He almost said no. He almost said it was fine. Instead, he said, "Thank you. I'd like that."

Mack nodded.

The dogs had each inhaled their chicken pie, nosing the flimsy foil dishes a foot in one direction and then the other. Then they swapped, checking to see that the other hadn't left anything behind.

"That's enough," Mack admonished them.

Neither paid him any mind.

July had stayed inside. The hood of her coat was down, but she'd untucked her hair from behind her ears, letting it fall close around her face.

"Don't mind me," Tiny sighed. "I'm just having a bad year is all."

She waited for the girl to smile, and she did, but it wasn't honest. That she smiled at all was more than Tiny knew she deserved. She didn't use to be this way. She used to drink, which was its own problem, but it did have a way of taking the sting out of the rest of life. Now she didn't drink, and everything stung.

"You're Anita's new girl," she said, changing the subject. "I was sorry to hear about your mom."

This kept happening. In the store. In school. July wasn't used to it, and she wasn't certain she ever would be.

"Oh . . . thanks."

"Felicia came by a while ago," Tiny said, which July knew was supposed to tell her something, but she wasn't sure what. Tiny leaned her hip against the counter. "You got classes with any of her boys?"

"One of them, I think."

July didn't think. She knew. His name was Dylan, and he'd sat down next to her in algebra. He had a dirty black backpack that he'd dropped onto the desk and then laid his head on, face down. His hair was cut almost to the scalp, revealing a constellation of dark moles under the blond bristle. It wasn't his desk, and he didn't bother looking up at the kid whose desk it was, who said his name and started to poke him before thinking better of it. Dylan didn't move or speak until Mrs. K had walked in and told him to go back to his seat.

Finally, he'd lifted his head, looked over at July, and whispered, "Next time my mom comes in the store, tell her I talked to you. Say I was nice, okay?"

She'd expected him to sound menacing, but he didn't. He sounded like a kid who didn't want to get in trouble with his mom. It made her sort of like him.

July didn't say this aloud, but Tiny nodded a little, as though she had. "Most times, I don't know whether to feed 'em or crack their heads together."

July could imagine both.

"Anyway, can I get you something?" Tiny asked.

"Um." July pointed at one of the whole pies. "How much is the coconut cream?"

Tiny's coconut pies were legend. She made hers deeper than deep dish with a perfect crust scalloped along the edge. The custard inside was a golden yellow, made from cream and farm eggs, a whole island's worth of coconut, and—her secret ingredient—a good bit of sea salt. It balanced the sugar and brought the brine of the ocean to the tropical dessert. Something you didn't know you wanted until you had it. She piled a mountain of whipped cream over that, twice as thick as the custard itself, made with a whole vanilla bean and sugar that she melted and caramelized before blitzing back down to a powder again. Over top, she sprinkled on a snowstorm of toasted coconut shavings. They cost a fortune to make, and she didn't make many. It was a special-occasion dessert.

"A whole one?" she asked.

July nodded. She had the money Anita had been paying her, but it wasn't a lot of money and there was still one big purchase she was going to need to make.

"Five dollars," Tiny said.

July didn't move, and she didn't say anything. She didn't know what to say. She thought maybe Tiny was making fun of her.

Tiny, a little quicker on the uptake this time, realized her mistake. She reached under the table and pulled out one of her signature blue pastry boxes, stored flat. With a practiced hand, she quickly folded it into shape. Then she slid open the case and pulled out the pie, setting it carefully inside. The box was extra deep, meant for double-decker cakes, and it barely closed without squishing the pretty finish.

Tiny pushed it across the top of the case toward July.

"Five dollars," she said again, "and you promise to make sure your uncle keeps those dogs out of my shop from now on. Deal?"

July reached into the pocket of her coat and pulled out a small green wallet. "Deal," she said.

By the time she came out, Jim had already gone back to his table, a lightness in his step that hadn't been there before. Mack was still on the bench.

"Anita can drive us all to the church," he said, inviting himself along.

He wanted to trust July, but a part of him couldn't help think it was an awfully big gesture coming from a fourteen-year-old, who might have sooner avoided the scene of her crime than return to it. He wanted to see for himself that it was the pastor and not the son who was on the receiving end of whatever was in that box.

"Fine," July said.

. . . .

July opened the front door, carrying a large box from Tiny's shop. Carol was sitting on the sofa next to her neatly folded blanket and pillow, a book in her hands. She was dressed in slacks and a sweater, her hair pulled back, as though she was expecting to go somewhere.

"Hello," she said.

"Hi."

"Dessert?"

She hadn't been to Tiny's shop since everything had happened, and she missed it. She missed Tiny, although not the apple pie. Carol thought she'd eaten enough apple pie to last her in this life.

"It's not for me," July said, meaning it wasn't for any of them, which Carol understood. "Is Anita home?"

"She's in the office," she said. "Working."

"Oh."

She sounded disappointed. Carol could've told her it was fine, to go on in, but she didn't. July was still standing just inside the front door, which she hadn't shut. Cold air swirled into the apartment, chilling it. Carol had forever been admonishing her children to shut doors when they were young.

"Did you need something?" she asked.

"A ride. To the church?"

She said the last part like it was a question, which Carol doubted it was.

"I'll drive you," she said, and stood up, setting her library book on the coffee table next to the mug of tea that had gone cold.

"Mack wants to come, too," July said.

"I don't doubt it."

Carol put on her coat, and the two of them left without saying anything to Anita.

CHAPTER TWENTY-THREE

July had failed to mention the dogs, but Carol, having considered the alternatives, decided to risk it. For the first time in her life, she didn't have a thousand small tasks that needed her attention. She wasn't taking care of her children or her husband or that big house on the water, and if she had felt invisible before, she was something else now. Unmoored. Undefined. Anxious. So if the price of being outside her own mind for thirty minutes was a fifty percent chance of anaphylactic shock, so be it. Death comes for us all.

That said, Carol was still Carol, and while she was willing to accept her own demise, she was not going to be allowing any nonsense on the way.

The five of them—three human—were standing on the sidewalk next to her car, which she had not yet unlocked. She looked from the pastry box to the dogs and said, "Can they be trusted?"

Mack tried to look as though this were a terribly unfair question but could not manage it. Instead, he lifted his chin and nodded. "They'll be good."

Carol was not looking at him. She had locked eyes with Gideon. She did not know either dog, but this one smelled like trouble. Gideon looked back, then down and away. Samson, happy not to be the center of attention, was willing himself invisible and was fairly sure he'd succeeded.

Carol made a noise that suggested to Mack she'd believe it when she saw it, but Gideon understood it for what it was: a show of dominance with the promise of bloodshed just below the surface. After she'd unlocked the door and spread out an old towel from the trunk for their dirty paws, both dogs filed in, heads, tails, and ears slightly lowered. The other two humans followed suit.

Seven minutes later, Carol pulled her BMW into the church lot behind Pastor Chet. He parked near the door in a spot marked with a metal RESERVED sign, and Carol took another two spaces down.

Wearing a puffy brown coat that looked like it had been pulled from the donation bin, he got out and waited while Carol turned off the engine. July opened her door to climb out, while Mack rolled down his window.

"Hello," the pastor said, glancing at July and then leaning down to see who else was inside. "Carol, Mack." He raised his hand.

Carol waved, and Mack nodded. The dogs were still a little afraid to move.

"July has something she wants to give you," Mack said.

Chet turned his attention to her, and she held out the box. He took it and opened the lid. He stared a moment, surprise lifting his eyebrows, and then quickly closed it.

"I'm sorry," she said, "about the other day."

July had her hands in her coat pockets and her long hair tucked inside the collar.

Chet looked from the box to her, opened his mouth, and then changed his mind. She gave him a small, tight smile, and he cleared his throat, glancing over at Mack, who still had the window down.

Shifting his weight from foot to foot, the pastor nodded for July to follow him.

Tucked in under the church's overhang, he whispered, "Is everything okay?"

He might have been talking about the fight with Anita, but they both understood he was not.

She nodded. "Everything's fine."

"Because if you need—" He stopped. "I can always—"

July interrupted. "It's okay. You should enjoy the pie."

"No, I don't think—"

But she dipped her head and hurried back to Carol's car before he could finish.

Mack was irritated he hadn't been able to make out the conversation. His hearing wasn't what it had been, and it was made worse by Carol, who had pointedly turned on the radio.

"What did Chet say?" They had bumped out onto the road, and Mack was twisted around in his seat to look at July.

"Not much."

"Said something."

"Just some church stuff."

Mack glared at her and turned back around. "Didn't look like church stuff, if you ask me."

No one had asked him, and July didn't answer. She was looking out the window and petting Samson's head. He let his mouth hang open as she rubbed behind his ear. Gideon wanted in on that action but, under the circumstances, allowed himself only a high-pitched whine. July reached over and patted him.

"Well, I'm sure he appreciated the gift," Carol said.

She saw July shrug in the rearview mirror, which she thought was a shame. Carol believed in acknowledging the kindness of children.

How many dandelions with one-inch stems had been brought home to her, all of which she'd dutifully floated in water glasses?

She could feel her mind grabbing hold of the pastor's slight and preparing to hang on to it. Mack, meanwhile, was brooding in the passenger seat. He'd come intending to make sure things were on the right track, but he had the distinct feeling he hadn't accomplished that.

Both adults were preoccupied with their thoughts, but none of those thoughts were for the pastry box itself. Only Pastor Chet had seen the note July had scribbled inside the lid, and so what he was thinking, as they drove away, was that it might be best to set the whole thing on fire right there in the parking lot and then back over it with the car a few times before driving away into the night.

. . . .

Declan had always felt like the mutt his father had been guilted into adopting. Doc fed him and clothed him. He paid for braces and baseball cleats and six years of college, but Declan had always sensed it was an obligation.

So when he'd called his father and offered to come stay with him, the muted response wasn't a surprise. But Declan couldn't take it back, and Doc couldn't wave him off, so there they had been, one on each end of the phone, the discomfort settling on their shoulders.

Things started off as stilted as Declan had imagined. His father worked as much as was possible, but the occasional dinner couldn't be avoided. When they did sit down to a meal, it was like eating takeout at a funeral.

Every patient his father saw knew Carol had licked old Gordy the Drunk's balls, and his father knew they knew. Like wildfire, the gossip would burn itself out, turning to embers and then blackened ash before blowing away, but knowing it would end didn't lessen the horror while it was happening.

That was when the universe, as it sometimes does, provided. The two men discovered college basketball. Neither of them had given two shits about basketball of any kind in their lives, but one morning over two sad bowls of Corn Flakes, Declan, to avoid having to speak, had turned on the small set in the kitchen while they ate. Soon it became a regular thing, and the two men made a silent agreement to each care about this thing neither of them cared about for the sake of common ground. Within a week, they'd chosen a team to support and could sit side by side on the couch for hours.

It was also the only time Declan could talk to his dad, which might have been the universe's broader point above and beyond free throw percentages.

"You know the old movie theater?" Declan asked when the screen went to commercial.

It was Saturday, and they each had a folding TV tray in front of them, along with an Italian sub Declan had picked up in town.

"Yeah." His father pulled a potato chip out of the single-serving bag on his tray.

"How long's it been closed?"

Doc paused before throwing the chip back in the bag and wiping his hands on the napkin in his lap. "A while."

Declan picked up the other half of his sandwich, trying to make his interest seem casual. His father was still on his first half and not very far into that.

"How long's a while?"

Doc balled his napkin up and dropped it on the sandwich wrapper. He'd been losing weight since Carol left, which was maybe fine. He had a little pooch that had appeared over the last few years. It wasn't enough weight to be a medical concern, but he'd noticed.

Carol'd never said anything about it, but he didn't know what that meant anymore.

"What's that?" he asked, trying to remember what they'd been talking about.

The TV switched to a car commercial. He hadn't bought a new car in almost twenty years. Maybe he was due for one.

"How long's the theater been closed?" Declan asked again.

He wondered if Doc's hearing was starting to go. He was at that age.

Doc shrugged. "Ever since the Shifflers retired."

He said it like Declan was supposed to know when that had been, which was a slight irritation, but one it was better to let go.

"They still own it?" he asked.

Declan knew the Shifflers. Mrs. Shiffler had been the one to hire him, although, in the way of teenagers, he'd paid them very little attention after that.

"Far as I know."

Doc leaned back against the sofa and crossed his arms over his chest. He was certainly due for a new car. He'd need to do some research, of course. Really put some thought into it. He liked the idea of making a project out of it. A project would be good for him.

The commercials ended.

"You got a number for them?" Declan asked.

Doc was looking at the screen and didn't respond. Declan was now pretty sure his dad was going deaf.

"Maybe in your files or something," he said, raising his voice several decibels.

Doc winced. The damn kid was two feet away and shouting like they were on opposite sides of the Grand Canyon. Declan had never been the sharpest. It was a disappointment, but one Doc had come to terms with a long time ago. At least he thought he had, but it was still the first thing he thought whenever his son did anything to annoy him.

"I don't know," he said. "Why?"

Declan picked up one of his own chips and fingered it. Unlike his father, he put it in his mouth, a mistake, as it forced him to talk around the half-chewed bits. "There's this idea I had."

Doc stopped thinking about a new car and the basketball game. He even stopped thinking about the shouting. His eyes closed without his permission, and the air leaked out of his lungs with an audible *whoosh*. It was the sound a body makes when faced with a foreseeable and yet unavoidable disappointment.

CHAPTER TWENTY-FOUR

Two days later, Pastor Chet pulled the old black sedan up in front of Preston Daly's house. It sat on a piece of property at least twice as large as the others near it with a wrought iron fence that ran all the way around. It wasn't but chest high, hardly enough to keep in a dog, and was softened in the summertime by wildly overgrown rosebushes that ran along the two public-facing sides of the corner lot. The fence had a gate that could swing across the drive, but Chet couldn't remember the gate ever being closed, and it wasn't that day either. He turned off the engine and looked out the passenger-side window toward the house. Next to him on the seat was the coconut cream pie, July's note still inked on the inside of the lid.

He expected to see some sign of her, but she was not standing in the drive or sitting on the porch stairs. He had not passed her walking on the road, and no drapery twitched at his arrival.

To say he hadn't wanted to come was putting it mildly. Unfortunately, that had been all the more reason he needed to. That was what his father had told him growing up: "The community doesn't have pastors to do what's easy. They have them to do that which is all but impossible." His father had meant ministering to the dying, the shut-in, the addicted, the bereaved. He had meant keeping the community faithful in times of disharmony, depression, and war. He had not meant seeing to the needs of a young girl. Her presence should not have been difficult to bear, and yet, for Chet, it was. He would've taken three hospice patients and a full day in the locked memory care facility on Bainbridge over this. But July had left that note for him, and despite all of his misgivings, he had come.

When Chet had told his father he was going to seminary, the man's first word was "Don't." Chet had never told anyone that, and as far as he knew, his father hadn't either. It hadn't been much of a conversation after that. Chet reasserted his intention, and his father did not object again.

"If you feel called," Chet thought he remembered him saying, but he wasn't entirely sure now. He did know they didn't speak about it again. His father, already a widower, had died while Chet was in seminary. And in the years since, he had thought about that conversation at least once a week. Had he meant that Chet did not have what was necessary to do the job? There were those in town who would agree with that. He suffered from periods of serious depression, and even in between those times, he often felt as though gravity pulled more forcefully on him than on others. Or had his father blurted the truth of his own experience, his own unhappiness with his life and choices?

Neither of them had been the sort of men capable of having that conversation then. Chet did not blame himself. He had been barely twenty and trying to hide so much. But he wondered, if they would've talked, would it have changed anything? So much of their lives had turned out eerily the same on the surface, but Chet had no idea if they felt the same underneath. They had been respectful of each other, but they had not been close.

While he sat in the car, the rain had started up again, and the windows were blurred with splattered droplets turning to rivulets that ran down the glass. His breath fogged the inside. He needed to get out before not getting out became conspicuous.

The house sat on the hill that overlooked the town and the sea beyond. The view had, for more than a hundred years, attracted the town's wealthiest citizens, and Preston's slice of it was perfectly unobstructed. The Victorian had a roof that came up into three separate peaks with a wind-vane-topped tower over the front door. The porch jutted out toward the driveway and was weighed down with all manner of bric-a-brac. In fact, the whole house was so covered in various sorts of trim, it was hard to find a bare bit of wall at all. It had taken the painters four different shades of blue just to differentiate them.

The rain was starting to come down harder, but Chet didn't bother with his hood, only held the heavy pastry box close to his chest as he hurried, ducking under the overhang as quickly as he could. Up close, he could see the paint was beginning to crack and flake in the salt air, and the front stairs creaked loudly underfoot as he stepped out of the rain, which speckled the top of the box.

July's note said to meet her here at the banker's house with the pie. It was a weekday, and he could think of no good reason she should be here. He had, before leaving the parsonage, considered calling Anita or perhaps the school, but he'd have had to explain, which would have breached pastoral confidentiality.

Pastor Chet pressed on the bell and, after a second's delay, heard a deep and muffled *ding-dong* from inside the house. After a minute, there were footsteps, and the door opened.

Mr. Daly looked taken aback. "Pastor! What a surprise."

Preston liked to come home for lunch. It had been his habit ever since he'd purchased the house, which was a three-minute drive from the bank, but it was only in the past few weeks that he'd started liking it. A lot had changed in that time.

The piles of discarded magazines were gone. The gray fur that had collected on the edges of the baseboards was gone, replaced by the shiny, warm glow of well-cared-for wood. The windows were clear as vodka. The rugs were clean, and the colors bright and rich. The scuff marks on the walls had been repaired. The burned-out bulbs had been replaced. Everything smelled clean and vaguely of citrus. The trash was removed on a regular basis. His clothes were laundered and hung in his closet grouped by type—shirts, pants, jackets. His boxer shorts were folded, and there was food in the refrigerator, all of which—despite his being an indifferent cook—could be made into real meals. Pasta, roasted chicken, Parmesan cheese, bags of salad, bread and eggs, thick slices of ham.

He found, if he concentrated on one small task, he could keep his mind from being overwhelmed by all the tasks. And the finishing of one thing led naturally to the starting of something else. It had an effect on him. He made his bed. If toast crumbs fell to the floor, he wiped them up. He'd started reading at night again and listening to music, even pouring a glass of wine, rather than working from the moment he woke up to the moment he went to bed.

It was almost absurd the difference he saw in himself. He'd thought, just that morning, that he might take up jogging. He'd been a jogger in college, some forty years ago. Could he jog now? He'd looked down at his body, dressed only in his underthings. He was reedy, with a chest that was ever so slightly concave. It would probably be best, he'd thought, to start slowly.

Just now, he'd been in the kitchen. He'd tucked his tie in between two buttons on his dress shirt to keep it out of the way while he made a sandwich at the counter. He'd spread the mayonnaise and piled on the ham and cheese and was adding lettuce—he had lettuce!—when the doorbell had rung, and he'd gone to answer it.

This was the first time anyone had come calling during his meal, and he found himself as surprised as anyone that he was able to receive them. "Come in," he could say without needing to worry or apologize over the state of things. It was such a new feeling. And so he did.

"Come in, come in." Preston held open the door and stepped aside.

Mr. Daly was dressed for the office but for his navy blue stocking feet. With his crisp white shirt and pressed gray pants, he wore a pale blue-striped tie that highlighted the unusual color of his eyes, which was something Chet tried not to notice. He was always trying not to notice.

Under the best of conditions, Preston made him feel shy and sweaty. Chet could speak in front of an entire congregation, counsel a couple on the verge of divorce, ask anyone on the island straight-out for their tithe, but standing in front of Preston made Chet feel like he had three arms.

"Mr. Daly," he said, the formality of which he instantly regretted.

Chet wanted to go back to his car and start this whole thing over again from the beginning. He could do it better. He was sure. But Preston only smiled at him. It made the small wrinkles at the corners of his eyes bunch together.

"What's this?" he asked, nodding at the box in Chet's hands.

Chet looked down, surprised to see the box was still there.

"Pie," he said. "Coconut cream."

"You're kidding." Preston clapped his hands together and squeezed them tight in front of his chest. Chet had never seen an adult show so much open joy over dessert. "That's my absolute favorite."

"July asked me to bring it for her."

"July? God, isn't she wonderful?"

Chet was not entirely sure she was wonderful.

"But she's not here, of course," Preston said.

"Are you sure?" It was a silly question, but Chet couldn't help it.

Preston made a show of looking behind himself and then faced the pastor. "Pretty sure."

"She asked me to meet her here."

Preston cocked his head. "Really?"

Chet lifted the lid of the box and watched as Preston looked down and read it.

Come to the banker's house.
Noon on Monday. Bring the pie.

Preston lifted his eyebrows and looked back up at Chet.

Chet was wearing his usual black pants and clerical collar under a shabby brown coat. He wished he were wearing something else, something less godly. He also needed a haircut. Sometimes, when money and time were tight, which was often, he trimmed around the ears himself.

Preston's face had changed. "Chet?"

"Mmm?"

"I don't think that pie is for her."

Chet didn't know what to say, but he did notice that Preston had stopped referring to him as "Pastor." The banker reached out and took the box from him. Chet let him have it.

"Have you had lunch?" Preston asked. He gestured down the hall toward the kitchen. "I was making sandwiches."

"Sandwiches?"

"Unless you'd like to go straight to the pie?"

"Straight to the pie?"

"Are you going to answer all of my questions with questions?"

Preston was smiling. It was a nice smile that went all the way to his gray eyes. They really were striking. Everything about Preston was unusual in the best way. Nothing about himself, Chet feared, was interesting at all. But he could, at the very least, pull himself together for the next half an hour. He was being asked to visit, after all. He did that all the time.

"I would love to join you for lunch. Thank you."

"Excellent, and do you drink wine at lunch?"

"Not usually," Chet said. "But . . ." There was the briefest of pauses. "I think I would like to. Just this once."

"That was what I was thinking," Preston said. "Just this once."

. . . .

That afternoon, Anita was in the store. She breathed in the earthy smell of produce as she walked through cool storage. Someone had sliced open a box of bagged lettuce and removed one. Peggy, no doubt, doing a favor for a customer. Anita told her to say that what was out was what they had, but Peggy had her favorites. It meant Anita would be stuck tossing lettuce already on the shelf. That was the way it went on the island. People traded favors, and nothing Anita could say was going to change it. She wasn't even sure it ought to be changed, and so she pretended not to see the open box and moved on.

She stopped on her way toward the front of the store to pull a row of tomato sauce cans forward on the old wooden shelf, filling in the gap and making it look neat, each label facing exactly forward. It settled her. She did the same with boxes of macaroni, noting the off-brand was selling faster than usual. They were nearly out, and she knew there wasn't any more in the stockroom. She would need to adjust the next order and check to see what else was changing. Folks switching to generic didn't mean anything good. If it was more than macaroni, she'd need to pay attention, maybe change up the specials they ran each week. Tourist season—and the extra money it brought—was a long way off.

She was thinking about that when she came around the corner and ran straight into the front of Henry's cart.

The three-quarter-sized ones they used at the store were better at navigating the old building, with its narrow aisles, but in Henry's hands it looked sad, like a grown man pushing a child's toy in public. It reminded her of when her father was in the rehabilitation hospital, how some of the very old women with memory problems were given baby dolls to soothe them. But Henry did not look soothed.

"Oof," she said, stepping quickly out of his way. "Sorry."

Not once in all her life had Anita seen Henry do the grocery shopping, and from the looks of things, it wasn't going all that well. He was wearing his work clothes—khakis, a checked shirt, and a tie so plain you hardly saw it. The corners of his mouth were turned down, not in an active frown but as if the fight with gravity had been lost. The cowlick he had in the back that was usually smoothed down with a bit of pomade had escaped its bonds, and one of his soft-soled shoes had come untied. She would've thought he'd hear the *slap-slap* of the little plastic ends of the laces against the wood floor, but he was either deaf, distracted, or had lost the will to care.

"Your shoe's untied," she said.

He blinked, as though her words needed translating before he could understand them. Then he looked down. "So it is."

She thought for a moment he'd leave it that way, but he gathered himself and crouched down to fix it.

While he did, Anita scanned his cart. Bologna. Grape-Nuts. A box of Hamburger Helper but no hamburger. A frozen pizza. A six-pack of Sam Adams. A head of iceberg lettuce. She'd seen worse, but she'd seen a lot better, too.

She reached into the cart and picked up the lettuce. The cut where the stem had been had oozed brown under the plastic shrink wrap, and the whole thing felt too light. Iceberg should be dense, heavier than you expected for its size. She could tell he'd picked up whatever his hand first touched and put it in the cart without even looking.

When he stood back up, she said, "I've got some better in the back. Let me get you one."

He straightened his shoulders and gave her a quick nod. She'd caught him with his defenses down. It was like that moment, first thing in the morning, when you see yourself in the bathroom mirror on the way to pee. That was a private face, one you didn't show to the world, but somehow his had slipped out. He wasn't himself lately.

Doc followed her toward the back with his toy cart. Halfway there, it occurred to him she might not have meant for him to follow, but he was in it now. No way back.

"How's the nose?" he asked, trying to sound confident.

She made a noncommittal noise. "Still can't sleep with a pillow over my face, but that's about it."

The bruising was mostly gone. He could catch the last bits of yellow spreading out under her eyes like jaundice. Nothing most people would notice, and nothing that couldn't be covered with a little makeup, which didn't seem to have occurred to her.

"I didn't know you drank beer," she said.

He almost said he didn't before remembering the six-pack in the cart.

Beer had always been something pushed onto him at other people's houses back when Carol was still getting them invited to one place or another a few times a year. He'd rather have stayed home and apparently hadn't been very good company. Months would go by before there'd be another invitation. A few times, Carol had people over to their house, but he'd usually walk in after everyone had finished, sinking into an empty chair only in time for pie and to pick up whatever loose threads of conversation were left after he'd apologized.

But no, Doc would not have called himself a beer drinker. Even Anita's small selection had been overwhelming to him. He'd chosen this one because he liked the name. It seemed like a beer he would drink if he drank beer. He planned to try it. Have one after work. See how it felt.

"Declan is visiting," he said to excuse himself. Sixty-six was an embarrassing age to be trying on a new identity.

Doc assumed she knew about Declan, just as he knew about Carol, a fact relayed to him by Mack, who seemed to think it was some sort of favor rather than the impending catastrophe it might turn out to be. Doc nearly blew his stack when Mack told him and then had to do a lot of backpedaling to cover it.

Even after all this time, Doc didn't want Carol to know about Anita. He barely knew how to handle the situation with Gordy now. If he had to negotiate his hurt feelings and hers—to say nothing of the gossip that would be stirred up—Doc might even have to stop going to the Philosophers' Club meetings. It would all be too much to handle.

They were at the big swinging doors that read EMPLOYEES ONLY. Anita pushed through, and he waited, staring down into his cart. He didn't want any of these foods. He'd never eaten Hamburger Helper and had never wanted to, but he also didn't want to keep eating lunch meat every night. He knew what it was doing to his colon. The box in his cart said "Salisbury" flavor. He didn't know what that meant and thought about putting it back, but then he'd have to choose something else, which felt insurmountable. He'd never been one to think much about food, and now he knew why. It was depressing.

Doc closed his eyes. Anita was taking too long. He wanted to leave, but he couldn't. He was trapped, held hostage by the fetching of lettuce that would be exactly the same as the lettuce he'd already fetched, which he also did not want. How had it come to this?

Doc didn't know how Anita felt about their relationship now. He hadn't really known what she'd felt about it then. It had happened in stages: a look here, a touch there, a kiss. And then, when they were sleeping together, they'd fallen into that, too. Every Wednesday evening they would meet at the apartment upstairs. It was the night Mack and Connie had a card game over at Bill's house. Anita had been in her early twenties but still living in her childhood bedroom, which had made Doc uncomfortable. There'd been stuffed animals on the bed like in Sarah's room, and he'd have to push them out of the way when they were having sex. He'd never stayed, obviously, and every time he hurried down to his car, which he left parked on another street, he'd felt embarrassed.

On top of that, being with Anita did something to his feelings for Carol. It changed them in ways he had begun to worry couldn't be undone. In the end, this had turned out not to be true. He had been able to put Anita behind him, to go back to things as they were, but he hadn't known that then.

He knew the way he'd ended things with Anita hadn't been perfect, although she'd taken it reasonably well, he'd thought. When Doc did the math, he realized she was twice the age now that she'd been then. She'd lived a whole second life since they'd last been together.

The swinging door burst open, and Doc jumped. Anita paused,

watching him, and he felt ridiculous. She held out the head of lettuce, which did, in fact, look exactly like the first one. It might have been the first one, for all he knew.

"Thank you," he said, taking it from her and setting it down next to the Hamburger Helper.

Behind the drape of his tie, Anita could see the dip of Henry's chest and the small bump of his belly below it, like his shoulders were being pulled down to his hips. The skin on his hands had thinned, and his cheeks looked like they were melting and starting to slide down his face. He looked old, and more than that, he looked defeated, a man with bad lettuce and no idea that box didn't have a lick of hamburger in it.

"Would you like to go out for a meal sometime?" Anita asked.

Henry looked up from his cart like he'd been startled.

"Friends," she added, feeling a hot flush at her neck.

He opened his mouth and started to shake his head.

She wished she could take it back. *Don't interfere.* She knew the rules. She'd created them. They'd kept her life as smooth as it could be. Gave her predictability. Ease. Maybe it wasn't what someone else would've chosen. There were no great joys, but there were no great hurts either. She was, if nothing else, safe.

"I . . ." Henry started.

Anita opened her mouth. She would tell him "Never mind" before this got worse for either of them.

"All right."

Anita stopped. Henry stopped. The answer had surprised them both. He pulled himself up straight, settled his shoulders back where they were supposed to be.

"Might be good to get out," he said, framing it for himself, keeping it in bounds.

"Might be," Anita said.

"I don't really like to cook."

"No," she agreed.

"Good," he said.

"Yes."

She rang up his groceries, and he left. They didn't discuss it further, giving Anita time to wonder what in the hell had gotten into her.

CHAPTER TWENTY-FIVE

Sarah shouldn't have called her brother from the school pickup line. She was trying to be efficient. The line of cars wrapped around three sides of the school, and she was three-quarters of the way back, despite having left work thirty minutes before the bell time.

Sarah spent half her life dropping off and picking up her kids from school and then, at least once a week, driving them back for some damn thing or another—craft night, book fair, PTA bingo, trunk-or-treat, winter choir practice, which was distinct from spring choir practice, neither of which did she remember agreeing to. Or maybe it was *her* turn to be at school because she was expected to go almost as often as her kids. Volunteer for the pumpkin patch, the Valentine's Day party, the science fair, the multicultural fair, the spelling bee. Drop off fifty toilet paper rolls, plastic bags, Halloween candy (no peanuts, no chocolate, no soy). Did you do your shift in the library? In the reading circle? Last week, Jack had handed her homework he'd been assigned for PE. Who the fuck got homework in PE? Sarah, that was who, because Jack was seven and didn't do anything independently.

The buses were starting to arrive. There was nothing Sarah would

not have given—including the family dog—for her kids to ride the
bus. But Ariel had flipped the hell out the first time there was a substitute driver, and there was always a substitute driver. It got so bad,
the bus had to pull over, and somebody down the street had to be
sent to their house just as Sarah was about to leave for work. Ariel
apparently thought she was being kidnapped, and so now neither of
her kids rode the bus, meaning this was the only time she was alone
and could call her brother, which was still a mistake. Sarah needed
two glasses of wine and a Valium to talk to her brother, and nobody
was handing those out in the pickup line.

"You're checking on Mom, too?" she asked.

"We had lunch," he said.

Sarah didn't ask who paid. She knew, and her blood pressure was
already climbing. She didn't need this.

"How was she?"

"Fine. She's always fine. She's Mom."

"People who are fine don't do what she did, Declan. She's not fine."

Sarah could hear her brother on the other end of the phone breathing. It was crazy that that made her crazy. She was aware other big
sisters grew to love and appreciate their younger brothers. (She
didn't actually know any of those people, but they had to exist.) And
she liked the sound of this. She really did. She would like to work
with her brother to get their parents through this crisis, which was
surely only the first of what would be many in their final years. But
Declan was the same at thirty-five as he'd been at six. Impulsive,
distractible. He'd always left a trail of crayons, Hot Wheels, and
Ding Dong wrappers behind him, and it wasn't because he assumed
there would be someone to clean up after him. It was that he never
thought about the cleanup at all.

"You can be figuring things out and still be fine," he said.

"What does that mean?"

"Just because she's not with Dad anymore doesn't mean her life is falling apart."

"She's in her sixties. She's never worked. That's exactly what it means." God, it was like talking to a dog.

The parking lights ahead of her were blinking off. People who'd turned off their engines were starting them again.

Sarah took a breath and tried to sound reasonable. "I think it would be best for both of them if they could work this out."

"Okay."

"Do you think you could encourage that?"

"Nooooo." He dragged the word out in that adolescent way of his that he knew made her nuts.

"Why not?"

"Because it's none of my business."

Sarah almost said it was certainly his business because if their mother ended up destitute, all of the work would fall on them, but that wasn't true. It would fall on her. And she wasn't the one there trying to manage things because she had a house and a job and a husband and two small children and pickup and pumpkin patch and PE homework. So the fact that she couldn't drop everything meant that everything would, in the end, get dropped on her.

For a moment—less than a second—Sarah thought about taking her foot off the brake and gunning it right into the back of the Toyota in front of her.

"Have you checked your email in the past couple of days?" Declan asked.

He was using the nonchalant voice she didn't trust.

"Not my personal one, no." Sarah couldn't remember the last time she'd looked at her personal email. All the bills went to Kurt, and all the kids' stuff went through the school's apps—plural. There were three.

"I sent you some information. I'm hoping you could take a look."

"Information about what?"

The line in front of her was inching forward.

"Remember the old movie theater?"

What were the odds she didn't remember it? Declan had worked there part-time in high school. Their mother had hoped it would teach him some responsibility. Obviously that hadn't worked out.

"Yeah?"

"It's for lease."

Sarah didn't say anything, but she knew, in that moment, it would be a cold day in hell when she opened her email again.

CHAPTER TWENTY-SIX

While Carol had packed her bag, Henry had been standing in the door of their bedroom, watching her. The sheets on the bed were still in disarray, and he had done everything he could not to look at them. On her way out, she had stripped the bed and shoved everything into the washer, even the comforter, which was too much. But it wouldn't have been fair to leave it for him to do.

She'd grabbed up whatever of her clothes had been to hand. She'd taken her toothbrush and deodorant, the book she'd been reading, and a pillow from the guest room. She'd forgotten her reading glasses, her vitamins, and her dignity.

She knew she'd need to go back eventually, but she'd done a good job of putting it off. Squinting—and the subsequent headache—had turned out to be preferrable to walking back into the home she'd had for forty years without knowing what it was to her now. It wasn't that Henry had asked her to leave so much as she had not been able to stay. She'd run. Plain and simple. Maybe those nights, bare butt to the moon, had been practice. It was hard to say, but avoiding the trip was now something adjacent to, if not exactly, cowardice. She knew that, and she accepted it. She'd have gone right on accepting it if it hadn't been for July.

When Carol had come through the door the day before, July had been sitting at the kitchen table, her face turned toward the window, a sad, unfocused look in her eyes.

"What's up, buttercup?"

It was something she used to say to Sarah, a phrase she'd nearly forgotten until it came out of her mouth.

July blinked, as though surprised to see Carol there. She'd had a load of clean laundry in her arms, which had become slightly damp during the short trip up the stairs from her car.

"Nothing," July said. "Math."

She didn't bother to look down at the book in front of her.

Carol carried her clothes to the couch and dropped them. She sat next to the pile and began refolding a pair of pants that had been folded well enough already. "Didn't look like nothing."

Carol'd been sleeping on the couch for a week before she'd noticed that Anita didn't have a washing machine. It shouldn't have come as a shock, but it had. When she'd asked, as nonchalantly as possible, where Anita did her laundry, the answer had not been helpful. Carol was certainly not going to ask Mack if she could use the washer-dryer in the trailer.

Anita, who'd answered without turning away from the computer screen, had said, in a voice so dry Carol could not tell if she was being mocked, "There's a laundromat out on Old Harbor Road."

"Yes," Carol had answered. "I know."

The Suds-in-a-Bucket wasn't far from the junkyard that pretended at being an auto-repair shop. She'd driven past the laundromat for more than half her life without going in. The first time, she carried her dirty clothes in a trash bag, which, when combined with the scuffed linoleum and vending machine full of powdered detergent, proved to be almost unbearably depressing. But she'd gotten on with it and had been moving an armful of wet corduroy pants and

old-lady briefs from one machine to another when the door had
swung open and Tiny had come in. It was late in the day, and the
interior had been dim. (In time, Carol would learn the hour wasn't
the issue. The laundromat was always near to dark, no matter the
time or weather. It was as though the building itself had the power
to repel light.)

It had taken Tiny a minute to notice her. When she did, she only
nodded and said, without comment or question, "Carol."

Carol said her hellos and watched as Tiny dropped her plastic
hamper in front of a bank of machines, pulled a fresh roll of quarters from her coat pocket, and bent to sort her mountain of laundry.

Carol was glad to see her. She was always glad to see her, but she
was a little bit surprised. It hadn't occurred to Carol that Tiny didn't
have her own machines either. That Carol hadn't realized this felt
like a small embarrassment, as though she were out of touch. She
was just to the point of telling herself that was ridiculous when the
door swung open a second time, and Felicia walked in. She had two
of those rolling carts that she pulled behind herself, the clothes in
various mesh and polyester laundry bags piled into them, one for
each of her sons plus herself. It took some doing for her to negotiate
the door and the carts, and in the process one of them tumbled over.

"Fuck me, Jesus!"

Carol hurried toward her, but by the time she got there, Felicia had
righted the cart and was scooping up one of the bags, which looked
a lot like some sort of giant larva. Carol stopped where she was, and
when Felicia looked up, she said what Tiny had not.

"You really are on the outs, then?"

Carol was not sure she'd ever been so out of place. She felt her
cheeks start to flush when Tiny's voice rang out behind her.

"All the best people are."

"Ain't that the truth," Felicia said. She held Carol's eye for a moment and then nodded, as though deciding something. What, Carol would never know.

Felicia rolled her carts over to a bank of empty washers. Tiny continued what she was doing, seemingly unbothered, and Carol went back to the molded plastic chair where she'd left her library book. It took her a moment to realize, when Felicia started talking, that she was talking to her.

"The important thing," the woman was saying, "is to pick the right machine. You gotta look here." She had one of the washers open and was pointing to the rubber gasket along the inside. "If something nasty got shoved in here anytime recent, you'll know it."

"Have you ever found anything?" Carol asked.

Tiny let out a bark of laughter.

"Lord, you would not believe," Felicia said. "People on this island."

"Depraved," Tiny said.

Felicia nodded her agreement, pulling open one of the bags and shaking out a cascade of soiled boys' clothing.

"This one time," Felicia began, and by the end of the story, Carol had started to think she might not have failed to write her second book if she'd spent more time at the laundromat. She wouldn't go so far as to say she looked forward to going every week now, but she didn't avoid it either.

On the couch, she waited, watching July out of the corner of her eye. She'd folded half a dozen things that didn't need it before the girl said, "Do you know the *Church Mouse* book? About the mice who live in a church with—"

"A cat," Carol said, smiling. "My kids had those books. They loved them."

"My mom had a copy," July said. "I was just thinking about it."

"She read it to you?" Carol asked.

July didn't answer, and when it was clear she wasn't going to, Carol said, "Maybe we can get you another one."

July looked down at the math book in front of her. Carol couldn't see her face, which she suspected was the point. "I already asked Jim. He said it's out of print."

"Well, then you can have mine." Carol matched a pair of socks, rolling one around the other into a ball and tossing it into her open suitcase that she was still using as a bureau.

"Really?" July had raised her head.

"We kept a few of the kids' books for old times' sake."

"Are you sure?"

Carol couldn't tell from where she sat if July's eyes really were damp or if she was imagining it.

"Positive. I'll go by the house tomorrow."

Carol went back to her folding, doing her best to suggest all of this wasn't any big deal—not the book, not the going, not July and the tears that might or might not have been there. She'd gotten up from the sofa and was crouched over, rearranging her things in the bag, trying to get it to shut, when July nearly knocked her to the ground, her arms wrapped around Carol's middle.

"Thank you," the girl said before letting go and, before Carol could say anything, hurrying away.

There really was no choice after that.

. . . .

Carol didn't tell Henry she was coming back for her things. They hadn't spoken since she'd left. Everything she knew came through Declan and Sarah, and everything they told her were things she could have guessed anyway. The things she wanted to ask, she didn't: *Did he remember to pay the electric bill? Fill the bird feeder? Take the supplements for his arthritis?* She'd always put them next to his coffee mug in the morning. But those were things her children would not know, and she wouldn't put them in a position of asking on her behalf. And if Henry was asking them questions to pass to her, it wasn't obvious.

"Are you doing okay, Mom?"

"Do you like it there?"

"How long are you planning to stay?"

She had no idea what the true answers to any of those questions were, so she said things she thought would satisfy them and then tried to remember what she'd said so as not to contradict herself.

The one question she could clearly answer came from Sarah: "Are you still seeing that man?"

"No."

"Are you going to?"

"No."

Gordy hadn't called her once, and she was fetching her mail from her box after-hours to avoid him, too. They were embarrassed of each other now. It had been one thing in private. In private, she called him Gordon and bought his favorite cookies. He complimented her voice and brought her dozens of eggs from his hens, choosing only the prettiest blue- and green-shelled ones. But in public, they were other people entirely. He was Gordy, and she was Doc's wife. His chickens were a problem, and so was his drinking, which—in the confines of their short afternoons together—she hadn't had to see. She was older than he was, too. Not by a conspicuous amount, but when it's the woman, any amount is considered to be conspicuous.

They did not have very much in common. He was a reader, which had surprised her, but he read what she thought of as "man books." And so while she asked what he was enjoying, she did not go out and read those books herself, and he did not ask after what she liked at all. She had noticed, but it was so terribly clear that they were not and could not be a couple, even before the blowup, that it only mattered somewhat, and that somewhat didn't overshadow what he did do for her. Gordon wanted her, and she wanted to be wanted. She didn't even want him. She realized that now.

He probably felt some related version of that himself. She had not been special to him beyond her willingness. Carol did not think Gordy was awash in willingness. He was not, to be honest about it, terribly popular, and in a small community, that was much harder. In a city, it wouldn't have mattered. No one is popular in a city. Cities are too big for such a word to have meaning. She did think Gordy would have been happier in a city. Maybe not now, but when he was young and still malleable.

She could have called him, but she didn't. What she had to say was only "Goodbye" and perhaps "I'm sorry." The better part of her knew those things were worth saying, but she was sometimes weak and did not always do what her better self knew to be right. She soothed herself by thinking that he could find her. He had to know where she was staying. And if his better self was not pushing him to do so, then it was only a little bit bad that she was hiding, too.

Carol chose a time she knew Henry would be at work. Declan was less predictable, and until she pulled up to the driveway, she hadn't known if she wanted him to be there or not. She pushed the button to open the garage and found it was empty. Declan was out. She felt a twinge of disappointment and also great relief.

In addition to the mouse book, she needed her glasses and the rest of her clothes, some toiletries, vitamins, and another pair of shoes—she'd made a list for herself on her phone—but what she really wanted was her laptop. Anita let her use the office computer for the internet and email, but her writing was on her laptop. And after everything that had happened, with all the time she had now to fill, she thought she might be able to do it again. Things were different. She was different. It felt, for the first time in a long time, worth trying.

Upside Down in the Salish Sea had been a local bestseller. She'd made the Pacific Northwest Booksellers Association list at number ten, and her name had appeared in the *Seattle Times*. To her, it might as well have been *Oprah*. But when she'd tried to write a second book, it was as though she'd never done it before. Everything felt clichéd or stilted. The plot fell apart halfway through, or the characters failed to interest even her. A second book was crucial. It needed to do as well, if not better, than the first and would be the thing that would decide whether she would have something she could call a career. She had started and abandoned half a dozen ideas, sometimes writing two or even three hundred pages before walking away. And while it was possible that all of those attempts hadn't been good enough, it was also possible she was afraid to finish. As long as the second book didn't yet exist, there was the possibility of it being a success. But once it was done, possibility became reality. It would sell or not. Reviews would be written, and she would be judged. And she'd been unable to face it.

She'd been afraid to fail because failure felt like loss, but it was the loss of a fantasy. In the past weeks, she'd endured real loss. She'd lost her home, her marriage, and her financial security, to say nothing of her reputation. Writing suddenly felt like the only solid thing she had.

In the garage, she lifted the ladder they kept next to the metal storage shelves full of old paint cans and children's life preservers. She was careful carrying it in through the kitchen and had to stop and readjust her grip. There were footprints on the linoleum floor. Someone had traipsed through a puddle and in through the house. A stack of dirty dishes was in the sink, and newspapers were piled on the kitchen table next to the mail, which had not been sorted. She made note of all of it but didn't feel the usual pull to clean it up.

Careful not to bang into the walls, she carried the aluminum ladder through the dining room and up the staircase, stopping to rest every few steps. By the time she positioned it under the hatch that led to the attic, her heart rate was higher than it had been in a long time.

Carol could not remember the last time she'd climbed a ladder. Even when she'd done a little interior painting, she hadn't used it. They had those telescoping handles for rollers now. Henry had been the one to put things away up here. "Away" summed it up. It was the place they put things they couldn't justify throwing out but were certain they'd never use again. For things they actually needed, there was the basement or the garage, both of which were much easier to access. But the attic was where their old set of luggage had been consigned. It was the large, rectangular kind that had fallen out of fashion decades before. They'd replaced it with matching rolling bags, and she'd taken one with her the night she'd moved out. The other was rightly Henry's, so the floral-print canvas suitcases it would have to be.

Slowly and carefully, she climbed the ladder, pushing the hatch door out of the way when she reached the top. It occurred to her that she'd never actually been in the attic before. It had been over her head for decades but was Henry's domain. Standing there with her hands on the edge, her shoulders peeking up above rolls of pink insulation, she felt accomplished. This was new, and she was handling it fine.

Truthfully, it wasn't terribly exciting. Theirs was not the sort of attic found in storybooks with trunks full of antique bridal clothes and a haunted dollhouse. Theirs didn't even have a floor, just a patchwork of plywood Henry had cut to bridge the gap between supports. She remembered him warning her they couldn't put anything heavy up here for risk of it falling through onto their heads.

She'd worn tennis shoes for the job and had left them on as she'd traipsed through the house. (No one would notice her smeared prints among the others.) And it proved a wise choice. Carefully, she got herself up, placing first her bony knees and then her feet on the wooden slats before gradually standing—or rather hunching—up. There was a bare bulb with a tiny string dangling down. She pulled it, and sixty watts of yellow light lifted the gloom immediately around her and intensified the shadows farther away. Terrified that if she tumbled onto the insulation, she'd fall through to the floor below, she inched toward the piles of discarded things ahead.

Far to the right were the things they'd moved out of Henry's parents' house after they'd gone to the retirement home. She knew the suitcases were unlikely to be there. To the left was a similar pile that had come from Carol's mother's home. Carol would need to think of what to do with it if she really wasn't ever coming back. What she wanted to do was nothing at all. The things she'd cared about—a few photographs and some jewelry—were downstairs. Everything up here was what her mother had insisted she take. The woman had been dead for ten years, and Carol still had a crystal punch bowl with a dozen matching cups in its original box.

Their own things, which would be the punch bowls around the necks of Sarah and Declan, were wrapped in black plastic lawn bags. Why they'd been so concerned about dust, Carol really couldn't have said, but the bags turned everything into amorphous, dark shapes. The drawstrings had been tied tight, and her fingernails were useless, scrabbling at the knots. It had not occurred to her to bring scissors. And while she could have reversed the whole process and gone down to the kitchen to fetch some, it seemed an absurd waste of effort. Instead, she grabbed hold of the plastic and ripped for all she was worth. They were quality trash bags, unfortunately, so it took some doing, but she managed. Once a hole got started, it wasn't too much trouble to keep widening it until she could reach inside.

The first bag turned out to contain boxes with flaps closed but not taped. Out of curiosity she lifted one. Inside was an army of gold plastic participation trophies from Declan's high school baseball days. She let the flap fall shut and shifted the bag to the side. Behind it was another small plastic-wrapped mountain, which felt a little softer and more promising. She got that bag ripped open and lo! There was a piece of luggage, but it was the smallest of the set, the soft-sided overnight bag, smaller than a duffel. Carefully, she twisted around and set it behind her, reminding herself it was there and not to trip. She might use it, but it wasn't what she'd come up here for.

The next bag held board games. She could not imagine what had possessed either her or Henry to save board games. They did not like them and, as she remembered, the children hadn't particularly liked them either. They could have donated them to charity or the church or tipped them into the bin.

Underneath not one but two Monopoly games (Carol could not imagine) and a special-edition Trivial Pursuit, there were yet more cardboard boxes. She was no longer curious, but when she tried to shift them, to push the whole thing over to reach what was behind, the bag would not move. The boxes had to have weighed fifty pounds each, and there were several of them.

Carol balanced her weight on her right leg and hiked the left one over the whole of it to reach the bag behind, but it, too, felt like it contained a load of concrete blocks. She pushed another and another. All of them were horribly, terribly, unimaginably heavy, and now she herself was horribly, terribly, unimaginably frightened that she and all of this crap really were going to fall right through the ceiling.

Henry had told her the supports up here weren't built for weight. He'd made that very clear, but it had obviously been Henry who had carried whatever the hell this all was up here. Carol couldn't have done it with a gun to her head.

Cursing, she turned back to the games bag that she'd already ripped open and shoved the boxed Connect 4 aside. She heard one of the games spill open and the clatter of little plastic pieces going everywhere and ignored it. She got down to the unmarked cardboard box, the one so heavy she couldn't even shift it, and lifted the flaps. Unlike the trophy box, the flaps weren't loose, but they weren't taped either. They were folded, one edge over and one under, around all four sides, so they held one another closed like flower petals. With a yank, the cardboard flower bloomed.

She was far from the little yellow bulb, and her body was blocking most of that light anyway. But it didn't matter. She needed very little light to recognize what this was. And while she did, of course, recognize it, she didn't understand it. Not in that precise moment. She reached in and pulled out a copy of her own book. *Upside Down in the Salish Sea* had come out twenty years before, but this copy was perfect. Not a mark or a dent. It could have rolled off the printing press two minutes before. And below it was another perfect copy. And beside it and beside that and below it and below that. Copy after copy in box after box. Carol began digging faster and faster, tossing books aside, letting them land soundlessly in the snowy pink piles of insulation around her. She ripped open more bags, pulled open the flaps of the boxes. They were endless. Absolutely endless. And finally, she stopped.

Her breath was coming heavy and fast. She reached overhead and grabbed a beam to steady herself. She was going to have a panic attack if she didn't stop it. Carol closed her eyes and tried to concentrate on filling her lungs like children's party balloons. A minute passed and she no longer felt like she was drowning on dry land, but still, she didn't open her eyes. She couldn't bear to. She couldn't bear to see what was in front of her because what was in front of her was nearly every copy of her book that had ever been printed and sold; what was around her was enough to make the bestseller lists in all the tiny bookstores on all the tiny islands between Ebey's End and Anacortes. It was enough, if you were careful about when and where you bought, to make the Pacific Northwest Booksellers Association list for one single week at number ten. And that's exactly— *exactly*—what this was. It was her whole writing career, as modest as it had been. The one thing she'd done and achieved all on her own, and she hadn't even done that at all.

Later, Carol would not know how she had gotten out of the attic, although she would remember putting the ladder away. She had done that carefully. She did not want anyone to know she had been up there. She was nervous and shaky, as though she were running away from a dead body. Everyone in town knew she was a published writer. She'd been in the paper. She'd talked to the high school English classes for three years running. She dropped it into conversation from time to time, letting people know she wasn't only Doc's wife, not only a mother—although, as the years had passed, she'd dropped it in less and less for fear of the follow-up questions: "When's the next one coming out?" "What are you working on now?" Those had been too scary to face, and now there was this.

When she climbed back into her car, she was dusty and itchy, invisible bits of insulation having made it into her clothes and against her skin. She took nothing with her when she drove away. Not her reading glasses or her clothes and certainly not her laptop.

She'd forgotten all about the mouse book, and July wouldn't remind her. In fact, it was almost suspicious how much she wouldn't remind her.

CHAPTER TWENTY-SEVEN

A few days later, Anita locked the store, turning the key a little too sharply. She looked up, hoping to spot the moon through a break in the clouds. No such luck, but she was sure it was full. Everyone who'd walked into the store that day had been squirrely—even by island standards.

Her father had come in fussing about "that Liddle boy" and keeping July away from him. It had taken Anita thirty seconds to figure out he meant Malcolm, which made even less sense. On the trustworthiness scale, Malcolm was somewhere between a guide dog and Mister Rogers. Then, not more than an hour later, Norah Streeter had walked in. Norah was president of the women's ministry and wouldn't spare five words for Anita if the building were on fire, but she'd leaned all the way across the checkout counter, getting close enough for Anita to identify her toothpaste, and, in a low voice, asked if there was anything "unusual" going on with the pastor.

When Norah started consulting Anita on local gossip, some fundamental piece of the universe was coming undone. She'd be down to the post office next, talking to Gordy, and then they really would be serving snow cones in hell. And Anita couldn't help but notice that the can of Campbell's cream of chicken soup Norah bought every week was missing from her cart. So unless she was planning to layer up that iceberg lettuce with a can of baked beans and some Chips Ahoy! and toss it in the oven, the Liddle men were going to be without a women's ministry casserole for the first time in living memory. And what the hell that had to do with her father and Malcolm, Anita did not know, but she no longer believed in coincidences. There was not one coincidence left on the whole damn island.

Coming around the corner of the building, through the alley, she bumped into July. The sun had set, and the only light between the two buildings was at the top of the stairs. The air smelled faintly of popcorn.

"You were out?"

"Studying," July said. "At Tiny's."

"Again?"

July shrugged, and Anita followed her up and onto the old wooden staircase that shook slightly as it took both their weight. When they were almost to the top, July said, "There's something I need to talk to you about later."

Anita stopped climbing.

"What?" she demanded, but July was already opening the apartment door and stepping inside, leaving her alone on the stairs.

"Fucking full moon," Anita hissed.

Inside, pans were clattering in the kitchen, drowning out the sound of NPR. Onions and peppers sizzled in rendered pork fat that was atomizing and settling into the upholstery. Anita and July were pulling off their coats when Carol popped up from the oven and spun around, a tray of buttered and toasted hoagie rolls in her oven-mitted hand.

The sight of them almost made Carol drop the tray on her own foot. It had been years since she'd cooked for someone who came home to eat before it cooled and congealed. She still wasn't used to it. If anything, they were early. The Italian sausages were done and waiting on a paper-towel-lined plate, but the peppers could use another minute in the cast-iron skillet. They were really at their best when the skins bubbled and blackened in spots, and the onions went the color of a Coppertone tan. She had a bag of Ruffles open on the table next to a bowl of homemade dip that she'd been taste-testing now and again. The place settings were out, and she was four sips into one of the two individual beers she'd bought on impulse.

Carol couldn't remember the last time she'd had a beer. Long enough that she'd forgotten how terrible it was. But medicine wasn't supposed to taste good.

July kicked off her red high-tops. "I'm starving," she said, going straight for the bag of chips.

If July were hers, Carol would've told her to wait until dinner when everyone was at the table, but July wasn't hers.

Anita took more time undoing her shoes and leaving them neatly side by side, which she saw Carol had also done. The mud and pine needles that got into every crevice like sand—not to mention actual sand—were a Pacific Northwest scourge.

She slid into the kitchen, feeling like she needed to slide herself in, like there wasn't space for her. "Thanks for cooking," she said, turning on the water and soaping her hands.

Carol pulled down a platter that had belonged to Anita's mother and dropped on the hot rolls, filling them with sausages and the caramelized peppers and onions that dripped with seasoned grease.

"There's another beer in the fridge."

"Thanks."

Anita had no intention of getting it. Beer, in her estimation, was what you drank when the water wasn't safe. What was interesting was that Carol was drinking it. Outside of her annual New Year's bottle of cheap champagne, she never bought booze. It made Anita think of Henry and the Sam Adams. Even apart, they were the same.

July helped Carol carry the food to the table. Anita wanted to open the window and let the smell of pork fat dissipate, but it was cold and July was sitting closest, so she refrained. Carol brought her beer and set it next to her plate, and July got two glasses of water, setting one down in front of Anita before taking her seat. Everyone was settling, adjusting in their chairs, reaching for the bag of chips and spooning dip onto their plates, when July sat up a little straighter and put her hands in her lap. Carol, who sat across from the other two, noticed half a second before Anita.

The girl cleared her throat, reached into the pocket of her jeans, and pulled out a neatly folded stack of tens and twenties. She set it on the table next to Anita's spoon and knife before folding her hands again.

"I want to take a DNA test," she said. "They sell them online. It's a hundred dollars. I have the money, but I need a credit card."

July looked up at Anita, her interlaced fingers squeezed tight together in her lap. Anita glanced at Carol, who'd paused cutting into her sandwich with a fork and knife.

It occurred to Anita that this was exactly the sort of thing she'd been worried about in the beginning. The thing she was unqualified to handle and that would, over time, compound with all the other things she couldn't handle until one or both of them turned to drugs.

Lacking any instincts of her own, Anita did what she thought her own mother would've done. She began the interrogation.

"What are you hoping to get out of this?"

"Information," July said. There was a slight pause. "About myself."

Anita knew a half-truth when she heard one. "What kind of information?"

"Genetic information."

Anita sighed. It had been a long day. A lot had happened. A lot more was going to happen, and she wanted to have this out, not dissect an elephant with a pair of cuticle scissors.

"I think you know what I'm asking," she said.

July squeezed her hands tighter. "They'll tell me if there are any matches in their database, people who might be related to me."

"You want to find your birth mother."

"I want to find anybody."

This wasn't untrue, but she could see Anita wasn't buying it.

"I'd like to find my birth mother," July amended, "if I could, but even, like, a long-lost cousin would be something. That would be worth a hundred dollars to me."

"What if there aren't any matches?" Anita asked.

"There might be later." July was talking faster. "They keep the information on file, so if in the future someone takes a test, they can still find you. I can wait if I have to."

Anita took a breath and slowly let it out. "Can I think about it?"

July's face fell.

Anita held up a hand. "I just need time to think."

July looked ready to cry, but she nodded and turned her face to her plate. Anita turned forward again, too, her eyes catching on Carol's.

No one ate much after that.

. . . .

July finished not eating first, pushed away from the table, and carried her mostly full plate to the sink. On her way back, she said "I'm going to my room" and did.

Anita, who had eaten less than a quarter of her sandwich, balled up her napkin and dropped it onto the plate. Carol expected her to push up, too, take her dishes to the sink, and disappear into the office. Carol had no reason to get up because she had nowhere to go. The area she controlled had shrunk to the space inside her own skin. But Anita did not get up. She put her elbows on the table and her face in her hands, pressing the tips of her fingers into her hairline. Carol stayed where she was. She took a sip of the beer. It was still terrible.

"I don't suppose you have anything to say about all this?" Anita asked, a tired edge to her voice.

Carol crossed her arms and rubbed her triceps. Cold leaked through the glass pane of the window next to them. February was the hardest month on the island. It was the time when warmth started to feel like something you'd only once imagined. Daylight was short and feeble, and moods were low.

"It's your decision," she said, but Anita wasn't having it. She felt, perhaps rightly, that she was owed.

"Pretend, for a second, it's not."

Carol picked up her beer again and then put it back down. The room was quiet. Nothing from down the hall either. Out on the street, a car door slammed. Carol was thinking, and when she finally spoke, she did so slowly.

"She might not find anything, which, no matter what she says, will be a whole new hurt."

Anita grunted.

"Or she might find something, and it'll be tragic—a teenage mother almost certainly, maybe homelessness, maybe drugs."

They both thought about that for a moment.

"Well, as long as we've got something to look forward to," Anita deadpanned.

Carol shrugged. "No one gives up a child because things are going well."

Anita sighed.

July used "malice aforethought" in conversation. She had a 3.8 GPA, and despite having every reason, she had somehow avoided a complete nervous breakdown. She'd made friends with the pastor's son; wooed Tiny, which no one would've believed possible; and was unquestionably Mack's favorite person. For Anita, it was different. It wasn't that she liked July. It was that she would run into fire for her, which wasn't something she'd expected—not so soon and maybe not ever. But here they were, and it meant that this decision, along with every other decision, carried so much weight she didn't know how to lift it.

Carol was probably right, at least in part. Whatever had happened, it wasn't good. It wasn't the beginning anyone would imagine for a kid like July, and she doubted it was what July was imagining for herself, which was the point.

"You think I should say no."

"I think you should say yes."

Anita opened her eyes. She wasn't sure how long they had been closed. "What?"

"You should say yes."

Carol looked unfazed, like they'd been discussing how to divide the electric bill.

"Because . . . what?" Anita sat back and held out her hands. "In for a penny, in for a pound. What's one more trauma?"

Carol, who wasn't very good at replying to sarcasm, chose to ignore it. It was one of the things she disliked most about Anita.

"She's going to do it one way or another. This way, you're involved. You get to be the safety net. You say no, and there's no net."

Anita stared at her and then let her head fall back. "I hate this."

She expected Carol to respond to that. She didn't, and when Anita straightened, she was still there in her neat clothes and her precious

French twist. She was so calm it made her look smug, which was why Anita said it. And anyway, it was supposed to be a joke. Sort of.

"I hate you a little, too."

"That's fine. I've hated you for twenty years."

The words came out quick and snappy like she'd been holding them in her cheek. Anita felt like she'd been slapped. Her neck and face flushed; she opened her mouth and then didn't know what to do with it. Carol didn't say anything.

Anita's first instinct was to lie. *I don't know what you're talking about.* But there was no doubt on Carol's face. This wasn't a trap. It was a statement of fact.

Enough time passed that it was possible neither of them were going to say anything else. But in the end, it was Anita who broke.

"Twenty years is a long time to hate someone."

Carol picked up her beer and took a long drink. When she set it down, she was making a face. "I suppose it would be. Truthfully, I should say I hated you twenty years ago. It's not the same thing."

"You don't anymore?" Anita was starting to wish she hadn't passed on the beer.

"Not really. Or at least only intermittently."

Anita thought intermittent hatred was probably better than she deserved.

"What changed?"

Carol let out a long breath. "Time. Kids." She kept her arms crossed but slumped back. "Sarah got to be the age you'd been, and I saw what that was like. Then Declan, who could barely . . ." Carol shook her head and didn't finish the thought. "Anyway, seeing that, it got harder to hold you responsible."

Anita thought about that. Then she thought about July and how few years were between her and that age. It wasn't half enough. If a middle-aged man put a hand on July, Anita would take him apart with a butcher's saw and sell the pieces on special.

But even still, she looked back and saw herself differently. She'd been naive, and she'd made mistakes. The girl she'd been was probably deserving of forgiveness, but that wasn't the same as not being responsible.

"I don't hate you either," Anita said. "I never did, and I'm sorry I said it."

Carol was quiet a moment. "What did you think of me?"

"Back then?"

"Yes."

"I didn't much." It was true, and it was terrible. Anita knew it.

"Well," Carol said, "I suppose that must've made it easier."

There was a lot Carol didn't understand, and that Anita would never try explaining to her. It wouldn't do either of them any good. But it boiled down to this: The fantasies she'd had about being with Henry long-term had required so many alterations to reality—Henry single, Henry without children, Henry not her father's best friend— that it was hardly Henry at all. It was an open place she'd been trying to fill, and she'd given up on that a long time ago.

At least she thought she had. Then she'd gone and invited him to dinner. She wasn't sure what that said, but she knew she didn't want to tell Carol about it.

"Sometimes I have to remind myself that you're a different person now than you were then," Carol said. The look on her face was philosophical and tired.

"I forget that, too."

Carol nodded. "We all look back and think we knew then what we know now. It's natural."

Anita shifted her weight. The conversation was getting to be too much. Her body wanted to get away.

"Wrong." Carol was looking up at her, which was how Anita knew she'd stood. "But natural."

Anita cleared the table and, for once, did the dishes. Carol didn't object. If it was penance, it was a paltry one, but Anita did feel a bit easier in herself.

While she worked, Carol went to take a bath, carrying her library book down the hall with her. When the bathroom door shut and the tap turned on, Anita dried her hands, went to July's door, and knocked.

"What is it?"

Anita opened the door. July was lying on her bed, face down with her arms around her pillow.

She looked up. "Did you decide?"

Anita had July's money folded tight, and she laid it on the night-stand. July looked at it, and her face fell.

"Come with me."

Anita saw a ripple of argument run through July, but she didn't say anything. She pushed herself up and took a giant step over Anita's mattress, not quite clearing it and landing with her foot half on and half off the edge. She put her hand out to grab the door of the closet, but Anita reached out and caught her before she could. She held on to her until both of July's feet were firmly on the ground, and then, without a word, they crossed the hall to the office. She stood next to the desk and gestured for July to take the chair. July did, staring straight ahead at the swirling screen saver, her hands limp in her lap.

Anita reached into her back pocket and took out her wallet. It was small like a man's but closed with a snap. She opened it and took out a credit card.

"It's a Visa," she said. "Tell me when you're ready for the number."

CHAPTER TWENTY-EIGHT

I t took less than a day for everyone in town to hear about Declan reopening the movie theater. Folks stopped and pressed their faces against the glass lobby door, cupping their hands to block out the gray outside light. There wasn't much to see for a while, but then deliveries from the mainland started to arrive. The FOR LEASE letters on the marquee came down, and OPENING SOON went up.

One particularly wet and miserable day, Malcolm had been allowed to drive to school, and per their new, unspoken agreement about such good fortune, he shared it with July, picking her up at the bus stop before she was soaked all the way to the bone. When he drove her back that afternoon, all the spots in front of the grocery were taken. Both ground beef and toilet paper were on special that week. Anita still put the big, old-fashioned, hand-lettered signs up in the front windows advertising like it was the 1960s, and it still worked as well now as it did then. The store was hopping, which July knew meant she'd be on bagging duty.

She much preferred to work the register, even though it meant she would be sacking the orders, too. But when it was like this, Anita always stepped in. No one, not even Peggy, was as fast as she was with no mistakes. There were a lot of things that could get under

Anita's skin, but a customer having to come back inside because they'd been double-charged for something made her a special kind of crazy. She always gave the person the item for free to apologize, and whoever the culprit had been would hear about it.

Malcolm parked the old sedan in front of the theater. When he pulled the key out of the ignition, the engine shuddered before going silent. It was fifty-fifty whether it would start up again. The pastor said there was an upside to it. It kept the two of them humble as, from time to time, they were reliant on the kindness of their congregation for rides or a jump start, often in the most inconvenient weather. It was good for the soul, he claimed, and instructed Malcolm to think of it as a sort of gas-powered alms. Malcolm did not think of it this way. He thought, if the church was to provide the pastor (and his family) a car, they should also see to it that the car was in working order.

Chet had stopped responding to that argument. He'd stopped responding to most things, and Malcolm found himself having to repeat himself two or three times to get his father to look up. It wasn't unusual for the pastor to be distracted, but the length and depth of this current bout was worrisome. Worrying about his father was Malcolm's part-time job. (The school counselor called it "hypervigilance.") But this past week, his worry had taken a turn toward something else. These suspicions were still vague, and he hadn't yet decided to face them. So instead, he sat in the old sedan with July, looking through the windshield.

They could see through the lobby door, to the left of the empty ticket booth. The door was held open by a large work bucket and shielded from the wet by the marquee that jutted out over the sidewalk. There was movement inside. Malcolm usually dropped July off, as she had to go straight to work anyway, but this time he undid his seat belt and climbed out with her to see what was going on.

They walked up to the door, keeping their feet just this side of the threshold to be polite. Inside, the carpet was an intricate black-and-red swirl, the sort of low pile that was easy to vacuum and showed less wear. A glass candy case ran along the wall. It was now half stocked with theater-sized boxes of Junior Mints, Milk Duds, and, July noticed, Hot Tamales. To the right was a popcorn machine, and although it was empty, they could smell the ghostly scent of butter. Behind all that was a counter with a soda fountain and a nacho cheese dispenser, along with a glass-sided warming box waiting for the hot dogs and containers of tortilla chips to come. They were both hungry after a long day of classes, and seeing it all there made them hungrier.

Just then, one of the interior doors swung open, and Declan came striding out. Despite the cold, wet weather, he was wearing cargo shorts that went down to his knees along with a faded black hoodie. His hair was mussed. (It was always mussed, which July knew but Malcolm didn't.) And in his arms was a stack of large cardboard boxes that went all the way up to his chin.

When he'd taken over the lease, he'd imagined the whole thing would be plug and play. The Shifflers had implied—perhaps even outright stated—that this was the case. But every time he turned around, he found something else was broken. (The warming box, the soda fountain, the machine that spit out the tickets in the ticket booth, one of the projectors, six—no, seven—seats in the theater. And he didn't even want to talk about the plumbing.) He'd never worked this hard in his life. Up until now, it had been a series of white-collar jobs with flat-screen monitors, communal coffee machines, and watercoolers that dispensed both hot or cold, depending on your preference. The only maintenance he'd ever had to deal with was the occasional malfunction of a copy machine, and if the answer to that wasn't immediately obvious, he'd walked away from it, maybe calling someone to report the problem and maybe not.

Now there was no one to call. He'd tried pressing his father into service, but he'd been immovable on the subject. This was Declan's bed, and he could "right well lie in it."

Declan had adored the lobby when he'd worked there as a teenager, and he'd adored it even more the first time he'd come in, using his very own key, but now, struggling under a literal load, he barely noticed it. He did notice the two high school kids peering in at him, one of whom he recognized right away. It only took a second for him to get one of his ideas.

"Hi," he said.

"Sorry," Malcolm said. "We were just looking."

"No problem."

Declan sounded slightly out of breath. The boxes weighed a ton, and his shoulders were screaming. He muscled them the rest of the way to the far wall and squatted down to drop them, nearly losing his balance in the process.

When he turned, he was talking only to July. "You were the one who told me this place was for rent."

She gave him a small smile.

"You didn't tell me you were Anita's cousin."

She shrugged. "You didn't ask."

"True," he admitted.

The lights were off in the lobby, and so, even with the clouds, she was backlit, making her hard to see clearly. The boy looked older and familiar in the way everyone in town did.

"Do I know you?" Declan asked, shifting his gaze.

Malcolm shook his head. "No, but you probably know my dad, Pastor Chet."

Declan sucked air through his teeth. "Jesus Christ," he said. "You're Malcolm."

If Malcolm was surprised or put off, he didn't show it. He just shoved his hands into his pockets. "Yep."

"You were practically a baby the last time . . ."

Neither July nor Malcolm was old enough to understand the ways in which time could pass in one place but be reasonably expected to stand still somewhere else. How it might be possible to age slowly yourself, largely without your own noticing, until you saw that age reflected in the body of someone you'd once known and didn't anymore. And how this could lead to a sudden wave of years crashing over your shoulders.

Malcolm was looking past him, toward the popcorn machine, with something that almost veered toward lust.

"You like popcorn?" Declan asked, recovering himself.

Malcolm nodded.

"Movies?" Declan looked between them, deliberately including July this time.

They both nodded.

"You want to see movies for free?"

They both nodded again, Malcolm enthusiastically, July with hesitation.

"I need a little help getting things up and running is the thing," he said. "Are either of you good with a mop or, better yet, a wrench?"

. . . .

Malcolm and July were sitting on the floor of the lobby. It was Saturday. They'd struck a deal with Declan to work Saturday afternoons doing odd jobs for as many movies as they wanted to watch when the theater finally opened, which wasn't that great a deal as it only had one screen, so it was the same movie over and over again for at least a week. But it came with all the soda and popcorn they wanted, which was better, especially for Malcolm, who had to live on church-lady casseroles and food pantry leavings. The pastor wouldn't even let him take the halfway decent stuff that people donated. That, he said, should be left for those in need.

Malcolm was pretty sure a lot of the people who used the food pantry had more money than they did. He and his dad might not have been the neediest of the needy, but they weren't needy one-percenters either. They deserved the Rice-A-Roni as much as anyone.

July didn't know everything about Malcolm's situation, but she knew enough. Enough that, when it became clear Declan saw them as a package deal, she'd agreed.

On the floor between them was the food warmer. It looked a lot like a smaller version of the popcorn maker—a glass-walled box— but with a big bulb recessed into the top that let off a little bit of light and a lot of heat. It reminded July of the lamp people got to keep their pet snakes warm, except you'd probably end up setting your snake on fire. She said this to Malcolm, who'd taken the whole thing apart, trying to figure out why the bulb, which was new, wasn't turning on. Declan had given them access to all of his tools, which were technically his father's tools, although he never used them.

"I've never known anyone with a snake," Malcolm said, not looking up from the tangle of wires he was poking with a screwdriver, something that seemed unsafe to July, even after they had unplugged it. "But Kevin—the kid with mono—his mom let him get a pet ferret like five years ago. He trained it to use a litter box."

"Really?"

July had never seen a ferret in person, but she was pretty sure they were small weasels and possibly not even legal as pets, although someone had told her Gordy's chickens weren't legal either.

"Yeah, it was kind of cool. The ferret just ran around the house like a dog or, I guess, a cat, considering the litter box." Malcolm stopped his poking. "Plug it in, would you?"

July crawled a few feet across the red-and-black carpet to do as instructed. Nothing happened.

"Okay, unplug it. Anyway, so one day the ferret is running around like usual, but it's, like, the day before Thanksgiving, so his mom has the oven going, like, all the time, making pie and turkey and whatever else. It's a gas stove, right? So it has a pilot light."

Malcolm was stripping the plastic coating off two of the wires with something that looked like pliers but wasn't.

"Apparently ferrets really like tiny spaces, and when no one was looking, it squeezed under the oven and caught its fur on fire."

"No!" July's eyes widened.

"I swear to goodness."

Malcolm never blasphemed.

"And so the ferret runs out from under the stove all on fire and crazy, and then it runs straight for the sofa and runs under the sofa. The whole family was over by this point—aunts and uncles and everything."

July put her hand over her mouth.

"So the sofa caught on fire, and when the sofa caught on fire, the drapes caught on fire."

July spoke around her hand. "Did the whole house burn down?"

"Not the whole house, but there was a lot of damage. Kevin and them had Thanksgiving dinner with us that year. His mom cried, like, the whole time. It was pretty depressing."

"Did the ferret die?"

Malcolm stopped what he was doing and looked at her out of the corner of his eye. July blushed.

"Plug it in again," he said, pushing back off his knees and falling onto his butt with an *oof*. He'd been at it for forty-five minutes, and his neck and back were starting to cramp.

July plugged it in. The light bulb switched on. Malcolm let out a whoop and held his hand in front of it. "We have achieved nacho warmth!" he shouted.

July cheered and grinned at him. He grinned back and then asked, "How did you get that?"

"Get what?"

He pointed to the spot on his own forehead, which made July's finger go to the same place on hers, right above her eyebrow.

"Oh, I ran into a sliding glass door when I was three."

"Oops," he said. He was smiling, but he wasn't laughing at her.

"How about you?" she asked. "How did you learn to fix all this stuff?"

"Parsonage," he said, leaning back. "Everything's always breaking. I watched my dad when I was a kid. Now I can do most of it." He paused. "Well, a lot of it anyway."

"I don't think my mom owned a screwdriver."

"She didn't have to fix anything?" he asked, picking up the tools that were scattered around them on the carpet and putting them in their case.

"We had a bunch of those L-shaped metal things, the ones that come with, like, boxed furniture."

"Allen wrenches."

"Yeah, and superglue. But mostly she just called the landlord when things broke."

Malcolm finished with the tools and sat back down next to her.

"I guess your landlord is, like, God," she said.

"More like the board of directors."

"God has a board of directors?"

He laughed. "That's probably how they see it. It's basically church members who give the most money. Technically the pastor reports to them."

"Is Norah Streeter on the board?"

"I'm pretty sure she's on every board. It's a law or something." He paused. "Why?"

"Just curious."

"About Nosy Norah?"

"Did you make that up?"

"No," he snorted. "Everybody calls her that except the pastor. He gets mad when people do."

"Maybe he shouldn't," July said.

Malcolm wasn't sure how to take that. "He says everyone is doing their best with the tools they have at the moment, and it's our job to help them if they need it."

July didn't answer that, which wasn't a surprise. Malcolm was used to people trailing off when he talked about church stuff. He started to get up. He needed to put the tool bag back in the utility closet and see if Declan needed anything else before they left.

"I bought a DNA test online. It came, and I took it."

Malcolm froze. "Wow," he said. "You did?"

"Yeah, I'm just waiting for the results now."

She had wanted to tell him sooner, but they mostly saw each other during their lunch period. The cafeteria was small and crowded. The tables were close together, and anybody could overhear. She was still the new girl, and she still felt people watching her. Conversations stopped when she stepped into the girls' room and resumed only when she'd closed the stall door, stopping again when she opened it. She'd almost told him in the car the other day, but he was busy talking about the video game he'd downloaded and was trying to play without using any microtransactions, which was pretty much impossible. He knew that but was getting frustrated anyway and telling her about it in the sort of excruciating detail that made her want to peel off her own fingernails.

"It's from one of those family tree websites. If my bio-parents or any of their relatives have ever taken one of the tests, I'll get an alert about the match."

"It'll just, like, tell you who your parents are?" He sounded amazed.

"Well, it's not *that* easy. It'll tell me what percent match I am with the person who took the test. Like, if you took a test and your dad took a test, you'd both get a fifty percent match back. But the numbers are usually a lot smaller, like all the way down to a fraction of one percent, which is a sixth cousin or whatever."

"So if your mom's sixth cousin also takes a test, you could figure out who your real mom is from that?"

"My *bio-mom*, but, yeah, maybe."

The correction seemed to go over his head.

"If somebody asked me who my sixth cousin was, I wouldn't know," he said.

"A lot of people who do these things are really into family trees."

"Yeah."

Malcolm said it like he was agreeing. He supposed he was, but he didn't know anything about it. All of the men in his family, at least on his father's side, where right outside the parsonage door, a whole line of them in black and white staring down at him in their clerical collars. If July knew too little about her relatives, Malcolm felt he knew too much.

"Does Anita know you bought it?"

"Yeah, she let me use her credit card."

"Wow." His eyebrows went up. "That's cool."

"Yeah."

After July had ordered the test, she'd tried to give the money to Anita again, but she'd refused. She'd said she was the adult, and she would be responsible for all "care and feeding." It made July sound like the family pet, but that was how Anita talked when she didn't want to talk about something.

"What will you do if you find her?" Malcolm asked.

July was sitting on her butt with her arms wrapped around her knees. The lights in the lobby were all the way up, but it still wasn't very bright, which was fine. She wasn't sure she wanted to be seen right then. With the heel of her red high-top sneaker, she traced the edge of one of the black swirls in the carpet.

"I'll ask if she wants to meet me, I guess. I mean . . ."

Thinking about coming face-to-face with her biological mother made July aware of her pulse in a way she didn't want to be. The mechanical, meaty pumping of it; the swish of the blood that she couldn't quite feel but could easily imagine. Rubber tubes of blood going all through her body.

"It's like . . . She doesn't even know my adopted mom died. She thinks I'm just living a happy life somewhere."

Words started to come out of Malcolm's mouth, but then, at the last minute, he pulled them back with a sort of strangled noise that made July look up from the pattern she was tracing with her heel. The carpet was so industrial her shoe didn't even make a line in the pile. It was hardly carpet at all. Even grass showed where you'd walked on it.

"What?"

July flexed the muscles in her jaw without knowing she was doing it. Her hair was tucked behind her ears, which weren't pierced because by the time Catherine said she was old enough, July knew too much about how it worked. A gun would shoot a metal dart through her ear, which would stay in the wound, forcing scar tissue to grow around it. She'd have to turn the earring every day to keep the scar tissue from growing *onto* the metal and hope it didn't get infected. It seemed a barbaric thing to do, even though she'd begged for it a few years before.

She could see Malcolm deciding if he should say what he was going to say. His mouth moved around on itself like he was tasting the thought, and when he did say it, it was like spitting it out.

"But you do have a happy life, right?"

July blinked.

"I mean with Anita and Mack and the store and everything?"

He didn't say, . . . *and me.* He did think, . . . *and me.* He kept going.

"I know Ebey's End isn't Seattle, and it's small and poor and whatever, but it's still, like, good. Like the people are mostly nice, and it's really pretty with the ocean and the woods and everything. And yeah, the weather sucks, but we're all, like, *making an effort.*"

He'd started out genuinely asking: Didn't she think this was good? And then he'd switched into making a case for why it was because obviously she didn't think it was or she wouldn't be saying everything she was saying and doing everything she was doing. And then, when he got to the end of that, he realized he was actually kind of mad. Because Ebey's End might not be perfect, but it was his and his dad's, and it had been his mom's, and she'd chosen to come here and even die here. So yeah, it was good, and if July couldn't see it, then, well, fine. She could go if she wanted. They didn't need her. Mainland people were a pain in the ass anyway.

July stared at Malcolm, who had so completely missed the point it was as if he hadn't been listening at all.

Of course her life wasn't happy. Her mom had *died,* and unlike Malcolm and Anita and apparently everyone else, she'd only ever had one parent. She was alone. Anita was her state-approved guardian, which felt tenuous and temporary because it was meant to be. It was basically the same thing as foster care, only slightly less random. So it didn't matter where July was or who else was there or what stupid job she had. Her mom had died. She had died because of something July had told her, and now July was alone. It was like a black hole had opened up in the center of her universe, and it was sucking everything into it. It was sucking her into it, and the only thing she could think of to do to not get sucked in was to find her other mom. Because whoever she was and whatever had happened that made her do what she did, she was all July had left.

"Yeah," July said. "The view is great. I don't know what I was thinking."

She was already up off the floor and dusting her backside. Declan had one of those motorless carpet sweepers that you could move back and forth a million times and pick up maybe four dropped popcorn kernels.

"Okay, I think you know that's not what I meant," Malcolm said, even though that was sort of what he'd said, if not all he'd said.

He was braced for an argument, but he didn't get one. July was already heading toward the door, and his words didn't stop her.

CHAPTER TWENTY-NINE

The true depravity of the human soul can only be known to someone who has cleaned a public toilet, and Anita had been cleaning this one since before she could drive. It was a single-person lavatory tucked into the corner of the store between the dairy case and a stand-alone Little Debbie display. ("'Got Milk?' Don't forget the Zebra Cakes!")

Knowing what she knew, Anita elected not to touch the floor. She took off her tennis shoes and stood on top of them while she pulled down her jeans. It was going all right until she had to pick up one foot and then crashed into the sink, raising a bruise on her hip and landing her socked foot in a puddle of wet. Anita closed her eyes and tried very hard not to have any thoughts. No thoughts at all.

Anita regularly found condoms in this bathroom, which was adjacent to the deli meats. The proximity to bologna shouldn't have mattered, but it did. Sometimes they were in the trash can, and sometimes they weren't. But she knew whoever had left them had never wiped excrement off these walls. If they had, a condom would not be enough.

Anita recentered her dry foot on top of her shoe, her soiled foot raised behind her like the paw of a wounded dog. She reached for the ADA-mandated grab bar and pulled the wet sock from her foot.

She hesitated a moment, remembering her mother, who admonished her several times a week growing up: "Waste not, want not." But as far as Anita knew, her mother had never stood half naked on a shoe island surrounded by flesh-eating bacteria holding a sock that might or might not be soaked in human urine. Anita threw it in the trash.

Holding tight to the grab bar, she reached for her canvas tote looped over the purse hook, but it was too far away. She had to let go and scoot herself on her shoe skis closer to the door. The bag was printed with the library's logo, a gift from Jim when she'd begun supplying refreshments for the Friends of the Library meetings. He hadn't minded that the boxes of cookies were slightly damaged, sliced open by an exuberant stock boy whose own mother would never have let him near a box cutter.

That morning, she'd stood in front of her closet with no idea which clothes to stuff in that tote bag. The last date she'd gone on had been in high school. Keith Warner had asked her to go to a school dance with him. She supposed it had been homecoming because she knew it wasn't prom. She had gone, and it had been a very adult lesson in not getting your hopes up. No number of balloons and streamers could change a junior/senior high school gym into anything else, especially when the balloons were all on the ground because who-ever had been in charge of helium was only one generation removed from whoever was in charge of her box cutters. Black scuff marks still had marred the gym floor. The blue vinyl tumbling mats still had been up against the wall. And the gym still had the thick, musky odor of too many teenage boys nervously sweating together.

For the next few months, Keith had waited for her at her locker and walked her to class. Once or twice, they got hamburgers at the diner her father went to now, and there had been kissing, wet and uncoordinated. The blind licking the blind, it seemed to her now. She remembered how he'd make his tongue into a dart and would piston it back and forth into her mouth. It did not bode well for any future sexual activities, although things never went that far. He'd broken up with her on a piece of paper torn from a notebook and slipped inside her locker. She hadn't been particularly upset about it, other than wishing she could have been the one to leave the note for him. But she also hadn't known that would be it for her. Everyone else paired up, split apart, and paired again like globules of oil floating in water. Her globule had turned out to be different, solitary, and the honest-to-God truth was that she didn't know why.

She was not pretty, but pretty was thin on the ground in Ebey's End. She was not, by local standards, objectionable. She didn't have a hump or a goiter or even a port-wine stain. Under her clothes, things were starting to show wear. Gravity pulled on her breasts, and time had softened the skin of her neck. The veins in her legs and hands were more visible than she remembered, and something was happening to the backs of her arms that she didn't trust. But even still, she'd have put herself solidly in the middle of the pack.

Spinsters, which she was, had always been around. They appeared frequently in children's books and fairy tales. In biographies of the Founding Fathers, they got single-sentence mentions as the "sister of." When Anita imagined a spinster, she thought of a schoolteacher sometime between the 1880s and 1910s. She thought of poetesses, which she blamed on Emily Dickinson. She thought of lesbians at a time when no one—maybe not even the lesbians—knew the word "lesbian." And she thought of herself. She was a modern-day spinster, which could've been empowering had it been by choice, but it was not. She was simply the one left standing when the music stopped. Everyone else had clamored for and gotten a chair, and she had been distracted. Living with her parents. Losing her mother. Running the store. Pining over a married man.

Anita had not gone to college. She hadn't even traveled much. If she added up every night she'd spent off the island, it would've been barely more than a month. She wasn't alone in that, but the others seemed to have understood the limits of their circumstances early. A lot of people married their high school sweetheart. Those who didn't left and, she assumed, married other people, foreigners from Ohio or Maine.

Quickly, she'd given up trying to figure out what she *should* wear and instead had settled on finding the inoffensive. It had taken weeks to make the arrangements, long enough that she thought Henry had forgotten or changed his mind, which was almost a relief. But last week, he'd called at the store with a day and time. They were meeting at the Salish Grill, which was the nicest restaurant in town, a step up from the diner and the pizza place, but not so nice that you'd wear anything but jeans. It was the place you took a date if you had a date, but also a place you might go on a Tuesday if you were a doctor with more disposable income than she had.

Anita had chosen her darkest denim along with a white button-down shirt that had gotten wrinkled in the tote bag. Not so worrisome, as she was planning to pull a navy blue sweater over top of it. Once she had a clean pair of pants on, she stepped into her old brown leather loafers and looked in the mirror. The greenish fluorescent light made her cheeks and the tip of her nose look flushed. The black elastic headband she wore looked like a timing belt stolen off a car, but it held back the loose curls that would otherwise fall into her eyes.

Her hair was medium brown with individual strands of silver that caught the light like Christmas tinsel. It was long enough to tuck behind her ears and short enough to fall back out. She wasn't wearing makeup, because she never did. She owned some—a tube of mascara, concealer that looked like beige lipstick, brown eyeshadow. But it was all more than ten years old, and she was afraid to use it. Not that she would've minded looking a little bit better than she did, but she didn't know how to achieve that. When she put on makeup, she saw the makeup—not a better face but a makeup face—and if she saw it that way, she assumed other people would, too. And anyway, she doubted the wisdom of smearing anything as old as July across her lids. She imagined breaking out in a rash, her lashes falling out in clumps like they did when she was a kid and had the chicken pox.

This would have to do.

She washed her hands and dried them, refusing to give herself one last look before she walked out into the store, her tote bag stuffed with her work clothes, her favorite tennis shoes in her free hand. She walked straight ahead and out the door, not looking to see who was around and might be wondering where she was going "all dressed up."

Anita walked to the Salish Grill. The building had once been a house, old like everything else in this part of town, which was up-hill, a few blocks from the store and surrounded by other houses, some of which also had been turned into businesses. The Grill had a wide wooden deck worn gray by the salty air and speckled with gull droppings. Standing on it, she could look through the windows and see the back of Henry's head. He'd smoothed down his cowlick and was sitting in a booth, the only occupied table in the restaurant. He was looking down at something in front of him, maybe a menu.

Anita watched the bartender, who'd been unloading a rack of glasses at the bar, come around and over to Henry's table. Henry looked up, and they spoke. She could see the bartender's lips mov-ing, but all she heard was a car going down the street behind her. Next to her on the deck rail, a gull landed. In the summer, tourists sat outside and dropped French fries. No one sat outside in the win-ter, and the gull flew off, disappointed. It was March and thirty-nine degrees outside. She wondered what it had expected. She wondered what she expected.

When she'd impulsively invited him to meet her, she'd said "a meal." A normal person understood that to be dinner or maybe lunch. Breakfast was technically a possibility, but only if you were having scheduling difficulties. When he'd called with the details, he'd said four o'clock. Four o'clock was the one time of day you could not reasonably be having any meal at all. None whatsoever. All other times of day could be a late something or an early something, but four wasn't anything. She didn't even know if they were eating. Maybe they were only having drinks. You could drink at four o'clock if you had nowhere else to be, but they both had other places to be. They were busy. They worked. They each had a business to run. But the restaurant was empty now, and standing there, she realized that had been the point. That was why it had taken him so long to call.

More than twenty years had gone by, and he was still afraid of someone seeing them. And she was still walking right into it. She was stunned—actually stunned—by her own stupidity. She'd thrown away socks for this. She'd betrayed Carol *again*, who before hadn't really been hers to betray and now, surprisingly, was. Just by being here, she was betraying her, and she was betraying herself. Maybe she was a lonely globule, but even lonely globules could have self-respect. She looked down. Her tennis shoes were still in her hand.

You don't get to do this, she thought. *Not this time.*

She might have been talking to Henry. She might have been talking to herself. It didn't really matter. She walked away.

. . . .

Anita made her way back into downtown to the only real bar, moving fast enough that it was an effort to keep breathing through her nose. The tavern was next door to Tiny's place and did steady business all day. Inside, it was dim despite the large window on the far side that looked out over the bay.

Anita wasn't social enough on her best day to sit at the bar, and so she dropped her tote bag and shoes at a table by the wall and went to ask Nicole for a brandy Manhattan. Neither of Anita's parents had done much drinking, but on New Year's Eve, after the store had closed at noon, her mother would come upstairs and mix a batch of brandy Manhattans for herself and Mack and eventually for Anita, too. It was the only mixed drink Anita knew, aside from a margarita.

While Nicole mixed, Anita read the list of washed-up flotsam pinned to the wall behind the cash register. In addition to the unofficial cooler full of condoms, the bisected rowboat, and the wringer washing machine, there was now a rusted metal Superman lunch box with matching thermos and part of a Sinclair gas station sign. It didn't say which part, and when Nicole set down her drink—reddish brown in a martini glass with two maraschino cherries in the bottom—Anita asked.

"The part with the dinosaur's butt," Nicole said. "You want to open a tab?"

Anita didn't intend to have more than one drink, but she gave Nicole her credit card to hold anyway, picked up one of the bowls of pretzels off the bar, and carried it and her drink back to her table.

The Manhattan tasted like her mom's, aside from not being served in a juice glass, which gave Anita a pang. Her mother had died of a heart attack no one knew she was having. She'd told Mack her stomach was upset. She was tired. She'd been feeling lousy all day, and she was going to bed. He'd asked if she needed anything, and she'd said she didn't. She went into their bedroom and closed the door. Mack, not wanting to disturb her, stayed out on the couch. Anita had been twenty-three at the time and still imagining she might somehow find a reason to move out, which she knew would also mean moving away. It had been a reasonable thing to want that night when her mother was tired with an upset stomach, and it was not a reasonable thing the next morning. Mack had been the one to go in and check on her. Anita knew from the sound he made. Nothing else could've accounted for it, and she never thought seriously about leaving again.

She took another sip of her drink. She was maudlin and wished she had something to read. She had her phone, but Anita didn't keep books on her phone. She wasn't on social media, and she didn't have it in her to read the news. She got the phone out anyway, typed in her PIN, scrolled through all the icons, and set it back down. She ate a pretzel, expecting it to be stale, but it wasn't. It did make her thirsty, and she drank some more, enough to expose the end of the cocktail pick, allowing her to eat the brandy-soaked cherries without getting her fingers wet. A small win.

She was facing away from the door, but she heard it open, felt the rush of cold air go up her back. Nicole greeted the new person, and then there was a rush and rustle at Anita's side and Jim flopped down in the chair opposite her. He laid a copy of *Upside Down in the Salish Sea* on the table and pushed it toward her. It was a library copy with the thick plastic-wrapped cover and a Dewey decimal sticker on the spine.

"Here," he said, panting. "Oh." He let his head fall back and put his hand to his chest. "I know I'm late. I'm sorry." Each word came out breathy.

Anita's eyes fell to the book, but she didn't touch it. She could feel the cold coming off of his clothes, and his cheeks were alarmingly red.

"Late?"

He nodded. He was still gasping for breath and loosened his scarf.

"July— Whew," he said. "Sorry. God, I ran. I never run. July asked me to bring you this today at exactly 4:10. She was very specific, but my volunteer didn't show up today. I couldn't get away on time." He pushed back his coat sleeve and looked at his watch. "I'm not that late, though, am I? Where is everybody? They didn't leave, did they?"

All of Jim's sentences came out stacked one on top of the other. She might have blamed oxygen deprivation, but he'd always been that way, even in high school.

"Who?"

He was looking around, but no one except Nicole was looking back. "Your book club. I didn't know you had a book club. I usually know because sometimes I can order extra books. Although if it's toward the end of the fiscal—"

She interrupted him. "July arranged this?"

"Yeah."

He was eyeing her drink. It would've been polite for her to order him one, but she didn't. He took a pretzel instead.

"Did she say anything else?" Anita asked.

"Like what?"

"Lord knows."

He stopped chewing. "Are you okay?"

"Yeah," Anita said, fighting the urge to lay her head down on the table. "I'm just having a bit of a day."

"Yeah?" Jim put his elbows on the table. "Want to tell me about it?" He reached for another pretzel.

Anita did, and she didn't. And either way, it didn't matter. She couldn't.

"Okay," he said, getting the idea. "Well, you know where to find me."

"I do," she said, and pushed her drink toward him. "Thank you."

He smiled, picked it up, and, in one gulp, drank most of what was left, then grimaced.

"It was no problem. July gave me a free package of pork chops to do it. Not that she had to, but she'd already offered so . . ."

"Right," Anita said.

He stood up. "Did you like it?"

"What?"

"The book. July said you lost your copy. Oh my God, did you not get to finish it?"

"Not yet."

Jim pressed his lips together like he was holding back his words. Then he exhaled through his nose and said, "Okay, just so you know, there's a pretty big reveal toward the end, so maybe cover your ears when people talk about that."

"Sure."

"A spoiler would really change your experience of the book."

He looked deeply concerned. It was the same way Anita felt when someone bought canned spinach.

"Noted," she said.

He started to walk away. Anita twisted in her chair and called to him, "Say hello to your sister for me."

Jim stopped and looked back. He gave her a small smile and nodded. "I will."

When he was gone, Anita looked back down at the book. The horizon line on the cover was down near the bottom of the photo. The green water, which stretched from edge to edge, was choppy and churning, and a small red boat was capsized in the waves. Above it, grayish-white fog blotted out the rest of the world. The title, in navy blue type, floated in the air, wisps of fog blowing over the words. Below it, unobscured, it said, "Carol Bell."

Anita hadn't read it. When it had come out, Henry was gone from her life. And she was still standing behind the counter in her apron, selling Carol her weekly allotment of boneless chicken breasts and

SunChips. It was all that could have been asked of her. She didn't need to read the book, too.

Nicole appeared at her table.

"I read that," she said, putting her finger on the cover. "It was good."

"Yeah?"

"You want another?"

Anita knew she probably shouldn't. "Sure."

Nicole took the glass away and left Anita with the book and nothing else to do.

"Goddammit, July," she said, and reached for it.

CHAPTER THIRTY

The next day, Anita found her front door locked. They locked the door at night because even on Ebey's End that was the general habit. But when someone was home, they left it unlocked, and nowadays someone was always home.

In the beginning, when July moved in, Anita would stick her key in the lock when she knew the girl was home, only realizing she didn't need her key when the key was already turning. It was a habit, like zipping her coat or bumping the cash drawer closed with her hip. Then Carol came, and Anita stopped taking her keys from her pocket the minute her foot hit the first stair. People adapt. She'd adapted. And now that adaption had failed her. She fished her keys out of her pocket and opened the door.

Inside, she kicked off her shoes and listened for signs of life. There were none. A house is quiet in a different way when it's empty. Even if everyone is asleep, it's not the same. People can feel one another. A soul moves the air.

A small zap of electricity went through Anita. She hadn't been home alone in months. It was as though someone had been choking her a very little bit for all this time, and suddenly, they let go. The relief was palpable. It made her almost giddy. She looked around for what she would do, excited by all the possibilities and simultaneously disappointed by them. Whatever she chose, it couldn't live up to the moment.

Anita knew there were people who didn't like to be by themselves. She also knew light was a wave. It didn't mean she understood it. She looked at her watch. It was coming on five, which meant July would be home in an hour. She wondered, briefly, where Carol had gone, careful not to dwell on the thought in case it might summon her. Anita had started Carol's book in the bar and had taken it home when Nicole started dropping hints about wanting her table. She'd read it that night, lying on the floor next to July, neither of them mentioning it, although Anita did give her a long look that July pretended not to notice.

When she went to sleep, Anita slid it under the mattress where Carol wouldn't find it.

The book was about a young widow, living alone on an island in the Salish Sea that sounded a lot like Ebey's End but without the people. The woman, who never did get a name, spent her days gathering mussels and mushrooms, hunting island deer and building the wooden boats she sold on the internet to people who weren't half as capable as she was but who had a lot more money. At night, she went behind the house and visited her husband's grave.

Even with the grave, it didn't seem like a bad life. Not for a few chapters anyway. Anita wasn't a fast reader, so she was just getting to the part where the widow might not be okay. She was going outside without her clothes, even when it was cold and wet. She was dressing in the morning and then undressing on the front porch, leaving her things in a neat pile by the door next to her work boots. She was wandering into the woods, running until the trees and the sky and the ground were a blur. She came home bloodied. She took cold showers. Anita was starting to wonder what exactly had happened to the husband and maybe if he had ever existed.

It wasn't the book Anita would have expected Carol to have written, although the rumors from a month or two back made a lot more sense now. Anita hadn't put much stock in those stories to begin with, but now she knew they were hokum. That a certain subset of her neighbors couldn't tell the different between fiction and a true fact did not surprise her. That they'd go say those things about Carol did, but then again, with that nice house and that nice life it had seemed she was living, there were those who would want to take her down a notch.

Anita let her eyes rest on the suitcase by the sofa. Carol was usually home by then. She liked to have dinner started most nights by a little after five. After checking for a note and not finding one, Anita changed into plain gray sweats and pulled the book out from under the mattress. She decided to give herself forty-five minutes to do exactly as she pleased. If Carol wasn't home after that, she'd go downstairs for jarred spaghetti sauce and a pound of ground beef.

. . . .

An hour and a half later, Carol opened the bedroom door, and Anita screamed.

The noise scared the hell out of Carol, who arched her back like a Halloween cat and gripped the edge of the door like she might need to rip it off the hinges and kill something with it. Anita shoved whatever had been in her hand under the blankets, and Carol's first thought was *vibrator.*

"Pardon," Carol said as Anita shouted, "Sorry!"—having temporarily lost the ability to modulate her voice.

Carol was looking up at the ceiling. Anita, whose heart rate had not yet recovered but probably would without killing her, raised an eyebrow. "Carol?"

"Are you decent?"

"I'm making an effort."

"What's going on?" July's voice came from behind Carol, who shuffled to the side so she could see in.

"When did you get home?" Anita asked, trying to crane her head to see up at the clock radio on the nightstand over her head.

She was sprawled out across the mattress. She'd piled her pillows into a backrest against the nightstand, and there was an open bag of microwave popcorn beside her, scorch marks visible on the paper. Kernels had spilled out across the blue corduroy comforter, and the burned smell of it was in the air.

"Thirty minutes ago," July said.

"She was doing homework at the table when I came in."

"The door was closed," July said. "I figured you were napping or"—she paused meaningfully—"whatever."

Anita didn't catch her meaning. "I didn't hear."

"Yeah." July smirked.

Catherine had taken her every Saturday for a month to the local women's health clinic for the "Your Body, Your Sexuality, and You" classes. They were mother-daughter classes. July assumed that alone was as bad as anything could be. Then they'd gotten to the two-hour "unshaming masturbation" lesson, and July had realized how wrong she'd been. During the "introduction to bedroom aids" portion, Catherine had raised her hand *three times.*

"I'm hungry," July said. "Can we get pizza?"

"If it's okay with Carol," Anita said, picking up the stray popcorn and putting it back into the bag.

"You know that makes you sound like a couple."

"What?" Anita asked over Carol's "That's enough."

July rolled her eyes.

"Go downstairs and pick out two," Anita said, pushing up off the mattress, an undignified process involving all fours and hanging onto the corner of the nightstand. "And some salad," she added when she was standing.

"Can't we order pizza?"

"No," both women said in unison.

July threw up her hands and spun on her heel. "You really are a couple."

Neither of them answered or moved until they heard the front door open and close. From the bedroom, they could hear the *clomp-clomp-clomp* of July's feet down the wooden stairs. The girl looked like an angel and walked like an arthritic hippopotamus.

"Sorry I'm late," Carol said.

"You're an adult, and we don't have plans," Anita said, wadding up the popcorn bag and dropping it in the wastepaper basket.

She stepped toward the door, and Carol moved aside to let her pass. Anita disappeared into the room at the far end of the hall, and Carol heard the pop and slide of a dresser drawer that tended to stick. When she looked down, she saw the corner of something that looked familiar poking out from under the blanket.

CHAPTER THIRTY-ONE

July had been skipping lunch in the cafeteria. It was the one place she couldn't keep from running into Malcolm. It had been two weeks since their fight, and while they nodded at each other in the halls, they still weren't actually speaking. Instead, she bought granola bars and grape Gatorade from the vending machines near the teachers' lounge. Food wasn't technically allowed in the library, but if no one else was there, Mrs. Hirsch let her keep it, as long as she was careful.

July sank into one of the wooden chairs in front of a student computer terminal, letting her backpack fall off her arm onto the floor. The school kept the internet access locked down pretty hard, but she could still check her email and do her homework. She always started with the former, even though there usually wasn't anything.

She cracked the seal on her drink and took a sip, wiping her lip on her black sweater sleeve while she waited for the screen to load. When it did, the subject line of the first message stopped her breath and made her heart race, a dizzying combination.

DNA RESULTS—MATCH(ES) FOUND

Goose bumps raced up July's right arm and down her side as she moved the mouse, hovered, and then clicked.

"Oh my God," she said, nearly spilling her Gatorade and catching it just in time.

A surreal feeling washed over her. The room and the school and everything expanded away from her like a bubble blowing up and leaving her alone and floating in its center. She read the words and then read them again, afraid she was making some sort of mistake.

"Oh my God," she said again.

She tried to click the print icon in the corner, but her hand shook so much she couldn't keep the mouse steady. She had to click two more times before the enormous machine at the end of the row hummed to life.

July grabbed her things, shoving it all into her bag before snatching the three pages out of the print tray on her way out the door. She forgot to close her email. She forgot everything that wasn't this. There were only ten minutes left, and she had to get to the cafeteria.

. . . .

The library had once been a house, and Jim's desk sat in what had once been the parlor. A yellow globe light hung in the center of the room warming up an otherwise dark and gloomy day, but it did little to illuminate the page he was attempting to fix, which was why he had a small flashlight gripped in his teeth, his glasses pushed to the end of his nose, and a length of repair tape hovering over *Plants of the Pacific Northwest Coast.* It was a perennial favorite and was always being slid into the overnight drop box the worse for wear. Patrons shoved it into hiking packs and left it out in the rain. This particular copy had wrinkled brown edges that Jim was fairly sure came from being dropped into a mud puddle. (At least he was hoping it had been mud.)

The electronic bell dinged, letting him know someone had opened the front door, but he didn't look up. He'd been at this for more than five minutes, and his neck and jaw both ached. The page he was trying to stick back in had been ripped fully out, right through a whole block of text, which made lining it all back up nearly impossible. He did almost have it, though, and he was trying not to breathe as he carefully nudged it a quarter of a millimeter up with his pinky, the tape hovering and ready to stick down the second he got it just right.

Whomp.

Anita dropped a copy of the latest Faye Kellerman novel on his desk, sending his loose page rippling three inches away. Jim didn't move except to close his eyes and force a lungful of air out through his nose.

The online support group he belonged to for long-term caregivers had brought in a meditation instructor to teach them how to breathe through their rage, which they all had but couldn't admit to having outside of the group. Jim found those lessons worked just as well outside the home. In fact, it was astonishing anyone who didn't meditate got through the day without murdering someone. Since last Tuesday, his deep breathing had saved half a dozen people. Seven now.

Jim took the flashlight from his mouth, wiped it on his sweater, pushed his glasses back up to the bridge of his nose, and managed something like a smile.

"I'm returning this," Anita said, "but I need another copy of the other one, the *Flipped Over in the Sea* one."

"*Upside Down in the Salish Sea.*"

"Whatever."

"Why do you need two?"

"I don't need two. I need one. Mine disappeared."

"Again?!"

Anita stared at him before remembering the story July had made up. The book club. A lost copy. Dammit. Now he was going to think she was irresponsible and revoke her borrowing privileges. She tried to think of something that would both cover the previous lies—hers and July's—and exonerate this one real loss.

"It was Dad's fault," she said.

Jim sighed and actually appeared to soften. If Anita wasn't mistaken, he had a soft spot for Mack. On the one hand, this played in her favor. On the other, it was confusing. It wasn't like her father was a library person. He was more of a *People's Court* person. Jim's indulgence didn't make sense, but neither did anything else.

A day had gone by before she'd noticed the book was even gone. Initially, she'd blamed July, but the girl had held up under interrogation, although she'd looked a little smug that Anita had been reading it in the first place. Together, they had searched everywhere it could possibly have gone, including the store and Anita's car. The damn thing had simply vanished.

"I'm afraid you'll have to pay for it," Jim said. "If it turns up in fair condition, I can issue you a refund."

Anita pulled her wallet from her back pocket.

"It'll take me a minute to look up the cost," he said. "You can go up to the Blue Room. There should be two more copies on the shelf."

She left him tapping at his keyboard and went up the ornate wooden staircase. Each of the rooms on all three floors of the library was wallpapered a different color. The parlor, where Jim sat, was the Green Room, which housed most of geography and history. The Blue Room was the largest of the second-floor rooms, allowing for a rectangle of half shelves in the middle, in addition to the ones lining the walls. In between the shelves were strips of dusky blue wallpaper that featured embossed trees with roosting peacocks. Several years ago, Anita had stated with certainty that peacocks couldn't fly and therefore would not roost, but Jim had proven her wrong. (It's never a good idea to make a bet with a librarian.) Peacocks, it turned out, could fly, just not well or far or high, but if it were a very stunty tree and a very motivated peacock, it could theoretically come to roost. Anita still thought about that every time she came looking for fiction by authors A–De.

Anita found the Bs near the bottom of one wall and skimmed from Behrens to Bennett. No Bell. She looked again, expanding her search from Bates to Bradley. Still nothing. One of the peacocks looked at her. She stood up, holding onto a shelf for support, hoping belatedly that it was anchored to the wall. Her knees creaked, and she had to shake them out before heading back down to complain.

"Yes, it is," Jim said.

"No, it's not."

Jim spun in his chair to face a computer screen. It was one of the modern mesh-backed office chairs with lumbar support, and Anita envied it. Hers was faux leather and peeling. Every time she stood up, little flakes of black pleather stuck to the butt of her pants. It wasn't that she thought a lot of people looked at her butt, but it was undignified nonetheless. She tended to walk around compulsively brushing herself.

"Two copies available." Jim pointed to the screen.

"Available to whom might be the question."

Jim pushed up from his chair and walked around his desk toward the stairs. Anita followed.

In the Blue Room, he went to the same shelf Anita had, crouched down as Anita had, and scanned the same spines Anita had.

"Huh."

He pushed up without holding on to anything, and if his knees made a sound, it was very quiet.

"Well," he said, scanning the area around himself, as though the two books might have made a jump for it and then army-crawled toward the nearest shadow. "That's concerning."

"Maybe they got misshelved."

"No," he sighed. "One copy maybe, but not two." He put his hands on his hips and was quiet for a few seconds before starting up again. "It's either a prank, and I'll eventually find half of cookery mixed up with mathematics. Or they're gone, stolen probably."

He looked around again, as though he could spot a missing book among thousands. For all Anita knew, he could. A man who knew the physical limitations of a peacock and was willing to wager on it was not to be underestimated.

"Don't you have an alarm or something?"

Jim crossed his arms. His olive-green sweater had a small hole in the elbow. Anita could see through it to the plaid button-up he wore underneath.

"The only reason I have sugar for my coffee," he said, "is because I bring it from home." There was a pause. "Actually, I bring the coffee, too."

"Folgers is going on sale next week," she told him. "Dollar fifty off."

"Save me two?"

"For you, buy one, get one."

He shook his head. "You don't have to do that."

She shrugged. "You're Dad's friend now."

"I am," he said, sounding a little surprised by it.

"How are the meetings?" she asked.

"Good." He paused. "Bill scares me a little."

"Bill scares everyone. It's the handcuffs."

Jim nodded, and they stood companionably for a moment.

"Do books go missing often?" she asked.

Jim shrugged. "Depends."

"On?"

"Sex mostly. I stopped buying *Fifty Shades of Grey.* Nobody wanted to be seen checking it out, but half the town wanted to read it. I lost a copy a week."

If there was sex in Carol's book, Anita hadn't gotten to it yet. There was nudity. Maybe that counted.

"Anyone steal *Inside Out in the Ocean* before?"

"*Upside Down in the Salish Sea,*" he said, and raised an eyebrow to say that was the last time he was playing that little game. "And no, not that I can remember. It's not very popular, honestly. It came out quite a few years ago. We wouldn't normally have so many copies still, but I can't bring myself to put them in the sale bin. It would hurt Carol's feelings, you know?"

The idea of hurting someone's feelings appeared to cause him actual pain, and Anita made a mental note to just give him the coffee.

A few minutes later, she was nearly to the front door when she stopped and turned back. Jim was at his desk, bent over a book with a long piece of tape in his hands.

"Hey," she called, "how'd you get that fancy chair?"

"Friends of the Library," he said around the flashlight in his teeth. "Gift for twenty years of service."

Jesus, she remembered when Jim had started at the library. If forced to guess, she'd have thought it was five, maybe six years ago. She might have said eight to cover her bases. Her life had hardly changed at all in that time, not until recently.

"What do you get for thirty?" she asked.

"I'll let you know."

. . . .

Malcolm got free lunch. Every year, his father filled out the applica-
tion, and every year, he qualified. It wasn't as bad as it used to be.
There used to be a list attached to a clipboard that the cashier would
check off for the poor kids. Now each student had a plastic ID with
a barcode on the back. If you had money in your account, your lunch
was deducted. If you were a free-lunch kid, it gave you a pass. No
one had to know anymore, but Malcolm had never gotten over how
it had felt. His whole body flushed every time he checked out, his
neck getting red and hot. So even though no one had to know, he
was pretty sure everyone did.

For a minute, it had gotten better. He'd go through the line with
July, who told him all foster kids, which she technically was, got free
lunch and a bunch of other stuff, too, from the state. It was her first
time getting free lunch, and she wasn't embarrassed about it. She saw
it as a really shitty consolation prize. She even took an extra milk.
Chocolate because she could. Malcolm could have, too, but he never
did, even though he was thirsty, and the milks were the same size
now as they had been when he was five. July thought she deserved
the milk, and Malcolm didn't think he did. He was self-aware enough
to see that, but he had no ability to change it or even to think it ought
to change, which probably meant self-awareness wasn't for everyone.

He was sitting in his usual seat at his usual round table. There was
an empty chair on either side of him, which felt like two yawning
chasms. Other kids sat in the other chairs, but they weren't talking
to him. It wasn't that they *never* talked to him, but he had to work
to make himself part of the conversation. It was easier to sit alone
with his free "Western cheeseburger," whatever that meant. It didn't
even come with fries. The other divots in his tray were filled with
steamed broccoli and a plastic cup full of tiny orange slices. It seemed

like the sort of food you'd get in a hospital if the doctors still had hope. If there wasn't any hope, you'd get the fries.

He'd eaten the burger because he had to eat something. If he didn't eat every two hours, it felt like his body was consuming itself. He'd drunk the milk and had picked up the orange slices, which swam in some kind of syrup. There was an eighty percent chance he was going to eat those because the broccoli was absolutely off the table. The question was really if he should eat the orange slices and then drink the syrup or the other way around, and he was thinking about it when July punched his shoulder from behind, negating the question. He knew it was her without turning around, and he didn't even care that his broccoli was now swimming in fruit cocktail juice.

"Come with me," she demanded when he turned. "Now!"

He stood up, grabbing his book bag and his tray, which he took to the dishwashing station. You had to take your tray to the dishwashing station. It was a rule, but July stood there making bug eyes at him.

"Come on!" she said, grabbing his sleeve—not his arm, just his sleeve—and pulling him out of the cafeteria. They went through the student lounge with the cardboard shamrocks dangling from the acoustic tiles and out to the covered walkway that stretched between the junior and senior high buildings.

You were only supposed to go outside if you had a reason to go outside, but it seemed like July had a reason. She kept walking. She was ahead of him and still had hold of his hoodie sleeve, so his arm stretched straight out in front of him, making him trip-walk behind her. When they were halfway between the two buildings, as far from other people as they could reasonably get, she dropped his arm and spun around.

"The DNA results came back," she said, leaning forward, so he could smell the Gatorade on her breath, which should've been gross but wasn't.

"Okay," he said, which he knew wasn't really the right answer, but she hadn't told him the right answer yet.

"I got a match!"

It looked like she was squeezing herself without actually squeezing herself. If she were another girl, she would've jumped up and maybe squealed or something.

"That's great," he said, and meant it. Mostly.

If she saw the hesitation, she didn't say anything. She was acting like they hadn't fought at all, and he wasn't going to bring up anything that would remind her of it, even though this whole conversation should be reminding her of it.

"It's twenty-five percent," she said. "*Twenty-five.*"

"Yeah."

"Do you know what that means?"

He didn't know what that meant, but she didn't wait for him to tell her that.

"Twenty-five percent is a half sibling." She'd grabbed his sleeve again and was shaking his arm with it. "I have a sister!"

"Holy shit." Malcolm was genuinely stunned, and it wasn't even happening to him. July didn't seem stunned, though. She seemed high.

"Can you contact her?" he asked.

"Through the site, yeah. But it's all, like, quasi-anonymous. You can choose what to share and what not to. She only uses her initials, S.N., and her city."

July's words were coming out in spurts like she was out of breath.

"Where does she live?" he asked.

She made the bug eyes at him again. "Seattle."

"Whoa."

"Whoa," she agreed, and then she smiled. She smiled so wide he thought her whole face might split open.

CHAPTER THIRTY-TWO

I t was 3:30 in the afternoon. July had been home for fifteen minutes and was already getting on Anita's nerves. She'd dropped her bag by the door, then went to the kitchen sink, turned the water on, changed her mind, went back to her bag, pulled out her books, sat down, stood back up, went back to the kitchen, opened the fridge, shut the fridge, went to her room, came back out, went back to the sink—

"Are you on drugs?" Anita demanded.

After the library, she'd spent the rest of the afternoon in the office, balancing the books and processing the payroll. Her numbers were still in the black, but they were shrinking steadily. It was depressing on its way to frightening, and so Anita was now standing at the counter with an open gallon of rocky road. Not even the good kind because she could no longer justify buying herself the good kind. She was eating directly from the container with the big spoon, which had been both helping and not helping, when July had come in and started acting like a squirrel trapped in a car.

"What? No!"

"Then what's wrong with you?"

"Nothing's wrong with me."

"What happened at school?"

"Nothing."

"I have many faults, July, but stupid isn't one of them."

Unlike her new butcher, Anita thought.

Darryl, the old butcher, had quit. He was married with two kids and lived on a farm that cost him more than it made him. The Blue Bird had offered him two dollars more an hour. Anita couldn't even blame him. He'd volunteered to come in nights, free of charge, to train whoever replaced him. It was an offer Anita had accepted even though it made her feel worse. Finding someone willing to disman-tle animal carcasses for two dollars less an hour than at the Blue Bird, who wasn't also drunk or high and didn't scare the hell out of the customers, had turned out to be a pretty small needle to thread. She'd ended up hiring a recent high school dropout who'd already been fired from the car-repair shop.

Darryl had been coming in every day for a week. A dog could've learned to quarter a chicken in that amount of time, but all the kid had done was come close to chopping off his own thumb.

July reached into the cabinet and took down a drinking glass. "Where's Carol?" She was playing at subtle and failing.

"Why?"

July set the glass down. "Just asking."

Anita was about to say something about not being her brother's keeper when the front doorknob turned and, as though summoned, Carol rushed in. She was harried and wet. Her purse had slipped off her shoulder and had taken the sleeve of her coat down with it. Whole hanks of blond-gray hair had come loose from her twist.

"Have either of you seen my debit card?"

"What?" Anita asked, her brain still trying to catch up with what-ever this was turning out to be.

"My debit card!"

Carol was yelling. Carol never yelled.

"No," Anita said. "Not since you used it at the store."

Carol turned to July, who shook her head.

"Goddammit!"

July leaned back like the word had pushed her.

"Do you have the rest of your wallet?" Anita asked.

"Yes, *of course.*"

Anita didn't know why the "of course," but Carol was too flustered to make sense. She was yanking off her shoes and dropping them in front of the door, letting her purse fall and taking off around the apartment, coat half on like a silk blouse falling from a hanger.

July's eyebrows crept up. She glanced at Anita, who glanced back. Carol, meanwhile, had dropped to her knees by the sofa and was pulling everything out of her suitcase. More sweaters and sensibly cut pairs of pants than could reasonably be expected to fit in one bag were piling up and tumbling down around her. If she'd yanked out a full goldfish bowl, Anita wouldn't have been surprised.

"When did you last use it?" she asked.

"At the diner!"

July's face had gone from alarmed to frightened. Carol, who had thrown an entire stack of mated socks, didn't notice.

"Did you call them?"

"No, Anita, I thought tearing apart my own underpants first made the most sense!"

Carol turned and threw a handful of lady briefs across the sofa. They were shiny and synthetic, and each of them had a seat large enough to re-cover a barstool.

"Right," Anita said, feeling more in control of her life in that moment than she had in years.

Carol stopped like someone had pulled her plug from the socket.

She sat back on her heels and let her hands fall, palms up, on her thighs.

"I went to the diner and the bakery and the hair salon. I've looked through my purse a hundred times. I pulled the floor mats out of my car. I got down on my knees in a parking lot to search under the seats. It's not there. It's not anywhere!"

Anita glanced down at Carol's jeans. The knees were wet and dirty, and her voice sounded very near to tears.

"Did you go to the bank?" Anita asked, finally finding her store of sympathy.

"I haven't been to the bank in two weeks!"

"To cancel the card."

Carol opened her mouth and then shut it. She pulled her spine straight and said in her most reasonable voice, which, under the circumstances, came out a little creepy, "It wasn't my card."

Anita's bottom lip flattened. The turn toward larceny was unexpected. She chanced a glance over at July, who was two seconds from crawling under the table.

"It was Henry's," Carol went on, "and Preston won't let me cancel it."

Understanding dawned. "And you don't want to tell Henry you lost his card?"

Carol's spine slackened.

"I don't want to tell Henry I had it in the first place." She let herself fall to the side, her shoulder leaning into the sofa next to the discarded underpants. "We kept two accounts. The one in my name ran out of money, so I've been using his."

No one said anything.

"We're still married," she said.

"You are," Anita agreed. "It's your money, too."

Carol didn't answer. She pulled her legs out from under herself, closed her eyes, and propped her elbows on her knees. Cross-legged and hunched over, she put her face in both of her hands. The room around her had gone silent, and there wasn't any telling how long it would've stayed that way if Carol hadn't spoken first.

"Jesus."

She dropped her hands, tears running out from the corners of her eyes. They were slow-moving and quiet and could easily have been missed.

Hesitant, Anita sat down a full couch cushion away from Carol, who did not turn to look at her. She didn't seem ready to look at anyone, which was a feeling Anita understood. After a moment, she scooted closer, which wasn't close enough, and then closer still, finally reaching for Carol's shoulder.

"It won't be such a big deal," Anita said.

The last time she had felt this way touching another person was when she'd first slow-danced with a boy in the sixth grade, the two of them shuffling one step left and one step right for three minutes. It was a strange mix of hyper-self-consciousness, tingling excitement, and a barely suppressed urge to run away.

Carol, who appeared unaware of all of it, shook her head. "I've been so stupid."

"Everybody loses things."

"It's not about the card." She moved away from Anita, surprised to find the other woman so close. "I don't have anything."

Anita tucked her rejected hand under her thigh. "That's not true."

Carol looked at Anita, incredulous. "I have to go," she said, standing up.

Anita understood she had failed to help and had possibly made things worse, although exactly how remained unclear.

Carol stepped over her feet in a rush to get to the front door. She was in such a hurry Anita thought she was going to forget her shoes.

She didn't, but she was still cramming her heels into the backs when the door closed behind her.

An unnatural quiet descended on the apartment like something essential had been sucked out of it. It took Anita a moment to remember July was still there.

"She'll be fine," Anita said when she caught the look on the girl's face. "She's just upset. It's okay to be upset."

It sounded juvenile, but she'd heard the good-seeming mothers say this to crying children in her store before. It sounded natural coming out of their mouths and, she was afraid, condescending coming out of hers.

She was still sitting on the sofa. Some of Carol's underwear was under her butt. She looked over. The pair next to her had fallen so she could see the cotton gusset that went between Carol's legs. Anita looked quickly away. Behind her, there was a bang that was so loud and sudden it made her squeeze her privates.

July had knocked over a kitchen chair grabbing up her things. "Sorry," she said, righting it. "I'm going to Tiny's."

Anita thought about stopping her, but that was as far as she got. Instead, she watched as July shoved everything into her backpack and snatched up her coat. After the door slammed, Anita listened to the wooden staircase rattle against the building as July ran down and away.

. . . .

Dylan was bouncing his basketball down the sidewalk. His mom had gotten it used, and it didn't hold air as well as it used to. He had to pump it up every time he played over at the church, which was more often than he wanted. But when he didn't show, the pastor called his mom at work, and then she got on the radio and asked one of the deputies to keep a lookout for him, which was a lot worse than just going to basketball.

It irritated him, but he had to respect an effective system. He'd been listening to a lot of podcasts at night on his mom's phone. He liked the self-improvement ones, the ones about building habits and creating or reducing friction. He even liked the ones about stuff like that in bigger contexts, like how making people opt out of retirement savings was a lot more effective than asking them to opt in, which was how he learned that there was such a thing as "organizational psychology" and that you could go to college to study it. It was the first time in his life he'd ever thought maybe it would be cool to go to college, a thought he'd quickly tried to squash because no way could his mom afford that.

"Hey."

Dylan caught the ball on the next bounce and held it. "Hey," he said back.

July had just come running out of the alley next to the grocery store. He was pretty sure that was where she lived, like, in an apartment or something above the shop. Living where you worked was definitely an efficient system, and part of him wished he could go up and see it. Also he just kind of liked her. She was weird and sometimes shy, but she wasn't shy because she was weird. He didn't know if that would make sense to anyone else, but it made sense to him.

He rubbed his hand over his bristle of blond hair, back and forth, an old habit. "What's up?"

"Have you talked to Tiny?"

"Tiny?"

"At the bakery." July had her backpack on her shoulder, and she hitched it up higher. "I mentioned you to her a little while back."

"Me? Why me?"

Dylan couldn't think of a time when his name coming up had been a good thing, and whatever this was, he was ready to deny it.

"She's been looking for some help around the shop forever. Kind of seems like it would be a good fit." July shrugged. "I wasn't sure you'd be interested, though."

"Oh."

Dylan had seen the HELP WANTED sign in the window. He'd seen it so many times that he didn't see it at all anymore. Probably no one did. Also no one had ever recommended him for a job before, which was what he thought she'd said, although a careful parsing might have proved him wrong.

He didn't know what to say. "Okay, sure."

She tucked her hair behind her ear and give him a small smile, which made him rub his head again, a little faster this time.

"Thanks," he said.

"Sure."

"Okay." He knew the conversation was over, and it was time for him to leave, but he couldn't remember how.

She took two steps toward him, and he froze, held his breath, tried to be cool. But then she stepped around him. By the time he turned around, she was jogging across the street. She didn't look back, and he looked down before she caught him staring.

. . . .

Carol stepped into Henry's waiting room. She'd smoothed her hair in the rearview mirror and straightened her clothes. The knees of her pants were still muddy, but there hadn't been anything she could do about that.

When Shannon looked up from her computer, her eyebrows raced each other up to her hairline.

"Hi?" she said. It was a question.

Carol stepped up to the counter. "Can you tell Henry I'm here." It was not a question.

She knew he had a break between patients this afternoon. He'd given her the password to the scheduling system years before, and if he hadn't, it wouldn't have mattered. He used the same one for everything. So did she.

Carol watched Shannon consider making up an excuse. Henry was her boss, and that was where her loyalties lay. It wasn't as though she'd taken this job just to keep herself occupied. She and her husband had their heads above water but barely. Brian worked landscaping and tree trimming when he could and handyman gigs the rest of the time. They had three kids. Their youngest son's teeth had come in as crooked as a nineteenth-century graveyard and would stay that way. If any of them wanted to go somewhere other than community college, they were going to have to discover some hidden talent that would win them a scholarship because otherwise they were on their own.

Carol, who was wrapped up in her own drama, looked pointedly from Shannon to the phone, and Shannon sighed. "You can have a seat," she said, picking up the handset.

Carol hadn't come often to Henry's office. If she'd needed to talk, she'd called. If she'd needed to drop something off, she had and then left. This was, she realized, the first time she'd ever sat down, and it was uncomfortable.

When Henry came around the corner, he was wearing his glasses, and he needed a haircut. Carol could see that he'd done his own laundry—surely not at the Suds-in-a-Bucket—but he'd left it to sit in the dryer too long. His shirtsleeves were wrinkled.

"I'm sorry to bother you, but there's . . ." She could feel Shannon listening. "Preston said there's been a mix-up at the bank."

Henry held out a hand, directing her down the hall to his office.

Once there, she took the chair opposite the desk, which had so many papers scattered across it, the surface was invisible.

"What kind of mix-up?" he asked.

He was using what Carol called his "doctor voice," firm but sympathetic. His patients always got the best of him, and it had made her jealous. She'd often wished he would save some for home.

"I lost your debit card," she said. Tears pricked at the corners of her eyes, and she hated it. She felt stupid when she cried about things like this. "I tried to cancel it, but Preston said it had to be you."

"All right."

That hadn't been what she'd expected. Anytime one of the kids made a mistake, he was the first to snap. He never out-and-out shouted, but he hadn't been kind either. He'd never told them everyone makes mistakes. He'd never told them it was fixable. That had been her job.

"I'm sorry," she said, wiping the corner of her eye with one knuckle and rolling her shoulders back.

"There hasn't been any fraud, has there?"

She shook her head and cleared her throat, trying to get rid of the sticky feeling she always got there when she cried.

"Well, then that's fine."

"That's fine?"

"I'm sure it will be."

Henry placed his hands lightly on the desk in front of him like he was about to play the piano. His sleeve rode up, and she could see the brown leather band of his watch. She'd bought it for him on their twenty-fifth wedding anniversary. It was the one gift she'd gotten him that he'd seemed genuinely happy to receive.

"I'll call over to the bank and get things sorted."

Carol still had her coat on. Her purse was crammed uncomfortably between her hip and the arm of the chair, the strap still over her shoulder, but she made no move to adjust it.

"I've been using the account," she said. "For essentials."

There was a pause.

"Use it for whatever you want."

She squeezed her toes inside her shoes. "I thought you might not appreciate that."

"Why?"

The sticky spot in her throat was growing larger. It wasn't why she couldn't find the words, but it didn't help.

"It's yours," Henry said when she didn't answer. "Do what's best."

She had always been the one to manage their money. He had trusted her with that. The retirement accounts and college savings accounts, bills, emergency funds, investments, refinancing their mortgage all those years ago. He didn't look through any of the statements that came through the mail, and he signed all the tax forms she put in front of him without a glance.

She'd done well. They were in a good place. Not rich, not on a country doctor's salary, but they were fine. Better than most. Although none of her calculus had taken into account two households. That would change things.

"I wasn't sure you'd still feel that way," she said, fingering her purse strap, "after everything."

His eyebrows conferred, coming close enough to whisper to each other over the bridge of his nose. This wasn't the sort of conversation he'd ever been comfortable with.

"I do."

Carol waited for more, but when he looked for something to add, he couldn't find it. Instead, he let his shoulders relax as much as he could. It wasn't much. He felt stiff and awkward all over.

"Are you . . . well?" he asked.

She nodded but then stopped and shrugged. "I'm sleeping on Anita's couch."

He almost opened his mouth and told her she could, if she wanted, come home. He got so close his jaw loosened and his lips started to part, but then he didn't. He didn't want her to have to sleep on anyone's sofa. Maybe at first he had, but not now. But that was different from living together, which still seemed— He wasn't ready to share a bed yet. That was all. He thought of suggesting she find her own place, but that sounded permanent. And he didn't want permanent. He didn't want either thing—not her home and not her gone either. It was an unsettled and confusing feeling, and he wished to hell it would go away.

"And you?" she asked. "You're well?"

"Yes."

"You have Declan there."

"We don't see each other much."

"No?" Carol was surprised, and then she wasn't.

The point of Declan coming back had been for him to be with his father, but if he had come back and then done something else entirely—renting an old movie theater, for example—it wasn't out of character. In fact, it was to be expected.

She didn't say any of this aloud. She didn't need to. Instead, without much forethought, she said, "You should know I found the books."

It came out in a rush, the words trying to beat the door that would slam shut on them.

"Books?" He frowned, confused.

"My books. In the attic."

"Oh."

She saw it hit him, and then watched as he tried to figure out what to do with it. He lifted the corner of a piece of paper with his thumb and forefinger, bent it, smoothed it down. "I wanted . . ."

She waited, but he let out his next breath and no words came with it. "You wanted what?"

It came out harsher than she'd expected, and she thought she saw him wince.

"To make sure that you were"—he exhaled—"happy, I suppose."

"I'm not," she said, the tears rushing back. "I've never been so unhappy in my whole life."

"Humiliated" was the word that came to mind. She was humiliated. So much so that she couldn't even say it aloud.

He nodded. He looked saddened, but he did not apologize.

"You shouldn't have done that." The words came out strangled.

"Why?"

Henry looked up at her, and Carol blinked at the question, at the stupid, stupid question.

"It ruined everything!"

He shook his head. "No."

The surety with which he said it made her want to pick something up and throw it at him. He'd destroyed the one piece of real success she'd thought she'd had. It was all a lie, and it was his lie. She never would have done that to him. Not ever. That he had— She was so angry and so embarrassed it paralyzed her.

"You needed a chance for others to see what you could do," he said. "Just a little boost to catch people's attention."

Carol didn't say anything. She didn't know what to say, and Henry was looking right at her, willing her to see this his way. As though this horrible thing could possibly have two sides.

He tried again. "When Sarah was applying to college, you wrote her essay."

Carol gripped the armrest. "That is not the same thing! And I didn't write it."

Sarah had always been an excellent student, but she took after her father. Words had never come together right for her. Whenever she'd had to write anything personal, the essence of who she was got lost. It was the act of trying to press her thoughts down onto the page that killed them. And it would have been a travesty for that small thing to have gotten between her and getting into the one school she'd had her heart set on. And so Carol had helped her. Only *helped*. Sarah had written the admissions essay, and then Carol had rewritten it. Edited, really. All of the ideas had been Sarah's, all the intent, all the real work. Carol had simply made sure that the admissions officer could see it properly.

"You gave a running start," Henry amended.

That was closer to the truth, and Carol nodded. "She earned it."

"So did you."

"No, I didn't!" She slapped the arms of the chair. "That's just it. I didn't earn it. All of those sales were you. The whole time. I was like . . . like a little kid sitting on your lap, holding the steering wheel in the parking lot thinking I was driving."

She mimed this, and Henry gave her a sad smile.

"You're good with words."

"Oh, shut up."

Carol crossed her arms and then leaned forward over them. She was no longer flexible enough to rest her forehead on her knees, so her upper body hung there, her head drooping.

"Success isn't given fairly. I wanted your second book to have the best chance."

"That didn't exactly work out."

Carol was still bent over. Henry's words, when they came, floated out over her head.

"I'm still waiting."

CHAPTER THIRTY-THREE

Gordy had thought, being that it was the grand opening and all, the tickets might be free. He should've known better. The line stretched all the way down the sidewalk, past the grocery store to the corner. It was ridiculous. He was about to turn around and go home when he saw Tiny coming down the street. She was dressed in her work clothes, too, although in her case that meant sweatpants and a muscle tee, even though it was late March and threatening snow. She had a coat over top, unzipped. He noticed she wasn't wearing an apron. He also noticed he could see the outline of her bra, one of those sports ones.

"Jesus," she said when she caught up, getting into line behind him.

Her presence meant, by definition, that he was in the line rather than leaving it, something he couldn't be blamed for and didn't try to change.

"Ridiculous," he agreed.

"Wouldn't have expected to find you here," she said, crossing her arms over her chest in lieu of zipping her coat. "Are you becoming social in your advanced years?"

Gordy snuffed. "Are you?"

Tiny raised her chin in acknowledgment, if not agreement. "Gotta get out sometimes," she said. "How are the chickens?"

He sighed. "I think Pearl's got something wrong with her foot again."

"Oh?"

"She's not wanting to put weight on it. Could be bumblefoot. You remember last year when she broke her toe?"

Sadly, Tiny did. Pearl—she couldn't believe she knew this—was one of Gordy's older birds, and old birds sometimes fall, especially if they live in a poultry high-rise. Gordy had called Tiny over to help him splint it. She had shown up with oven mitts on both hands. She'd have preferred something thick and leathery, but oven mitts were what she had.

"Take those off," he'd said.

"When hell freezes over."

Tiny's lifelong fear of birds was, she felt certain, justified. Chickens, in particular, were vicious, nasty creatures whose natural place in the world was enrobed in pastry. She had absolutely no compunction about eating them. In fact, she relished it. She considered it her civic duty, one less murderous beast among them, which was why, when Pam had come to her door with a box full of baby chicks, all those years ago, she'd turned her right out, made her sit outside in the rain to wait for her order.

In retrospect, the whole thing had been odd. Pam didn't often come to the bakery. Gourmet pies weren't within the budget of a pastor's wife, although Tiny had, from time to time, donated one to the cause. Moreover, there had been no good reason for her to have chickens in any stage of development. Unless she had been planning to turn the playground into a barnyard, there was no place on the church grounds for chickens. But there the woman had sat, her brown hair pulled into its usual ponytail, waiting for her small coffee with a cardboard box and a sign:

Chickens: free to a good home

A minute later, Gordy had come walking down the street. Gordy always came to the shop on his ten o'clock break. You could've set your watch by it. He'd stopped in front of Pam.

Later, he'd told Tiny that Pam had found the chickens in the box on the side of the road after nearly running them over on her way to the bakery. She was a chicken savior, he'd said, which was plausible, at least. She'd come to the island to study eagles. A bird was a bird.

Through the window, Tiny had watched the exchange. Gordy, who'd never owned any animal before, had stopped. The two had spoken. He'd reached in to pet one of the beasts and eventually picked it up. Miraculously, this didn't result in a mauling. Tiny had even seen him raise the baby chick to eye level, look it over, and then bring it to his stubbly cheek, rubbing the down against his face, which both ensured the transfer of salmonella and broke Tiny's understanding of who Gordy was in the first place. He'd put the chick back in the box, and Pam had handed the whole thing to him, walking away without her coffee.

Walking. Not driving. She didn't have the car that day. Chet did.

She missed Pam. The whole town did. After she got sick, a gray film fell over everything. Tiny, who counted her as a friend, had expected a miracle. Pam was the sort of person who would get one of those, but that wasn't the way it had gone.

Whatever the town had lost the day she'd died, Malcolm had lost triple. Gone was the happy, silly boy he'd been, and it broke Tiny's heart every single time she saw him.

A chorus of laughter broke out up ahead. Tiny leaned to the side and stood up on tiptoe to see. (It felt like she spent half her life on tiptoe.) It was the Old Philosophers, who were, on average, somewhat less old now that they had Jim. Doc was there with them, and it made her wonder where Carol was. Surely she was coming to the grand opening.

On the one hand, Doc, Gordy, and Carol in the same place could be explosive. On the other, there hadn't been any good gossip going around the bakeshop in a while.

"What's so funny?" Tiny called out to the cluster of men.

Mack turned and smiled. "What do Alexander the Great and Winnie-the-Pooh have in common?"

"I don't know," Tiny said. "What?"

"Same middle name."

Tiny groaned and looked over at Gordy, who was forcing the corners of his mouth not to turn up.

"What do French bakers say about old age?" Tiny called back.

"What?" Mack asked.

"It crêpes up on you."

"Ha!" Mack said. "Mine's better."

Tiny shrugged, and Mack turned back to his friends.

Doc, who was holding himself still and straight, had made a point of not turning around, which Tiny had to admit was probably for the best.

Gordy cleared his throat. Tiny ignored him. He did it a second time.

"What, Gordon?"

"After this, I'm going to check on Pearl's foot."

"Uh-huh." She was careful not to look over at him, but in the end, it didn't matter. He waited a few seconds and then said the thing she knew he would.

"I could use a hand."

A white fleck landed on the sleeve of Tiny's coat and then another and another and more. She looked up. Gordy looked up. Everyone in line looked up. For a moment, they all went quiet. The snow was coming down light but fast, melting when it touched them, sticking for a moment in the scrubby bits of grass along the sidewalk. If it kept up, they would wake to find the forest flocked in white, roofs blanketed and dollops balanced on their mailboxes. Ebey's End was always beautiful. It was a mild beauty in the summer, and a fierce, brutal beauty in the rain and wind. But snow on the island was something different. It slowed time.

Ahead of them, a few hoods flicked up. Tiny zipped her coat.

. . . .

July had to wait until Anita and Carol left to join the ticket line. They'd planned to leave later, but through the windows, they could see the queue already backing up an hour before the show.

"You're coming, aren't you?" Carol asked.

Declan had chosen a Bond film for opening night. She'd not have said so, but Carol was surprised he'd managed to think of something most people on the island would want to see and then follow through. It was actually a good business decision, something she found hard to square with the son she'd raised.

"I'm coming," July said without looking up from her notebook. "I just want to get these problems finished. Hold my place?"

July listened to the women's footsteps on the outside stairs, waiting until they were all the way down to the alley and then as many seconds after that as she could bear. Then she hurried into Anita's office and booted up the computer.

All messages had to be sent through the DNA family tree website. She logged in, went to her results page, and clicked on the blue

underlined initials at the top of her list of matches. It showed their
mutual percentage (24.1) and the number of matching DNA segments
(fifty-nine). She wasn't July's only match, but she was the only one
above three percent. There was a time when July would've taken
three percent. Three percent was better than no percent, but with
24.1 on the table, she hadn't even bothered to look at the others.

The click took her to the woman's public profile, which was about
as spare as it could be. July took a breath and clicked the message
icon. A pop-up window opened. In the subject line, she typed: "Sisters?" Then she stopped, looked at it, and hit the backspace key once.

Sisters

July finished her message, read it five times, and then hit SEND,
tapping the mouse button fast, like it was red-hot, and then jerking
her hand away. The pop-up disappeared. No turning back. Not that
she wanted to, she told herself. Definitely not.

Before her brain could run away with itself, which it was already
starting to do, July hurried out of the office and speed-walked down
the hall, stopping to grab her coat in her room. She was headed toward the door when it hit her. She tried to push it away. She wanted
to get downstairs. The line was already moving, people were going
in, and she didn't want to be late. But there was no getting around
it. She pivoted and ran back to the bathroom, yanked open the medicine cabinet, and grabbed the half-empty box of Band-Aids, looking
to make sure the Neosporin was still tucked inside.

With it clutched in her hand, July ran out of the apartment and
down the stairs, snowflakes landing in her hair and melting into
little drops. She had to find Tiny before the movie started. She didn't
know why, but Tiny was really, really going to need some Band-
Aids.

CHAPTER THIRTY-FOUR

O h, hi, Mrs. Bell. Is July home?"

Carol had answered after the second round of knocks just when Malcolm was about to give up and go back down the side stairs.

"She's not. In fact, I thought she was with you."

Malcolm could smell onions and garlic coming from the kitchen.

Recently, there had been a lull in casserole deliveries. He'd complained about them before. He never got any choice in what they ate, and he didn't like green peppers or mushrooms or anything that was too soupy. But now that he was left to poke through the church's food pantry for something that could be cobbled together, preferably without having to use the stove, he missed them. In fact, the food smells wafting out the door at him were distracting, and he took a second longer than he should have to answer.

"Right, uh, she's supposed to be. At least I thought that was what we'd decided. But . . ." He gestured to the blank space behind himself.

Declan had been true to his word. Malcolm and July had both gone to opening night at the theater for free, although not exactly together. He'd stood in line with his father, and she'd stood with Anita and Carol. She'd been late then, too, and he wondered if that was going to start being a thing. But once everyone was inside with their tickets, crowding around the concession stand and loitering in groups, they'd found each other. It had been like a big party, everyone talking and mixing, and when they'd gone in to get their seats, they'd chosen two together away from their families.

It had been fun that night, but they'd decided to do things differently the next time they went. There was a plan. They'd worked it all out, but Malcolm had been waiting in the alley for fifteen minutes and she hadn't shown.

"Maybe I misunderstood," he said.

Carol cocked her head in a way that made his stomach drop. She wasn't like a lot of the other women in the church. She didn't look past him or condescend to him. In fact, it always seemed like she paid too much attention. The look she was giving him made him worry she was reading his thoughts—or that he'd accidentally spoken them aloud.

"Well," Carol said, "I'm sure she's just running late."

Malcolm exhaled. "Right."

"Why don't you come in and wait?"

Carol stepped aside, making room for him to pass. Malcolm hesitated, letting in cold air.

Her mind was going as fast as his. School had gotten out hours ago, and July didn't have a shift in the store that day. If she wasn't with the boy, where was she? Carol could call Anita downstairs, but that might stir up more trouble than the situation called for. She could call Mack, which would be a different complication. Or she could sit tight and talk to the boy, at least until she'd decided how concerned she ought to be.

Malcolm shuffled his feet. "Um . . ."

Enough was enough. "In," she said.

Malcolm came in. She shut the door behind him, and he bent automatically to remove his damp shoes.

"I just took a pan of enchiladas out of the oven," she said.

Malcolm's stomach growled loud enough to hear.

"Sorry," he said, his ears going pink.

"For what?" Carol asked. She was already in the kitchen, opening a cabinet and taking down a plate.

"That was loud," he said.

"Doesn't make it something to apologize for," she said. "Sit."

Malcolm stepped to the table and sat. It was smaller than his at home, but there was more room to eat. It wasn't covered in papers.

"Do you like sour cream?"

Malcolm didn't but was afraid saying so would be offensive. Maybe the sour cream was already in the enchiladas.

"Malcolm?" Carol was holding a full plate, waiting. "Have you ever had sour cream?"

His ears pinked more. "Yes."

"Did you enjoy it?"

"Not really." His ears went fuchsia.

"All right, then," she said. "No sour cream."

She brought the plate and utensils to the table and set them in front of him, taking the seat opposite.

The table was pressed up against a window. He knew, because July had told him, that she had to eat dinner with the two women every night. She said it like a complaint, but he didn't think she really minded. He wouldn't have minded. He would've given anything to be able to eat dinner with his mom, and July got two. Malcolm knew Carol wasn't really her mom, but she seemed an awful lot like one. And Anita definitely counted. She was July's foster mom and her cousin, which he supposed made Mack both her great-uncle and her grandfather. It was like half the island was rushing in to be her family, grabbing up every title they could get their hands on. And now she'd maybe found a sister, too.

Malcolm only had the pastor, who he knew very well didn't always sleep at home. Malcolm had heard him sneaking out. He'd gotten up the first few times and watched him drive away. Malcolm tried to stay awake to see when he'd come home, but he hadn't made it past one in the morning. It turned out he didn't really need to. The parsonage door swelled in the winter, so when you pushed it open, you really had to push, and it made a sort of pop as it sprang free of the frame. It was 5:10 every time. The first morning, he'd expected his dad to say something at breakfast, but he hadn't. He'd put coffee in a travel mug and had taken a plate of toast to his office, all hustle and bustle—visits to make, souls to save—like it was any other day. But he'd seemed happier. A lot happier.

Malcolm wasn't stupid. He figured out pretty quickly the pastor was seeing someone, and he didn't want Malcolm to know. A lot of single parents were like that. Malcolm had seen a bunch of TV shows and movies with that kind of thing. Plus, it meant the pastor was having premarital sex, and while their church wasn't on a super-high horse about it, you weren't going to get a round of applause either. And that was just if you were a member. The pastor and his family were held to a higher standard. Chet was always telling him that. Lecturing, more like. So what was this?

"You look an awful lot like your mom," Carol said.

Malcolm had his head down over his plate, the longish curls he was always brushing back hiding her from view as he shoveled one forkful after another into his mouth.

"What?" he asked, then realized his mouth was full and put his hand in front of it, trying to swallow quickly. The food was hot, and he nearly choked.

"Sorry," he said, his voice froggy.

Carol stood, he thought, to get him a glass of water, but instead, she opened the fridge and took out a gallon jug of milk.

"You look like your mom," she said again as she poured. "I'm probably not the first person to tell you that."

"Yeah," he said. "I mean no. You're not the first person."

She wasn't, technically, but people didn't like to bring it up. They didn't like to talk about her in front of him at all.

"I didn't know her well, but what I knew I liked. Pretty much everyone did, I think."

Carol brought the full glass over to the table and set it down.

Malcolm only ate dinner with the pastor once or twice a week, and they drank water if they drank anything at all. Their meals were unceremonious, eaten on top of papers, at the sink, on TV trays or their laps. It was moms, he thought, who made you drink milk, who made you sit at the table.

"Thank you," he said, taking a long drink that drained half the glass. "This is really good."

"Ready for seconds?"

She nodded toward his plate. It was empty, which surprised him. He was sure it had been full a minute ago. She hadn't even sat down from getting his drink.

"Sure," he said. And then, "If it's not too much trouble."

He was sure it was.

"You're very worried about being trouble."

Malcolm wasn't sure what to say to that, and so he said nothing.

She took away his plate and glass and brought them both back full. "Henry knew your mom better than I did. He could probably tell you some stories about her, if you ever want to hear them."

Malcolm knew his mother had been Doc's patient. Everyone was, but it was Doc who'd diagnosed her cancer, who'd sent her to Seattle for treatment. It had worked the first time. Malcolm had been two and didn't really remember. He remembered afterward, though. He remembered them talking about it. His parents told him she had been sick and had to go away to get better. And she had—been sick, gone away, gotten better. Things had been fine for a while. Then, five years later, the cancer came back. Five years was supposed to be the magic number with cancer. If it was gone for five years, you were good. Doctors stopped monitoring you so closely. Your family breathed again. But that hadn't been the way it had gone for them.

She went away again, and he remembered being worried but not as worried as he might have been. They'd done this before.

That was what he felt most guilty about. He hadn't worried enough about her, and what if that was the thing that had been different the second time? Malcolm knew that was probably ridiculous. Cancer didn't care if people worried, right? But people still prayed for the sick. His father organized prayer chains for congregants. If you were sick or your kid was in the military or somebody had a difficult pregnancy, everyone in the chain got the message. Everyone prayed. If that helped, maybe Malcolm's worries might have helped, too. Maybe worry and prayer were sort of the same thing.

His mother had lasted two years the second time. Then she'd died.

"Mack was the closest to her, though."

Malcolm's mind had gone away, but Carol's words brought it back.

"Really?" No one had ever told him that.

"He helped her with her fieldwork when she first came to the island. Maybe it's hard to imagine, but he was strong before the stroke, outdoorsy. He knew his way around the woods."

"How old was I?" Malcolm asked, trying to place himself in the picture.

"Little," Carol said. "She was always taking volunteer helpers. I never went, but Declan did. It was part of his senior project."

"They knew each other, my mom and Declan?"

He'd been working with Declan for weeks. That he'd known Malcolm's mother without Malcolm knowing it felt strange.

"A bit," Carol said. "It was maybe a month's work. Declan thought it would be more fun than tutoring at the library or picking trash off the beach."

"Right."

Those senior projects still existed. He'd have to do one next year. Complete x number of volunteer hours, write an essay about it, say how it made you grow as a person even if it didn't. Malcolm had barely thought about it. The pastor already made him do a million things. He'd just pick one.

Carol looked at her watch.

"Anita will be home soon," she said, even though she wasn't thinking about Anita at all. Her level of concern was notching its way up with each five-minute increment that passed.

Malcolm had finished his second plate. There was a cake in the kitchen, a chocolate-buttermilk Bundt she'd made that morning and stored in an old-fashioned aluminum cake carrier. It had probably belonged to Anita's mother. Maybe even her grandmother. Under other circumstances, she'd have cut the boy a piece, but now was not the time.

"I'm going to make a few calls," Carol said, standing up. "You can wait here."

Malcolm stood up, too, but once he was standing, he didn't know what to do with himself. He had been more irritated at July's no-show than concerned, but now that Carol had decided to *do something*, it seemed more serious. If she was worried, it was worrisome. He kicked himself.

Carol picked up the phone in the kitchen. Landlines were still common on the island. Cell phones were convenient but unreliable,

especially when the weather kicked up, and it looked like it was fixing to.

CHECKOUT was the first number written on the little speed dial
paper attached to the cradle. ANITA DAD was the second. DOC was
third. Carol had already tried that one when she'd first moved in.
The paper was written in Anita's hand, not Mack's, but Mack wasn't
likely to have known how to program a phone. Carol had wanted to
see if it rang through to her husband's office or their home. It was
his office, and there were good reasons Mack might need to get hold
of a doctor quick. Carol had decided only within the last few weeks
not to be bothered by it. Now she didn't even notice it. She'd already
pushed one for checkout and was tapping her fingers on the counter
while it rang.

Anita picked up on the fourth ring. "Island Grocery," she said. "How
can I help you?"

Carol didn't identify herself. They were past that stage with each
other. "Is July there?"

"No. Why?"

"She was supposed to meet Malcolm for a movie."

"She hasn't been here all afternoon," Anita said, matching Carol's
tone of concern.

"All right. I'll call the library and Tiny's." Carol looked at her watch
again. Both would be almost closed.

"I'll call Dad," Anita said.

They both hung up without goodbyes.

Ebey's End still got the Yellow Pages every year. Stacks of them
would appear for the taking in public buildings around town. Carol
got hers at the post office and kept it by the kitchen phone. Anita did
the same. The size of the island was reflected in the thickness of the
book—not more than half an inch. Carol was flipping through, planning to call Tiny first, when the front door opened.

Malcolm jumped. He'd been standing by his place at the table, frozen there like Lot's wife.

"There you are," July said, shoving her hands into the pockets of her coat. "I was waiting."

Carol closed the phone book but didn't set the receiver back in its cradle. Not yet. July glanced over, but Carol didn't say anything. July looked at the table.

"You were eating?" she asked.

Malcolm opened his mouth and then closed it before trying again. "I was waiting for you."

"I was in the lobby, like we said."

"We said the alley."

Malcolm's face looked less sure than his words sounded.

"Why would we say the alley in this weather?"

"I don't know," he admitted.

He didn't know, but he really had been sure they were meeting in the alley. Why would they go into the theater when they weren't planning to sit in the seats? Recently, Declan had given Malcolm permission to sit in the old projection booth, which had the best view and was for employees only, which made it cooler. But old buildings being what they were, you couldn't get to the projection booth from inside. You had to take the outside stairs, like the ones to get to this apartment. Declan had given him keys, which had been kind of exciting.

Malcolm should have thought to look in the lobby, though. It would've been an obvious place to start rather than coming here and bothering Carol, getting everybody all worked up. He felt his ears pinking again.

"Well, hurry," she said. "I don't want to miss anything."

Malcolm reached for the dirty plate.

"I'll clear it," Carol said. "You go on."

That seemed to make him uncomfortable, but he obeyed. "Thank you for dinner, Mrs. Bell," he said. "It was really good."

"You're welcome anytime," she said.

He bobbed his head.

"I mean it." She was still holding the phone.

"Okay."

He turned and picked up his shoes. July had already stepped back out onto the landing of the stairs. Malcolm was in such a hurry to follow her he was trying to tie his sneakers and walk at the same time.

When the door closed, she heard their feet on the stairs, both fast and clunky with youth. Once they were at the bottom, though, that peculiar quiet of an empty home descended, and Carol looked out the window. Not at the kids but at the asphalt. It was wet, but it wasn't raining hard. Just sprinkling for now. The clouds—thick and dark—promised more later.

Carol pressed the speed dial again. Anita picked up before the first ring finished.

"She showed up," Carol said.

She heard Anita exhale relief. "Where was she?"

"Not where she claimed."

"What does that mean?"

"Her coat was soaking wet."

July's coat was wool. She would have had to have stood outside for a long time in just a sprinkle to soak herself.

"Do we worry?" Anita asked. She sounded exhausted.

"We're alert."

"Do you think she's gotten into anything?"

Anita made her sound like a dog that had found a bag of Halloween candy.

"I don't know yet."

That wasn't what Anita wanted to hear. "I'm closing up soon."

"Enchiladas for dinner." Carol looked over at the baking dish, which was now more than half empty. "Don't come too hungry."

. . . .

The booth wasn't used for showing movies anymore. Everything was run by computer with a digital projector that hung from the ceiling at the back of the theater. The whole setup was smaller than some Bibles Malcolm had seen. The booth was used to store cleaning supplies, toilet paper, and those rolls of red paper tickets, which didn't really seem necessary since people paid at the ticket booth just before walking in. But Malcolm had figured out pretty quickly that what Declan did wasn't always motivated by what made the most sense.

The pastor hadn't been overjoyed when Malcolm had started working with Declan. It took a lot for Chet to come out and say he didn't like someone. Pastors were supposed to like everybody, but he'd gone so far as to use the word "dilettante," which for Chet was practically a swear. Malcolm thought maybe the pastor didn't like some of the movies Declan was planning to show. The Bond film hadn't exactly gotten them off on the right foot, but Malcolm had shrugged and said it was only an after-school job. Chet had pressed his lips together but didn't say any more.

Malcolm knew what his father said was true, but he also thought— quietly and to himself—that Ebey's End needed a few dilettantes. One, at least. Without Declan, the movie theater never would've reopened. Not in a hundred years. It was too much work for too little money. No one practical would ever have taken it up, and the whole island would've been the worse for it. Sure, they could watch movies at home, but even the pastor had to realize that watching alone in your living room, pausing to answer the phone or let the dog out, wasn't anything like a real theater. A real theater was an experience, an event, something you did with other people. It took you out of your normal life in a way TV never could.

In Malcolm's opinion, the whole town had gotten a little more color since the theater opened. There was something to look forward to every week, and Declan was talking about more than just first-run movies now that things had gotten going. He was talking about showing classics on weekday nights, back-to-back showings of Bogart and Hepburn or *Gremlins* double-featured with *The Goonies*. He'd even talked about doing a midnight showing of *The Rocky Horror Picture Show* once a month for the high school kids.

It was hard to say if any of that would actually happen. Having it not happen would be pretty in character for Declan, too, but it might, and that was good enough for Malcolm for now. It made him start to think about what other things the town might have if there were a few more people like him around. They could get a bookstore or a comics shop or maybe even Thai food. (Malcolm had never actually had Thai food, but it sounded promising.)

He and July were sitting close together, their metal folding chairs touching, their hips almost touching, so they could both see through the little window where the old-fashioned projector had once been. They had missed the previews and the first ten minutes of the movie, which had apparently been important. That or the plot was generally confusing. Either way, it was hard to pay attention when paying attention didn't get him anywhere.

He fiddled with the box of Milk Duds he'd fished out of one of the extra cartons of candy that were stored in the booth, which was part of his wages now. He had a second box down by his feet. July had picked Red Vines and Peanut M&M's. He really wanted a Sprite, too, but not yet badly enough to get up and go all the way outside and in through the front to get it.

"Hey," he said, testing the waters to see if July was really into the movie and would shush him or if they could talk.

"What?"

She didn't sound annoyed, but she didn't look over at him either. She didn't really have to. They were so close they could hear each other fine even over the Dolby 5.1 surround sound, being that it wasn't an action movie. (Declan had cared a lot about the audio. Malcolm didn't care at all, but he'd heard it enough that he could recite the specifications even while not knowing what they meant.)

"Mrs. Bell said Mack was friends with my mom."

July put another M&M in her mouth and talked around it. "Okay."

He waited a minute in case she was going to pick up the thread on her own. She didn't, and the movie played on. It was set in the 1950s and was about three people who—Malcolm wasn't totally sure about this—might have witnessed a murder. It was supposed to be like a Hitchcock movie but wasn't. Things that were stretched out for tension were stretched too long, to the point where he got bored and no longer cared. (It was possible those first ten minutes had been really, really important.)

When the scene cut, Malcolm tried again. "So would you mind if I asked him about my mom sometime?"

July finished chewing before leaning over enough that her shoulder touched his. She was still wearing her coat, which he thought was weird. It was wet, and the theater, even up in the booth, wasn't cold. She still didn't look at him, though.

"Why are you asking my permission?" she fake whispered.

"I don't know. He's your family."

"You've known him a lot longer than I have."

Malcolm wasn't sure what he was supposed to say to that, but before he could figure it, she said, "We can go over for dinner this Sunday, if you want."

Malcolm hesitated. "Don't you need to ask first?"

"I'll tell him we want to come. He won't mind."

Malcolm was glad she'd said "we." It would've been weird to go by himself.

"If it's really okay."

"It is."

Malcolm tried to shake out some more Milk Duds. They kept sticking to the box. They were also really hard to chew, but that was the part he liked. It made them last longer, so he could really only get through two boxes in one movie, especially without something to drink. Declan hadn't put a limit on how much candy he and July could have during a film, but more than two movie-sized boxes apiece seemed greedy.

"Did you hear back from your bio-sister yet?" he asked.

Malcolm was getting the hang of the terms July preferred.

She slumped back in her seat. "No, nothing."

"Oh," he said. "Sorry."

"Yeah."

Malcolm didn't say anything else. There didn't seem much more to say. He was genuinely sorry she was disappointed, but also, he kind of wasn't surprised. The whole thing hadn't seemed like it would work out well. Having it not work at all might turn out to be a blessing.

CHAPTER THIRTY-FIVE

After dinner, Carol went to take a bath while Anita cleaned up the kitchen. The apartment didn't have a dishwasher, and it had taken some time to scrape the burned-on cheese out of the old Pyrex baking dish. She might have given up and thrown the whole thing away if the trash weren't already overfull.

When the counters were wiped down and her hands dried, Anita took the top off the pedal-operated can in the corner and tried to wiggle the trash bag free without spilling old napkins and Styrofoam meat trays across the floor. It was not a resounding success. She lost a wadded-up bread bag, an apple core, and a plastic hanger with the hook broken off that had been awkwardly crammed down inside. She'd have been annoyed, but the hanger had been her own doing.

Anita had to lift the bag, which was unusually heavy, almost up to her head to get it out of the extra-tall can. When she dropped it to the floor, it made a distinct *thud*. Holding it from the top, Anita nudged the bottom of the bag with her socked foot. Whatever was in the bottom was solid, sharp-cornered, and responsible for most of the weight. Not relishing the idea of sticking her arm into a week's worth of garbage, she bent down and stretched the bottom of the white bag as taut as she could, trying to see through it.

"You have got to be kidding me!"

No longer reticent, Anita dropped the bag, pulled off her shirt, and shoved her bare arm straight into the stinking, wet, salmonella-laden trash.

. . . .

Anita did not knock. She walked right into the bathroom, all but flinging open the door and brandishing three hardback books, one of which she'd had to pull out of a microwave popcorn bag, which made it slightly greasy and hard to hold on to.

"What the hell is this?" she demanded.

Carol was naked. The water went up over her breasts, but Anita was not the sort of woman to stock bubble bath even if Carol had been the sort to use it.

"Jesus!" she exclaimed, pulling her arms protectively up over her chest. "What are you doing?"

"Making a citizen's arrest."

Anita shook the books in her direction, all of which had library call numbers on the spine and one of which had the pink-and-white-striped tail end of a register receipt roll still between the pages that Anita had been using as a bookmark.

"Did you steal these?"

Carol ignored the question. "Where's your shirt?"

Anita was standing between the tub and the bathroom sink wearing nothing but jeans that cut a little too tightly into her soft abdomen and an ill-fitting beige bra nearly as old as July. Something that might or might not have been barbecue sauce was smeared across her right forearm, and the foil seal off a new bottle of ranch dressing was stuck to her tricep, although she didn't know that yet and wouldn't for an unacceptably long period of time.

"I took it off."

"Yes," Carol agreed.

There was a pause while the discomfort of the situation settled. Anita, who could see Carol's pubic hair beneath the surface of the water, was losing some steam.

"I had to pay twenty-eight dollars and seventy-six cents for this," she said.

"A rip-off."

Carol let her arms drop and her head fall back against the yellow tiled wall. The tub was old, and even Carol, who was not tall, could not straighten her legs out all the way. Her knees poked up out of the water like two little sun-starved islands. The room had been steamy but was starting to cool, the warmth escaping out the open door. Carol noticed but didn't say anything. She didn't really have anything more to say, although she doubted Anita would accept that.

"I think it buys me an explanation," Anita said.

Carol disagreed. "I'll pay you back."

"That's not the point."

"What is the point?"

It did not come out as confrontational as it might have. It was simply a question, albeit one spoken by a woman who was tired and not very interested in the answer.

"Why did you do it?"

"I'm sorry, but that's not your business."

The same straightforward tone. Carol was naked and wet. She had been confronted suddenly by another woman, only somewhat less naked, about what was technically a crime for which the evidence was damning, and she wasn't giving an inch. It occurred to Anita that she would not want to cross this woman in a business deal.

Anita did the only thing she could do. She took one step to her right and sank down on the closed toilet lid, stacking the sullied books on her lap. She wasn't going anywhere. This was her home and her bathroom. Carol was her guest, here only on her say-so. Under the circumstances, she was owed something, and it was not just twenty-eight dollars. Anita was also not a woman anyone should want to cross.

Not that she felt crossed. She did not really care about the money, although she had, at least a little bit, a few minutes ago. What she cared about now was Carol and that something was clearly very wrong.

Anita propped her forearms on top of the books and laced her fingers.

"July will be back in less than an hour," she said. "We can talk about this now, or we can talk about it while she's in the room. Your choice."

Carol closed her eyes. She hadn't moved. Nothing in the room did but for two sets of lungs expanding and contracting. Anita expected she had her answer and would have to sit on that hard toilet lid for much longer than anyone would care to.

The light over the mirror was on. If Carol had preferred to take her baths in the dark, Anita never would've seen the tears start to roll down her cheeks. There was no sound and no movement. Only a steady, wet flow like the woman in front of her—who had somehow become a friend, maybe her best friend—had sprung a serious leak.

Even under threat of July's presence, it took a while for Carol to tell her.

"I didn't suspect for one second," she said after laying out the facts. "I was all puffed up. You should've seen me."

Carol's arms were still limp in the water by her sides. She was speaking to the knobs and spigot that jutted out from the wall above her feet. They were easier to look at than Anita.

"I bought every newspaper I could find with my name in it. I printed reviews off the internet and left them out for my kids to read. I knew they didn't really care, but it was proof. I was somebody who had done something more than keep house."

She shifted, trying to find a new position for her sit bones, which, despite their padding, were starting to grind into the old porcelain. The water, which was cooling, moved around her. One of her nipples responded to the dropping temperature, and one did not.

Anita had been quiet while she talked, but Carol didn't want to talk anymore. "This is the part where you say there's nothing wrong with only keeping house," she said.

Anita, who had been hunched over, sat up, lifting the stack of books off her knees and sitting them on the floor by her feet. She brought her shoulder blades together and leaned back, trying to work out some of the kinks. Her feet were starting to go numb, which happened sometimes whenever she sat too long on the toilet, although it was usually because she'd read far longer than nature had required.

Little relieved by the adjustments, she put her palms flat on her knees and let out a long breath. "I agree with Henry."

"What?" Carol pushed up. Her back, no longer sloped against the tub, was painfully straight.

"You have another chance."

"I can't publish after this!"

"Why not?"

"Do you know what would happen if people found out?"

"Who's going to find out?"

Carol leaned forward and pulled the bath plug. "Nothing here stays quiet forever," she said over the suck and gurgle of the drain.

"Plenty of things do."

Carol stood up and reached for the sea-foam-green towel she'd left folded on the bath mat. Her hair was still up. Only a few stray pieces at the nape of her neck had gotten wet. She dried quickly and a little roughly and then wrapped the terry around herself. There was barely enough to cover her boobs and her bottom at the same time.

"Name one thing," she said.

"I can't. If I could, it wouldn't be a secret."

Anita saw the muscle in Carol's jaw squeeze, and she knew, if Carol could have, she would've sent Anita to her room for sass.

"The only reason you know," Anita went on, "is because Henry was fool enough to keep the boxes."

Carol's look did not soften.

"So we get rid of them," Anita said.

"How?"

"What do you mean, 'how'?"

"I can barely lift one of those boxes on flat ground. I certainly can't get them out of the attic, and neither can Henry anymore."

"He got them up there."

"That was twenty years ago. He is not the man he was, believe me. It would kill him."

"We could—"

Carol held up one hand, the other over her left breast holding her towel closed. "Stop. Please. I appreciate that you want to help, but the boxes aren't the problem. All I want is to put this in the past. Just forget it."

CHAPTER THIRTY-SIX

D ylan had shoved his one button-down shirt into his backpack that morning and forged a note from his mom saying he could get off the school bus at the stop behind Connor's Pharmacy. When the bus pulled away, he stepped into the alley, yanked off his coat and the old sweatshirt under it—the one that had, like, five holes in it. The dress shirt had gotten wrinkled in his bag. He put it on anyway, but when he went to do up the cuffs, they were an inch shorter than they had been last time he'd worn it.

"Shit," he said.

He reached for the top button, ready to pull the whole thing off, snapping threads as he went. He'd shove it all back in his bag and walk the forty-five minutes home from here, feeling like the idiot he was. He couldn't do this. This wasn't for him.

"Dylan?"

He looked up. Mrs. Connor had the back door of the building open, a bulging black trash bag in one hand. He mumbled a hello, and she put her free hand on her ample hip. Even though it was still cold, she was wearing a flowered dress that screamed spring and a pair of purple leggings underneath it. On her feet were ankle socks and a pair of red plastic clogs.

"That shirt does a million things for you," she said.

Dylan didn't know what that meant and must've looked it.

"The blue brings out your eyes and freshens up your complexion."

Never in his life had someone mentioned Dylan's complexion, at least not in a good way.

"Where are you going looking so handsome?"

Coming out her mouth, it didn't sound mocking.

"Job interview," he said. "It's probably stupid."

"Doesn't sound stupid to me," she said. "I think it makes a whole lot of sense."

"It's wrinkled," he said, looking down at himself and realizing for the first time that the shirt looked ridiculous with his jeans, which were worn and the kind of dirty that you couldn't get out.

"Oh, I can fix that," she said. "Come on in."

Mrs. Connor dropped the sack of trash into the bin next to the back steps and waved him toward her.

Dylan felt a flush start to creep up his neck and reached up to rub his head. Part of him, maybe all of him, wanted to disappear into the sidewalk.

"Come on," she said again, coaxing, like he was an alley cat that needed feeding.

He gave up and went to her.

Inside, she headed down one of the packed pharmacy aisles, the one with all the laundry stuff. She crouched down and pulled a pearl-colored bottle off a low shelf. She turned the nozzle to ON, then looked over her shoulder at him and gave a wink. "Don't tell," she said.

She was talking to the right person. Dylan never told anyone anything.

"Now close your eyes," she said.

That made him nervous, but if there was anyone in town he

trusted, it was Mrs. Connor. He did what she said. A spray of cold water hit him square in the chest, and his eyes flew open. What the—

"Hold still," she instructed. She was spraying the shirt with him in it, reaching for his arms and pulling on the sleeves, trying to get it all over. "Turn around," she said.

The spray hit his back. Not water. He could smell it now, sort of like flowers but not real flowers.

"That should do," she said.

He turned around, and she was putting the bottle back on the shelf. His shirt was now too small, too wrinkled, and half wet, which didn't seem like a whole lot of improvement to him.

"Next aisle," she said, and gave him a gentle shove in the right direction when he hesitated.

Mrs. Connor took a blow-dryer off a shelf and guided him to a back corner, where she unboxed it and plugged it in. She turned the dryer on him, pulling the fabric tight as she went and smoothing it with her hands, sometimes handing the dryer to him so she could do a proper job of it. When all the wet spots were dry, she turned it off, and he looked down at himself. The wrinkles were gone.

"Now," she said, wrapping up the cord and nestling the appliance back into its box, "let's just do this."

She reached for his sleeve, which was still hovering well above his wrist bones, and started carefully rolling it up, more like she was folding something real neat, like a letter, than the way he'd have done it. She stopped when it was just below his elbow and then went to work on the other side.

"Now tuck it in," she instructed, and he did what he was told.

When he looked up, she was beaming at him. "Now that's a young man about to get a job," she said, and for the first time, Dylan believed it.

. . . .

Tiny was seriously considering throwing something, and not something small either. She'd thrown more than her share of towels, spatulas, and, quite recently, a whole blueberry pie that had the audacity not to set right. But none of those things had done one bit of good, and now she realized she'd been thinking too small. Maybe if she ripped the microwave right off the counter and flung it over the display case, things would start to improve. Maybe if she set it on fire first.

At this very moment, she had a sink that was overflowing with dishes, a dishwasher that had broken, and an oven that was acting funny. There was a stack of special orders she hadn't touched, a line of customers almost to the door, and that afternoon, when she'd gone to get her mail, there'd been a letter from the IRS. Probably the microwave wasn't going to be enough. Probably what needed throwing, she couldn't pick up.

Tiny was so angry that it was making a funny feeling behind her eyeballs, a feeling that—and she hoped she was mistaken about this—might mean she was close to crying.

When the bell over the door rang, she didn't look over. She kept right on with what she was doing—taking orders, flinging cookies into paper sacks, banging on the espresso machine, and making change. When she did look up, what she saw was one of Felicia's boys in his church shirt, shifting his weight from foot to foot like he was going to pee.

Tiny, along with the rest of Ebey's End, tended to think of Felicia's boys as interchangeable: four stairstepped versions all stamped out with the same pale skin, buzz cut, and dirty jeans. When together, as they often were, one was usually in a headlock. They made trouble, but not, it should be said, the worst sort of trouble. What they got into could pretty much always be cleaned up and apologized for, and there was still the possibility some or all of them would grow out of it. Not all boys did, of course, but Tiny would've set decent odds, mostly due to Felicia.

When Dylan made it to the front of the line, Tiny let her eyes flick up and over him.

"Dressed up," she said, pouring milk into the little metal frothing jug for Lynette's cappuccino.

"Yeah, well," he said, touching the rolled-up sleeves self-consciously. Then he cleared his throat and set his shoulders. "Uh . . . Mrs. Tiny?"

She released the steam wand, letting it clear itself with a burst of hot air that hissed loudly and hid her snort. "Ms.," she said.

(Tiny had, in fact, been married once. But she was fairly certain no one on the island knew that. There were still some secrets, after all.)

He nodded and swallowed. "Ms. Tiny." Deep breath. "July-said-I-should-come-talk-to-you-about-the-job."

The words ran out of his mouth like a mob trying to push through a door, and Tiny had to give her brain time to parse what he was on about.

"What job?" Tiny genuinely could not imagine.

Dylan pointed at the sign taped to her front window, the one that had been there so long the edges were beginning to curl.

July had, in fact, come running through the door half an hour before like she was late for her own wedding. Tiny'd watched as the girl had scanned the room and then let out a breath, her shoulders falling down away from her ears, before she'd calmly joined the back of the queue. Tiny looked over to where the girl sat now, a textbook propped open in front of her that she was only pretending to read.

Tiny knew there was something different about July. Maybe something had tickled the back of her mind before the Band-Aid Incident, but that was the thing that had sealed it.

"Trust me," the girl had said, pressing the half-empty box of bandages into Tiny's hands at the theater's grand opening.

That had been weird enough on its own, but then two things had happened. The first was that Tiny would see that damn chicken of Gordy's in hell. And second, she still had several of those bandages, which had turned out to be a godsend, wrapped around her right index finger. Chicken bites, as it turns out, don't heal up as fast as you'd want.

So when July had come in that afternoon acting squirrely, Tiny had taken note.

"July told you. To ask me. About a job."

It was one sentence, but the way Tiny said it, it didn't sound that way. It sounded like she was making fun of him, and every worry Dylan had had standing behind the pharmacy in his stupid, mismatched clothes came flooding back. He felt the tips of his ears flame. He felt ashamed, and feeling ashamed made him angry, and feeling angry made him want to tear into something. He balled up his hands and shoved them into the pockets of his jeans.

"You know what," he said, all diffidence gone. "Never mind."

Tiny, who knew a little something about shame, held up a chicken-bit hand before he could walk away. "Cool your temper now."

Dylan thought that was pretty rich coming from her, but he stayed quiet.

There might have been those in town who, if asked, would've said one of Felicia's boys was the perfect person to work for Tiny. They were the only ones who could match her, ornery for ornery, and therefore might be convinced not to quit. But whatever Tiny had to say on the matter, he didn't get to hear. Just as she opened her mouth, a terrible crash turned every head toward the back booth.

July, who did at least try to look sheepish, was absolutely surrounded by bits of broken crockery and glass, ruined food, spilled drinks, and silverware. Her order had been unusually large and specific: one latte with a saucer and a spoon, a piece of chocolate pie with fork and knife, a cookie on a separate plate, and a glass of water. None of which she'd touched and all of which was now on the floor.

Dylan's eyes went from the mess to Tiny, who looked not so much angry as done. If she had taken off her apron and walked out the door and all the way to the ferry and from the ferry to Maine, he would not have been surprised. His mother got the same look sometimes.

"I got it," he said, the same way he did at home when things got out of hand.

He reached across the counter and grabbed Tiny's towel, snagging the trash can from by the door on his way. Next thing anyone knew, he was down on his haunches, gathering up the broken bits and wiping up the worst of the smeared chocolate and spilled drinks.

July crouched down beside him with her back to Tiny.

"How's it going?" she whispered.

He started to look behind himself and then didn't. "She doesn't want me."

July did look over. People at other tables had mostly gone back to their own business, and Tiny was pouring a cup of coffee, one eye on the cup and one eye on Dylan.

"I think she's changing her mind," July said. "Keep it up."

"How?"

"Tiny needs help, but she won't ask for it. You just have to start doing things so she doesn't have to ask. Then it's like she's letting you."

Dylan snorted, dropping the last of the glass into the trash and carefully folding over the towel so the cleanest part was on the outside. He bent and reached under the table to get to the last bit of spilled pie.

"She sounds like my mom," he said.

"Then you know what to do," July said, sliding back into her seat and pulling her history book closer.

Dylan stood up, took a breath, and then, chancing a look over his shoulder, went to go bus some tables.

This time it was Tiny who stayed quiet.

CHAPTER THIRTY-SEVEN

Malcolm and July weren't even halfway up the front walk before Mack opened the door. Gideon and Samson squeezed
around him, tails whapping like windshield wipers turned
to high in a storm.

"They heard you pull up," Mack said. "'Bout lost their minds."

The dogs knew better than to run off the porch, but they scooted
right up to the edge, their toenails hanging off, trying to be the first
in line for sniffs and scratches.

"Thank you for having us over, Mr. Odom."

July let Malcolm make the pleasantries for both of them. She had
dropped the grocery sacks and was sitting on the single step that led
up to the porch, a dog on either side of her. She was scratching under collars and behind ears. Samson and Gideon leaned into her, the
weight of them forcing her to lean back. Every inch she gave, they
took, pressing forward as she moved back more and more until her
elbows were on the cold ground behind her.

"Hey!" Mack called to them. "Knock that off."

"I want you both to come home with me," she said, getting a mouthful of fur as Gideon attempted to climb into her lap.

"I'd pack their bags in a heartbeat," Mack lied. "But Anita would skin me alive."

That last part was true, but July still imagined sleeping with both of them piled into the bed around her. Sometimes she woke up in the middle of the night and stayed awake, choosing to read one of the library books Jim had recommended with a flashlight rather than face her dreams.

Gideon bumped her gently with his forehead. The hot *pant-pant* of his breath in her face smelled like dry kibble. She moved her scratches to his chest, and he let his tongue loll. The corners of his mouth turned up and his eyes drooped. She pressed her face into his neck.

"Please," July said. "Just for one night."

"We can talk about it later," Mack said, which she knew was a no, but she wasn't planning on giving up.

"Everybody inside before you catch a cold," he said.

July kicked off her shoes and padded into the kitchen to unload the food. Both dogs sighed and dropped to the floor at her feet. Malcolm's presence had been accepted on a probationary basis, and they didn't move when he edged around them.

Mack took his usual spot at the kitchen table, parking the walker at his side.

"You want tea?" July asked, already opening up the refrigerator and pulling out the plastic pitcher he kept there.

"Thank you," he said when she put the glass in front of him, ice halfway up like he liked.

July and Malcolm had done the shopping together. Neither was a great cook, but both had been left to fend for themselves in the wake of working parents, which made them better than some. Standing in front of the meat counter, which was unoccupied, July had said she could make spaghetti or crunchy tacos. Malcolm could make loaded baked potatoes or bacon-and-egg sandwiches on those biscuits that exploded out of the cardboard tubes. July would have voted for the sandwiches herself, but they both figured Mack would rather have the tacos.

In the kitchen, Malcolm was opening all the cabinets looking for cereal bowls to fill with shredded lettuce and the overly strong onion he would dice too big. July had a skillet on the stove and was ripping the plastic off a tray of ground beef—80/20, Mack guessed from his vantage point.

When July had told him they were coming over for dinner, she hadn't said why, and he hadn't asked. She came with Anita at least once a week, sometimes more. He'd started keeping peanut-butter-flavored cereal in the cabinet after she told him it was her favorite dessert, and she usually had a bowl—sometimes two—after they'd finished dinner. She'd clear the table while Anita rinsed the dishes. Then the girl would take her cereal to the living room and turn on the television, the dogs piled around her.

Mack would've fed her fifteen bowls to keep her there where she was, paying him no mind with whatever reality show nonsense she watched jabbering in the background. It wasn't so different from when Anita was her age, and he missed those times, when they were all together and Connie was alive. It hadn't been anything anyone else would've thought special. They worked six days a week, and one or the other of them was nearly always running downstairs for a shift, scheduled or not. But one or the other of them was nearly always with Anita, too, whether it was upstairs or down. They'd been close, and they'd stayed close. And when he looked back with nearly his whole life behind him, that was the thing of which he was most proud.

July had been a surprise, but now that she was here, it made him gladder than anything. So glad he could just about bust. Now Anita could have what he had. It would be harder for her, he knew, in a lot of ways. The whole situation was as mixed-up as anything, but when July ate her cereal in front of his TV, he thought maybe it would be all right. At first, he hadn't thought so. It had kept him up nights, and he wasn't the only one. But now he could see a path through. So long as everybody who had a script stuck to it, which was why Mack was sitting at the table with ants in his pants.

July came to visit him with Anita. She didn't come by herself, toting two bags of groceries like a little grown-up, and with *that* boy besides. Now she was in his kitchen, overbrowning the meat, and he knew there had to be a reason. She kept glancing over at Malcolm and making big eyes, which made the boy look over at Mack and sweat.

The Liddle men had always been heavy sweaters. Half the time, by the end of services, Chet looked like he'd walked through somebody's sprinkler. Now here was Malcolm wearing that black T-shirt. All Mack had to do was squint, and he could see the short-sleeved, black button-up the boy's father wore every day of his life, topped off with that white collar. Mack figured he slept in it, figured he'd conceived that boy in it.

Malcolm jerked his hand away from the knife he was using to mangle an out-of-season tomato that didn't even pretend to be red. He looked down at his fingers, apparently found them intact, and shook them hard before going back in. Mack imagined a slow bleed oozing into the produce, and he couldn't keep quiet any longer.

"All right, you two," he said, slapping his hand on the glass-topped table. "Say whatever it is you've come here to say so we can do the eating in peace."

July turned the heat off the skillet. It had been up on high the whole time by the sound of things. She moved it to a cold burner and left the plastic spatula sitting inside, threatening to melt against the bottom of the pan. Malcolm stopped mangling vegetables and looked over at her like he needed permission, which made Mack so damn impatient he could hardly keep from saying something he shouldn't.

"I was talking to Mrs. Bell the other day, and she said you and my mom were friends."

It had not and would not occur to Malcolm that the reason he'd talked to Mrs. Bell was because July was not where she said she'd be when she said she'd be there. It definitely did not occur to him that she might have done that on purpose.

Mack shifted in his chair, and Samson lifted his head up off his paws, ears and nose alert.

"I knew her."

July, who'd been opening a box of taco shells, caught the shift in her uncle's words. She paused and looked sideways toward Malcolm, but he didn't react.

"I was just wondering if you could tell me about her."

Mack twisted his iced tea glass around inside the sweat circle it had made on the table. There were coasters around someplace, but he hardly ever used them.

"I'm sure your father could tell you a lot more than I could."

"Yeah, but . . ." Malcolm deflated.

"But what?" Mack asked.

Malcolm stayed quiet, and Mack thought he was going to have to shake it out of him. "Go on."

Malcolm looked down at the cutting board and then back at Mack.

"It's like, if I died, and you asked my dad about me, he'd tell you his version of me, right? And maybe that's not wrong, but if you asked July, she'd tell you something really different. And then, if you asked my teachers, you'd get something else, and on and on. Like collecting pieces, right? But every time I ask about my mom, it's like it's too sad and people don't want to talk about her, or they only want to say these, like, platitude things. And it's already been a long time, so everything everyone did know they're forgetting. Every single day more of her is gone. And it's just . . ." Malcolm looked lost. "I've only got, like, one piece."

Mack didn't speak right away, and there was a tightness in the air even the dogs could feel. Finally, he said, "Finish what you're doing there, and we can talk about it."

Malcolm nodded. "Thank you."

He'd picked his knife back up and turned to the cutting board before Mack said, "But if you're looking for the side of her *you'd* have seen, I can't give you that. Nobody can."

Malcolm didn't look up from his work. "I know."

There was a toughness in his voice then that almost made Mack respect him.

July poured an envelope of "taco spice" over the slightly burned meat, and Malcolm put the hacked bits of onion, lettuce, and tomato into separate cereal bowls. They carried it all over to the table, laying it out with a bottle of mild taco sauce, a package of pre-shredded cheese, and the box of shells neither of them had thought to warm up.

Mack didn't object. He'd been more or less living on bologna sandwiches made with that pink sandwich spread Anita complained was harder and harder to get. Most times, he didn't even bother with lettuce, just ate it as is with a handful of plain Ruffles chips on the side of the plate. Each night, before he went to bed, he washed the knife, the plate, and his glass by hand. Wasn't worth turning on the dishwasher only for that. If he saved up every dish he dirtied the whole week, there might not have been enough, which saddened him in a way he couldn't quite articulate and sure as hell wasn't going to try. Who would he even tell? Doc wouldn't understand. He still had Declan at home, and now, with the theater, he probably always would. Bill's wife was alive and well. Chet had Malcolm, at least for a while, and even Jim lived with his sister. Mack had had to replace his family, first his wife and then his daughter, with dogs. It was a good thing he and Connie hadn't had more children; Mack would've ended up with a goddamn pack.

The kids fetched place mats, plates, and silverware, forgot the napkins and had to go back, but it turned out Mack had forgotten to buy napkins last time he was at the store, so Malcolm took the roll of paper towels off the dowel instead.

"The pastor never buys napkins," he said, setting it down in the center of the table with the taco fixings. "We just use these. Same with Kleenex. We use toilet paper. He says it's the same thing."

Both kids had the good manners to let Mack fill his plate first, which he appreciated. Not because he cared much, but because he figured, in some unknown future, manners like that would serve them.

He took two shells and started talking while he filled them. "I met your mom before your dad did. She got off the ferry and came straight into the store, that big hiking pack of hers on her back. I swear that thing was magic. She had everything in the world in there, more than you'd ever think could possibly fit, and she could reach right in and find anything without even having to look."

When Mack finished assembling his tacos, July started on hers. Malcolm didn't. Later, she'd poke him in the ribs and nod down at his still-empty plate to remind him to eat.

"She'd come to study the eagles," Malcolm said, trying to push things along.

Mack nodded and swallowed his bite. "Except the organization she was working for—some nonprofit hooked up with a university or some such—had screwed up. They were supposed to have found her some short-term rental place to stay in, but the person in charge of that had quit, and nobody told the new guy anything about it. So your mom—not your mom yet, of course," Mack said, gesturing with his taco, some of the filling falling out onto the plate, "shows up with nothing but the pack. Nowhere to go, nothing."

"I didn't know that," Malcolm said.

"Mmm-hmm," Mack said, looking pleased. "I was working the register that afternoon, and I started up a conversation."

Both kids knew Mack would have started up a conversation with a lamppost if it were new in town.

"And she tells me what happened. Now, this was twenty years ago. Ebey's End wasn't nearly so built up then as it is now."

July felt her eyebrows inch toward her hairline. Even today, there wasn't a single stoplight on the island.

"So, I picked up the phone and called over to Aaron, who had a secondhand shop with a little clock-repair business in the back. This was where Tiny's is now. Aaron and them had a farm, too—inherited it from his wife's people—so they weren't using the living space above the shop for anything but storage. Your mom didn't mind scooting around a few boxes, so fifteen minutes after buying a box of granola and a carton of milk from me, she was moving in."

Malcolm looked like he'd hit the RECORD button in his brain. July was certain, if she asked him two months from now, he'd be able to recite every word Mack said. That kind of attention didn't leave a lot of space for analysis, but July had room in her own mind for listening, chewing, and thinking. Who, she wondered, if they don't have a place to stay, buys a carton of milk? She glanced at Malcolm to see if he was thinking the same thing, but he wasn't. She could tell. But she couldn't help thinking it and thinking about those pencils he'd mentioned, the ones that always appeared in his lunch box at just the right time.

"That's how you got to be friends?" Malcolm asked.

Mack had finished off his two tacos. He didn't eat as much these days as he once had, but with a little extra sauce to cover over the burned parts, the tacos weren't bad. He reached for another shell.

"She came into the store every few days after that, and pretty soon she was looking for volunteers to help with the fieldwork she was doing. Your mom knew everything there was to know about birds, and she could spot them like nothing I ever saw. We'd be walking some trail, and she'd freeze right in front of me and point. I couldn't see a damn thing until it took flight, but sure enough, there'd be some winged creature tucked into the crook of a branch thirty yards off. It was like she could sense them out there."

July could see Malcolm picturing it.

"Did you talk while you worked?"

Mack shook his head. "Not much. You had to stay pretty quiet to keep from scaring the birds."

That was a disappointment. Malcolm wanted more. He would always want more. Losing his mother had opened up a hole in him that had no bottom.

Mack went on, describing her as best he could. There didn't seem much harm in that. Pam had been smart—even smarter than she let on, which was pretty damn smart to start with—and she had one of those senses of humor that made it so it didn't seem like she was telling a joke until half a beat later. Sometimes he'd only cotton to a punch line an hour after she'd told it, but she never made him feel silly about it. She'd just smile and wink like they were in on it together.

Mack didn't say he'd been surprised as all hell when she'd taken up with Chet. Not that Chet didn't have his positive points. He did a good job running the church, which wasn't easy. Even aside from the fact it left him without two cents to rub together, the politics of the place were and had always been ridiculous. Couldn't move a damn trash can without pissing somebody off. And it wasn't like preaching was all Chet did. It wasn't a quarter of it. The whole town would damn near collapse without him, and folks pretty well knew that.

Still and all, Mack never had been able to square the two of them together. It was like a muskrat taking up with a fish, but the only person he ever heard say so was Connie and only in private. Maybe that was the way of it, everybody saying but not anywhere anybody else could hear. And in any case, it wasn't their business. Pam and Chet got to courting, and it seemed like fifteen minutes later they were getting married. She kept up with her fieldwork, even when she wasn't always getting paid for it. The eagles had become a passion for her, and she could get herself twelve kinds of worked up when talking about all the human-type activities that were killing them off. That was the part Mack told the boy about. He stretched it out as much as he could, throwing in every detail he could remember. By the time he'd finished, even the dogs had wandered off.

Mack knew Anita would be calling soon, wanting to know where July was.

"Other people helped her, too, right?" Malcolm asked, not paying any attention to the time.

"Oh, sure. Quite a few over the years. I don't know if she ever really needed any of us, but I got the impression she liked the company. There aren't many times in a life you can sit with somebody not talking. There's a peacefulness to it."

Neither of the young people commented on the irony of that coming out of Mack's mouth.

"Mrs. Bell said Declan worked with my mom for his senior project."

Mack picked up his paper towel napkin and balled it up, tossing it into the middle of his plate. "May have done. A fair number of kids did."

"I thought I'd talk to him next."

"I wouldn't."

That last sentence was like a string breaking in the middle of a violin solo. Malcolm blinked. "Why not?"

"He won't know anything."

Mack pushed up from the table. Malcolm still had three-quarters of a taco on his plate. Later, he'd be so hungry he'd eat half a loaf of bread off the parsonage counter, not even bothering with margarine or a plate.

"It's late. You kids better get on the road before your parents start worrying."

"The pastor never worries," Malcolm said.

"Like hell he doesn't," Mack countered, setting his dirty plate on the little padded seat of his walker to push into the kitchen.

Malcolm stood, feeling stung. "We'll clean up," he said, grabbing for as many bowls and plates as he could carry at one time.

Mack wanted to object, but he didn't have it in him to clean the kitchen, the state it was in. He let them at it. Nobody said too much, and within fifteen minutes, they were doing their goodbyes.

After they left, Mack sank back down into his seat at the table. There were crumbs all over the counter and water splashed across creation. The place mats were still out, and later, when he got up to get himself a glass of water, he'd find the sink full of dinner's cast-off food, but he was too busy thinking about the past to worry over the present.

CHAPTER THIRTY-EIGHT

There's something weird with the electric bill," Sarah's husband said.

He'd just gotten home from work and had his head in the cupboard. Sarah was mixing up pancake batter from a box. Dinner would be done in less than thirty minutes, but he came out with a box of spicy Cheez-Its anyway. Ariel had mangled the box trying to open them and, after one, had declared them "disgusting." That had been three weeks ago, so now they sat on a shelf slowly going stale, which was the only reason Sarah didn't complain about him eating them. They threw out so much food it was criminal. She blamed the kids. She was certain this had not been true before they had kids.

"Weird how?"

"Weird wrong."

"So, call them."

"I was hoping you could take a look at it first. I forwarded it to your email."

"Fine," she said, which it wasn't.

"Also, the check-engine light came on this morning."

Sarah didn't even answer him.

Before they'd had kids, coming home from work had signaled the end of work. Now it was the beginning. Dinner was no longer eaten on the couch watching whatever violent TV show they'd DVR'd earlier in the week. (Those had been the days of DVR.) Now dinner had to be eaten at the table so that everyone could talk about their day, even though none of them—not even Jack—wanted to. The forced togetherness led to whining and arguments, which segued into homework time, which was more whining and arguments, then bath—ditto whining and arguments—and finally pajamas and bed.

Sarah and Kurt alternated kids each night. She did stories and back rubs with Jack while Kurt took Ariel. Then, the next night, they switched, which sounded a lot more organized than it was because the kids shared a room but were too different in age and temperament to share a bedtime routine. Sarah had never had to share a room with Declan, although she did have to share their mother, who was essentially a single parent. Kurt did more with his kids in a month than Doc had done in his entire life, which Sarah tried to remember when he failed to handle a simple billing error without her supervision.

By the time they turned on the sound machine and the sleepy-time clock, which was the opposite of an alarm, telling Jack, who would otherwise get up at 4:30 in the morning, when to stay in bed, all Sarah wanted was to go to sleep. Not that she could. There was always something. That night it was the electric bill.

She found her laptop, which was almost ten years old, shoved under her side of the bed, where she'd put it after a late night spent shopping for kids' rain boots. (Ariel had outgrown hers in the middle of the season.) The battery had twenty-seven percent left, which she knew from experience would fall rapidly and somewhat unpredictably. She had no idea where the charger was. It had almost certainly been cannibalized, the power brick separated from the cord, each now attached to some other device that belonged to one of the other three people in her house. The size of it—smaller than most two-bedroom apartments—should have made it easier to find things, but that would only have been true if the number of things inside the space was proportionate to the space, which had stopped being true the moment Sarah had gotten pregnant.

It only took eight minutes to figure out the electric bill, six of those minutes dedicated to typing in the nine different passwords the two of them used for everything, trying to figure out if the ones that were wrong were wrong or if she'd made a typo because there was no "show password" option.

"You didn't pay the bill last month."

"What?" Kurt was in his boxer shorts, digging through the hamper for the pair of old sweats he usually slept in.

"It's twice the amount because you didn't pay last month's bill, and now there's a fee."

"I paid it!"

"It says you didn't."

"I'm sure I paid it."

"Well, cross-reference the credit card, then. If you did pay it, call customer service."

She closed the power company tab on her browser. She would not do the rest for him. Bills were supposed to be his chore, and there was no way she was going to let him make it hers just by screwing up.

The next open tab was her email. She deleted Kurt's forwarded message and went on deleting. She had more than three hundred unread messages, almost all of them some version of "Don't miss out!" or "80% off! President's Day Clearance!" Halfway down, she found the email from Declan, subject line "Theater Info." She didn't open it, but she didn't delete it either. Deleting it felt like a decision, and she was done making decisions that night.

Kurt found his pajama bottoms and turned off the light without asking. In the darkened room, her screen glowed pale blue, illuminating her face and chest as she lay back against a small stack of pillows. He cracked the window closest to his side of the bed even though it was freezing outside. Her husband regularly sweated through the sheets, staining them yellow on his side all the way down to the mattress pad. Laundry was her chore, which was why she knew a drop of bleach would ruin a pair of jeans, but a whole bottle was useless against a man's sweat stains.

When she'd deleted all the ads, ignored Declan, and filed a few electronic receipts for tax season, there wasn't much left. She could have turned it all off and gone to sleep. The battery was down to twelve percent, but Sarah had always been a completionist. There were three emails unread. She could do three before the battery ran out. It was like a race, which was almost a game, which was almost not irritating.

She opened the message second to the top of the queue. It was from the ancestry website she'd signed up for two years ago. Her mother-in-law had sent her a DNA test for Christmas. Sarah had not been particularly interested in donating her most personal data to a corporation to be used for God knew what until the end of all time, but that disinterest had not held up against family peace. The woman wouldn't stop asking her about it, so Sarah had done the test, mailed it in, and, in order to receive the results, had chosen yet another log-in and password.

Sarah had almost deleted the email in the ad purge, but the subject line was just interesting enough—"New Relative Match!"—and the email above it read "Message from Your Match: July H."

"What?" Kurt asked.

He was reading a Terry Pratchett paperback. The weight of the book light threatened to tear off the flimsy cover, but it, along with the light of the screen, was enough to see the storm brewing on his wife's face. (In fairness, there was usually a storm brewing on his wife's face.)

"That DNA site your mom signed me up for"—this wasn't literally true but still factually correct—"it says I have a twenty-five percent match."

"Okay."

Kurt had no idea what that meant. His mother had sent him the same DNA test that she'd sent Sarah. He'd kept it on the dresser for a few months before, without much thought, throwing it into the plastic garbage sack he was dragging around emptying all the waste-baskets into fifteen minutes before the trash truck arrived.

Sarah looked over at him and widened her eyes. He understood he was not going to get to read any more Pratchett that night and sighed.

"Is twenty-five percent good?"

He did not actually care. His general philosophy of relatives was that if he needed to know about them, he would already know about them. And if he didn't, that was for the best.

"Twenty-five percent is a half sibling."

Neither of them spoke while the potential ramifications of that soaked in.

"Maybe it's a mistake," he said.

Kurt also had a general philosophy of unpleasantness, which went along with the one about relatives. If it seemed bad, there was prob-ably a reason why it wasn't that bad, and the most likely reason for that was an error. The world was filled with humans erring con-stantly. Every single person got at least one thing substantively wrong every day. There was no reason to think your bad thing wasn't one of those.

Sarah didn't like the feeling that was starting to spread from her hands up her arms to the rest of her body. She felt shaky like she'd just had a close call on the interstate.

"DNA tests are pretty much never wrong." She didn't actually know this, but she was sure it was true anyway.

"It has to be," Kurt said.

"The person sent me a message."

"What does it say?"

"I haven't read it."

Kurt had been lounging on his own stack of fifteen-year-old pillows, but he was now sitting upright, his book still in his hands but dropped down to his lap, so the light shone on his groin. Even being a mistake, this was interesting.

Sarah didn't actually want to read the message. She wanted to be the person she had been thirty seconds before who was deleting advertisements and racing her battery to sleep. Now she probably did need to find the charging cord and said so.

"I'll get mine." Kurt shoved back the covers. "Don't read it without me," he said as he padded out of their overcrowded bedroom, like this was a new episode of *Succession* and not her actual life.

She didn't read it without him, though. She wanted—needed—the support because something in her stomach told her this was about to be very bad.

Kurt came back with the cord. "Okay, what's it say?"

Opening the email didn't tell her. She had to click on the link, which took her to the website and another round-the-mulberry-bush of password guessing, which finally took her to the site's internal message system. Other than the original "welcome" note she'd never read, the one from July H. was the only message there, bold and black, signaling it was unread.

"They sent it over a week ago," Kurt said.

Sarah didn't answer him. She clicked.

Kurt read over her shoulder. "So, she got the same report you did, the twenty-five percent?"

"Apparently."

The message was short, written by a teenager. (Kurt had paused to do the math. The girl had given her birth year.) The tone was inquiring and upbeat. She had questions and hoped they could talk. Clearly whatever situation she was in was very different from theirs. Simpler. Or maybe it was that she was a kid and hadn't any idea the mess she was stirring up. Kids didn't. And anyway, it might all still be a mistake, he thought.

"Your dad wouldn't do that, would he?"

Kurt wasn't sure what "that" was: An affair in general or unprotected sex in particular? A sperm bank? The thought zapped Kurt like touching his tongue to a nine-volt battery. God, could Doc have been donating sperm? He'd read stories of doctors doing some really crazy stuff, but that was, well, gross.

Doc was old, with a chest that looked like someone had scooped it out and then applied the excess to his stomach. On the two occasions he'd come to visit them—following each of the kids' births—he'd worn a tie. Carol came more often, dressed more casually, and was easier to be around, but he could still see how they had ended up together. They were nothing like his parents. His parents played on the floor with the kids, were happy to eat boxed macaroni and cheese, and wore sweatshirts with old vacation destinations emblazoned across them (BERMUDA, CANCUN, KEY WEST). Sometimes the sweatshirts matched.

"Dad was fucking half the island when I was a kid," Sarah said. Her eyes were still on the screen.

"What?!"

She hushed him. The walls were thin, and if he woke the kids, it was going to be his job to get them back down.

"You never told me that," Kurt whispered.

"Why would I?"

Half the island might have been an exaggeration. Sarah only knew about one affair for sure. That her mother would later move in with that woman was more than Sarah's brain could process.

Kurt leaned back into his pillows and stared across the room. There was a chest of drawers a foot from the bottom of the bed, which was pressed up against a bookcase overflowing with paperbacks, which abutted one of those plastic sets of drawers college students buy at Target. But he didn't see any of it.

"Do you think your mom knows?"

"She knows about the affairs."

"Not about this?"

Sarah wanted to say "Of course not," but she couldn't make the words come out. Maybe her mother did know. Maybe that explained an awful lot of what had been happening recently.

"I don't know," Sarah finally said.

"If she doesn't, are you going to tell her?"

Sarah didn't answer, and when he looked over at her, she didn't have the same assured expression he'd come to see not as an expression but as simply his wife's face.

"I have to, right?"

He couldn't remember the last time Sarah hadn't known what to do, and he definitely couldn't remember the last time she'd brought that unknowing to him. But all Kurt could do was look at his wife, who he did love very much, and give his most sincere shrug.

The openness she'd had a moment before vanished, and she looked away from him.

"What about the girl?" he asked.

"What about her?"

"What are you going to say to her?"

Sarah had her eyes on the screen, and when she spoke, it was as if the answer were written there and she was only reading aloud.

"Nothing."

Kurt blinked. "Really?"

"Really."

"Oh."

Sarah lay awake that night, trying not to look at the clock. Next to her, Kurt slept, but all Sarah could think about was calling her mom and what she would say when she did. The more she thought about it, the worse it made her feel, but keeping the secret wasn't better, only different. In her message, the girl said she'd been adopted. If her mother didn't know, it was possible she wasn't the only one. The more Sarah thought about it, the more probable that seemed.

She pressed her fingers against her closed eyelids. This whole thing was awful. Her parents had never had a *great* marriage. Who did? Like, four people, and Sarah didn't know any of them. A "good enough" marriage was what most people got if they were lucky. How many times had she wondered if she really wanted to stay in her own? God, she imagined getting her own apartment all the time. She wasn't going to *do it*, obviously. They had kids and a mortgage, and none of that would get better or easier split between two crappy, overpriced apartments. So you made do. She made do, and she knew her mother had made do, too. You ignored things you shouldn't because the argument would be worse. You lowered your expectations until getting through the day in good enough shape to do it all again was all you were asking.

They were a whole fucking country of women with kids who were making do, and getting through, and hoping somehow it would, eventually, get better. When the kids were older. When the kids were grown. When the mortgage got paid off. But maybe you never actually got there because things kept happening. Your son turned out to be a fuck-wit. Your husband had an affair. Your husband had an affair and a baby. Your *father* had an affair and a baby, and your mother hadn't held a job since Reagan was in office, and all of it was absolutely going to end up in your lap one way or another. In fact, it already had ended up in Sarah's lap because that baby grew up to get a DNA test and the internet. And so maybe calling her mother first wasn't the way to go. Maybe there was someone she ought to talk to first. Someone who might know exactly who had put that baby up for adoption. Someone it would be easy to call at work because she was always at work. It was her store, after all, and someone had to ring up all those groceries.

CHAPTER THIRTY-NINE

Anita, are you out of apple butter?"

Ms. Akers had been the high school algebra teacher in Anita's day and nearing retirement age then. She'd worn a black sweatshirt she'd covered in puff-painted equations and taught her students their order of operations by writing songs she'd sing in front of the class, accompanying herself on a ukulele. It had been more than twenty-five years since Anita had been her student, and still, every time Ms. Akers walked into the store, Anita started humming to herself: *Parenthesis to exponents, multiply, start on the left . . .*

Anita didn't know what had happened to that sweatshirt. Surely all the sticky bits of puff paint had peeled off in the wash by now, but Ms. Akers still stood as straight as she ever had, her hair shorn nearly to her scalp. She'd always worn it that way, and she'd never married. The rumors had been almost obligatory. Now, with her hair thinning and white, the cut made her look as though she were recovering from chemo, and Anita worried about her.

"Shouldn't be," Anita said. "Top shelf with the other jams right next to the syrup."

"That's where I looked," Ms. Akers said. Then, "Hell-oo there, Mack. What's the news?"

"Nothin' worth knowing. That's for sure."

Mack was spending the morning in the bagger's spot at the check stand with no intention of bagging anything. He'd turned his walker so he could sit on the little padded cushion and had that morning's edition of the *Island Examiner* in front of him. He was flipping through the pages for a second time with thirty more minutes to kill before he'd start his walk toward the diner for lunch.

"Leaving in a bit," he said. "Going over to meet Jim."

Anita looked at her father. Jim had called that morning. He had a stomach bug and needed to cancel. She'd told her dad about the call two hours ago.

"No, Dad. Jim's sick, remember?"

Mack blinked and then, after a moment, shook his head. "Right, right."

He went back to his paper without looking at either woman. Anita knew her father's occasional memory lapses embarrassed him. She didn't know if it was a normal part of getting older or some residual effect of the stroke, but when she'd tried to bring it up in the past, he'd been brusque, followed by a standoffishness that could last for days. Having it happen in front of a witness wasn't going to make it any better. Anita turned to Ms. Akers.

"Let me look for that apple butter," she said, and stepped out from behind the register.

They both walked past the Easter display, already picked thin. Ms. Akers was pushing one of the carts. Her weekly haul had been slowly shrinking for a long time. Seven years ago, when the district forced her to retire, the amount she bought halved. It was worrisome, but she kept ticking along. Then, a month ago, she'd stopped buying cat food. Anita hadn't asked, but Constant, the tuxedo stray who'd never fully taken to being an indoor cat, had been old enough to vote.

Anita walked toward jams and jellies, matching her pace to Ms. Akers. The only things in her cart were a bottle of orange juice, a loaf of rye bread, a pound of ground chuck, and a single yellow onion that rolled unimpeded toward the back of the basket as they walked. Despite herself, Anita wished July were there. If Ms. Akers needed something—something other than apple butter—she'd have gladly given it to her. As it was, she reached up to the very top of the shelf, took down the jar, and handed it over.

"Right in front of my face," Ms. Akers said, shaking her head. "Sorry to be a bother."

"You're nothing of the sort."

After Ms. Akers moved on to canned goods, Anita shifted the remaining jars of apple butter to a lower, more accessible shelf, moving the price tag along with it. It was the best she could do, and it was woefully inadequate.

When Anita got back to the check stand, her father was standing by the register holding the receiver.

"Who are you calling?" she asked.

It took him a moment to respond. "No one."

He went to hang the phone up, missed the cradle, and had to do it again. He was gripping the edge of the counter with his other hand, and Anita thought she saw him sway. His walker was down by the bagging area. He didn't usually walk away from it, even on good days.

"Dad?"

He shook his head. "Just a wrong number," he said. "It wasn't anything."

She hadn't heard the phone ring.

"Are you feeling okay?"

"I'm fine."

"You don't look fine. Maybe we should go see Henry."

"I'm not going to him!"

Anita blinked. She couldn't have said the last time her father had raised his voice, if you didn't count yelling at the dogs.

"All right," she said. "Settle down."

Mack was shuffling sideways along the check stand toward his walker. "I'm going out," he said.

Adrenaline was flooding Anita's system, giving everything a sharper edge. There was no way she was letting her father out of her sight. He was pale and confused. He wasn't moving right, and she'd spent enough time in neurology departments over the past couple of years to know a personality change was not a good sign.

"It's pretty slick out there. How about I drive you?"

She didn't want him riled up. His blood pressure would be high as it was, but she did need him in the car. Once he was strapped in, she could take him anywhere she damn well pleased.

"There's nobody to watch the store," he said, which was true and coherent, for which she was grateful.

"I'll close it."

Mack had finally made his way to his walker. He'd hated the thing at first. Now he sought out the familiar feel of the grips and held on tightly.

"My store doesn't close in the middle of the damn day. It never has, and it never will. I said I'm going out, and I'm going out." He nodded over Anita's shoulder. "Ms. Akers is ready to check out."

Anita glanced over to see her old teacher making her straight and steady way to the register. The only thing she'd added to her cart since the apple butter was one individually wrapped Hostess hand pie. Cherry.

When Anita turned back, Mack was wheeling himself toward the front door. The motion sensor found him, and it swooshed open.

Ms. Akers started unloading her basket.

"One moment, please," Anita said. "I need to make a phone call."

Ms. Akers, interested but respectful, nodded. "I'm in no hurry."

Anita picked up the receiver, paused, and turned back to her teacher.

"Could you go to the door and watch my dad? Someone needs to keep an eye on him."

She thought the woman would have questions, but she didn't. No one got to be her age without understanding what time could do to the mind and the body, and no one got to be the teacher she was without strict efficiency. She was at the door before Anita finished dialing Henry's office.

"Shannon," Anita said into the receiver, "go get Henry right now."

. . . .

Mack moved carefully. They'd had a few days of false spring here and there, but winter didn't give up easy. The temperature had dropped overnight, and the sidewalk had frozen in spots. A fall was the last thing he needed.

He stopped under the theater marquee and pulled his cell phone from his pocket. His hand wasn't as steady as he'd have liked it to be, and he'd never really gotten the hang of touch screens. It took a couple of tries before he got the thing dialed.

Just a minute before, while Anita had been helping Ms. Akers, the store phone had rung. Mack had put down the paper and pushed himself to standing. Using the side of the check stand for balance, he'd shuffled over. It was only a few feet, after all, and he'd had a little something to prove. Every time he forgot anything, no matter how small, Anita started acting like his brains were draining out his ears. Yes, he forgot Jim had called. He was old. He had a lot more to remember than she did. It irritated him, and he'd never been particularly good at hiding that sort of thing so he'd walked to the phone on principle.

"Island Grocery," he'd said. "Mack speaking."

"Mr. Odom? Mr. Odom, this is Sarah Bell." She gave her maiden name.

Mack had leaned against the register. He figured she was calling for her mother, but that didn't mean a small chat wasn't in order.

"Sarah, I haven't seen you in an age. Did you come out for Christmas this year?"

"Is Anita there?" she'd asked, ignoring his question.

She'd sounded agitated, but Mack remembered her always sounding agitated. Even as a girl, she'd been the fussy sort, always worried about what other people were doing and tattling about it. That was still how Mack thought of her, probably how most folks on the island did. That was the way of a place like Ebey's End. Your identity got solidified early, and nothing would ever change it.

"Anita stepped away for a bit. Is there something I can help you with?"

She paused, and he thought she was fixing to hang up. But she surprised him.

"Mr. Odom, I have a personal question to ask you, and I need you to trust me that it's important."

Mack's eyebrows had gone up. "Go on."

"Has Anita ever had a baby?"

"A baby!" She might as well have asked if Anita were the pope. "Lord, no," he'd said, and then gave a little laugh.

"Are you sure?" Sarah'd pressed. "There wasn't a time when she went away for a few months maybe?"

Something in the back of Mack's mind had started to ping a warning alarm. He didn't like where these questions were going, and he needed to shut them down.

"What's this all about?"

Sarah had made the call from her office. Her door was closed. She had her work phone pressed to one ear and the other hand over her eyes. Her elbow propped on her desk was the only thing keeping her upright.

"Sarah," Mack had said, "are you crying?"

"My dad's been having affairs. A lot of them, it appears."

Mack's mind tried to put that together. "I don't know about any affairs."

"Yeah, well . . ." Sarah almost laughed. It was the only emotion she hadn't hit yet.

"Whatever this is about," he'd said, speaking to her like she was still a teenager, "I'm sure there's an explanation."

"Jesus Christ!" Sarah couldn't take it. Not for one more second. "He had affairs. I know he had them, and now there's a kid with a DNA test to prove it. So you know, I thought I'd check because Anita is on the list."

Mack had felt like his knees were about to give out on him. "Don't be spreading lies like that, Sarah."

"Ask her if you don't believe me. Hell, ask my mom. She knows all about it."

Mack had felt dizzy. He was afraid to let go of the checkout stand.

"Anita's your age," he'd said, which wasn't true but was near enough.

"Yes, well, it would seem he liked them young."

Sarah had pulled a handful of tissues from the box on her desk, and now she threw them, aiming at the trash basket and missing.

"I don't know where this is coming from."

She could practically hear the wagons circling. It took everything she'd had not to bang the phone against the top of her desk. This would be how it would go. That's how Ebey's End was and how it would always be. It was why she'd left.

"Okay, sure, fine. Goodbye, Mr. Odom."

She'd hung up on him, but Mack had been slow to put the receiver down himself. He'd still been holding it when Anita had come out of the bread aisle toward him.

Standing out there under the theater marquee, Mack listened to the phone on the other end of the line ring. It went on longer than he'd expected. It was a full ten rings before the girl finally picked up.

"Shannon," he said, agitated and short, "is Doc in? I need to see him."

"He's right here," she said without asking why he was calling, which should've been some kind of clue, but Mack wasn't thinking straight. "How fast can you make it?" she asked.

"Fast as I can," he said. "I'm gettin' a ride."

Mack hung up and considered his options. Bill came to mind first but was discarded. Jim was sick. With a breath, Mack dialed the only number left to him. On the second ring, Chet picked up.

. . . .

Anita hung up the phone. "Doc said my dad was calling him."

Henry had put her on hold to talk to Mack before clicking back over to her.

Ms. Akers, who still hadn't taken her eyes off her quarry, nodded. "He made two calls, and now he's waiting."

"Waiting for what?"

"A ride, I'd guess."

Anita turned, headed for the break room and her coat.

"If he wanted you to take him, he wouldn't be standing outside," Ms. Akers said, as calm as someone could be.

"What he wants isn't the point."

Anita's voice was sharp. She was upset and scared. She had been on this ride before, and she knew exactly what was around the next bend.

Ms. Akers shrugged and walked back to her cart, taking up her position by the checkout stand like it was any old day and she wanted to pay.

"You can have the groceries."

"Oh, I know," she said. "But I'm going to pay for them because you need something to occupy your mind."

Anita opened her mouth, and Ms. Akers held up her hand.

"I'm not saying he's fine. I'm saying he's sitting on that little stool of his, watching down the road. Whoever he's waiting for is on their way and close by, you can bet on it. You do what you think is best, but I'd let him go on his own terms. You know where he's headed, and you can call a hundred times in the next fifteen minutes if it makes you feel better."

Anita had been the one to find her father after his stroke. They'd life-flighted him off the island and wouldn't let her go with him. She still didn't remember getting to Seattle. Someone told her Tiny took her.

She took care of her father like her mother would've done it. She did it for her mother, and she did it for Mack, and she did it for herself, too, because no one had ever loved Anita as much as he did, and no one ever would. Maybe no one would ever love her at all because she had already gotten all she deserved to get. Mack had done everything for her. Everything she'd ever needed or wanted, and a million things she never even knew about. Mack would've stopped the earth turning if she'd needed him to. He'd have reversed gravity and made time spin backward. He'd loved Anita so much that sometimes he couldn't even see other people. She was his girl, and it was supposed to be that way always.

Anita had already lost her mother, and she couldn't imagine herself without him, too. Sitting in that hospital, she'd cried so hard, she'd vomited. The nurses had had to call someone to clean it up. She'd known her father was dying. She had been absolutely sure of it, and the grief had felt like an amputation.

He'd recovered, but she hadn't. She couldn't. Anita was not whole, and so nothing else could ever happen to him again because the thing that would get ripped out next would be some vitally important part that was, at this moment, keeping her alive. And before, maybe that would've been okay. Maybe Anita being upright and aboveground wasn't so important. But she had July now. July depended on her, and whatever happened to her could not also happen to July, because her parts had been ripped out, too. She could not grieve anyone else either. So really, what everyone had to understand, especially Mack, was that he had to live forever. He just did.

"Tell you what," said Ms. Akers, looking like maybe she read minds. "Let's me and you stand right in the doorway. It'll stay open, and we can lean out sneaky-like and watch him. And if you don't like what you see, he's right there."

Anita didn't say anything. She wasn't sure if she was supposed to. Ms. Akers walked up to her and with her dry, papery fingers wiped at her cheeks.

"No need for that now," she said, patting Anita's arm. "Come on."

CHAPTER FORTY

Mack told Chet he needed a ride to Doc's. He said it was urgent. Chet did not ask questions. When you had a walker and shuffled your feet like someone perpetually wearing clogs two sizes too big, nobody asked what was wrong. They assumed everything was wrong, and if you said it was urgently wrong, there was almost no one who wouldn't drop everything to avoid being partially to blame for your imminent demise. It took Chet less than five minutes to pick him up. He'd run straight out of the church's trustee meeting, leaving the treasurer and secretary to squabble over the slush fund without supervision. (There was $128.74 remaining for the month, and Chet suspected they would soon come to blows.)

Declan had yet to arrive at his place of business, and the sidewalk in front of the theater was slick and unsalted. Chet came to a too-quick stop and threw himself out of the driver's door in an attempt to catch Mack before he inevitably broke a hip. Mack was fine, but the pastor's foot went out from under him. He'd been wearing the same pair of black dress shoes every day for ten years, and whatever tread they'd once had lived only in memory. His knee hit the sidewalk with a hard crack. His other foot stayed planted, his leg bent, so he appeared to be either proposing or readying himself for the hundred-yard dash.

"You all right?" Mack asked.

"Yep," Chet said, coming up somewhat more slowly than he went down. "I'm fine."

Mack doubted that, but if he'd cracked his patella, they were going to the right place.

Chet reached out toward Mack as though to steady him, but Mack was more afraid he'd pull him down.

"I got it," he said, doing his best to dodge. Chet was limping a little in his pursuit, which reminded Mack of those old monster movies. He supposed that made him the pretty young girl in the high heels.

Doc's office was less than a mile from the store, and Chet didn't touch the brake once, despite three stop signs encouraging otherwise. Pastor's privilege, Mack supposed. Everyone in town, including the constabulary, knew Chet's car, and no one was going to pull him over for anything less than firing live ammunition out the window while driving blindfolded, in reverse. It was simply bad karma to ticket a man wearing a clerical collar. Add that to his friendship with Bill, and the bullets would have to hit somebody before a patrolman would get involved. They made it to Doc's in less than a minute.

Chet got out to fetch Mack's walker from the backseat.

"I'm going in by myself."

"I can help you."

"Don't need help."

Mack had pulled himself up and was headed toward the brown shingled building. Chet hadn't given up and was keeping to Mack's flank despite the shooing motions Mack kept giving him. The pastor was dead set on at least opening the door, but Shannon beat him to it. She was holding it wide before they were all the way across the five-car parking lot.

Chet fell back and called out, "I'll wait in the car."

Mack shooed him again. He'd just as soon the pastor went back to his committee meeting, but he wasn't going to take the time to argue it.

"Doc's waiting for you in Room One," Shannon said.

As far as Mack knew, there wasn't a Room Two, but Shannon always said it like there was, which, on that day, pissed him off. Putting on airs. He walked past her and down the hall without a word.

Inside the exam room, Doc was sitting at the little built-in desk, tapping on a computer. He looked up when Mack opened the door.

"How are you feeling?"

Mack pushed the rest of the way in and closed the door behind himself. He didn't sit. "Someone told me you put hands on my daughter, and I am bringing that to you."

Doc pushed back from the desk. The stool he was on rolled a bit too far on the old linoleum floor.

"Anita called and said you were having symptoms. I sent Mrs. Prince home so I could see you. She was already in the paper gown and everything."

Mack was sorry for her sake, if it was true. Mrs. Prince used a wheelchair and was older than Moses. Nobody was sure what kept her alive, but Mack was there and he had business.

"I said I am bringing what I was told to you, and I am asking you about it."

Doc put his hand on his knee. "Can I at least take your blood pressure?"

"No, you can't."

"Can I ask who said it?"

"It shouldn't matter."

"It matters to me."

In Mack's mind, his daughter should be nothing but that to Doc. Mack would never, not for anything in the world, have laid a hand on Sarah. He'd never even imagined such a thing, not one time, not in the deepest, darkest part of himself. It was not a thing that should need discussing. There were lines you didn't cross. He could feel himself getting red in the face, which was probably what got Doc up and onto his feet.

"Mack, it was a long time ago."

"How long?" His jaw was so tight he didn't know how he got the words out.

"Too long to matter."

Doc reached out a hand like he was going to guide Mack into a seat. Mack let go of his walker and knocked the hand away.

"I asked you how long."

Doc let out a breath like doing the math was an imposition. "I don't know. Twenty-odd years probably."

Twenty-odd years ago, Anita had barely been an adult. Barely legal to drink. She'd still been sleeping in her childhood bed, for God's sake. She'd still been— Mack tried to stop thinking of what she'd been. It was tearing him up, but he couldn't stop seeing her. Because he could do that. He could see her that age. He could see her at every age all the way down to the moment she'd been born, and sometimes he did. Sometimes he'd catch sight of her in the store doing one thing or another, and between blinks his mind would switch the picture, and there in front of him she'd be at six, at sixteen, at twenty.

And how old had Doc been then? Doc, who had taken care of every one of Anita's sore throats and scraped knees since she was big enough to fall down. What had been going on in this room? Mack had trusted him. Connie had trusted him. Carol had trusted him. The whole damn island had trusted him.

That was what he was thinking about when the door went flying open, and Shannon started shouting. It wasn't until then that Mack realized he'd been hitting Doc. He'd been hitting him with his walker over and over again. It wasn't but aluminum and plastic, but he was wielding it as hard as he could. Smashing into his former friend, who was pinned to the far wall, his glasses fallen off and his lip split. He had one arm up to protect his face and the other wrapped around his midsection.

Mack put the walker back down on the floor. He was breathing hard, and his vision was swimming. He was afraid he was going to lose his balance. He was afraid Anita had been right. Maybe he was having symptoms. Maybe something was wrong with him, and if that was true, then he was probably going to go ahead and die because there was no world in which he ever again went to Doc for anything.

Mack turned and faced the door, pushing the metal frame along with him. It wasn't going right, not moving like it used to. Shannon backed away from him, her mouth hanging open. She was a ridiculous woman being ridiculous, but he didn't stop to say so. He didn't do anything but grunt, which sent her flailing back even farther.

Mack shoved the walker ahead of him down the hall, through the waiting room, and out the door. Chet must've been watching for him. He was out of the car and halfway across the lot in a second, limping slightly on his bum knee.

"What did Doc say?" he asked. "Did something happen?"

Mack wanted to ask Chet if he'd known, but he didn't. Anita'd been too young to have known what she was doing, not with Doc full-grown and married, kids of his own even. Mack was disgusted by it, he could admit that, but he didn't blame his daughter. And he wouldn't spread it.

"Take me home," Mack said.

. . . .

Malcolm was awake at eleven o'clock that night when the door to his father's room quietly opened and closed. There was the pop and scrape of the coat closet and then a strange static in the air as his father froze, listening to see if he would stir. Malcolm imagined the parsonage as a stage set, the audience able to see both of them, separated by a single wall, breathing in tandem like nervous rabbits.

Several times, in the past few days, his father had started to say something to him. From the look on his face, Malcolm knew it was serious, and he wondered if it was this. But he hadn't been sure. A full minute passed before Malcolm heard the front door open and close and then that peculiar, weighty silence that meant he was alone. Malcolm didn't get angry often, but he was then. It felt like being lied to. It felt that way because it was.

He heard the car start and the crunch of tires backing out of the parking lot, and he knew Chet wouldn't be back anytime soon. Malcolm sat up and pushed aside the curtain next to his bed. The motion-sensor light around the front of the building was still on, and Malcolm could see a light snow coming down in the yellow haze. It was almost Easter, but winter wouldn't let go of them.

He let the curtain fall closed. If he lay back down now, he knew he'd only listen to every creak and hush of the old building. He thought about where his father was going and then decided not to think about it. He wished he had a cell phone and that July did. He wished they could be awake together. He thought about quitting his "job" at the theater and getting one that paid real money. He wondered if Anita would hire him, and if it would be enough to get a phone, and what, if anything, the pastor would say about it.

Malcolm's stomach growled. Dinner had been "church supper," a box of store-brand macaroni and cheese with a can of tuna and a can of peas mixed in. He'd invented it back in junior high and called it "church supper" because all three ingredients could usually be found in the free pantry. With enough black pepper, it wasn't terrible. He'd eaten two plates sitting at his desk while his father had his at the table, his plate to one side and a yellow legal pad in front of him. Chet liked to have Sunday's sermon written by Friday night, and Malcolm knew better than to interrupt. Before bed, Malcolm had eaten the last of the saltine crackers with margarine and a sprinkle of sugar on top, which had pretty much cleaned out the cupboards.

With as much decisiveness and rebellion as he could manage, Malcolm threw back the comforter and put his feet to the brownish-orange industrial carpet. He had a hole in the heel of his right sock that let the cold seep through. Under the covers, he'd worn a T-shirt and sweatpants, but the temperature in the room—in the whole church—was set to sixty-three degrees. Malcolm grabbed a long-sleeve thermal shirt that was draped over the footboard and an oversized hoodie to put over that. He shoved his feet into a pair of blue velour slippers and dumped everything out of his backpack before carrying it, gaping and empty, out the door.

The free pantry was basically an extra-large walk-in closet, probably intended to hold parishioners' coats. Now it was lined floor to ceiling with shelves covered in floral peel-and-stick paper. He flipped on the light and started on the right, making his way around the shelves from one side to the other. He'd never been allowed to take the things he really wanted. The pastor had always insisted they leave the good stuff for someone else, and Malcolm had a hard time not making up for all of that in one night. Into his backpack, he shoved a box of chocolate Cheerios branded for Valentine's Day, a package of Neapolitan sugar wafer cookies, a jar of crunchy peanut butter, and a loaf of bread, which he decided to carry in his arms so it wouldn't get smashed. At the last minute, he added a canister of powdered lemonade, too, because why not. He remembered to turn off the light before he shut the door, and when he made his way back to the parsonage, he went as fast as he could without breaking into a run.

Inside, he stopped in the kitchen to grab a spoon from the drawer and then went right to his room, stripping off the hoodie and thermal as he went. He left out the wafer cookies and the peanut butter and slid everything else under his bed, pushing it to the very far side where the bed touched the wall.

With his bedside lamp on, Malcolm fetched a George R. R. Martin book from his desk. July had given it to him the day before with a cavalier "You like him, right?" Malcolm did like him, and he liked the book—the actual object—just as much. It was brand-new, the pages crisp and unread. No weird library binding with the plasticky cover. No call-number stickers. No stains from other people's food. No weird smells from other people's houses and bodies.

He opened the jar of peanut butter, peeling off the inner seal and stashing it back in his backpack. (He'd have to dispose of any trash at school.) Then he opened the cookies. The way they were packaged, you'd have to eat all the vanilla wafers to get to the strawberry and then finally the chocolate or the other way around, depending on which end you opened. Malcolm chose to start with vanilla, being that he had the chocolate Cheerios and all.

He stuck his spoon into the peanut butter and pulled out a big scoop, before leaning back against his pillows with his book propped up against his knees. He put the spoon in his mouth. It was salty and oily and delicious. He had to swallow a few times to get it down before biting off half a cookie. White wafer crumbs rained down onto his T-shirt like snow. He expected to feel guilty, but he didn't. Not yet anyway. He wanted to be like everyone else for a couple of hours. Junk food and dragons and staying up late with a book that was actually his. He wanted to forget about his dad, dead moms, and whatever was going on with July. He figured he'd earned it. He figured God would understand.

If Malcolm had been asleep, he'd never have heard it. The *eh-eh-eh* sound was like an alarm clock shoved under a mattress behind a door. He was deep into the book, which was even better than the last one. Things were starting to pick up steam—and get steamy— and he was happy, very happy, to ignore the noise, whatever it was. It didn't seem serious. It wasn't loud enough to be serious, but it was irritating, and that irritation compounded minute after minute as it went on and on. Whatever it was would not stop and, if anything, seemed to be getting more intense. Things were happening—both in the book and, as a consequence, to him—that he did not want to be distracted from. Finally, Malcolm threw back his blanket and shoved his feet back in his slippers to investigate.

When he opened his bedroom door, the sound got louder. He followed it through the living room to the front door of the parsonage. When he opened that, the sound got even louder, which was not the alarming thing. The alarming thing was that he smelled smoke.

Malcolm's heart seized, and he froze for longer than he should have before taking off at a run, winding his way down the narrow halls, past the photo timeline of pastors, the Sunday school and meeting rooms and his father's office. The smell got stronger and stronger the closer he got to the sanctuary. Panicked, he shoved open the double doors, but inside, the pulpit and pews, windows and tapestries were all still and unharmed.

He whirled around and started to retrace his steps. That was when he saw the dark gray wisps escaping from under the door to the basement. Remembering the fire safety drills they'd done in elementary school, he put his hand to the door. It did not feel hot, and he opened it. That was as far as he got. The smoke was too dense. He choked and squinted, his eyes stinging. He couldn't see the stairs in order to go down them, and if there was anything he could do, he was too afraid to do it. He slammed the door and ran to his father's office to dial 9-1-1.

The dispatcher, who knew Malcolm, told him to hang up and evacuate. A fire truck was on its way. Malcolm did hang up, but he didn't run. He stayed there in a burning building long enough to find the old-fashioned address book his father kept in the middle drawer. With his hands shaking, he flipped to the Ds and dialed, messing up once and having to start over.

A middle-of-the-night call is universally understood, and no one, no matter what they might be doing, will fail to answer it. Mr. Daly's voice was even and calm when he picked up. The "hello" the same as if it were two o'clock in the afternoon.

"Tell my dad there's a fire in the church basement. He has to come back right now."

Malcolm all but yelled it into the receiver before slamming it down and running back down the hall and out the front doors of the church, down the concrete steps to the gravel parking lot in nothing but sweatpants and a T-shirt.

It was quiet at first. The sirens on their way but too far still to hear. For a whole minute, there was nothing but his own panting and the falling snow. Then Malcolm's ears caught the distant wail of a siren. People were being woken in their beds and were shuffling to their windows, pushing back the curtains, opening doors, and stepping onto porches. One or two of them might even get in their cars and follow the truck. Those folks near enough to the church would pull on boots and put coats over their nightclothes, making their way on foot, following the flashing red of the lights they could see over the tops of the trees.

But it wasn't a fire truck that Malcolm saw first. A foggy, discolored pair of old headlights swung into the lot, brushing across him and coming to a quick stop. It was only then that Malcolm felt the cold and started to shake. His father threw open the driver's door, turning off the engine at the same time, which rattled its protest.

"Malcolm!" he shouted. "Thank God. Are you okay?"

Malcolm began to cry. He couldn't help it. His father had covered the distance between them and was somehow squeezing him and rubbing his bare arms all at the same time. He smelled like himself but also not like himself, like something Malcolm couldn't yet identify.

The fire truck pulled into the lot, men jumping out and down and swarming around, the lights and sounds overwhelming and dizzy-making. Chet grabbed hold of his son and pulled him farther from the building, out of the way of both the work and the harm. He steered him toward the car, old and worn but comforting and familiar. He opened the passenger door, and Malcolm slid in, his body shaking.

On the other side, his father got in, starting up the engine. He reached for the knob and turned the heat up as high as it would go. "I'm so sorry I wasn't here."

"The fire alarms didn't go off," Malcolm said, his voice still stuffy with tears.

"What?" The pastor blanched, reached a hand toward his son, and then glanced into the backseat.

Malcolm followed his eyes. Directly behind him, his gray hair neat, his eyes sad but gentle, was Preston Daly. His arms and legs were folded into the tight space. He looked uncomfortable but uncomplaining. He wore, Malcolm saw, a T-shirt and sweatpants, too. Malcolm had never seen the banker in anything but a suit. He'd even worn one to the church's summer barbecue.

"Hello, Malcolm," he said. "I'm very relieved you're not hurt."

Malcolm opened his mouth, but for everything he knew—or thought he knew—he couldn't manage to say anything.

"There's something we need to tell you," Chet started, but that was as far as he got. There was a fireman on the other side of the driver's window, bent down and knocking against the glass with one knuckle.

The pastor jumped and then reached for the door handle. When the door opened, the smell of smoke rushed in.

Malcolm and Mr. Daly watched as the pastor was escorted toward the building. The flashing lights changed the color of everything: the church, the gravel, the falling snow, and the two men, who disappeared behind the fire truck.

Malcolm was having trouble holding everything in his mind at the same time. He'd heard the rumors. He assumed everyone had. He assumed the pastor had, which had made his silence all the worse. And without his father saying anything, one way or the other, Malcolm hadn't known for certain if he believed it. He would have taken a lot of pleasure in Nosy Norah being wrong. But then, he guessed, he must have believed it because it had been Mr. Daly's number he'd called. In extremis, he had known. And now it was here in the open, and whatever was going to happen was going to happen. And Malcolm wished that it wouldn't.

He was sorry for feeling that way. He meant no offense. He supported everybody's right to do whatever and all—as long as that "whatever" wasn't this and that "everybody" wasn't his dad. And if it was his dad, then only so long as his dad was not the pastor because he was not sure his dad could keep being the pastor after this, and if his dad was not the pastor, he didn't know what would happen to him. Or he did and that was worse.

Malcolm could feel Mr. Daly in the backseat, his body folded awkwardly into the small space like a creature about to hatch from an egg. Even without turning around, Malcolm could tell he was on the edge of saying something, but he kept not saying it and that was fine. Malcolm didn't want to talk.

He pressed his face closer to the glass, trying to see over the two fire trucks between him and the church. The parts of the building he could see remained intact, lit only by the flashing emergency lights. He didn't see flames, and he prayed he wouldn't. He prayed for the firefighters and for the building, and while he was praying, a voice came from the backseat.

"Are you making your devotions, Malcolm?"

There was something formal in how Preston spoke. Malcolm had thought maybe it only seemed that way because of the bank and the suits, but Preston wasn't wearing a suit and he certainly wasn't in a bank. It was the way he was, and Malcolm would have to get used to it, he supposed.

"Yes," he said.

"Would it be all right if I prayed with you?"

Mr. Daly was a member of the congregation, although his attendance was confined mostly to major holidays and special events. Malcolm had always assumed he was only keeping up appearances and that his tithe was more of a general community donation, intended for things like the after-school program and the food bank. Malcolm did not, in short, imagine that the banker thought much about God. But there were a lot of things Malcolm had not imagined.

"Yes."

"Would you lead?" Preston asked.

Malcolm led. It was the first time anyone had asked him to do that.

Afterward, he said, "How long have you and . . ." He didn't finish, but Preston didn't give any indication that it mattered.

"Not long. July, well, I can't say that she introduced us, but she opened the door."

"July?"

Malcolm turned and looked over his shoulder. Mr. Daly was looking out the window. He nodded. A lot of people had gathered in the parking lot. Some had gotten dressed, and some had coats pulled on over nightclothes. They were watching the firefighters and the church, but it was inevitable that some of them would notice the two of them. Soon someone would knock on the window, and Malcolm wasn't sure how he'd handle it when they did.

"I don't know how she knew," Preston said. "But she did."

Malcolm felt like he'd been shoved hard. He understood why his father wouldn't have wanted to tell him, but that July hadn't felt worse.

"You said the fire alarms didn't go off?" Preston said it offhand, as though it were a minor point that he'd just thought to mention.

Malcolm blinked. "Yes, I mean no. No, most of them didn't go off. Just the one in the basement, but that's far away from the parsonage."

"I'm surprised it woke you."

"It didn't," said Malcolm. "I mean, I was up late reading. I had a new book. July gave it to me. It's my favorite author, and I was excited about it . . ."

Malcolm's voice trailed off as he thought about what could've happened if he hadn't been awake, if it weren't for that book.

Later, the firefighters would discover a problem with the alarm system. The connection that should have set off the other alarms in the building had malfunctioned, but that knowledge wouldn't come for days.

Mr. Daly closed his eyes and took in a sharp breath like he himself had had the close call. "Imagine," he said, his eyes still closed, "if you had been asleep in there tonight."

Malcolm was imagining it, and the thought sent his heart beating faster again.

Preston opened his eyes and looked at Malcolm. "Thank God for that book," he said. And then, after a pause, "And for July."

CHAPTER FORTY-ONE

T he next day, all anyone talked about was the fire. It had started in the semicommercial kitchen tucked into the church basement. The Easter egg hunt and spaghetti suppers were all canceled, and anyone planning any sort of reception—wedding, baptismal, or otherwise—in the fellowship hall was out of luck. (It wasn't even noon before two families had called on Tiny to ask if they could move their events to the bakery.) But the sanctuary was relatively unharmed. The basement was concrete and cinder block, which had contained the worst of it. Some joists between the floors would need replacing. Sections of the church nearest the damaged area were taped off, and work would need to be done to make sure they were safe. Water from the hoses had done as much damage as the fire, and everything was sooty and smelled like smoke. But it could've been worse. It could've been a lot worse.

Half the town had been over to help clean up what they could, and the other half was planning to go. The insurance company was sending someone over from Seattle, and Calvin Budds, who owned the one construction company based in Ebey's End, had offered to start work as soon as they cleared it. He didn't have a lot of guys, but most of them were church members and willing to work weekends and evenings to see to it.

. . . .

Carol was back over at the house for the second day in a row. It didn't hurt to check on Henry again. Shannon had called her as soon as Mack had stormed out. Henry hadn't been hurt too badly, although he still refused to tell her why it had happened, and Mack wasn't talking either. And while Carol might have done well to be more concerned, what she really was was irritated. It seemed like exactly the sort of thing those two would eventually do, some offense to each other's manhood that demanded redress, neither of them willing to behave like fully grown adults with working minds. She blamed both of them—Mack and Henry—specifically, and she blamed the whole gender more generally, and she found herself being short even with Declan when he finally came home and gave a low whistle when he caught sight of his father's split lip.

She might have thrown up her hands and let them deal with their own problems if it weren't for the church fire. Peggy had called up to Anita's, doing her part of the phone tree, to ask if food might be donated for all the helpers, which, of course, it was. But that food needed cooking, which obviously couldn't happen at the church, and Anita's kitchen was too small to sneeze and fart in at the same time. Henry's house was still technically Carol's, and it was for a good cause. So she'd loaded up the car and had driven more than twenty bags of hot dogs, cold cuts, breads, cheeses, sodas, chips, fruit, and half the cookie aisle over to assemble into individual lunch bags.

It was too much for her to do on her own, but July was on cleanup duty with Malcolm at the church, and Anita had to work. Henry, though, was home and would be for some days. It wasn't that he couldn't see patients in his condition. It was that he preferred not to. Not until either his face healed or he could think up a believable story. The current front-runner was car accident, but he was undecided. In the meantime, he was taking shallow breaths until the pain in his ribs receded.

When the phone rang, he was standing at one counter, assembling ham-and-cheese sandwiches. He'd set the whole thing up like an assembly line and was silently praising himself for his efficiency. Carol was at the stove. She had her four largest skillets out, one on each burner, with a whole package of hot dogs browning in each one. The phone, which was four feet from Henry's left hand, rang again.

Carol glanced over her shoulder. He hadn't even looked up. With a snap of irritation, she wiped her hands, walked to the other side of the kitchen, squeezed in next to him, and picked up the phone on the third ring. Henry didn't even scoot over. He was too busy tearing off leaves of iceberg lettuce and stacking them next to a pile of American cheese slices he'd unwrapped, which would certainly stick together now.

"Hello," Carol said, turning her back to keep from adding something else to his list of injuries.

"Mom?"

"Sarah?" Carol looked at her watch. It was unusual for her daughter to call in the middle of the day. It was unusual for her daughter to call at all. She was busy in the way working mothers of young children are always busy, which is to say borderline homicidal.

"How are you?" Carol asked.

"I tried your cell."

A low ping of concern sounded in Carol's mind. "Did you? I didn't hear it. It's in my purse."

"Anita said you were at Dad's."

"You called Anita?"

"You're still living there, aren't you? Wait, did you move home?" Sarah's voice went up an octave, which Carol found surprising. Her daughter had so obviously been worried she'd show up at her doorstep.

"No, I just needed to use the kitchen. Sarah, what's going on?"

Carol glanced over at the stove. She'd left the hot dogs on, and she was in danger of burning them.

"I'm calling about Dad."

Carol's shoulders dropped. Declan had obviously told his sister about the fight. "He'll be fine," she said, "but he's calling in sick for a while."

"He's there?"

The only memories Sarah had of her father at home revolved around major holidays. But even on Christmas, after the presents had been opened and the cinnamon rolls eaten, he would disappear into the small bedroom he'd turned into an office. As a teenager, she'd suspected he wasn't even working, that he was only avoiding them. Now she suspected other things.

"He is. Here, I'll put him on, and he can explain."

Carol had no intention of cleaning up her husband's mess. If he wanted to make up some ridiculous fiction, he could do it without her. And anyway, she could smell the hot dogs.

"No—" Sarah started, but she could hear the clatter as her mother set the phone down and her voice, more distant, telling her father that the call was for him and that *he* could tell her about Mack.

Mack, Jesus. Of course he would have gone straight to her father. The last thing Sarah wanted was to listen to whatever lies Doc had already told her mother. It was disgusting. He was disgusting.

"Sarah?" he said into the phone. His ribs were hurting, and he had to take breaths between words. "This really isn't . . . a big deal."

Sarah recognized that tone. It was the one he'd used when she was growing up and upset about something that had happened at school or some fight she'd had with her mother. Doc, if he bothered to talk to her, always did it with some big sigh, like he couldn't imagine why he had to deal with any of this. It was belittling, and it had worked. She'd gotten the message. But she wasn't thirteen anymore. She had a lot more experience dealing with men and their tones now. Doc might have been an early practitioner of that gaslighting "this isn't anything, Sarah" bullshit, but he didn't hold the patent. She'd been dealing with that for decades now. She was a fucking expert.

"Actually, Dad, this is a very big deal," she said, and laid it all out in chronological order. The family tree website; the DNA test; the message from the half sister, which she read aloud. She'd even printed out the match results that had shown up on her account: twenty-five percent. She offered to send him a copy or, better yet, she'd send it to Mom.

When she stopped speaking, the line was quiet. He was still there. She could hear him taking short breaths, which she assumed was fear. *Good*, she thought.

"You don't have . . . a sister. It's not . . . possible."

He had no intention of describing his vasectomy to his daughter. He didn't care how old she was.

"Apparently it is possible," she went on in that tone of hers that had always made Doc crazy, largely because it was identical to his own. "I think you know how DNA works."

"Yes," he said, tucking the phone against his shoulder and putting his palm gingerly to his side. "But you don't."

"Excuse me?"

"Twenty-five percent," he breathed, "could be . . . a half sibling. Could also be . . . a niece."

Sarah was stunned. She'd confirmed what the girl had told her. She'd confirmed the match. She'd just assumed—the girl had said half sister—she hadn't considered— The blood that had flushed her face ran back down. It felt like it ran all the way out of her body.

"Declan has a kid," she said.

Her father didn't answer. There was a clatter, and her mother's voice was back.

"What is all of this about?" she asked.

As an adult, Sarah no longer felt the glee of ratting out her brother, but it didn't pain her either. When she'd told her mother everything else, she said, "The girl calls herself 'July H.' I'm guessing that's her birth month, if it helps narrow things down."

Carol made a noise Sarah hadn't ever heard before, and for a moment, she was afraid her mother was having some kind of attack. "Mom?"

"Don't write the girl back. Don't do anything," her mother said, and hung up.

Sarah sat with the dead receiver next to her ear for a full five seconds before putting it down.

. . . .

It was Doc, in the end, who called Mack.

"What do you want?" Mack asked.

"I don't suppose," Doc said in that painful way he had of speaking now, "it was . . . a coincidence . . . her ending up . . . with Anita."

The dogs always knew. Maybe they could hear the change in his heartbeat or the way he breathed. Maybe they smelled it somehow. But Gideon lifted his head off Mack's knee, looked at him, and began to pant. Samson, on the other side, gave a short, high-pitched whine.

"Anita doesn't know anything about any of this," Mack said.

"How . . . is that?"

"Because I didn't tell her."

Mack had had a long time to prepare himself for this, and yet the more time he'd had, the less prepared he'd become.

"Declan had . . . a right."

A flash of anger went over Mack, fair or not. "Declan was twenty and barely managing that."

"Not . . . your call."

"And I didn't make it."

"Who?"

Doc wanted one name, but that wasn't how it had been. So, Mack gave him the name of the man who had the right, at least more than anybody else, to say how it had gone.

"And I need to call Anita," Mack said. "Before you do."

He and Doc had been best friends for a long time. Mack wasn't sure they still were, and it wasn't the time to hash that out. A lot had happened in two days, and maybe neither of them had done right by the other. But they were going to have to find a way to work this out. There wasn't any real choice.

"Fine," Doc said, and hung up.

CHAPTER FORTY-TWO

When the call came, Chet walked away from the volunteers, climbed into his car, and drove away. He didn't say where he was going or why. Half the town watched him go. They had a lot of questions and nobody but one another to ask.

When Chet got to the Bell home, he asked to come in and sit. All three of them were there. Carol listened with one hand tight around her middle and the tips of the other hand pressed to her lips. She had questions and took a deep breath before she asked each one. Doc was as angry as he'd ever been and made statements rather than questions, some of them threatening, a few warranted.

Chet did his best to speak directly to Declan, but Declan, who looked like he'd been told it was terminal, wouldn't look him in the eye.

"She didn't tell me," he said.

"I know," Chet replied.

"She told you, though?"

"Yes."

They'd sat side by side on the bed Chet still slept in, Malcolm asleep in the next room. He'd just turned two, not yet potty-trained, not yet ready for a big-boy bed. He sucked on his knuckles and loved his mother, and Chet loved both of them. He did love his wife. Still loved her. Pam had cried, and he had cried. She had asked him to keep her secret, and he had agreed. For better or for worse, he had agreed, and while he understood that there were those—some of them in that room—who would disagree, he knew he would do the same again. Knowing everything, and there had been much, he would do it again. He would do it as Pam's husband, and he would do it as her pastor. He would keep the confidence, and he would deal as best as he could with all that came after.

Declan looked down at his knees. "She knew you could handle it."

"You were twenty," Chet said.

"She'd have told you at twenty."

Chet started to speak, some platitude, no doubt, and then changed his mind. He'd been a pastor a long time, and he understood better than most how trust was built and how it was broken. The truth was Pam had told him, and there had been so much he had not told her.

"None of us did exactly right back then," Chet finally said, "but it's still possible what we did was the best we could have done."

Declan didn't answer, but after a long moment, he nodded.

Chet would wonder, looking back, if he ought to have said more. But if there was anything he knew from all his years of service, it was that most trouble was caused by thinking there was only one right way. Life was too complicated—for some more than others—and what was good or bad usually depended on where you stood and how much time had passed. And most of them would not live long enough to judge the long tail of any of it.

. . . .

Mack called Anita at the store.

"Something's happened," he said. "It's about July."

"What is it?" Her voice was sharp and protective.

"You'd better come" was all he said and hung up.

When she pulled up to the trailer, Mack opened the door, but the dogs stayed inside. The wind had picked up. A gull overhead was trying to fight against the air current and appeared only to bob in place.

"What's going on?"

Anita'd already called the church on her way over. Peggy, who was manning the phone in the pastor's office, coordinating volunteers, told her July was mopping up the multipurpose room and fine, as far as she knew. It was all Anita could do to take the woman's word for it. She wanted to drive straight there, find the girl, and pat her down, looking for injuries.

"Let's talk inside," Mack said.

In the dining room, Samson and Gideon each came over, dipping their heads and butting against her thighs. It was friendly, but their hearts weren't in it. Their tails didn't wag, and Gideon's eyebrows were huddled together over his muzzle. Under any other circumstance, she'd have thought they'd been drugged, but the heaviness in the air pressed down on her, too. It pressed her right down into a chair.

"Is July all right? What happened?" Her stomach felt like fat snakes fighting inside a balloon.

"I know who July's biological parents are," Mack said.

Anita was stunned. "How?"

Later, she would not be able to say why that had seemed more important than "Who?" Maybe she had an inkling. Maybe not. Maybe she was just confused and upset. A lot of that would be going around for a long time.

"Because I arranged for Catherine to adopt her. Pam and Chet asked me to."

Everything in Anita's brain was trying to arrange itself around this new information—what it all meant, what this would change. Everything, of course. Everything would change. Anita's heart was hammering in her chest, and she wondered if she should run. If she should grab July and run.

"July is theirs?" Her voice came out weak.

Mack shook his head. "Pam had this research project she'd been working on, and sometimes she'd let a kid from the high school help her."

"Yeah," Anita said. She vaguely remembered that. "So?"

"One of those kids was Declan."

Anita felt her limbs getting cold.

Mack shook his head. "Not then. A couple years later, when he was in college, grown."

That word snagged on something inside Anita. The way her father said it, dismissed it. Declan would've been the same age as she had been with Henry. She'd think about that later. Not then. Then she was only thinking of July. Her and July. The two of them and what all of this meant, but later. Later, she'd think about Declan, what she knew of him back then, what she thought she knew of herself then, too. She had been old enough—by whatever standard most people would use—but she had not been grown. And if she had not been, then Declan had not been either. She'd think, too, about how Carol had reacted to Doc's cheating, which was not to react at all, and how he had reacted when she had, and how the town had reacted, and that Carol was sleeping on her couch. There were two different measuring sticks. There always had been, and Anita wondered if there always would be and how she'd explain that to July because she'd have to.

Mack took a rattling breath. It sounded like he was getting a cold or maybe that he was going to cry. She hadn't seen him cry since her mother died. He'd cried then and for weeks after, and it had changed how she saw him.

"She was the pastor's wife," he said, gathering himself. "Malcolm still in diapers. Chet was . . ." Mack shook his head. "Undone. No good was going to come of it."

He'd been telling this story to his hands, folded tight on top of the glass table. His knuckles were changing colors, and he had to let go to keep from cutting off the circulation. He was quiet a moment. He might have been giving Anita space to say something, but she didn't know what it would be. He went on.

"When Pam told Chet, he offered to raise the baby as his own." He looked up to see if she understood. "He said he'd treat it just the same as Malcolm. But she already knew Catherine was looking to adopt and having a hard time of it. I'd told her on one of our walks. So . . . so she called and asked if I could put them in touch. Said she thought maybe this was the way to make a bad choice into something good."

"The pastor agreed?"

"He didn't really have much say, I don't think. It was her decision."

"What about Declan?"

Mack shook his head.

"I see."

"Pam went to Seattle before she started showing and lived with Catherine, lived in the room that became July's, as a matter of fact. Officially, she had the records sealed because of Declan, but they kept in touch until Pam passed anyway."

Anita remembered Pam leaving, now that Mack mentioned it. "I thought she went to Seattle because she had cancer," Anita said.

Mack closed his eyes. "That was what she told people. Everybody thought Doc must've diagnosed it, and he thought somebody on the mainland had. And when she came back, she said it was gone. It was a pretty good story until she actually got sick, a few years later."

Anita sat back, stunned. "She lied about having cancer, and then she *got* cancer?"

"Don't say it like that."

Samson got to his feet. They heard his nails on the linoleum, but neither of them looked over.

"Like what?"

"She died on her son's birthday."

Anita didn't need the reminder. No one did. It had cut that little boy off like a lopped branch, forcing him to grow a whole different way. They all loved Malcolm as he was, but everyone knew he wasn't who he had been and that there wasn't any going back.

To Mack's mind, it really wasn't any wonder Chet had fallen apart the way he had. The miracle was that he'd gotten himself back together. Mack wouldn't have. There wasn't a chance in hell. Mack would have gone right off that bridge.

"The thing is," he said, putting his hands on his thighs and pushing himself back in the chair, "July took that DNA test."

Anita had nearly forgotten it, so much had happened since then. Mack told her about the results and Sarah and how it had all come out. Then he went quiet. He was done talking, but the story didn't feel done to her. It didn't feel anywhere near done.

Gideon shook his head, and his metal tags jingled in the heavy pause.

"This is why you didn't want me to take her." The truth was dawning on Anita as she spoke.

Mack squeezed his hands again.

"You told me I wasn't fit"—Anita's voice rose—"but you all just didn't want to get found out. *You* didn't want her here."

For the first time, Mack looked her in the eye. "I am begging you not to tell her that. Tell her everything else, but please." He took a breath, and there were tears in his voice. "She needs to know that we all want her. That we've always wanted her. Tell her— Tell her we all love her—so much—we're just fighting over who gets to love her the most."

Anita stood up without answering. She'd never been so angry or so scared in her life.

Outside, there was an old white BMW parked on the street next to the mailbox. The passenger-side tires were in the scrub grass. Another six inches, and it would've tipped over into the ditch. Carol was standing by the front bumper, looking at the trailer but not moving toward it. Her hair was pulled back, but whole hanks had come loose and were blowing across her face. She didn't seem to notice.

They looked at each other, the space between them and around them separate from the rest of the world. As Anita made her way across the yard toward her friend, she imagined what this moment would've been like if July had not brought the two of them together months before, if they did not already know each other, if there had not already been forgiveness.

July had seen to them, Anita understood, so that they could see to her. That was how she saw it. She just hoped to hell Carol would see it that way, too.

The wind was blowing hard enough to bend the tops of the trees. By afternoon, the forest around them would creak and groan as the wood deep inside all those trunks and limbs was wrenched to and fro. Branches as big around as a man's thigh would come down, sudden with a sound like a gunshot. People had died being in the wrong place at the wrong time in storms like the one coming on.

"Mack's inside," Anita said.

She looked into the car. She expected to see Henry but didn't.

Maybe he was with Declan. Somebody should be. "You can go talk to him if you want."

"You going to the church?" Carol asked.

"I am."

Anita didn't know how the news of all this was going to break, only that it would, and it would travel faster than the storm. The most important thing was getting to the girl before anyone else did. Anita would defend her with fire if it came to it.

"Don't let her check her email," Carol said. "Sarah might have said something, and you don't want . . ."

Anita nodded.

"You want me to go with you?" Carol asked.

"No," Anita said honestly. "But I'd understand if you insist."

Carol shook her head. "You know what you're going to say?"

She didn't exactly, but she knew how she would start and that would have to be enough.

Carol didn't move, and for a moment, neither did Anita. She wanted to do it, but she wasn't sure. It wasn't like either of them, but maybe it needed to be. Anita held open her arms, stepped forward, and hugged her friend. And Carol, after a moment, hugged her back.

"Do you think you could call me later tonight?" Carol said before either of them had let go. "Tell me how she is."

Anita stepped back. "Where will you be?"

"The house. My old one. Not forever, I don't think, but Declan is going to need me."

Anita understood, but she didn't like it. "You can come back anytime," she said.

Carol smiled, but it wasn't a happy one. "You've got July, then?"

Anita nodded. She tried to look sure, but the question fanned the fear already burning in her chest. Did she have her? Anita was only her guardian, a piece of paper easily taken away. She'd barely agreed to it in the first place, and now it was all she wanted. She'd give anything—the store, the trailer, every dollar she had, and her arms along with it—to keep July. She was the child of her heart. She loved her more than anything in the world, no matter what happened. Even if they took her away—and Anita clearly understood that they could. Declan could. And Henry and Carol, too. These people who were so messily entangled in her life could take this perfect, precious thing. And even if they didn't make her go, July could choose them.

Carol climbed into her car. Anita stayed there where she was while the wheels spun on the slick mud inches from her toes. She watched her friend pull away, and she knew then what she would say to July. It was the only thing she could say.

Anita got in her own car. She drove to the church, and she said it exactly like she planned.

"Whatever you want, whatever you do, I will love you with everything that I have. I won't ever stop, so you don't have to worry. Whatever happens, I belong to you, and I will carry you in my heart forever. Nothing can change that. Nothing you could ever do or decide, nothing in this whole world, will take that away. I swear to God."

Anita's tears poured down her cheeks, hot and wet and soaking the collar of her work shirt. And July, sitting in the passenger seat with her bag on her lap, shook with sobs.

"I love you, too," she said, her throat so tight the words could hardly get out. "I just wanted to know. That's all the test was. I don't want anyone else. Please," she choked. "Please don't send me away. I can't. I can't lose another mom."

. . . .

Later that night, while the wind pulled fliers from posts and tossed branches against the building, Anita lay down on her mattress in

July's room. When they were both tucked in, July let her arm hang down, and Anita reached out and took her hand.

The next morning, Anita went down to the store and put a sign on the front door.

CLOSED FOR FAMILY

Outside, the street was so covered in leaves and small branches, along with bits of trash, she could barely see the asphalt. Anita only looked at it. Then she called everyone who was supposed to work and gave them the day off.

CHAPTER FORTY-THREE

When July opened the door to the projection room, Malcolm was waiting for her. He had the folding chairs set up. On top of hers was a giant soda and two boxes of candy: Red Vines and Peanut M&M's. He had Milk Duds, but he hadn't opened them yet.

"Hey," he said, standing up on instinct and almost knocking over his own soda.

July shut the door, and the room went dark again. "Hi."

Dark was better. It was easier to talk to her in the dark. She was his sister now. She'd always been his sister, he guessed, but now he knew it, and this was the first time he'd seen her since knowing it. She'd missed two weeks of school, which made sense. She'd had a lot to process. It wasn't like she could've also learned algebra. Malcolm wished Anita would've explained that to the pastor, who hadn't let him off one single day.

It was hard to know what to do with his hands. Like, should he hug her? She was standing two steps away, but she had her hands tucked up inside her sleeves, which might have been a sign. The truth was, he didn't know how she felt about everything. A lot of people had lied to her. He wasn't one of those people, but the pastor was, and it was hard to say how that would play out.

He'd heard July and Anita went to Carol's house for dinner. Declan hadn't been there, though. Instead, he'd opened the theater as usual, offering Malcolm an hourly wage to sell the tickets, which Declan usually did himself. Malcolm, for maybe the first time in his life, had refused a first offer. He said he'd only do it if it was an actual job with regular hours, not just whenever Declan felt like it. Maybe it was wrong to take advantage of his being so freaked out, but it had worked. Now Malcolm sold tickets three days a week and worked the concessions two more days while Declan pretty much hid in his office as much as he could. Malcolm had even started doing the schedules for all the part-time people, including himself, to make sure it actually got done.

"So, are you okay?" Malcolm asked.

"No, but also, like, yes?" She took her hands out of her sweater sleeves and tucked her hair behind her ears. "That probably doesn't make sense."

"It makes total sense," he said. They both shifted their weight.

"I'm sorry," she said, "for not telling you about your dad and Mr. Daly."

He shrugged. "It's okay."

It was, and it wasn't. It would be. Eventually. It was complicated.

"You want to sit?" he asked.

That night's movie was about a hit man who comes back from the dead. It was okay but also kind of stupid. Malcolm had already watched it once. The promised film festivals and *Rocky Horror* showings hadn't exactly materialized yet, and now, with everything, he didn't know if they ever would.

Honestly, the way Declan was acting, Malcolm wasn't sure how much longer he was going to be around. It was just a feeling for now, but Malcolm had already decided that if Declan did leave, he'd come forward and offer to manage the theater. It would be hard with school, but he was already a junior, and by the end of the year, he'd have most of his credits already. He could do work-study starting in September, and he'd have the whole summer off before then. He could open the place up for all kinds of special events, especially when all the summer people came, because the thing was, the theater wasn't just a movie theater. There was actually a little stage in front of the screen, and that made a lot of things possible. Malcolm had more ideas than he could hold in his head. He'd started keeping a notebook.

He and July sat next to each other. It was his day off, and the movie didn't start for another ten minutes, so it was just trivia questions and other filler stuff on the screen. July opened the Red Vines, but she wasn't eating them, just wrapping one around and around her finger.

"Do you feel weird knowing we have the same bio-mom?" she asked.

"A little," he admitted. "Do you?"

She shrugged. "Are you mad?"

"At my mom?"

"At me."

"No!" He was so surprised he actually jumped a little in his seat. The Milk Duds bounced in the box. "Why would I be mad?"

"I don't know," she said. "You might think I messed up your family."

"I'm pretty sure my family was messed up already." He paused. "Are *you* mad?"

She stopped twisting her Red Vine. "Not as much as everybody wants me to be."

What she said didn't surprise him, but he still didn't know how to answer it. The island had more opinions than people, which didn't make sense until you'd lived there awhile.

"*They're* mad, and so they want me to, like, validate that, I guess? So they can say they're mad on my behalf?" July sighed.

"Yeah."

Before, all Malcolm had wanted was for people to talk about his mom. Now he just wanted them to stop. He'd overheard all kinds of stuff. People talked while they waited in line to buy their tickets and their nachos, and then stopped all of a sudden when they saw him. At school, he didn't even have to overhear. People just came out and said shit. Some of it was really awful and gross, and the only reason Malcolm hadn't hit Ryan Streeter was because he wasn't really sure how to hit someone. But that was becoming less and less of a consideration by the day.

Malcolm *was* confused and angry. He didn't think what she had done was okay, but she was still his mom and she was still dead. And Ryan could still fuck the hell off.

He and his dad had ended up having to move into a rental after the fire. He was pretty sure Mr. Daly was paying for it, which was a good thing because after everything with July came out, his dad had resigned. He wrote a letter of apology to the board of directors and to the congregation. He was about to send one to the *Island Examiner*, too, but Mr. Daly, who had them both over for dinner every night now, intervened.

"There's a difference," Mr. Daly had said, "between taking responsibility and hanging yourself on the cross."

Malcolm had thought his dad might object to the analogy, but he hadn't, and he didn't send the letter to the paper.

It wasn't the end of things, though. After everybody found out he resigned, some members of the congregation started a petition asking him to come back. So far, they'd gotten seventy-four percent of church members to sign, plus pretty much everybody who came to

Sunday suppers, the AA meetings, the bereavement group, and the after-school group. Old Ms. Akers stood outside Anita's store a few days a week collecting signatures. And the Connors had offered to let her set up over at the pharmacy, too. Tiny took one of the petition sheets herself and made everybody sign before they could get pie, which meant Norah Streeter was pretty much banned for life.

Mack took one of the sheets and parked himself at the diner with it. Jim had his at the library, and Bill kept a stack in his patrol car. The Old Philosophers in full effect.

"Have you talked to Declan?" Malcolm asked.

"Once," she said. "On the phone."

"How did it go?"

July shrugged and took a sip of her soda. Malcolm could imagine. "Anita and I went over and talked to Carol and Doc, though."

"I heard."

"Heard how?"

Malcolm rolled his eyes.

"I told them I wanted to stay with Anita, and Carol and Henry said they didn't think 'anyone'"—July made air quotes—"would object to that."

"What about them, though? Will they be your grandparents?"

"Yeah, they said they hoped to be, if it was okay with me."

"What did you say?"

It was her turn to roll her eyes.

Malcolm smiled. "That's cool."

The lights in the main part of the theater dimmed. The previews were about to start.

"Then Anita said something else."

The theater went full dark. Malcolm could only see the outline of her next to him, although he could smell Red Vines when she spoke. That's how close she was.

"What?" he asked.

"She said she'd called my social worker."

"To tell her?"

"To ask about adopting me."

Malcolm opened his mouth so quickly a Milk Dud almost fell out. He tried to swallow and started to choke on his own thick, sugary spit. His eyes watered, and between gasps, he asked, "Adopt, like, forever?"

"Adopt like forever," she said.

CHAPTER FORTY-FOUR

Carol moved out of the apartment and back into the big house on the water. She'd put her things in the guest room, her books on the nightstand, and the clothes she wore most often in the chest of drawers, which made her wonder if she really needed other clothes. The comforter on the bed was stiff and cheap and reminded her of a motel, and so she'd ordered another one. It was fluffy with a pattern of dark green leaves and white flowers, which she never would've bought for the bed she'd shared with Henry. But this was her room now, and everyone knew it because this was the one room with a door that, as often as not, was closed.

Henry had, once, brought up the HVAC system and airflow and the "problem of doors." Carol had not said anything, but she had looked at him in such a way that he did not bring it up again.

She hadn't come back for the reasons other people might have imagined. She'd come back because, at least for the moment, Declan needed her more than Anita and July did. Anita and July were fine. They were better than fine, and despite everything, maybe they always had been. And really, there was not space for her there.

Carol needed to find her own space. She'd needed to for a long time. It hadn't occurred to her that she would find it back where she'd started, but then again, nothing in the house was the same as it had been. Things had changed and resettled in such a way that they hardly resembled themselves. Then there had not been space, and now there was. For her, but not only for her.

The whole island, it seemed, was resettling itself into a slightly different configuration. None of it had been easy, and not everyone was happy. Declan was not happy. Nosy Norah was not happy. Gordy would not be happy on principle. Carol herself wasn't sure she was exactly happy, but happiness was transient and unreliable. She wasn't, when she walked into Tiny's Bakeshop that morning, looking for happy. She was looking for something much truer and more complicated than that.

The bell above the door jingled, and Carol hitched her new tote bag a little higher on her shoulder. It was heavier than she was used to. Tiny was behind the counter, transferring extra-large chocolate chip cookies from a baking tray to a plate in the display case. Most people wouldn't have thought Tiny looked any different, but there was something about the eyes and mouth, just a little less tension than there had been these past years.

Dylan didn't bake, but he could clean and fix things. A couple of weeks ago, he'd rearranged nearly everything behind the counter and in the back of the shop. When Tiny saw what he'd done, she'd gone through the roof until, with panic in his eyes, he'd explained how much time it would save her, having things the way he'd put them. She'd bitten hard on the inside of her cheek and told him she'd give it one morning—one. She'd ended up giving it pretty much forever because it made her feel like she was running her bakery with skates on her feet. Everything was smoother and faster, and on the second day, she'd handed him an envelope with an extra $200 in it. She knew he'd been giving his paycheck to Felicia.

"You keep that for yourself," she'd told him.

He opened his mouth and then closed it.

"I mean it," Tiny had said.

"Yes, ma'am."

Tiny had to do it. She didn't have any choice. If she didn't, she was going to end up hugging him, regularly and possibly in public.

"I've got one apple pie left," Tiny said without looking up.

"No," Carol answered. "Thank you. I'll have a coffee, please."

Tiny paused but didn't put the tray down. "For here?"

"Yes."

Tiny's eyes went to the bag, despite Carol's attempts to keep it tucked behind her and out of sight. Her laptop had fit perfectly inside along with a new pack of pens and a fresh notebook, college-ruled, spiral-bound, single-subject, with a waterproof cover and reinforced storage pockets, as specified by the Ebey's End Junior High supply list, grades seven and eight, according to Mary Alice, who'd sold it to her at the pharmacy.

"You planning some work?" Tiny asked.

Carol thought about hedging, but where would that get her?

"Yes," she said. And then, after a pause, "I'm writing again."

And she was. She had been. She wasn't sure that it was going anywhere, but it was a start, and it was more than she'd had before. The whole thing still made her sick to her stomach. She wasn't even thinking about publishing again. She was specifically not thinking about it, which meant, of course, that she was thinking about it, but she wasn't ready to think about it. She just needed to put some words on the page and see if they were any good. It had been a long time, and it was harder than she remembered, which was saying something because in her memory it had been very, very hard.

Tiny put down the cookie sheet, which was blackened and warped and did not set flat on the counter. She put her hands on her boyish hips and looked Carol in the eye. The lines on Tiny's face were deeper than Carol had realized, and she had sun spots on her cheeks, which drooped a little toward her jaw. Her eyelids were heavy, and the skin on her neck looked a lot like Carol's own. Carol didn't know if Tiny was older than she'd always thought or if she'd just been used as hard as that cookie sheet. There were stories about Tiny's life before she'd come to Ebey's End, and they were not easy ones to hear for anyone who cared for her. Carol cared, but she also knew a good character when she saw one. The whole island was full of good characters, and Carol did not plan to let that go to waste.

"That one," Tiny said, pointing over Carol's shoulder to a booth in the corner.

Carol turned to look. If she sat on one side of the booth, she'd have a view through the large front windows to the street and everyone going by. Sitting on the other side of the booth, there would be no distractions. It got good light but not too much. There was an electrical outlet nearby if her battery ran low. It was, she could see, the best seat in the house.

"That one's yours now," Tiny said. "Anyone else is sitting in it when you come in, I'll make 'em move."

A hard knot formed in Carol's throat, and she had to clear it with a soft noise before she could answer. "You don't have to, but I appreciate—"

Tiny didn't let her finish. "Carol?"

"Yes?"

"Now would be a real good time for shutting up."

Carol did not, in general, let people talk to her that way, but she also knew that there were times when it was better to make an exception. Tiny put a mug of coffee down on the counter, and Carol picked it up. She turned toward her booth, and she didn't say anything else.

ACKNOWLEDGMENTS

'm sorry to tell you Ebey's End does not exist, although Whidbey, Bainbridge, and an entire archipelago called the San Juans do. Ebey's End looks an awful lot like bits and pieces of all of those places, and for good reason. My deepest gratitude to the locals, inn-keepers, restaurateurs, bartenders, bookstore owners, and all the rest who have made my family welcome on many, many trips over the years.

A particular thank-you to Malcolm Wynn, who kindly answered too many questions about what it was like to be a teenager growing up near Friday Harbor. Upon our meeting, the character of Malcolm had already been in existence for two years, and I could no more change his name than that of my own child. So, the coincidence has been left to stand. I consider it good luck.

Special thanks to Maggie Waltosz, who was my grocer for five years. Over the course of 260 Sunday mornings, we got to know each other across a conveyor belt loaded with extra-large jars of pea-nut butter, several gallons of milk, and enough Goldfish crackers to supply every preschool in the state of Washington. My daughter grew up with Miss Maggie and loves her more than most of our relatives. She did her best to guide me through the workings of modern grocery retail, with which I have taken unconscionable liberties.

Speaking of liberties, magazine aficionados will know that *Martha Stewart Living* went out of print in 2022, but there is simply nothing better for telling Preston that September is the month he should air out his pillows. And so, in these pages, the magazine lives on.

The name Ebey's End is an obvious and cheeky wink to Ebey's Landing, a National Historical Reserve. (I don't know what a "historical reserve" is either. But it's a place, and it's pretty, and you should go. Take a jacket. I wasn't kidding about the weather.)

It amuses me to borrow names I particularly like, and the closer you are to me, the more likely you are to suffer this abuse. Most notable is Carol, which is the middle name of my college roommate, Janice, whose last name, Shiffler, I borrowed, too.

The real Bill is a retired police detective and one of those family friends who might as well be blood. Al and Donald, former members of the Old Philosophers' Club, are named after my own grandfathers.

Book titles I only steal from myself. *Upside Down in the Salish Sea* was briefly considered for my second novel, which ultimately became *The 100 Year Miracle*.

As always, my deepest gratitude is reserved for my husband, Austin Baker, without whom writing this book and any other would be impossible.

Barbara Poelle has been my agent from the beginning. She is extraordinary, and I will go over the cliff with her.

Cassidy Sachs is the editor of which dreams are made. Her heartfelt exuberance for this story buoyed me, and when she described the worlds I create as being "better versions of reality," I had a North Star.

It takes a village to publish a book. My village at Dutton includes John Parsley, Stephanie Cooper, Nicole Jarvis, Amanda Walker, Sarah Thegeby, Christopher Lin, Sarah Oberrender, Lorie Pagnozzi, Melissa Solis, Clare Shearer, Erica Rose, LeeAnn Pemberton, Mary Beth Constant, and many others who do so much to get books into the hands of readers.

I rely on a small cadre of beta readers, who, for no discernable reason, agree to read shitty drafts, giving me notes and opinions until the book can be made fit for public consumption. It would be a thankless job except that I am thanking them here. I am thanking them from the bottom of my heart. Jessica Staheli, Megan Kenney, Aimee Granger, and Austin Baker, you are angels.

And finally, to my daughter, Abigail. I'll write you stories forever.

ABOUT THE AUTHOR

Ashley Ream is a former journalist and the author of two previous novels. Her debut novel, *Losing Clementine*, was a Barnes & Noble debut pick and a Sutter Home Book Club pick, and is being made into a major motion picture. Her second, *The 100 Year Miracle*, was named an Amazon Best Book of the Month and selected as the Whidbey Island All-Island Read. Ashley lives with her daughter and husband on the edge of the big woods outside of Seattle.